A MESMERIZING TALE OF GOOD AND EVIL, SCANDAL AND CORRUPTION.

CLAIRE CONNELLY: Beautiful, elegant— *ambitious…* This rising star of a syndicated TV newsmagazine is caught in a tangled web of love and aspiration. But is the pursuit of success worth the ultimate price?

JAKE SERINGO: Cynical homicide detective, wronged by the past… He throws himself into work with a vengeance, determined to extinguish the haunting memories—and his all-consuming passion for the woman he'd blindly trusted.

THE HAMPTONS: Gorgeous socialite **Veronica Hampton Forsythe,** her twin sister, **Vanessa,** and their cousin **Lily D'Angelo.** All three dead ringers for each other—only one to be sole heiress of the family fortune. Who is good, who's tainted by evil…and who is truly insane? Despite all their wealth and connections, this formidable dynasty cannot escape the family curse….

REBECCA BRANDEWYNE

GLORY SEEKERS

MIRA BOOKS

ISBN 1-55166-276-0

GLORY SEEKERS

For Roger E.,
my driving wheel.
For the rock and roll years.

CONTENTS

Glory Seekers

Roll on, you deep and dark-blue ocean—roll!
Ten thousand fleets sweep over you in vain;
Man marks the earth with ruin; his control
Stops with the shore of the vast, watery plain,
Where breakers foam upon the shifting sands,
And beyond, the riptide lies in deadly wait—
Men's lives entwine like the tangled strands
Of seaweed, and the madding storm does not abate,
But wreaks havoc on all in the name of fate.

Man's steps are not upon your paths—your fields
Are not a spoil for him—you do arise
And shake him from you; the vile strength he wields
For earth's destruction you do all despise,
Spurning him from your depths to the skies,
And sending him, shivering in your briny spray,
And howling, to his Gods, wherein lies
His wretched hope in some near port or bay,
And dashing him again to earth—there let him lay.

The armaments which thunderstrike the walls
Of rock-built cities, bidding nations quake,
Are born of all the eternal pitfalls
That men themselves, in their failings, make,
Comprehending not everlasting time,
That the past changes not unless change be wrought.
Men are in vain glory seekers sublime.
They suffer no sea-change, are, rather, caught
In their own decay, never learning aught.*

*Poem adapted from *Childe Harold's Pilgrimage: Ocean* by George Gordon, Lord Byron

Prologue

Tangled Strands

Oh, what a tangled web we weave,
When first we practice to deceive!

Marmion
—Sir Walter Scott

The Floater

She left the web, she left the loom,
She made three paces thro' the room,
She saw the water lily bloom,
She saw the helmet and the plume,
    She look'd down to Camelot.
Out flew the web and floated wide;
The mirror cracked from side to side.
"The curse has come upon me," cried
    The Lady of Shalott.

The Lady of Shalott
—Alfred, Lord Tennyson

A Small City, The Gulf Coast, The Present

Floaters were always the worst cases.

Worse than those involving victims of shootings, stabbings, or strangulations. Worse even than those that yielded up crispies—victims who had burned to death. Law-enforcement officers always thought they had seen it all until they showed up at a crime scene and got their first glimpse of a floater. Sometimes at the revolting sight, even the most hardened of homicide detectives turned green at the gills and lost his lunch. Jake Seringo hadn't even viewed the body yet, but his stomach already churned at the prospect.

Reaching into his trouser pocket, he withdrew a roll of antacid tablets and popped twice the recommended dosage into his mouth. It wasn't the thought of seeing the drowning victim, but all the caffeine he had ingested today that was making him so jittery and queasy, he told himself sternly, grimacing as he chewed the chalky, fruit-flavored tablets. More than a dozen cups of what passed for coffee in the squad room was enough to kill anybody. His doctor had warned him more than once to lay off it—and to quit smoking and drinking, too. But Jake hadn't paid any heed. If he didn't smoke, if he didn't drink to relieve the stress of his job, he might take out his automatic pistol some night and eat a bullet instead.

That was what dealing with the dregs of humanity day in and day out did to you—and the reason why he and every other cop he knew did their damnedest to avoid anything that might bring a psych evaluation crashing down on their heads. Psychological evaluations were supposed to be kept strictly confidential, but somehow word always managed to leak out within the department, anyway. When that happened, you were done for, washed up, labeled a nutcase, a ticking time bomb. Then the higher-ups demanded your gun and badge—and you were out on the mean streets yourself, all your years on the force counting for nothing and your pension down the toilet.

Without ever even consciously thinking about it, Jake knew that some dark part of him had long ago decided he would rather eat a bullet.

Covertly, he glanced over at his partner. Remy Toussaint was a big, decent-minded, good-hearted, and generally unflappable black man whose *laissez-le-bon-temps-rouler*—let-the-good-times-roll—attitude toward life was probably what kept him sane on the job. He was humming tunelessly under his breath as he guided their unmarked car along the quiet, winding, brick-paved streets of Forest Gables, the city's oldest, most exclusive, monied neighborhood. It had been built decades before the turn of the century, during the Reconstruction Era, when the South had boomed with upstart carpetbaggers, scalawags, and new money. Horse-drawn carriages and then trolleys had once plied these same wide streets; Englishmen, Frenchmen, and Spaniards had once dueled beneath the gnarled, leafy branches of the massive elms and moss-draped live oaks that provided cool, welcome shade during the long, hot, steamy summers.

Still, for all that it looked as though the twentieth century had passed it by, Forest Gables was nevertheless home to modern technology. High, foliage-laden, spike-topped, brick-and-stucco walls were pierced by automated black wrought-iron gates lavishly embellished with gilt. Elaborate security systems guarded the multimillion-dollar mansions nestled upon sweeping lawns whose gardeners, water-gobbling sprinkler systems, and towering, old trees kept them lush and green despite the blistering summer heat. At the edges of meandering walkways and elaborate bridges, the rims of gurgling fountains and lily ponds rippling with koi, stands of smaller, ornamental trees and blossoming bushes grew, and riotous flower beds burgeoned with brilliant color. The sultry breeze that drifted inland from the Gulf was almost sickeningly sweet with the profusion of fragrances that wafted from spreading bougainvillea, hibiscus, oleander, morning glory, and trumpet creeper. Everything that flourished here seemed wild and out of control, like the notorious kudzu, as though it were only a matter of time before the vegetation enveloped and suffocated all it touched, reclaiming what, over the centuries, man had dared to attempt to possess and civilize. Inhaling the moist, thickly redolent air tinged with its loamy whiff of death and decay was like being buried alive in the dank, dark earth, Jake thought, your heart pounding, your palms sweating as you gasped for each precious breath, wondering if it would be your last. He felt grateful he hadn't eaten any breakfast.

Toussaint, however, didn't seem in the least perturbed by either the humidity, the cloying scents, or the idea that he and Jake were shortly about to view a floater—much less one who had in life been a stunningly gorgeous, glamourous, rich socialite, at that. Now the unfortunate Veronica Hampton Forsythe was nothing more than another police-department statistic, a drowning victim floating lifelessly in her family's Olympic-size swimming pool.

Death—not Samuel Colt's infamous revolver—was the real great equalizer, Jake reflected grimly. All the money in the world couldn't save you from eventually rotting with the worms; nor could you take your accumulated wealth with you—not even in an asbestos briefcase. You could only pass it on to your heirs and hope they had sense enough to manage it as carefully as you had instead of blowing it all in one place.

Earlier, Jake had taken off his suit jacket, loosened his tie and collar, and rolled up his shirtsleeves. But it hadn't helped. He was still sweating like a jogger on an adrenaline high in the heat that, despite the fact that it wasn't even yet noon, was already stifling. His white cotton shirt was nearly soaked through, sticking unpleasantly to his skin. Not for the first time since the advent of the dog days of summer did he curse the fact that the unmarked car's air conditioner wasn't working worth a damn and that the department was either too broke or too cheap to repair it. But then, these days, life was tough all over. Even the wealthy, with all their walls, gates, attack dogs, security systems, and bodyguards, were no longer immune to its ravages. That he and Toussaint were here in Forest Gables this morning was proof enough of that.

Taking a crumpled pack of Marlboros from his shirt pocket, Jake shook out a cigarette and lit up, exhaling a stream of smoke out his open window. Toussaint's frown made his disapproval plain, but Jake figured anybody who started his day out with a fistful of jelly doughnuts didn't have any legitimate cause to complain about other health hazards.

But whether for good or ill, the nicotine took the edge off Jake's nerves and made it possible for him to get through each day. He drew deeply on the cigarette again, feeling some of his nausea recede. Not since he had been a rookie in uniform had he vomited his guts up at the sight of a corpse, and he didn't plan on doing so this morning, either. According to the uniformed officers already at the possible crime scene, there had been quite a party at the Hampton mansion last night. As a result, Veronica Hampton Forsythe couldn't possibly have been in the water for more than ten hours at the most. So how bad could she look? Bad enough, Jake knew from experience.

"Jesus Christ," he swore softly as they at last rounded a bend in the street and the baroque, wrought-iron gates emblazoned with the Hamptons' highly stylized, trademark H came into view. "The place is already a frigging three-ring circus!" He scowled darkly at the media vans lined up along the curbs, their camera crews jostling for position and angles, their reporters shoving microphones into the faces of the patrol officers attempting to cordon off the area, pushing back the neighbors who had come out of their houses to gawk at the unfolding spectacle. A couple of these last held small, squash-faced, begroomed and beribboned dogs that struggled and squirmed to break free of their owners' arms while yapping excitedly and ceaselessly, adding unpleasantly shrill punctuation notes to all the commotion. Private security vehicles and city patrol cars were parked helter-skelter, their lights flashing, their radios squawking.

"It just seems like everybody and his brother's got access to a police scanner these days." Toussaint sighed, shaking his head with disgust. "Hell, I think they hear the calls even before we do—and the damned media's got informants everywhere, even in the department!" Knowing that, realistically, there was little chance of getting the car through the melee, he eased it to a stop alongside the curb and killed the engine. Then he and Jake got slowly out, each bracing himself both mentally and physically for running the gauntlet that awaited. "Try to stay cool, Jake...and please, let me do all the talking," Toussaint insisted, glancing anxiously at his partner.

It was no secret that Jake ranked the media lower than vultures on the food chain and that he had nothing but contempt for them and their standard party line. As far as Jake was concerned, the public's right to know ended the moment it impeded a police investigation and invaded the privacy of shocked, afflicted individuals who had had the misfortune to become victims of crime. Dirty Harry had nothing on Jake. More than once, it had been all Toussaint could do to restrain his partner from forcing some hapless reporter to swallow a microphone, and sound bites from Jake were apt to be of the "Go fuck yourself" variety. While film at eleven seldom ever made Captain Nichols's day, Toussaint knew that if it included Jake's face, they would both invariably find themselves called on the captain's carpet shortly afterward, Jake rebellious and unrepentant, Toussaint doing his best to smooth the troubled waters between his hot-tempered partner and their irate superior.

"Don't worry, Remy," Jake drawled dryly as he slung his jacket carelessly over his left shoulder. "It's too damned early and too damned hot for a confrontation with those boob-tube buzzards. So you lead the way, and I'll just follow along quietly in your wake."

"Uh-huh." Toussaint's skepticism was unmistakable. Still, he made no further comment as he headed toward the hubbub.

Jake strode behind, his easy, fluid gait that of a natural athlete, concealing the tension coiled within his hard, muscular body, just as his mirrored aviator sunglasses veiled his dark-brown eyes scanning the crowd intently, alertly, missing nothing. Not the elderly bald man in the velour bathrobe and designer silk pajamas, morning newspaper in hand to explain his gaping presence at the curb. Not the officers speaking into their walkie-talkies, curtly motioning the throng and traffic away from the Hampton driveway, clearing the street so it could be blocked off with the city's orange-and-white-striped barricades, their reflectors gleaming in the bright, morning light. Not the cream-colored van that prominently displayed Channel 4's signature logo in bold blues and reds, and before which stood a beautiful, willowy blonde in a crisp, grass-green linen suit, not a single strand of hair escaping from her classic French twist, a microphone held casually but competently in one graceful hand. Amid all the cacophony and confusion, she stood out like a beacon of sanity, cool and composed, not frothing at the mouth, like the rest of her colleagues, to get the inside story—because that had never been her style. No, she was a good deal cleverer and more insidious than that.

Involuntarily, Jake paused when he spied her, his nostrils flaring, his mouth tightening, his body tautening, flooding with an ache that had nothing to do with his job this morning. He had known she would be here, of course. Still, the sight of her hit him like an unexpected punch to his midsection.

Fair-haired Claire Connelly, the ice queen of the local network media.

Even now, despite all the years that had come and gone since then, Jake could still smell the heady gardenia scent of her, could still taste her feverishly flushed skin, musky and glistening with sweat from their lovemaking, could still feel her naked body lying languorously beneath his own, her long, sun-gold hair spilling across the pillows, her heart beating in time with his. That he was assailed by these memories every time he saw her infuriated him no end. That, despite everything, he still wanted her was, as usual, the inevitable crowning blow. She had played him like a deep-sea fisherman played a marlin, and he had fallen hook, line, and sinker for the bait, drowning in the depths of her sea-green eyes.

Fool... Sucker, his conscience cried even now in his ear, as it always did when he saw her, taunting him mercilessly, filling him with guilt, shame, and anger that he should have succumbed to her wiles. That he had been drunk, grief stricken, and terribly vulnerable when she had caught him on her cruel barb was no excuse. That, if he were honest with himself, he must admit that while he had been brutal, she herself had been kind, caring, and had undoubtedly saved his life in the process only served as a further source of self-reproach, humiliation, and rage. He was a cop. He knew what humanity was like, the treachery it was capable of. He should have known better. No matter what, he should never have trusted her; he should never have *needed* her. Still, it was long over and done with now, and there was no going back to change it. She had taught him a hard lesson, but he had learned it well. He had never needed anybody since.

After taking a long, last drag off his cigarette, Jake dropped the butt onto the street and deliberately ground it out beneath his highly polished black boot. Then he continued on after Toussaint, both of them flashing their badges to get past the gates of the Hampton mansion.

"You think their guard dogs are out this morning, Jake?" Toussaint asked, scanning the area uneasily as they strolled up the long, serpentine drive framed by an assortment of elms, oaks, magnolias, and pecan trees. Unlike most things, dogs bothered Toussaint. He had once been attacked by a couple of Dobermans.

"Yeah, but I doubt if they're running loose right now, Remy. There're too many people on the grounds for the Hamptons to risk a lawsuit because somebody got attacked by their dogs," Jake observed as his gaze took in the elegant, rose-colored brick mansion embellished with forest-green galleys and hurricane shutters. It was situated upon the luxuriously landscaped lawn like an exquisite cameo set in a delicate, Victorian brooch, reeking of class and old money the way a wino stank of trash and panhandling. This was how the rich lived, why they were said to be "different." They could afford to be—because keeping a roof over their heads and putting food on their tables weren't a daily struggle for them. They didn't live in fear of winding up bedding down at night in an alley, eating supper out of a Dumpster. It was a far cry from the poor side of the city, across the river, where Jake had grown up, that was for sure. He had seen the inside of the place before, but this morning, he and Toussaint were directed by a patrol officer to the swimming pool around back. It was already cordoned off with yellow crime-scene tape that looked as garish and out of place in the tranquil setting as a clown at a funeral.

A small knot of people were gathered at the foot of the expansive, terraced patio that led down from the French doors lining the rear of the house, while the Crime Scene Unit worked around the huge pool itself, filming video and snapping still photographs from every conceivable angle. Until all that was finished, no one would touch anything at the possible crime scene. The department didn't want any screwups—like the big-time ones the LAPD had made in the Nicole Brown Simpson–Ronald Goldman murders. Senator Malcolm Forsythe might not be O. J. Simpson, but he *was* widely viewed by many as the next John F. Kennedy.

Jake and Toussaint introduced themselves to the private security guards and the two uniformed officers who had been first on the scene. "So…what've we got here?" Jake inquired once the amenities had been dispensed with.

The older of the two patrol officers flipped open her notepad. "One Veronica Hampton Forsythe, age thirty-five, married to Senator Malcolm Forsythe and the primary heir to the Hampton family fortune. The pool man found her when he arrived to clean the pool this morning. As near as we can determine, the victim was last seen between midnight and one o'clock a.m. last night, during a private fund-raising bash for the senator's election campaign. Evidently, she was drinking pretty heavily, and sometime during the evening, she and the senator had a heated argument, after which she stormed off. No one here at the house remembers seeing her after that. But there were a couple of hundred guests in and out all night long, so it's possible she was still alive after the party broke up. The initial theory is that she must have wandered out here by herself to the pool to cool off and either jumped in deliberately or fell in accidentally and, in her inebriated condition, drowned. Apparently, nobody saw what happened. But we'll know more after the M.E. gets a closer look at the body."

At that, Jake forced himself to turn to the carefully landscaped pool that, after glancing at earlier, he had studiously avoided. Veronica Hampton Forsythe floated facedown in the clear blue, chlorinated water that stirred gently from the running jets and the waterfall cascading over a jumble of artfully arranged rocks at one curve. Her long, red hair wafted like tangled strands of seaweed about her head; the filmy skirt of her black cocktail dress billowed like a lily pad around her corpse. Her thigh-high stockings had split open, and although she still wore one evening shoe, the other lay at the bottom of the pool, a somehow pathetic note.

Now that the videographer and photographer had completed their initial tasks, the medical examiner and the rest of the C.S.U. could begin their own—the latter bagging and tagging every piece of evidence discovered at the possible crime scene. Like Toussaint and the others, Jake drew a pair of surgical gloves from his pocket and pulled them on so as not to contaminate anything that might later prove relevant to the case, should it ever wind up going to trial.

Eventually, Veronica's body was hauled from the pool, and as Jake observed the foam that bubbled around her nostrils at the medical examiner's probing, he didn't need to hear the final verdict to know she had, in fact, drowned. The foam was a sure sign of that. He sympathized with the younger of the two uniformed officers first on the scene, who had abruptly disappeared behind a nearby clump of hydrangea bushes, from which retching sounds now emanated. Breathtakingly beautiful in life, Veronica was in death a bloated monstrosity. Determinedly, Jake fought back the gorge that rose to his own throat, and he forced himself to grin at and respond to the obligatory jokes cracked by his partner and the rest of those present.

The black humor was a common coping mechanism for those who daily dealt with the seamier side of life. If you didn't find something to laugh about, something to break the tension and hold at bay the horror of the endless crime scenes, you would eventually go insane. Jake had seen it happen before, to good cops who had just one day snapped without warning and either suffered a complete nervous breakdown, committed suicide, or gone on a killing rampage.

"There's a contusion here on the victim's brow," the medical examiner announced after a moment, pointing out the injury as he examined the swollen corpse. "In her drunken state, she probably struck her head when she went into the pool…might even have knocked herself unconscious, which resulted in her drowning. Other than that, I don't offhand see anything that would indicate foul play…no ligature marks, for example, or signs that someone attempted to strangle her into a state of oblivion before pushing her in. My initial guess is that this is an accidental drowning, but I'll let you know if the autopsy indicates anything different.''

"Fine.'' Jake voiced his approval tersely, glad to turn his attention away from the body and well aware that, statistically speaking, murders involving drownings were rare. Still, he had an uncanny sixth instinct for crime, and it was gnawing at his gut now, regardless of how accidental Veronica's death appeared on the surface. "Meanwhile as a precaution, I want every inch of this pool checked and then double-checked. We *are* dealing with the Hamptons, and Mrs. Hampton Forsythe *did* quarrel with her husband last evening, after all. And quite frankly, this entire family is too frigging accident-prone for my liking. Remy, let's get a dive team in here.''

His expression thoughtful, Toussaint nodded his agreement. If there were any mistakes made on this case, it wouldn't be him and Jake who made them, that was for damned sure. They would drain the entire Olympic-size pool if they had to, if that's what it took to be certain nobody had given Veronica Hampton Forsythe a vicious conk on the head last night before shoving her into the water to become this evening's lead story for the morbidly fascinated public glued nightly to their television sets and mentally congratulating themselves on having thus far eluded the criminals and lunatics running loose on the world's streets.

Book One

Shifting Sands

A daring pilot in extremity;
Pleased with the danger, when the waves went high
He sought the storms; but for a calm unfit,
Would steer too nigh the sands to boast his wit.
Great wits are sure to madness near allied,
And thin partitions do their bounds divide.

Absalom and Achitophel
—John Dryden

One

Awaking From a Dream

> Then we shall rise
> And view ourselves with clearer eyes
> In that calm region where no night
> Can hide us from each other's sight.

> *The Exequy*
> —Henry King

A Small City, The Gulf Coast, The Present

The dream came to Claire Connelly again, as it always did, in those misty, grey hours when darkness had not yet fled nor dawn emerged, when her slumber was at its deepest point but, perversely, somehow at its most restless, too, so she tossed and turned and muttered in her sleep. When she had been married, Paul used to shake her awake roughly and rudely at such times, so that when she had finally awakened for good for the day, she had done so feeling as though she had never slept at all, but had spent the entire night being battered and bruised by some unknown tormentor. But Paul was no longer a part of her life, so now there was no one to rouse her from the nightmare.

Claire didn't know whether to be grateful or not for that, whether it was better to have been jolted to consciousness by Paul cursing and shaking her or, as she did these days, to jerk bolt-upright in a cold sweat born of stark terror, her heart hammering in her throat, choking the screams that would otherwise have torn free from her lips.

Had the dream been the ordinary sort of nightmare, where you were being chased by some unseen but hideous monster and, despite how hard you tried to run away, your legs kept getting heavier and slower, until they finally refused to work at all, Claire would have forced herself to turn and confront her gruesome pursuer. But this wasn't that kind of a dream. Instead, she was caught in the violent clutches of a riptide, which was inexorably dragging her under, so she could feel seaweed tangling like chains around her ankles, imprisoning her, weighing her down. Huge, dark, swollen, white-crested waves pounded her mercilessly, leaving her sodden and chilled to the bone, gulping bitter saltwater as she gasped for air and attempted desperately to struggle toward the moonlit shore. But it was too far away, and Claire knew she would never reach it before she was swept away and drowned.

And then the hand was there, seemingly disembodied, because she could never discern more than a shadowy figure beyond it, reaching out to her. All she had to do to save herself was take hold of it. Yet, strangely, her fear of the strong, slender hand was as great as that of the riptide, and she couldn't make herself grasp it. Moments later, she felt the icy water engulf her again, and she knew she was going down for the last time, that she should have seized the proffered hand, no matter what it had held in store for her.

It was here Claire always awakened abruptly, fighting for breath, drenched in sweat, her sheets twisted wildly around her, her blood roaring in her ears, her heart feeling as though it would burst inside her. This time was no different, and she trembled for several long minutes before managing to convince herself she wasn't lying at the bottom of the ocean, but was safe in her own bed.

After a long while, she rose and stumbled from her bedroom to the adjoining bath, flicking on the light switch so the room was flooded with the harsh but comforting glare of the many fluorescent bulbs. Bending over the sink, she splashed warm water on her face, washing away the perspiration that beaded her brow and upper lip and trickled from her temples. Then, laying aside the washcloth that she had used, she stared critically at herself in the mirror.

"You look like hell, Connelly," she told her reflection as her gaze took in the snarled mass of blond hair that fell below her shoulders, the shadows that haunted her wide eyes, the crescent smudges of mascara beneath her lower lashes, the blusher faded to dull smears on her high cheekbones, the drop of blood caked on her full, lower lip, where she had apparently bitten herself during her nightmare. She should have cleaned off her makeup before going to bed, she thought wearily, but she had just been too damned tired to bother. "A woman's face is her fortune, Claire," she could almost hear her mother chiding disapprovingly, "and so must be properly taken care of at all times."

Despite how Claire had always argued that it was, instead, a woman's brain that was her key to success, she knew deep down inside that her mother was right, unfortunately. It was still a man's world—and the men who ran the realm of broadcasting didn't hire unattractive anchors and reporters, and she knew they found ways of getting rid of those who permitted their good looks to go to hell in a handbasket. She peered at herself in the mirror, searching intently for signs of forehead furrows, crow's-feet at her eyes, and minute hatching above her upper lip. Much to Claire's relief, the few lines she discerned were so faint as to be utterly neglible. At thirty-one, she could easily have passed for a woman in her early twenties. She had excellent skin and bone structure. If she were careful, stayed out of the sun, and underwent the discreet face-lift whenever it finally became necessary, she could continue her career in broadcast journalism for years, just like Barbara Walters—the woman Claire most admired and respected.

Walters had come up the hard way in a profession that had, at the time, been strictly a man's venue, paving the path for those women who had aspired to follow in her footsteps. She had asked the tough questions, yet she had done it so charmingly and graciously that she had snagged coveted interviews with everybody from heads of state to superstars—and entertained the public in the process. There were very few other people in the media who, whether male or female, could legitimately make that claim.

But Claire planned to be one of them. She already had a good start, as a reporter for the syndicated newsmagazine, *Inside Story,* aired by Channel 4 in her city. The hour-long show was a blend of national pieces interspersed with local news and features of specific interest to each market. This format made *Inside Story* an ideal milieu in which to receive the much-sought-after break, careerwise, since if the show's headquarters in Los Angeles liked a local story, they would broadcast it nationally. Claire had been lucky enough to have more than one of her clips seen by millions across the country. Channel 4 had rewarded her accordingly, cutting her workload at the station so she could devote more time to *Inside Story* and increasing her salary handsomely to prevent her from quitting and moving to a larger market. Her public-recognition quotient was one of the highest in the city. Had she so desired, she could easily have got a good job in Miami, Tampa–St. Petersburg, New Orleans, or Houston.

But the truth was that she liked the city in which she lived. It was small enough that the political and societal circles were limited in number and crime wasn't all-pervasive, and big enough to boast, among other things, a symphony and a concert hall that touring theater and ballet troupes didn't bypass. It was the best of both worlds, she had always thought, a relatively sane, healthy, and cultured environment in which to raise her seven-year-old daughter, Gillian.

Realizing suddenly that the water was still running

in the sink, Claire shut off the taps and padded from the bath to make her way down to the hall to her daughter's bedroom. The door was open, as always, in case Gillian should need her in the night and call out. On the nightstand beside the missionary double bed, a cheerful, clown night-light burned. Gillian herself slept peacefully, one small arm wrapped tightly around her stuffed Paddington bear. Their big, fat, calico cat, Mr. Whiskers, lay curled up on the quilt. He blinked and yawned, annoyed, when Claire shifted him so he no longer rested on Gillian's legs.

As she gazed down at her sleeping daughter, Claire was filled with the overwhelming sense of wonder and love she always felt whenever she crept in at night like this to check on Gillian. Her daughter was everything to her, the only good thing ever to come from her marriage to Paul Langley, the only thing she lived for, beyond her work. Pulling the sheet and quilt up a little, she tucked them securely around Gillian and Paddington both before bending to kiss her daughter gently on the brow.

"I love you, sweetheart," Claire whispered.

At that, Gillian's big, blue eyes fluttered open, recognition flickering briefly in their depths before they drifted closed once more. "Love you, too, Mommy," she murmured drowsily, as she sighed, stretched, and shifted to a new position. Reaching out, Claire lightly smoothed back her daughter's silky, blond hair, then laid her hand tenderly against Gillian's cheek for a moment before at last straightening and tiptoeing from the room.

In the kitchen, Claire poured herself a small glass

of red wine, knowing it would be difficult, if not impossible, for her to get back to sleep without it. She couldn't afford to lie awake until dawn—even if she didn't have to work tomorrow. Too many late nights always showed up on faces beneath the hot glare of the lights in a television studio, illuminating haggard skin and dark circles under puffy eyes. It was bad enough that the cameras inevitably added ten pounds to everyone's figure, no matter how svelte, without having to worry about looking like yesterday's news on top of it. That was one of the problems with film and video: It created an image—an illusion—that was indelibly stamped on the minds of the public, so that if you began to gain weight or lose your looks, people noticed and invariably started to label you a has-been. Claire had watched more than one good broadcast journalist go down the tubes that way.

Sipping her wine, she meandered back to her bedroom, where she switched on the big television set, punching the remote so the volume was set low. CNN filled the screen, updating viewers on the terrible crash of a commercial jumbo jet. Being a white-knuckles flier, Claire was glad she hadn't been assigned to cover that particular story. After deactivating her security system, she opened the French doors in her bedroom and stepped out onto the deck beyond. The night air was muggy but cool, tinged with salt from the Gulf, whose breakers washed gently upon the sawgrass-tufted beach just some yards from her house.

She shivered a little as she stared out at the dark, frothy waves. She knew most people would not have understood why, in light of her nightmare, she chose to live here, especially so close to the water's shore. It was not something she was certain she could explain herself, except that the sea had always thrilled her as much as it awed and frightened her. Standing at the edge of the huge, powerful ocean, you knew how truly small and insignificant you were in the vast scheme of the universe, how helpless against the monumental forces of nature. Men had conquered mountains, the skies, even space. But they had never truly tamed the sea.

It kept life in perspective.

Despite her best intentions, it seemed as though hours passed before Claire at last slept again—only to be abruptly wakened by the insistent pealing of the bedside telephone and, on the still-running TV, the CNN anchor announcing that "Dollars & Sense" was coming up next. At first, drowsy and disoriented and having forgotten today was Saturday, Claire mistakenly believed the telephone was her alarm clock buzzing. Groaning, she pushed the Snooze button, hoping to get in a few extra minutes of slumber. But the ringing continued, and finally recognizing the sound for what it was, she fumbled for the receiver and lifted it from the cradle. "Hello," she mumbled.

"Claire, rise and shine, toss on some clothes, and get down to the station *pronto*." The voice of her chief cameraman, Winston Nash, spoke in her ear, the hollow, hissing, background noise letting her know he was on his cellular phone. "Veronica Hampton Forsythe's body was found floating facedown in her family's pool this morning."

"What?" Claire exclaimed, startled into abruptly

sitting up and glancing wildly at her alarm clock to check the time. "Are you kidding me, Winston?"

"No. Hurry!"

The line went dead. But Claire was already scrambling from bed, grabbing the remote for the television set and pressing its buttons to see if any of the other stations had managed to scoop Channel 4, were even now interrupting their morning cartoon programming with a special news bulletin. She didn't see anything, but she knew that if Nash had the information, it was only a matter of time until an announcement at the very least was broadcast all over the airwaves. She would have to skip her morning shower, make sure Ana Maria, the live-in housekeeper, could get Gillian up and dressed, and stay with her until Claire returned home. As she rushed around, yanking open her closet doors and pulling out a grass-green linen suit and matching leather pumps, Claire mentally checked off all that needed doing.

To her relief, once she had got dressed and finished pinning up her hair and applying her makeup, she discovered that Ana Maria was already up and preparing breakfast in the kitchen.

"Just toast and coffee for me, please," Claire told the housekeeper. "I've got to get to the station right away. Veronica Hampton Forsythe was found dead in her family's pool this morning."

"Oh, no!" Ana Maria's eyes widened, and one hand flew to her mouth. "Oh, no. That poor family. Truly, they are cursed. So many tragedies…was it another accident?"

"I don't know." Claire shook her head as she accepted the cup of coffee the housekeeper poured for her from the automatic coffeemaker on the counter. "I don't think Winston had any of the details yet. Can you help Gillian get dressed and her teeth brushed this morning and stay with her until I get back?"

"*Sí*, of course. That is no problem. I can do the grocery shopping later."

"Thanks, Ana Maria. You're one in a million. I don't know what I'd do without you. Tell Gillian I'm sorry I had to run, but that I love her and that I'll see her later." Claire snatched up the piece of toast the housekeeper had finished spreading with red-plum jam, then grabbed her portfolio, handbag, and car keys, and strode toward the garage, her heels clicking on the hardwood floors. "And will you phone the station, please, and let them know I'm on my way?" she called back over her shoulder.

"*Sí*, I will do it right now," Ana Maria said, *tsk*ing with distress to herself over Claire not eating a proper breakfast and the tragedy that had struck the Hampton family. *So much for all that money,* the housekeeper thought, sighing. *Millions of dollars, and, still, such terrible misfortune, such great unhappiness.*

After backing her snappy, red, convertible BMW from the garage, Claire drove as fast as she dared through her secluded neighborhood, The Breakers, then headed the car downtown, where Channel 4 was located. Even during weekday rush hour, the city streets were relatively easy to navigate, with traffic moving along briskly. This morning, there was hardly anybody on the road at all, so that within twenty minutes, she was pulling into the station's parking lot.

Winston Nash was already there, along with their second cameraman, Booker McGuinness, loading equipment into one of Channel 4's live-action vans. Claire pulled into the parking space reserved for her and shut off the motor, then gathered up all her paraphernalia and hurried toward the two men.

"Claire...good, you're here," Nash observed in greeting. "Let's get cracking. If we step on it, we might be first on the scene."

Since scooping their rivals was the primary goal of all good journalists, the three of them climbed into the van without further conversation or delay. Nash took the wheel, it being the general consensus at the station that anybody who maneuvered through traffic the way he did had, in a former life, either driven a New York taxicab or else the getaway car for a cadre of professional bank robbers.

"So...what've we got?" Claire asked, hauling a pen and notebook from her portfolio.

"Not much," Nash admitted as he deftly steered the van along the city streets. "I was already up, hard at my morning workout, when I heard the call come over the police scanner. One white female, age thirty-five, floater."

"How do you know it's Veronica Hampton Forsythe?"

"The way the airwaves were burning up, it just couldn't be anyone else. The talk was all real guarded—you know, like it is when the police don't want the media involved, when they're trying to keep something quiet for as long as possible—and far too many cruisers were dispatched to the scene for just a simple drowning. So I called somebody within the department, a source who owed me a favor. It's Veronica Hampton Forsythe all right.''

"And you're sure the police said she was dead?''

Nash nodded, grimacing. "Yeah…evidently, she'd been in the water for some time, at least since last night. The pool man discovered the body this morning when he arrived to clean the pool. Right now, the police are calling it an 'accidental drowning,' but you know they have to send a homicide team out, anyway, in cases like that, just to make sure.''

At that, Claire momentarily paused in her note taking, glancing down blindly at her pad and swallowing hard. Of course Nash was right. At least two homicide detectives would indeed be at the possible crime scene—and given everything else that had already occurred these past few months, she knew just who they would be, too: Jake Seringo and Remy Toussaint. Her heart beat fast at the knowledge. She and Jake had been lovers once, long ago, and Claire knew he still believed she had greatly wronged him. Deep down inside, she herself still felt a gnawing sense of guilt that he was right about that. She had never meant to hurt him, but she had been young and ambitious, fresh out of college and newly embarked on her chosen career in life. At the time, she had thought she would be the world's biggest fool not to use Jake's story as a launch pad for herself. Now, older and wiser, Claire knew that if she had it all to do over again, she would do it differently.

But it was too late for that. You could never go back and change the past.

"Claire...Claire." Booker's voice jolted her from her reverie. "What kind of shots are you going to want?"

"Whatever we can get," she replied, determinedly forcing her mind to the story at hand. "The police will probably have the whole place cordoned off by the time we arrive, so I doubt we'll gain access to the house. But scout around, talk to the staff and neighbors, both...see what you can arrange. My guess is that we'll have to call for the helicopter to take some aerial film of the house and grounds, pictures of the pool. You'll need to comb the archives, as well, of course. I know we've got plenty of stock footage on the Hamptons and Senator Forsythe, which we can use with whatever we get today. Whatever we ultimately put together, though, it needs to be fabulous. This one has national exposure written all over it, guys!"

"You can say that again!" Nash grinned as he sped through a yellow light.

Within moments, he was pulling the Channel 4 van to a screeching halt alongside the far curb in front of the Hampton family mansion. As he, Claire, and McGuinness scrambled out, none of them could conceal the elation and excitement that gripped them at being first on the scene. The two men began hauling out their camera equipment, while Claire approached one of the uniformed officers who was attempting to bring order to the chaos already ensuing.

Over the course of her career, she had learned there was a fine line between doing her job and being obnoxiously aggressive, that you did indeed, as the old Southern saying went, catch more flies with honey than vinegar. She had further discovered that her good looks were both a blessing and curse—depending upon whom she was interviewing. So now Claire deftly selected a young, swaggering patrolman as her target. She knew instinctively that he would find her attractive, that he would want to impress her with his knowledge of the drowning, no matter how scant, and that the thought of having his handsome face plastered all over the news would mitigate any fear he might feel at having to suffer his superiors' wrath for it later.

"Excuse me, Sergeant," she said in greeting, laying one hand on his arm, smiling up at him brightly, and elevating him to a rank she knew he didn't possess. "I'm Claire Connelly, with Channel Four's *Inside Story*. Could I trouble you with some questions about the drowning?"

"It's officer, ma'am." He adjusted his cap and gun belt, preening. "Officer Edmond."

Claire soon had every scrap of information he knew pried out of him, and Nash had got film of the quick interview, before one of the senior patrolmen observed what was happening and stepped in to issue rebukes all the way around, ordering Claire and Nash away and young Officer Edmond back to his assigned duties. But it was enough to get on the air with—hopefully before anybody else, although other media had now started to arrive on the scene.

Seeing that, Claire and Nash hurried back to the Channel 4 van. The microwave dish on its roof and all the other equipment they carried on board enabled them to do live, remote broadcasts. Swiftly, they got in touch with the station, relaying what they had learned and setting up the remote. Claire reviewed her notes, then tossed them aside as just minutes later, Channel 4 interrupted its regular programming for a special news bulletin. On the tiny receiver in her ear, Claire heard the weekend noon anchor, Stephanie Roselle, break the news of Veronica Hampton Forsythe's drowning, then announce, "We go now live to Claire Connelly, at the Hampton family estate. Claire, what can you tell us?"

She had her back to the black, wrought-iron gates of the Hampton mansion, so that as she faced Nash's handheld camera, the lens would capture the hectic scene behind her. "Stephanie, as you can see, news of Veronica Hampton Forsythe's death has brought disruption to the normally quiet streets of Forest Gables, this city's most exclusive neighborhood, leaving family, friends, and neighbors shocked and saddened. Ms. Hampton Forsythe's body was discovered earlier this morning, floating facedown in the family's swimming pool, following a party held here last evening to raise money for her husband Senator Malcolm Forsythe's re-election campaign. According to Officer Edmond, one of the first patrolmen on the scene, the drowning is at this time being labeled an accident. No other information is currently being released, although we do understand that homicide detectives are en route. This is typical under the circumstances, however, so we don't as yet know whether there may, in fact, be some suspicion of foul play.

"Stephanie, as you and many of our viewers are aware, the Hamptons have over the years been plagued with a series of devastating tragedies, the most recent of which was the unfortunate death of Ms. Hampton Forsythe's younger twin sister, Vanessa, in an arsonous fire at the Seabreeze Sanatorium just a few short months ago. Investigators have as yet to make any arrests in that particular case, however, as all the available evidence appears to suggest the fire may have been ignited by a sanatorium patient, Billy Oxbridge, who had a long history of mental illness and perished in the blaze himself.

"Senator Forsythe is said to be distraught at his wife's death, and he is currently secluded here at the Hampton family estate, along with her only surviving blood relatives—her grandmother, Mrs. Nadine Hampton, who is the matriarch of this powerful and wealthy dynasty, and Ms. Lily D'Angelo, who is the deceased's cousin and now the apparent sole heiress to the vast Hampton fortune.

"It is not known at this time how his wife's death will affect Senator Forsythe's plans for re-election. As an incumbent, he has been largely favored to win this year's campaign, and has been widely viewed by many as having a shot at the presidency in the future, as well. His wife, extremely prominent in social circles and highly respected for her countless charitable works, was considered a major political asset to him. Her unexpected death can only prove a severe blow, not only to Senator Forsythe, but also to what remains of the Hampton family, which has now for decades endured so much more than its fair share of adversity that many people—including well-known Hollywood psychic Madame Zena—have declared that the entire family is cursed. This morning's tragic, untimely events have residents here in Forest Gables and this reporter wondering if there is indeed more than a grain of truth to that assertion.

"We will, of course, continue to remain on location and bring you updates as we receive them. Now, back to you in the studio, Stephanie."

Claire answered a few questions directed to her as follow-up, then waited until she heard the anchor thank her for her report, then end the special news bulletin, before she pulled the receiver from her ear and relaxed the poised stance she had assumed for the live broadcast.

Nash hefted his camera from his shoulder, smiled, and gave her the thumbs-up sign. "Great job, Claire, as usual—and I don't think anybody beat us to it, either. That ought to make the boss real happy. Hell, we might even eventually get a bonus or a raise out of this deal."

She nodded, knowing how glad she should be about that, how proud she should be of a job well done. But it was at that moment that she spied Jake Seringo and Remy Toussaint pulling their unmarked car to a halt at the curb across the street, and the sight of her former lover reminded her that, just like today, her success often came at the expense of other people's tragedies. Shadows haunted her eyes at the thought. Claire believed wholeheartedly in the work she did, that knowledge was essential in life, and that the media had a responsibility to provide it, especially in this technological day and age, when the majority of the public were glued to television sets and computers. Still, she couldn't deny the fact that the balance the media achieved was weighted heavily toward news that was depressing, shocking, and horrifying. While she knew that to a great extent, this was a reflection of life itself, she also wondered if perhaps the world wouldn't be a better place if the media concentrated on a more positive outlook. After all, when people were daily inundated with violence and other negativity, were not those aspects of their own lives, as a result, constantly highlighted and thereby reinforced?

Andy Warhol had once said that in the future, everybody would have fifteen minutes of fame. But getting it had driven many in both the media and the public to extremes. Claire often felt as though she walked on eggshells, striving never again to cross the invisible barrier that had sprung up in her mind after her brief relationship with Jake.

More than once, she had tried to apologize to him for how she had hurt him in the past. But he had brushed her off contemptuously, so she had known he didn't believe she was truly and deeply sorry for all the grief she had caused him, that she regretted it with all her heart, or that she had changed, that she was no longer the foolish, eager young girl she had been ten years ago. He still despised her as much as he had at the time of their breakup, and if the powerful, physical attraction they had always felt toward each other still pulled at them as strongly as ever, well, it must be diligently ignored.

So, although Claire was vibrantly aware of Jake's presence, she pretended not to notice him, forcing herself to concentrate instead on what Nash and McGuinness were relating to her. The Channel 4 chopper was on its way to shoot the aerial film they now knew for certain they needed for the segment they would put together for *Inside Story,* since the odds of getting onto the Hampton grounds appeared virtually nil at this point. It didn't matter. McGuinness was almost positive they had footage of the mansion—and maybe even the pool—in the archives at the station.

Her two cameramen continued their enthusiastic discussion, while Claire interjected what she hoped were appropriate responses, unable to prevent herself from watching surreptitiously from beneath her long, thick black lashes as, across the street, Jake Seringo dropped his half-smoked cigarette onto the old, uneven bricks. Despite everything, Claire had the strangest, most painful sensation that it wasn't the discarded butt, but her heart he was deliberately crushing beneath his booted heel.

Two

The Mean Streets

As a dog returneth to his vomit,
So a fool returneth to his folly.
Seest thou a man wise in his own conceit?
There is more hope of a fool than of him.
The slothful man saith, There is a lion in the way;
A lion is in the streets.

Bible
—Proverbs: 26:12-13

A Small City, The Gulf Coast, Ten Years Ago

Isabel Seringo had never liked working the night shift at St. Mary Hospital. But as a registered nurse, she had little say in the scheduling of her hours, and since she and her husband, Jake, needed the money, she punched the hospital's time clock whenever she was told to do so.

Tonight had been especially trying, with a seemingly endless string of trauma cases in the emergency room. The hospital's P.A. system had appeared to blast out "Code Blue" over and over, requesting this doctor or that to report to the E.R., S.T.A.T. It was that time of month, Isabel thought sadly, tiredly, as she finally left the hospital, its automated, glass doors closing with a soft swish behind her as she headed toward her old, compact car in the brightly lit parking lot. People went crazy whenever there was a full moon, as though its pull affected not only the earth's tides, but also humans' brains. The emergency-room patients had resulted from four shootings, two stabbings, several drug overdoses, at least three car accidents involving drunk drivers, and a motorcycle that had veered wildly out of control and crashed into a telephone pole. The victim of this last had been D.O.A., his neck broken from the impact.

It was just as well, Isabel told herself. The young man hadn't been wearing a helmet, so his head injuries had been extensive and severe. If he had survived, he would most likely have been a vegetable. At least his family had been spared that anguish and burden—although Isabel knew she would never forget the tortured expression on his mother's face when she had learned her son was dead on arrival at the hospital. Isabel couldn't imagine being able to survive that kind of loss. Gently, she laid her hand on her abdomen, distended with her first pregnancy, and said a silent prayer for her child within.

Moments later, she unlocked her car door, slid wearily into the front seat, and carefully buckled her seat belt. It was late, nearly midnight, and she was utterly exhausted. She wanted nothing more than to drive home as quickly as was safely possible, where she could pry her sturdy, white, rubber-soled shoes from her swollen, aching feet and collapse in bed. But she and Jake needed some groceries—not much, just a couple of things like milk and bread, so there would be cereal and toast for breakfast tomorrow morning. Still, it was enough that Isabel knew she must stop, however briefly, at the convenience store on the way home.

She comforted herself with the thought that it wouldn't take long to run inside and buy the few items they required. And since Jake was working the graveyard shift tonight at the police department, he would never know she hadn't driven straight home to their small apartment across the river, as he always strenuously insisted she do, claiming the streets of the poor side of the city in which they lived weren't safe during the daylight hours, much less after dark.

The Latino gang to which Manolo Alvarez and all his cronies belonged called themselves *Las Calaveras*—the Skulls—and this was the grisly insignia each member had tattooed on his right forearm during a brutal initiation rite designed to weed out from the start those who couldn't cut the mustard. The gang was primarily composed of youths ranging in age from twelve to twenty-five, and they were involved in any number of criminal activities—most at the direction of Colombian drug lords. However, this did not prevent them from branching out on their own when the need arose, and tonight was one such occasion.

"So...what're we gonna do to get us some fast cash

tonight, *amigos?*'' Manny inquired cockily and loudly of nobody in particular as he and three of his buddies cruised the mean streets of the city.

The radio in their jazzed-up old car was cranked up full blast. From the speakers, Gloria Estefan wailed "Turn the Beat Around" above the roar of the bad muffler, all the noise making it difficult to converse. However, this was not considered a liability, but, rather, an asset, since it informed those watching the garish convertible as it sped by that Las Calaveras were the kings of the city's ghetto, unafraid of being pulled over and ticketed. Nor did the young men make any attempt to conceal either the reefers or the tequila they passed around among themselves as they drove. They had already smoked two joints and drained one quart of Cuervo, pitching the empty bottle from the car to smash against the curb and hooting at the street hookers who had spat curses at them angrily upon being struck by the shards of flying glass.

"Whaddaya say we pull over at that convenience store and help ourselves to whatever they got in their till? We can grab us a couple of cartons of cigarettes while we're at it. I'm all out of smokes." Manny crumpled up his empty cigarette package and threw it from the car.

"Sounds good to me," Ramón Garcia drawled as he dragged on the reefer, holding the smoke in his lungs for as long as he could before exhaling and coughing violently, wiping at his red, teary eyes. "I don't like that fat, stupid slob who works nights in there, anyway. He's got Coke bottles for glasses…looks like some big, old, bloated, dead fish staring at you. People like that ought not be allowed out in public...'cept on Halloween, of course.''

The others laughed raucously, as though Ramón's observations about the night clerk were the funniest remarks they had ever heard.

"You know, I'll bet if we plugged old fish-face, he'd blow up and fly around like a punctured balloon...*whoosh, whoosh, grrr, splat.*" Enrique Lopez sniggered at the thought.

"And that's exactly what'll happen to him if he gives us any trouble," Hector Delgados declared as he upended the bottle of tequila, taking a long gulp before wiping his wet mouth off on his bare forearm. "*Bam.* Right between the eyes with my *pistola*, eh?"

"Not if I shoot the fat bastard first—which I will if he don't do exactly what we tell him." Manny hauled his Saturday-night special from beneath the car seat, checking the clip to ensure that it was fully loaded before jacking a cartridge into the chamber.

Spinning the steering wheel so the tires squealed on the asphalt, burning rubber, Hector guided the convertible into the pitted parking lot of the convenience store, narrowly missing the old, compact car that was the only other vehicle out front. He and the others stuffed their automatic pistols down into the waistbands of their jeans, so the guns were concealed by their T-shirts. Then, glancing around warily, they got out of the car to swagger determinedly inside.

When, from the rear aisle of the convenience store, Isabel heard the first shot, she thought it was just some truck backfiring outside in the street. It was only when the report was followed by a second bang and then a third that she realized the sounds were coming from inside the store and that something terrible was happening. Frightened, she instinctively crouched down in the aisle, hesitantly creeping forward until she could, in one of the large, round mirrors positioned to deter shoplifters, see what was occurring up front.

At the sight of the night clerk sprawled backward over the checkout counter, his thick glasses shattered, a stream of blood trickling from one eye that could no longer see, a larger, dark pool saturating his chest and dripping onto the counter, she clapped her hand to her mouth to stifle the screams that would otherwise have reverberated through the store. Four gang members were rifling the contents of the cash register and the counter shelves, stuffing cartons of cigarettes into plastic sacks and grabbing six-packs of beer from the cooler.

"Dios mio," Isabel whispered brokenly, tears starting in her eyes as she abruptly grasped the danger she was in. The young men were apparently unaware that Wyatt Jenkins, the night clerk, rode a motor scooter to work, which he parked in the alley behind the store. They must have assumed the car out front belonged to him and thought they were now alone in the store. If they found her... *"Dios mio,"* Isabel sobbed softly again, her jackhammering heart lodged in her throat, her palms sweating against the slick, linoleum floor, her head reeling and her stomach churning, making her feel as though she was going either to pass out or to vomit.

As quietly as possible, she began to crawl along the

aisle toward the small room at the rear of the store. If she could get inside it without being seen, she might be able to hide there safely until the gang members left. Surely, they would not risk hanging around. It was possible that before being killed, Wyatt had had time to press the silent alarm button, and that even now, the police were en route. Praying fervently that this was so, Isabel continued desperately toward the small room that offered her only hope of survival.

"That's it! We got enough! Let's get the hell out of here quick now before the cops come. *¡Vamanos, compadres, vamanos!*" Enrique cried, waving his gun around impatiently as he urged the others to take what they had and make good their escape.

"No, wait, Enrique! You gotta learn not to let panic get the best of you, to stay cool and think, man," Manny insisted, his voice a trifle mocking, his dark eyes narrowed shrewdly as he glanced suspiciously around the store. "We can't leave here yet—at least, not without the frigging video. Don't you watch no TV, fool? All them real-life shows about the *policía?* A place like this, they gotta have at least one camera, *amigo.* The cops'll be able to make us from the tape, and it'll wind up as the D.A.'s prime exhibit against us if we ever get caught. We gotta get it before we go. You and Ramón watch the front of the store, while Hector and I check out the back."

Heaving himself over the counter, from behind which he had looted the cash register, Manny started down the aisle toward the small room at the rear of the store, Hector hard on his heels. Reaching the closed door and finding it locked, Manny stepped back and kicked it open so hard that the frame splintered as the door crashed wide open, banging violently against the shelves inside against one wall, knocking various cleaning products to the floor. He flicked on the light.

"Well, well, well...lookee what we got here, Hector!" A wicked, supercilious smirk split Manny's leering visage as he spied Isabel huddled, petrified, on the floor in the far corner. "A pretty, young *señora*—and now, she's seen our faces." With one side of his mouth, he made a falsely regretful *tsk*ing sound. "Ain't that a cryin' shame?"

Three

A Shattered Life

When the lamp is shattered
The light in the dust lies dead—
When the cloud is scattered
The rainbow's glory is shed.

When the Lamp Is Shattered
—Percy Bysshe Shelley

A couple of high-school kids who had stopped at the convenience store on their way home from their Friday-night date had discovered the body of the night clerk and, distraught, had dialed 911 from a pay telephone outside. In their patrol car, Officer Jake Seringo and his partner, Frank Bollinger, were cruising the streets of the ghetto at the time, so they were first on the scene of the homicides when the dispatcher's call came through. After pulling into the parking lot of the convenience store, the officers warily got out of their patrol car to approach the two teenagers still standing at the pay telephone. In an attempt to comfort her, the young man had his arms around his equally young girlfriend, who was shaking and sobbing hysterically against his shoulder.

The sight of the two teenagers, obviously close, reminded Jake of himself and his wife, Isabel, when they had been dating. They had got married right after Isabel had graduated from high school, even though her parents had thought she was too young.

"Are you the ones who called in the murder?" Jake asked the teenagers gently, despite his knowing how unnecessary the question was.

"Yeah," the young man replied gravely, while his girlfriend clung to him and nodded tearfully, gasping and sniffling as she tried to compose herself.

"What's your name, *amigo?*"

"Tomás…Tomás Ortega. And this is my *novia,* Lupe Perez. We were—we were on our way home from a movie…thought we'd stop and get a couple of ice-cream cones, you know. They gotta machine here… We saw the—the body when we got inside. He was—he was all covered with blood and—and sprawled back on the counter. It was awful! I never saw so much blood in my whole life! Lupe started screaming… We didn't touch anything…just got out of there as quick as we could and called you guys."

"Did you see anybody else inside? Has anyone come out since you dialed nine-one-one?" Jake inquired, glancing sharply at the store's grill-covered front windows, searching for some sign of movement within.

"No." The young man shook his head. "We didn't see anybody, but then, like I said, we didn't stick around long enough to find out whether or not the killer was still in there. Nobody's come out, though. I'm pretty sure about that."

"Okay. My partner and I will check it out. In the meantime, we're going to need you both to hang around here so we can get a formal statement later. If you haven't already called your folks, you probably ought to do that now, let them know you're going to be late getting home, so they don't worry."

After that, drawing their revolvers, Jake and his partner started toward the store, so intent on what they might find inside that they paid no heed to the two cars parked out front, other than to use them for cover to avoid being easy targets for anybody lurking within.

"I don't see anyone," Jake announced quietly as, from where he was crouched behind the teenagers' vehicle, he peered intently again through the store's front windows. "How about you, Frank?"

"No, the place looks empty to me. My guess is that whoever murdered the night clerk is long gone by now. But let's be careful, anyway. We might be wrong, and barging in there could get us shot."

"Right." Jake wondered what was going through his partner's mind, if Bollinger were worried about him being just a rookie cop. Frank's last partner, fresh out of the police academy, had recently been killed in the line of duty. It wasn't the first time the department had lost a new officer in the ghetto; the place was virtually a war zone.

Alertly, guns held at the ready, the two patrolmen made their way to the store's heavy, glass front doors and slipped inside.

"Check him out." Bollinger motioned toward the night clerk before beginning cautiously to canvas the narrow aisles.

Easily, Jake vaulted over the checkout counter, only to draw up short at the sight of the night clerk's bloody corpse, arms outflung, glasses broken and askew. Abruptly, Jake felt his stomach lurch, as though the earth had suddenly dropped from beneath his feet. "Jesus! Oh, Jesus!" he gasped softly, momentarily frozen where he stood and hoping he wasn't about to be sick all over the place. Closing his eyes, he forced himself to take several deep breaths, fighting down the gorge that rose to his throat. All the videotapes and photographs of bodies he had viewed while in training had not prepared him for the reality of a corpse in the flesh. At last, moving gingerly to avoid stepping in all the blood puddled on the floor, he leaned over the body to lay two fingers at the side of the night clerk's neck. There wasn't any pulse, but then, Jake hadn't expected to find one. "He's dead, Frank," he called, turning from the corpse.

"We've got another one back here, too," Bollinger observed grimly as Jake joined him at the rear of the store. "Christ! Must've been a fucking animal who did this! Jake? Hey, you okay, partner? Shit! Get your head down between your knees and breathe, damn it!"

Jake paid his partner no heed, oblivious of his revolver sliding from his grasp as, without warning, his knees gave way beneath him and he dropped to the floor to bend over the pitiful corpse lying there. An anguished, animalistic cry of horror, rage, and disbelief erupted from his throat.

"Jake! For God's sake, Jake! What in the hell's the matter with you?" Bollinger grabbed hold of him, trying to haul him upright, only to be wildly flung away.

"You don't—you don't understand, Frank," Jake choked out after several long, terrible minutes, breathing hard and furiously blinking back the hot tears that stung his tortured eyes. "This is my—this is my...wife...."

"Oh, Jesus! Oh, Jake, I—I didn't realize... I don't know what to say. I am so damned sorry, partner. Christ! Come away, Jake. There's nothing you can do for her now— and we for damned sure don't want to contaminate this crime scene. We want Homicide to be able to catch the bastard who did this!"

"I—I think I'm going to be sick, Frank." Lurching to his feet, Jake stumbled blindly toward the toilet in the tiny, closetlike room in one corner, retching violently until, finally, nothing else would come up. After a while, his partner helped him to his feet, guiding him toward the sink and turning on the taps. Gratefully, Jake splashed his face with the tepid water.

"Are you going to be all right, buddy?" Bollinger asked soberly, his brow knitted with concern as he gazed at his partner.

"I don't know."

"Come on. Let me take you out front, Jake. You've had a severe shock, and I need to radio for backup and Homicide, too."

"Will you—will you at least cover her up, Frank? I just can't—can't bear to leave her lying there like that...."

"Sure...sure, buddy. You just wait here until I take care of that, all right?"

Jake nodded weakly, and after glancing at him uncertainly again, Bollinger stepped back into the storeroom to search for something with which to cover Isabel's corpse. She couldn't have been more than twenty-three or twenty-four, he thought, and she had been about six months pregnant, as well. Bollinger felt sick himself as he screened Isabel's body as best he could with a jacket he found hanging on a hook in the storeroom. Then he propelled Jake outside, not giving him a chance to linger over his wife's brutalized corpse.

"Sit down, buddy." He pressed Jake down on the concrete stoop that ran the length of the store out front. "I'm going to call in."

If there were anything guaranteed to get every cop in the city out looking for a criminal, it was the killing of one of their own. The murder of a policeman's wife was close enough, and presently, the parking lot of the convenience store was swarming with patrol and unmarked cars, the Crime Scene Unit's van, and the medical examiner's station wagon. Lights flashed, radios squawked, and officers and detectives combed the crime scene, while, across the street, the media gathered like circling buzzards. But Jake was numb to all the grim activity around him, shut up in a hell in his own tormented mind, unable even to think—except to assure himself that he must be suffering a hideous nightmare from which he would eventually awaken to find Isabel sleeping peacefully in his arms.

But deep down in his gut, he knew that wasn't so,

and he felt a second, staggering blow as his wife was carried out in a body bag atop a gurney to be loaded into an ambulance and transported to the morgue.

"Why don't you let somebody drive you home now, Officer Seringo? Your partner has already answered most all our questions, and if we need anything else, we can always give you a call at home."

At the sound of the deep, somber voice, Jake glanced up from where he still sat on the stoop of the convenience store to spy one of the homicide detectives, a big, black man by the name of Remy Toussaint. Instinctively, Jake liked the older man, felt somehow that he could trust him. "Shouldn't—shouldn't I...go with her?"

"No, son. Her body won't be released until after the autopsy, anyway, so you've done all you can do for her at the moment. You need to think about yourself now, take some time off to try to come to grips with what's happened here tonight. Seeing your first real corpse is always rough. That it should have been your own wife...well, nobody deserves that, and no amount of training in the world could have prepared you for it. So, come on. Let's get you home, son. You look like the walking wounded—and believe it or not, tomorrow's going to be even worse, when the reality of all this begins to sink in."

"You sound as though you're speaking from experience," Jake noted quietly.

Toussaint nodded slowly. "My son was murdered by a gang. He was our only child. Hardly a day goes by that I don't think about it. I ain't never been the same since—and you won't, either. But you've only got two choices. You can either lie down and die, or you can go on living—and try not to punish yourself too much because you're the one who survived. Still, you don't need to think about any of that tonight. Right now, all you need to do is get some rest. Trust me. Tomorrow will be time enough to try to make what sense you can of your wife's death, to come to terms with the fact that, for whatever reason, she's gone, and that none of us understands why the Lord lets bad things happen to good people.''

"It's a test—of faith, of strength," Jake said dully.

"Maybe so, son. Maybe so. That's as good an answer as any, I reckon."

Later, after Isabel's autopsy, Jake was informed of two things. The first was that the semen recovered from his wife's body indicated there had been at least four perpetrators at the crime scene. The second was that his and Isabel's baby had been a boy—as though knowing the sex of his child who had never had a chance to live was somehow supposed to make him feel better. In some dark corner of his mind, Jake knew the latter piece of news had been intended as a kindness, but the cruelty of it overwhelmed him. The sight of the small, closed coffin at the funerals of his wife and baby was as indelibly branded on his brain as the image of Isabel's bloody corpse was.

Once his family was decently buried, he returned home alone to their apartment, where he grabbed a half-full bottle of Captain Morgan from the clutter of dirty dishes now stacked all over the small kitchen table. Then he took his revolver from his holster and sat down on the battered couch in the living room to empty out all the chambers except one. After he closed the cylinder, Jake spun it around absently, then laid the gun on the coffee table before him. Silently, he smoked a cigarette and drank long swallows of the rum, not bothering to answer when the telephone rang off the wall. He didn't want to speak to anyone—not Isabel's grieving parents, not his own sorrowing father, and especially not any psychologist or well-wishers from the police department.

Finally, after a great while, Jake took one last, long drag off his cigarette and carefully ground the butt out in an ashtray.

Then he picked up his revolver.

Four

Hell's Gates

It is easy to go down into Hell;
night and day, the gates of dark Death stand wide;
but to climb back again,
to retrace one's steps to the upper air—
there's the rub, the task.

> *Aeneid*
> —Virgil

"Winston, please. Just listen to me for a minute, that's all I'm asking," Claire Connelly entreated, laying one hand on her friend's arm to draw him to a halt as he strode impatiently down the long corridor toward one of the studios of Channel 4. "We can do this. I know we can!"

"And lose our jobs over it in the process?" Winston Nash scowled at her as though she had lost her mind.

"That's not going to happen if Mr. Kendall likes the series—and it could be our means of getting a leg up the ladder! You know that, Winston."

"But that barrio shooting's already been aired, Claire. It's old hat now, yesterday's news—besides which, nobody in this city gives a damn about what goes on across the river, anyway, just as long as it doesn't spill over the bridges to trickle uptown."

"But that's my whole point! People *should* care! And that's exactly what our angle ought to be! That what happened to that night clerk and that policeman's wife could have occurred anywhere at any time—and will, sooner or later, if the persons in positions of authority in this city don't start cracking down on crime, especially across the river. Look, we can do the entire exposé based on two themes...the Great American Dream and the Great American Tragedy, beginning with Jake and Isabel Seringo's parents immigrating to the U.S., in search of a better life for themselves and their children. We can show how Jake and Isabel, despite growing up in the barrio, somehow managed to do all the right things—only to have their lives shattered by the very criminals Jake works to put behind bars and that I'm sure Isabel probably treated at St. Mary Hospital, too. It could be a masterpiece, Winston! Look, I'll even pay for all the film," Claire offered, in an attempt to sweeten her proposal. "All you have to do is handle the equipment we need."

"Somehow get hold of it, you mean! And what if somebody finds out I took it, Claire? Huh? Did you ever even stop to consider that? They'll think I stole it!" Nash protested, but she could tell he was weakening, and she pressed him still further.

"I wouldn't let you be accused of that. You must know I wouldn't. Besides, we don't even have to borrow the equipment from the station. I've already thought about that. We can probably check it out from the audiovisual department at the university, if necessary. I'm sure Dr. Younger wouldn't mind, that he'd authorize it if we tell him why we want the equipment. So, come on, Winston. What have you got to lose but time?''

"Well, when you put it that way... Oh, all right, Claire. I'll do it. Maybe I can even talk Booker into helping us.'' Nash shook his head as he gazed down at her, grinning ruefully at the realization that he had allowed himself to be persuaded. "But don't blame me if this little scheme of yours winds up costing us our jobs! The people in line ahead of us aren't going to like it one bit if we manage to put together a series Kendall actually decides to air!''

"No, but that's *their* problem, isn't it?'' Claire grinned back, excited at the prospect of putting her idea into action. "We've just got to do something to get ourselves noticed, Winston. Otherwise, we'll probably both be little more than glorified gofers for the next five years at least—and I don't know about you, but I intend to be Channel Four's top reporter by the time I'm thirty!''

"Yeah, right. Dream on, Claire...dream on.'' Nash rolled his eyes skeptically, laughing at her declaration. "But, hey, I like your style, babe.''

"One of these days, when I'm the next Barbara Walters, I'm going to remind you of this conversation, Winston. Meanwhile, it's quitting time for me, so I'm taking off. I'll drop by the university on my way home, speak to Dr. Younger. After that, I'll see if I can't track down Officer Seringo. Want to come along?''

"No, this is *your* series, Claire. That means you get to set it up—and that all *I* have to do is show up when and where you tell me, to shoot the film.''

Nash was right, of course. Claire knew that. So she didn't try to convince him to tag along with her. Instead, she made her way to her desk to shut down her computer for the day and grab her handbag and car keys. Minutes later, she was en route to the local state university, where—her student parking permit having now expired—she was lucky enough to find a visitor's parking space behind the Marconi Communications Building. She eased her vehicle to a stop, locked it, and hurried toward the big, redbrick edifice where she had spent most of her college years. From past experience, Claire knew her favorite former professor, Dr. Younger, the chairman of the department, was usually to be found in his office at this hour. After knocking quietly on his closed door, she discovered he was, in fact, in. Delighted to see her, he was, after she had explained her idea to him, more than happy to okay her and Nash's use of the necessary equipment from the audiovisual department.

"Thank you so much, Dr. Younger. We really appreciate all your help,'' Claire told him, sincerely grateful. "Keep your fingers crossed for us!''

"I will—and the best of luck to you and Mr. Nash with your potential series, Ms. Connelly,'' Dr. Younger called after her as, all her arrangements completed, she departed from his office. "I'll look forward to watching it on the air.''

Returning to her car, Claire sat there for a long minute in the parking lot, elated, as she searched her handbag for the scrap of paper upon which, before leaving the station, she had written down Officer Seringo's home address. It hadn't been difficult at all for her to obtain, since he was listed in the telephone book. She knew the street he lived on; it was across the river, in the barrio. She debated whether or not to call him first and try to set up an appointment, then finally decided it was better to try to confront him face-to-face. He couldn't put her off as easily that way, and deep down inside, she had a sneaking suspicion he wasn't going to prove nearly as enthusiastic about her plan as Dr. Younger had. After all, she intended to put the lives of Officer Seringo and his dead wife on display for the entire city to see. Still, no guts, no glory, she told herself.

At last, that thought spurring her on despite the momentary pang of guilt that had had her reconsidering, Claire shoved her key into the ignition, started her car, and pulled resolutely from the parking lot. Her heart thudded with anticipation at the realization that her imminent meeting with Officer Seringo might prove to be one of the most important of her whole life.

"I hope you don't turn me down, Officer Seringo, because one way or another, with or without your help, I'm going to tell your story to the world!" she insisted determinedly to herself as she headed toward her destination.

Originally in decades long gone by, that portion of the city that lay across the muddy, serpentine river had been its red-light district, a collection of brothel houses, street cribs, saloons, and gambling establishments that had provided entertainment for the city's rich and jaded young rakes. Over the years following the turn of the century, various attempts had been made to clean up the district and encourage businesses to open their doors there—all eventually to little or no avail. Despite its various pockets of prosperity, the ghetto had been unable to shake off the muck that clung to its roots; and one influx after another of both legal immigrants and illegal aliens had only compounded the problem. Poor whites, blacks, Creoles, Latinos, Asians, and just plain, old duke's mixtures, had all migrated to the crime-ridden mean streets of the city, so that now a trip across the river was like entering a region of small, foreign nations. There were countless blocks where, except for on the surviving street signs at the corners, English was nowhere to be seen, French, Spanish, and Vietnamese predominating instead; and in wooden stands arrayed along the cracked, uneven sidewalks in front of dilapidated stores, fruits, vegetables, and other staples unfamiliar to American palates were displayed.

Numerous buildings stood vacant, their doors and windows boarded up, the vulgar and boastful graffiti of the neighborhood gangs spray-painted on their exterior walls. Stout, iron grills or bars to deter burglars covered the doors and windows of those businesses still in existence. Empty beer cans and liquor bottles, cigarette wrappers and discarded butts, yellowed newspapers and old fliers, used condoms and needles, and other noxious garbage littered sidewalks, curbs, and alleys. During the day, the more respectable elements of the various neighborhoods were to be viewed upon the streets. But after dark, gangs, drug dealers and addicts, pimps and hookers, bookmakers, and other human refuse reigned supreme, and the patrol cars that cruised the ghetto were kept busy, their lights flashing and sirens wailing endlessly in the night.

Along the riverbank sprawled a seemingly interminable string of rail yards, factories, warehouses, and docks from which boats and barges laden with cargo journeyed upriver to other ports of call and which provided one of the major sources of employment in the ghetto. The other derived from the river's mouth, which opened into the Gulf and where fishing boats reeking of their daily catches clustered.

As Claire guided her car across one of the steel-and-concrete bridges that spanned the sluggish river, she felt another momentary twinge of uneasiness. She had ventured into this part of the city before, but usually always in the company of others. Rarely had she ever had cause to come here alone. Still, it was summer and not yet sunset. If she hurried, she would have time to speak to Officer Seringo and then get back across the river before dark—when the modern-day vampires who preyed on others made their appearance. As a precaution, she locked both her car doors and checked her fuel gauge. The needle indicated she had more than half a tank of gas, enough so she wouldn't find herself stranded across the river. Driving alertly and briskly, she made her way to the barrio, relieved that at least Officer Seringo's home address was in one of the better neighborhoods.

In fact, the white, two-story, brick-and-stucco apartment complex in which he lived had doubtless at one time been rather elegant, situated as the buildings were on a street lined with tall, old trees and dappled with forsythia, gardenia, hydrangea, lilac, and crepe-myrtle bushes now largely wild and overgrown. Each of the buildings was shaped like a U, each surrounding its own individual square of ground that probably had at one time been intended as a gardenlike court, but that was now mostly filled with grass that had run to seed and bare patches of earth from which a few forlorn flowers straggled. Still, wisteria, honeysuckle, and clematis climbed the lacy, wrought-iron balustrades of the galleries, lending a softer note, and Latino children played in the squares, their dark eyes curious but wary as they watched Claire cruise slowly down the street, then park her car in front of one of the buildings.

After a moment, she got out, carefully locking her door behind her before turning to scan the numbers on the apartments. Officer Seringo, she discovered, lived on the second floor. So she climbed the exterior staircase to make her way along the gallery above, marveling that the court below should be so peaceful, the air broken only by the sounds of the children at play and the bees that buzzed around the blooming vines. At this instant, it was hard to believe that just some few blocks from here, Officer Seringo's wife had been brutally gang-raped and murdered. Taking a deep breath to shore up her faltering courage, Claire raised one hand to rap softly on the apartment door.

The increasingly louder and more insistent knocking at Jake's apartment door hurt his head, as though a sledgehammer pounded mercilessly into his dazed and sorrowing brain. To ease the pain, he pressed the heels of his palms hard into his temples, kneading fiercely. But it didn't help. The ache—and the aggravating noise—persisted. At first, he thought the sound was coming from the apartment next to his own. Then, finally, he realized someone was standing outside his own door, rapping peremptorily.

"Go 'way," Jake called, slurring his words and waving his revolver haphazardly before taking another long swallow from his now nearly empty bottle of Captain Morgan. "Whatever you're selling, I don't want any. Now, go 'way. Lemme the hell alone, damn you!"

"I'm not selling anything, Officer Seringo," came the reply through the door—a young woman's voice, he grasped, slightly surprised and thinking, agonized, of his equally young, beloved Isabel, now lost to him forever. "My name's Claire Connelly. I'm a—a reporter with Channel Four news," she announced, fudging the truth, because in reality, she was only an assistant who had yet to get her face in front of one of the station's cameras—which was the whole point of her being here, she reminded herself stringently. "I'd like to talk to you for just a few minutes if I may. Could I come in, please?"

"What for? I don't have anything I wanna say to you people." A serrated edge of anger and disgust now sharpened Jake's voice, but outside, Claire obstinately refused to be deterred.

"Officer Seringo, please. It's very difficult to converse with you like this. If I could just step inside, I'll only take a few moments of your time, I prom—'' She broke off abruptly as, without warning, the door was ripped open so hard and wide that it banged violently against the interior wall, rattling the windows so brutally that for an instant, she was afraid they would shatter.

Quite the handsomest—and most terribly, dangerously drunken—man Claire had ever before seen in her life towered over her. He stood six feet two or three, she judged, and had the kind of lean, supple whipcord body that, in a man, had always reminded her of a panther. This initial impression was only strengthened by his sleek, black hair and dark bronze skin, the powerful, matted chest exposed by his unbuttoned, white shirt, the corded arms displayed by the rolled-up shirtsleeves, and the narrow hips and muscular legs encased in black trousers unfastened at his flat, corrugated stomach. A gold crucifix gleamed at his throat—in sharp contrast to the way he stared down at her furiously, his dark brown eyes blazing like hot coals, a muscle flexing in his taut, set jaw, and a big gun clasped in one strong, slender hand. Such was his threatening appearance, in fact, that Claire involuntarily cried out softly, taking an alarmed step back and instinctively clutching her handbag in case she needed a weapon—or a shield—against him. ''Officer Seringo, don't shoot. Please don't—''

''*Dios mio*, I told you to lemme the hell alone! Don't you have any respect for my grief or privacy?'' Jake snarled at her viciously, blinded by the bright, burning, orange sun slowly sinking on the western horizon and seeing nothing in that moment but red. ''Jesus Christ! I buried my wife and baby today—or doesn't that mean a damn to you vultures?''

"Oh, I'm—I'm so sorry...so *terribly* sorry. I—I didn't know...." Claire's voice trailed away awkwardly. She was stricken by his revelation and realized suddenly that she had allowed her excitement at doing his story to impulsively carry her away, so she had not even thought to check on when the funerals for his wife and child were to be held. She could not have got off to a worse start, made a more horrible impression. She swallowed hard. "I'm—I'm so sorry," she reiterated, mortified and continuing to eye the huge revolver anxiously. "I—I won't bother you right now...."

Still mumbling her apologies, she turned and began to stride hurriedly away, wondering if sorrow had so unhinged Jake's mind that he meant to shoot her in the back. But then, halfway down the gallery, as she heard him swearing and slamming the door behind her, what he really intended to do with the gun abruptly struck her. "Oh, my God," Claire whispered, stunned and horrified. Without thinking, she pivoted and raced back to the apartment, her heart thrumming as she beat frantically on the closed door, rattling the knob and cursing to herself when she found it locked. "Officer Seringo!" she shouted, beating urgently on the door. "Officer Seringo, open the door!"

At any instant, she expected to hear the fatal shot that would tell her Jake had killed himself. So an enormous amount of relief mingled with her fear as he once more flung the door wide. "What in the hell is your damned problem, lady?" he growled at her menacingly. "Are you deliberately looking for trouble—or just plain crazy?"

"Neither, but I think you might be the latter right now, Officer Seringo—out of your mind with grief, that is." Forcing herself to marshal her courage, Claire resolutely pushed past him before he recognized what she intended. Inside, it took her eyes a moment to adjust to the relative darkness after the brilliant sunset beyond. But presently, she was able to see the interior of the apartment, what an awful mess the place was, discarded clothes and empty liquor bottles tossed helter-skelter, ashtrays overflowing with butts and wrappers, and dirty dishes stacked from one end of the small kitchen to the other.

"Look, lady, I don't know what in the hell you think you're doing—"

"I'm trying to help you, Officer Seringo. You see, I'm afraid I have a terrible suspicion that you're thinking about putting that gun to your temple and blowing your brains out." Claire motioned toward the revolver he still gripped with almost careless familiarity.

"Mouth," Jake corrected, the softly, flatly spoken word and mocking half smile that accompanied it sending an icy shiver crawling down her spine. "People who're serious about suicide put the barrel in their mouths. That's the only real way to be sure the job gets done right. And what business is it of yours what I choose to do with my life? You don't even know me."

"No, I don't. But I understand pain when I see it," she insisted quietly, upset that he hadn't denied her accusation about intending to kill himself. "Please, won't you give me the gun and sit down and talk to me—or at least let me call somebody you *will* talk to?''

''Why in the hell should I?''

''Because it's important to me—and I believe it's important to you, too. I—I just don't think your wife would want you to do something like this.''

''How in the hell would you know what she'd want?'' he asked scornfully, although his thick, spiky, black lashes swept down, veiling his gaze so Claire couldn't guess his thoughts and she knew she had struck a nerve. ''You didn't know her, either.''

''No...no, I didn't. But I *do* know that no matter what, no woman ever wants anything bad to happen to the man she loves. So why don't you just put the gun away, and I'll...I'll make you some coffee, why don't I? And we'll talk for a while, and then I'll call someone to come stay with you...a relative or friend or your partner...whomever you'd like.''

''But then you won't get much of a story, will you, lady? And that's whatcha came here for, after all, isn't it? A story...film at eleven...every last detail of my entire damned life? So how about if I give you one hell of a lead story—an exclusive, in fact? Why, I'll bet you'll even wind up news yourself, just like so many of your muckraking cohorts. The only question now is whether I'm gonna shoot myself—or you, for making such a damned, interfering pest out of yourself!'' Jake laughed shortly, harshly, drunkenly, at Claire's suddenly ashen face and wide, terrified eyes. ''You see? It's not for no reason that people say the road to hell is paved with good intentions. So why don'tcha just get the hell outta here while you've still got the chance."

For a moment, scared and thinking she was in over her head, Claire almost did just that. But in the end, neither her conscience nor her ambition would permit her to leave. "You're a policeman, Officer Seringo, trained to protect lives, not take them. I know you're in a great deal of pain yourself right now, but I just can't believe you'd hurt me, too, because of that."

"Then you must be either a complete fool—or else as big a rookie as I am. Is that it? You a rookie reporter...whad'dyou say your name was? Claire? You so naive, so fresh outta college, so new to the game that you just don't know about doing your homework, haven't found out yet how many cops snap under the strain of their jobs every year? Is that it, Claire?" he inquired again, swaggering toward her in a way that made her think of some savage, wild animal stalking its prey and that had her backing away until she was flat against a wall and there was nowhere else for her to go in the small apartment.

Briefly, Claire debated over whether or not she should try to shove Jake aside and rush past him. But he was too close to her, too big and strong, too drunk and mentally unstable from grief at the moment for her to make the attempt, she thought. She might make him even angrier, unwittingly drive him into actually shooting her. She hoped that threat had been an idle one, but under the circumstances, she dared not take that risk, she decided. It was far better for her to try to remain calm and attempt to reason with him. At least as long as he was talking to her, he wasn't consuming any more alcohol. Maybe he would sober up soon, and it would be easier then for her to deal with him. Still, Claire's mouth was dry with fear, and her pulse fluttered at the hollow of her throat as, unhurriedly but inexorably, Jake placed his muscular arms on either side of her, so she couldn't escape.

"You're beautiful," he drawled as he stared down at her intently, his eyes hooded. "I didn't notice that before...but you are." Lightly, he drew his revolver down the side of her cheek, a terrible caress that made her shudder uncontrollably. "And now, you're frightened, too, as well you should be," he observed, his voice low, husky, as he deliberately moved in closer to her, so he was almost pressed against her and she could smell the liquor on his warm breath. "My wife, Isabel, was frightened, like you. I know she was, for how could she not have been? There were four of them, you know...four filthy animals who didn't care that she was young and pregnant and terrified. They held her down and took turns on her...used her as they would have a street whore—and then, afterward, they cut her throat and left her to bleed to death. By the time we found her, it was too late to save either her or the baby...."

Jake paused for a moment, then continued, seeming not to notice the tears that brimmed in Claire's eyes as he described what had happened to his wife and child. "I can't seem to stop thinking about it," he confessed emotionally, "imagining how she suffered before she died, wondering if she screamed for help—or only pleaded with them for mercy. What do you think you would have done in her place—a pretty *gringa* like you? What would you do right now if I were suddenly to put my hands on you...like this—" Without warning, he crowded her against the wall, roughly cupping her breasts through the linen of her suit jacket and thrusting his hips against hers. Then, before Claire, anguished, realized what he further intended, he hooked one leg behind hers, simultaneously jerking her away from the wall, so both of them fell hard to the floor. Jake sprawled on top of her, effortlessly weighing her down, despite how, panicked and gasping desperately for the breath that had been knocked from her by the unexpected fall, she began to struggle wildly against him. Easily, he grabbed her wrists, however, one hand pinning them firmly to the floor. "Now," he rasped ominously in her ear, "what would you do if I were to hold my gun to your head while I ripped off your skirt and panties and forced my way inside you? Huh, Claire?"

"I—I don't know," she whispered, unable to believe what was happening, horrified by all the pictures he was so brutally painting in her mind—and then by the startling and shameful thrill of excitement that shot through her, mingling with her terror, as his lips and tongue teased her ear before he sank his teeth lightly into her lobe.

"If you tried to scream, I could shove this gun barrel into your mouth—or something else that would gimme a great deal more pleasure. And you'd take it— all of it—however I chose to give it to you. You'd do whatever I wanted, in fact—no matter how vile or depraved—because you'd wanna live and you'd know I

might torture you, kill you if you didn't do whatever
I told you to. Wouldn'tcha, Claire?''

"I—I don't know," she choked out again, her tears
now seeping from the corners of her eyes to trickle
down to her temples and hair.

"No, you don't, do you? Because these aren't the
kinds of things you reporters think about, are they?
All you care about is getting your damned story,
scooping your competition. Well, the deaths of my
wife and child aren't for the public to shake their
heads over while feeding their fat faces supper and
watching the six o'clock news! And now that you've
had a taste of what it feels like to be the victim of a
crime, maybe you'll think twice about barging into
someone's home after they've just lost a loved one.
Now, go on, go 'way, get the hell outta here like I
told you to earlier—before I change my mind and do
something we'll both regret!''

At that, abruptly releasing her, Jake staggered to his
feet, running his hands through his hair and shaking
his head as though to clear it before lurching toward
the couch, where he flopped down amid a stack of
unopened mail and old magazines and newspapers,
muttering a heated imprecation tinged, Claire thought,
with both self-reproach and disgust. Much to her relief, after a long moment, he tossed the revolver onto
the coffee table, then grabbed a cigarette from the half-
crumpled pack lying next to one of the overflowing
ashtrays and lit up, blowing a cloud of smoke into the
air. Trembling violently in the aftermath of his assault,
she got slowly to her feet, leaning against the wall for

support while she caught her breath and gathered her composure.

"I'm sorry," Claire said at last in the taut silence that had descended. "I shouldn't have come here—especially today. You were right, I'm afraid. I'm fresh out of college, and I didn't do my homework. I—I didn't know you had buried your wife and baby today, and there's just no excuse for that. My timing couldn't have been worse. I apologize." She bent to retrieve her handbag, which she had lost during their scuffle. "If you'll...if you'll promise me you're not going to kill yourself, Officer Seringo, I'll leave now."

At first, Claire thought he hadn't heard her, or else that he had and meant rudely to ignore her. But finally, he replied. "Jake. My name's Jake. And it's I who should apologize. I've no excuse myself for my own behavior toward you. It was...unpardonable, and I can only attribute it to an instant of complete madness that has now dissipated—and with it, my urge to do away with myself, it appears. Perhaps I even doubted from the start my ability to go through with it. I only loaded one chamber, in case I changed my mind, I guess."

"And had you? Changed your mind, I mean, even before I got here?"

"No," he answered tersely. "It was only that the first two chambers were empty. Had you arrived a few minutes later, you might indeed have got yourself a story."

Perversely, that thought now no longer held the same appeal and excitement for Claire as it had previously. She felt like the most heedless and gauchest of intruders, and was ashamed of herself, even though in at least one respect, she was the injured party. "Believe it or not, that wasn't the kind of story I came here to get," she explained, quietly but insistently. "Truly. I wanted to do something caring and insightful, something that would move people, especially city officials, to take some action against the violent crime that goes on here on this side of the river. Perhaps that was naive of me—"

"It was."

"But if people aren't made aware of what's happening in their world," she continued as though he had not interrupted, "how will they ever be motivated to change it for the better?"

"You see yourself as something of a crusader, then, a champion courageously turning on a light in the darkness of the world?" he inquired, dragging on his cigarette again but not, to her relief, reaching for the nearly empty bottle of dark, spicy rum that sat on the coffee table.

"Well...yes. Isn't that how you see your own self, what made you decide to join the police force, for example?"

"Yes," he conceded slowly. "But these past several months on the street have shown me that we're living in a war zone, that there's always some fool or lunatic or tyrant out there intent on smashing that light you'd turn on."

"All the more reason for the media and others to expose them, then, wouldn't you say?"

"Not at the expense of invading the privacy of the innocent and grieving, and making a public spectacle out of them."

Claire did not know how to argue with that, how to defend herself against his implication that she was no better than a morbid ambulance chaser. She realized from his words that in some ways—and not without good cause—Jake thought of his wife and baby as casualties of war. But she also knew that public awareness of the horrors of the same could turn the tide, as it had in Vietnam, the Balkans, and elsewhere. When she remembered that, Claire did not feel as wholly disillusioned about her chosen career in life as she had just minutes before, only guilty that she hadn't proceeded more cautiously and with greater sensitivity. She would chalk that up to her inexperience and try not to make the same mistake again in the future, she told herself.

"Well, I guess I'll be going now." She made her way to the apartment door and opened it, unable as she did so to repress the small gasp of distress that emanated from her throat as she saw that while she was inside, the sun had set, leaving the barrio in darkness. Only a couple of porch lights shone now here and there, the streetlights few and far apart, their bulbs either broken or burned out.

"Shut the door," Jake demanded curtly as he glanced over at her and observed the cause of her dismay. "It's not safe out there now, especially for someone like you. I'll have to get myself cleaned up and take you home."

"You're in no condition to drive," Claire asserted firmly, "much less to take on any criminals. It's my own fault I'm here, and I'm certainly not your responsibility, anyway. Besides, I've had some self-defense classes. I can take care of myself.''

Jake swore. "You're a damned fool!" he spat. "You think my wife didn't know how to take care of herself, that I hadn't taught her what to do in case she was attacked? Get this through your head, lady. Criminals don't play by the same rules we do. They don't play by any rules at all! You might not have a chance even to *try* to defend yourself. After all, *I* took you by surprise, didn't I? And I'm not even sober. So close the damned door, and lock it. I'm not letting you go out there alone. If something should happen to you, I'm not gonna have that on my conscience, too!''

"Why, you blame yourself for the deaths of your wife and child, don't you?" Sudden understanding dawned in Claire's mind. "That's what's eating on you, along with your grief, isn't it? That's why you were thinking about killing yourself?''

"I'm a cop. I should have been able to protect them," Jake insisted grimly.

"But you couldn't have known your wife would stop at that convenience store.''

"No. If I'd told her once, I'd told her a hundred times to drive straight home after work. But if I'd had more money, if I hadn't had to work like a dog just to support us and take night classes to put myself through college, if I'd just taken a regular job right after graduating from high school and forgotten all about being a cop, I might've been in a position to move us away from here by now. But Isabel's folks thought she was too young to get married. They wanted her to get a degree and make something out of herself, so I put my own dreams on hold until she had her nurse's license. If I'd just given up my own plans entirely, she and the baby might still be alive.''

"You can't know that for sure." Claire's voice was filled with sympathy.

"No—and now, I'll never know, will I? Look, I don't wanna talk about it anymore, if you don't mind. So why don'tcha...ah...make yourself at home while I go take a shower and try to get myself into some sort of shape resembling a human being? Then I'll see that you get safely back across the river." Grinding his cigarette out in an ashtray, Jake rose and disappeared into the bathroom.

Moments later, Claire heard the sound of running water and knew he had turned on the shower. She glanced around, looking for someplace clean to sit, then decided as she surveyed all the mess in the apartment that she might as well make herself useful while she waited for him. Surely, she owed him that much at least for barging in on him at such a time, not to mention putting him to the trouble of driving her home.

The first thing she did was to search the kitchen cabinets for coffee and filters. Finding them at last, she filled the basket in the coffeemaker on the counter, then poured in several cups of water and turned the machine on. Presently, it was perking nicely, and the aroma of fresh coffee permeated the apartment, which was stale with cigarette smoke and booze. The apartment did not boast a dishwasher, so after running hot water in the sink, she put a load of dishes in to soak while she emptied ashtrays, collected the liquor bot-

tles, and bagged up trash. Finding no washer or dryer,
Claire folded all the scattered clothes so they could be
taken to a Laundromat, laying them neatly in the laun-
dry basket she discovered buried beneath them. Then
she tidied up the living room, sorting mail, newspapers, and magazines, straightening the cushions on the
sofa, and wiping down the coffee table and end tables.
After that, she returned to the sink to deal with the
dishes, washing and rinsing the first load, then stack-
ing them in the drainer rack to dry while she ran more
water and put another batch in to soak.

By the time she had nearly finished, Jake was
emerging from the bathroom. He had not only show-
ered, but was also freshly shaven, his jet-black hair
washed, combed, and gleaming like the feathers of a
rain-soaked crow. His white, cotton shirt was now but-
toned almost to the throat, its sleeves rolled down and
fastened at the cuffs, its tails tucked into his black
trousers, now belted at the waist. He appeared to be a
great deal more sober. Claire was slightly startled by
the transformation and struck anew by how very handsome he was. Jimmy Smits had nothing on Jake Seringo, she thought.

"You didn't have to do all this." He indicated the
now-clean apartment. "Really."

"I didn't mind the work, and I figured you could
use the help, besides. I've made some coffee, too, and
I found half a lemon meringue pie that hadn't yet
molded in the icebox, if you'd like a piece. It looks
homemade."

"Yeah, the wife of one of the homicide detectives—
Remy Toussaint—who're assigned to Isabel's case

baked it. He brought it by a couple of days ago, I think. I don't know for sure, though. All my days seem to have run together here lately. At any rate, his son was murdered by some gangbangers a few years back, so he knows what I'm going through and appears to feel some sort of responsibility toward me, as though he ought to drop by every so often, check up on me and be sure I'm eating, that kind of thing.''

"That's very commendable of him. I'm glad you're not without caring friends right now." Claire poured two cups of coffee, setting them on the kitchen table, then retrieved the pie from the refrigerator, cutting two slices and placing them on plates. To her surprise, Jake pulled out a chair for her before sitting down himself.

"I want to apologize to you again," he said as he sipped his coffee, "for putting my hands on you so crudely and pinning you down on the floor like that. It was inexcusable. I don't know what got into me. I was raised to treat women with respect, so I've never done anything like that before. Isabel...Isabel would have been shocked and appalled by my behavior."

"It's—it's all right," Claire replied gently as she cut into her piece of pie. "Please, don't give it another thought. I've already forgiven and forgotten the incident, I assure you. I know you weren't yourself in that moment and that the provocation was great, besides. I'm mortified that I should have intruded upon you at such a time, but perhaps you'll understand if I say that even so, I'm also glad I did under the circumstances. I'm afraid you might have killed yourself, otherwise. Officer Seringo...Jake, look. I don't want to make more of a pest out of myself than I already have, but...don't you think you should talk to somebody?''

"Maybe you're right," he agreed finally, sighing heavily. "But the problem is that if the department finds out you're suicidal, they don't want you on the streets, working, and no other cop wants to partner with you, either, because they don't know what you're likely to do under pressure. My mother would understand, but she died of cancer a few years ago, and I just don't want to lay all this on my father. He's not all that well himself, and Isabel's death has hit him pretty hard, besides. She was always very good to him, especially after my mother passed away, and he was...really excited about becoming a grandfather, too.''

"Well, you could talk to me," Claire suggested tentatively after a moment.

Jake's head jerked up sharply at that, his dark-brown eyes narrowing with scorn and disbelief. "Yeah, right," he sneered, "and watch everything I've told you show up on the six o'clock news later!"

"No, I didn't mean that. I still want to do a mini-series on you and what happened, yes," she admitted reluctantly. "I think stories like yours often motivate people to put pressure on city officials en masse, so that perhaps something good might come out of this tragedy...more cops on this side of the river, for example, or Neighborhood Watch programs—which cost very little to implement—stiffer laws against crime, whatever. It just seems to me that *something* positive ought to come out of this, something that might prevent other people from suffering the kind of loss you've suffered. I don't know why you can't understand that."

"Maybe I do—on some level, anyway. It's just that I can't cope with anything like that right now...maybe not ever. I don't want to be interviewed by you. I don't want myself and my private grief put on display for the public, as though I were some kind of an animal at the zoo. Maybe some people can handle that. But I can't, and that's all there is to it. So I thank you very much for cleaning up and for the coffee and pie, as well, but no thanks to the rest of it. Now, if you're finished, I'll take you back across the river." Jake didn't add, "Where you belong." But he didn't need to. His implication was plain, so Claire heard the words just as surely as though he had spoken them aloud.

"Yes, all right, I'll just clear the table and then get my purse." She forced herself not to badger him any further, to swallow her disappointment. His lack of enthusiasm and cooperation didn't matter, she told herself. Although she would have liked to have had both, she could do the miniseries without him if need be, simply shift its focus, making his tragedy the anchor but concentrating on life and crime across the river, in general.

After rising from the table, Jake shrugged on the shoulder holster he wore when not on duty, then carefully reloaded his revolver and tucked it into place beneath the casual jacket he also pulled on. "You ready?" he asked. At Claire's nod, he escorted her outside, flicking on the porch light and locking the door behind them. "We'll take your car," he said.

"It's not too late yet for me to catch a bus back. Do you mind if I drive?"

"No, I guess not." She handed him her keys, and he unlocked the passenger door, waiting until she was comfortably settled inside before closing it and going around to slide in beside her. He did indeed have very gentlemanly manners, she reflected idly—which made his earlier, barbaric behavior toward her seem even more of an aberration. When she reflected on it, a small shiver racked her. It had been unreal, like being attacked by some savage animal, and despite the self-defense classes she'd taken in college, she had found herself helpless against him. What, then, must have gone through his dead wife's mind when those four men had assaulted her? Claire could only imagine. It must have been utterly horrible, she thought.

"What kind of music do you like?" she inquired to take her mind off the tragedy and reaching out to adjust the volume on the radio.

"All kinds—except...I'm not too fond of country and western."

"I'm not, either." She usually kept the radio tuned to an adult-contemporary station, so she left it where it was. Then, not knowing what else to say or do, she lapsed into silence, studying her surroundings. This was a frightening side of the city in which she lived, an alien place as far removed from her own world as the moon. Groups of youths she could only assume were gang members roamed the streets, and women who were obviously hookers openly plied their trade. More than one speculative glance was cast in her direction, and she was glad Jake was at the wheel. She would have been extremely uneasy, otherwise. "Do you think the police will ever catch those men? The ones who... well, you know."

"It's hard to say. There weren't any witnesses—or, at least, none who've come forward, and the bastards were clever enough to yank the videotape from the surveillance system, which wasn't the best to begin with. Most likely, one or more of the perpetrators will be arrested for some other crime and try to use the information about what happened at the convenience store to make a deal with the D.A. That's what I'm hoping, anyway, if nothing else turns up. Where do you live?"

"Near the university. I've got a small bungalow there that I've rented for the last few years, ever since I left home to get out on my own, actually. So I'm used to it, and it's comfortable—besides which, I really can't afford anything better at the moment."

"I thought most reporters made a real decent living."

"Yes, in big markets, they do. But smaller markets like ours don't pay nearly as much unless you've worked your way up to the position of an evening anchor or something—and I'm afraid I'm a long way from that yet. It's only been about six months since I graduated at midterm, and the competition in broadcasting is fierce. I was actually quite lucky to land the job I have at Channel Four. Otherwise, I probably would have had to move away from here."

"And that didn't appeal to you?" Jake queried.

"No, not really. I've lived here all my life. It's

home. It's what I know best, and my family's here, besides. Take a right at the next corner.''

Presently, they were pulling into the narrow driveway of Claire's small, neat, white-stucco bungalow. Like almost all the houses in the immediate vicinity of the college, her own had been built during the Victorian era, primarily for young singles and couples just starting out in life, and then subsequently modernized through the years. It had a living room, a kitchen, a bathroom, and two bedrooms, as well as a modest, fenced backyard Claire loved to sit in during the summer evenings.

"Would you like to come inside?" she asked as Jake switched off the headlights and killed the engine. "I'd feel better about your driving me home if you'd at least let me call a friend or a taxi for you."

"No." He shook his head. "Thanks just the same, but I'd really better be getting back. There's a bus stop right up the street, I noticed, and I don't want to miss the next bus. It's getting late, so there might not be another one tonight." He got out of the car and came around to open her own door for her, then walked her up to the front porch illuminated by its light that automatically turned itself on after dusk. He handed her key ring to her.

After unlocking the front door and pushing it open, Claire paused momentarily before going inside, reaching into her purse to withdraw the pen and small, spiral-bound notepad she always carried with her. "Look, Officer Seringo...Jake. I know you've made it quite clear you don't want to grant me an interview—and that's fine. I've accepted that. But why don't I give you my phone number, anyway, just in case you decide you want to talk to somebody one of these nights, after all? I know you're not having an easy time right now, and I confess I'm still worried you might decide to play Russian roulette again. I'm not a police psychologist or a cop, so nobody within the department would need to know, and of course, anything you might say to me would be strictly off the record." She tore off the page upon which she had written her name and number, holding it out to him.

At first, Claire thought Jake was going to refuse to accept the piece of paper. But finally, he took it, folding it in half and tucking it into the inside pocket of his jacket. "Thanks. I doubt I'll need it, but I do appreciate the offer. I'm sorry we didn't meet under more congenial circumstances. Good night."

"Good night, Jake—and thanks again for bringing me home." From the doorway of her bungalow, Claire watched him turn and walk away, illuminated by the moonlight and lamplight that streamed down through the branches of the tall, shade trees, dappling the old, uneven bricks with which the street was paved. He had his hands shoved into his trouser pockets, his shoulders squared, and his chin resolutely lifted, so the breeze that stirred not only rustled the leaves of the trees, but also ruffled his hair gently, like a lover's caress. Except that his lover, his wife, was dead now. Claire thought she had never seen anyone who looked so lonely and bereft. Almost, she called out to him. But in the end, she bit back the soft cry that rose to her lips. She had interfered enough in his life—more than enough.

What was that old saying about two ships that passed in the night? That's what she and Jake Seringo had been. Their lives had come together, touched fleetingly, and then separated. That was all.

She would probably never see him again.

Five

Picking Up the Pieces

And the stately ships go on
To their haven under the hill;
But Oh for the touch of a vanished hand,
And the sound of a voice that is still!

Break, Break, Break
—Alfred, Lord Tennyson

The following morning at the television station, Claire explained to both Winston Nash and Booker McGuinness, whom Nash had persuaded to join them in their venture, that she had reconsidered her idea for the miniseries and thought they should broaden their focus to include the whole of life across the river rather than just concentrating on Officer Seringo's personal story. Since his tragedy was a recent event, they would include it, of course. But it would no longer be their centerpiece.

"Turned you down for an interview, did he?" Nash's eyes twinkled knowingly.

"As flat as a pancake," Claire admitted ruefully, choosing her next words carefully so as not to betray any of the rest of what had occurred at Jake's apartment. "Naturally, he's distraught over the death of his wife and child, and upon further reflection, I decided a wider scope would be more effective, anyway. People might be more motivated to take action if they understood exactly what life across the river is like on a daily basis. The only thing is, we'll have to go over there at least a couple of times after dark, to shoot film, really capture the essence of what happens after the sun goes down. I saw a little of it last night, and I confess it was something of an eye-opener. I knew it was bad, but I don't think I ever had any real concept of just *how* bad until last evening."

"Jeez, Claire, everybody knows it's rough over there. But when all is said and done, it's really no different from any other ghetto—and a hell of a lot better than some I could mention, especially those in the really big cities. Yet you act as though there were criminals lurking on every street corner across the river." McGuinness's skepticism was plain.

"Well, there *were* an awful lot of hookers out on the streets and young men I know were members of gangs. If you want to know the truth, I think the latter are really mostly to blame for the majority of crime that happens over there. Many of those who live and work across the river are actually law-abiding citizens. They're just poor, is all—compelled by their financial circumstances into a way of life that nobody ought to have to endure. The police department should have more patrol cars over there," Claire insisted stubbornly. "Neighborhoods like Forest Gables, Moss Oak, and Bayview have their own private security forces. They don't need a cruiser driving by every twenty or thirty minutes.

"It's not enough to say that's the way things are in a ghetto, Booker. You and I aren't afraid to drive home alone after work. We don't think that stopping at a convenience store for a few groceries will get us killed or that we're likely to be mugged on a street corner downtown. I'm not saying our side of the city doesn't have its share of crime, because it does. But we don't go to bed nights worrying that a bullet from a drive-by shooting is going to come through our bedroom window, either. *That's* what I want to get across in this miniseries, that those people who're living behind their spike-topped walls, with their security systems and guard dogs, had better wake up and realize that sooner or later, the whole city is going to be a war zone if something isn't done."

"Hell, Claire. This isn't a miniseries. It's a damned crusade!" Nash shook his head, frowning now. "I thought you were just interested in giving our careers a push in the right direction. You can't use the airwaves as your own personal soapbox and remain an objective journalist—and no matter how hard you try, you can't save the whole world, either, you know."

"I'm just trying to save our piece of it, Winston." Claire's voice was earnest. "And to prevent Isabel Seringo and her baby from having been murdered for nothing. If we can even get a few of the neighborhoods across the river to set up Watch programs as a result of our miniseries, then I'll feel as though we've accomplished something worthwhile. Yes, I want to help our careers along in the process, but I just don't believe anymore that it's the responsibility of the media only to report the news, no matter how horrible and depressing. We ought to be suggesting solutions, as well. People ought to know there *are* things that can be done, steps that can be taken to correct the problems we all have to live with. So are the two of you still with me or not?''

"We're with you," Nash said, after glancing at McGuinness for confirmation.

"Good. Then the first thing I want to do is to arrange interviews with some of those people I know will be sympathetic to this miniseries and interested in promoting their own ideas through it...police officers, Neighborhood Watch coordinators, whoever handles that MacGruff dog stuff about taking a bite out of crime. We'll have to do as much of this as we can on our own time, nights and weekends, so as not to interfere with our regular jobs here at the station. I don't want Mr. Kendall to think we've been neglecting our duties in pursuit of a story nobody assigned us to cover.''

"Do you really believe this idea will work, Claire? That the station will air the miniseries after we've finished with it?'' McGuinness asked.

"I don't know," she responded honestly. "I can't promise you that Mr. Kendall will like our work well enough to put it on the air. But I *do* know nobody ever gets anywhere in this life without taking some initiative. We've got a good concept. So all we can do now is run with it and see what happens.''

As she left the break room to return to her desk, Claire was not aware of the fact that she, Nash, and McGuinness were about to embark on a professional relationship that was to exist for many years to come and that would eventually lead them to national exposure. All she knew was that despite how busy her day grew, she couldn't seem to stop thinking about Jake Seringo. More than once, she picked up the receiver on her telephone and pushed the button for an outside line so she could call him—only to lose her courage and hang up at the last minute because she couldn't think of any excuse for getting in touch with him that wouldn't sound contrived. Nor could Claire explain to herself why she wanted to speak to him at all. Jake had made it quite plain he wanted nothing to do with her, and she had no reason not to let it go at that. Still, thoughts of him intruded into her mind all afternoon, so she found it difficult to concentrate.

Deep down inside, Claire knew that if she were honest with herself, she must admit that although she had, last night, seen Jake at what was surely his worst, she had nevertheless been physically attracted to him. But that recognition engendered both guilt and uneasiness inside her, the distinct feeling that there must be something wrong with her to think about him in such terms when he had just lost his wife and child—and under such brutal and tragic circumstances, besides. He would most likely be even more upset with her if he ever learned her interest in him had spilled over from the professional to the personal, that it had not been solely her caring, altruistic nature that had, after he had driven her home, prompted her to give him her telephone number.

"You'd better get hold of yourself, Connelly," she muttered under her breath, annoyed at and disgusted with herself. "For all you know, the man's an alcoholic." Many police officers were, she had discovered today during her lunch hour, which she had used to start researching and compiling information for the miniseries. And if not an alcoholic, Jake had certainly at least been on a drunken binge for the past several days, had turned to the bottle to drown his sorrows. "Oh, well, it's none of your business, anyway, Connelly," she told herself sternly. "You need to get your mind on your work—and keep it there."

Still, she couldn't prevent herself from feeling disappointed when she returned home that evening to find that Jake had left no messages for her on her telephone answering machine. There were a couple of hang-ups that might have been him, but that was all.

Sighing, Claire prepared supper for herself, which she ate in front of her television set, her remote control handy so she could change stations easily, catching bits and pieces of all the news broadcasts. She studied the female anchors and reporters, especially—not just how they worked, but also how they styled their hair and makeup, the kinds of clothes they wore. In broadcasting, it wasn't enough just to excel at your job; you had to look good doing it, too.

Claire knew she was—as Jake Seringo had so blisteringly pointed out to her—just a rookie in her profession right now. But she intended to get better.

After supper, she ran a hot bath, sinking gratefully

into the steaming water scented with her favorite gardenia fragrance. Laying her head back against the edge of the tub, she closed her eyes and let her thoughts drift. Inevitably, it seemed, her mind filled with images of Jake. She wondered how he was doing, if he were still sunk in the depths of depression and a bottle, or whether he had begun the long, hard, painful process of trying to come to grips with his loss and reassemble the pieces of his shattered life. She didn't know—or even why she wished she did.

His barbaric behavior toward Claire Connelly had demonstrated to Jake just how far over the edge he had slipped since the deaths of his wife and baby. He had totally lost control, and he knew that somehow, someway, he had to get it back if he were to go on surviving. Otherwise, if he didn't kill himself first, he was surely headed down the long, dark slide into alcoholism. So tonight he reclined on the couch in the living room of his small apartment and stared unseeingly at the running television set—all too aware of the still-sealed quart of Captain Morgan that sat on the coffee table before him. It was a comfort to know it was there, his security blanket, in case the pain got too bad for him to bear. But it was also a temptation. So far, however, although he had felt a desperate need for the liquor and had reached for it several times, he had prevented himself from opening the bottle.

He had reached for the telephone more than once, as well, thinking Claire Connelly had been right and that he needed to talk to somebody. The piece of paper on which she had written her phone number lay on the coffee table, beside the quart of Captain Morgan. But so far, he had resisted the urge to call her, too. She was a reporter, a snoop; she made her living by prying into other people's lives and putting them on display for the public. Jake was a very private man—and the fifteen minutes of fame he had unwittingly gained at the hands of the media as the result of the tragedy he had suffered had been more than enough for him. He didn't want any more of it. Yet, for some strange, unknown reason, he found he could not put Claire from his mind.

Despite his every moral value, his overwhelming grief, and how much he had loved his wife, Isabel, Jake had felt a savage, undeniable surge of desire for Claire when he had drunkenly caressed her so crudely, then knocked her to the floor and pinned her beneath him. The memory of that both shocked and shamed him—although he knew from the psychology classes he had taken in college that the urge to create life in the face of death was a powerful human instinct. Still, guilt gnawed at him. That he should have found himself so strongly attracted to another woman when his wife was not even cold in her grave disturbed him intensely. Why he had ever tucked Claire's phone number into his pocket, Jake didn't know. He would get rid of it right now, he decided resolutely.

Picking up the piece of paper, he set fire to it with his lighter, then tossed it into the big, glass ashtray on the coffee table, where it momentarily blazed brightly—like a candle in the dark—before dying down to a tiny pile of black ash. There. It was done. He no longer had anything for which to reproach himself. That he knew where Claire lived and that she was probably listed in the city telephone directory, anyway, were thoughts Jake determinedly shoved from his mind.

In the days that followed, Jake finally somehow managed to drag himself up from the black abyss into which he had toppled and forced himself to begin the slow, painful process of rebuilding his broken life. He returned to his job at the police department, throwing himself with a vengeance into his work so his thoughts no longer dwelled on his dead wife and child, and to make sure he was so exhausted once he got off duty that it was all he could do to prepare himself something to eat before he tumbled into bed, sleeping as soon as his head struck the pillow. If there were a mountain of paperwork to be completed, he stayed late at the precinct to finish it. If there were overtime hours to be worked, he took them. No one within the department applied himself more diligently to his job than Jake. He lived for it.

In his off hours, he set himself the task of trying to track down the murderers who had killed his wife and baby—even though he knew how thankless and fruitless the search was likely to prove, that the police had few leads and therefore little or nothing to go on. No eyewitnesses had come forward or been unearthed during the investigation. If the criminals had left any fingerprints behind, the ones found at the crime scene had yet to correspond to any already on file. The shell casings recovered at the convenience store had been enough to identify the kinds of guns employed during the commission of the murders, but the odds were that the weapons were Saturday-night specials and thus untraceable. The single-edged knife with which Isabel's throat had been cut might have been bought at any pawnshop in the ghetto. The semen samples taken from her corpse were useless without others against which to compare them for possible matches.

That gang members had committed the crime was only the primary theory. A routine examination of the apartment of the convenience store's night clerk, Wyatt Jenkins, had revealed a large stash of porno magazines and videotapes. It was thus possible Jenkins had been involved in some unsavory dealings that had led to his murder, and that Isabel herself had merely been an unfortunate bystander, in the wrong place at the wrong time. Jake knew this last to be true in any event, although the police had even speculated that Isabel's job as a nurse, the fact that she had had access to prescription drugs at St. Mary Hospital, might have played some unknown part in the crime.

"You understand. We just can't discount any possibility at the moment, Jake," Remy Toussaint explained gravely one evening when he dropped by with Chinese takeout. "You and I both know Isabel wasn't the kind of woman to have sold drugs. But still, we can't ignore the idea that some crazed, former hospital patient might have thought he could somehow force her to get drugs for him—and talked some of his dumb buddies into going along with him. It's a little farfetched, I'll admit. But, hell, Jake. These days, anything's possible.

"We got twelve-year-olds out there on the streets,

armed with automatic weapons, for Christ's sake. We got maniacs so hyped up on PCP that even a stun gun that would drop most people in their tracks doesn't faze them. And the gangs…well, hell, don't even get me started on those. They're the worst thing that's ever happened to these here United States. The gangs are at war with the rest of us—and most people don't even realize it, figure as long as the drive-by shootings and cold-blooded executions aren't taking place on their own streets, it's somebody else's problem.

"We're a society in an advanced state of decay, Jake, just like Rome at the end of her glory days. And those idiots up there in the White House and on Capitol Hill are just like Nero, fiddling away while Rome burned, too damned busy lining their own pockets with the taxpayers' hard-earned money even to give a hoot about what's happening in this country. I tell you, Jake, if things don't change for the better pretty soon, I don't know what's going to become of us all, and that's a fact." Remy shook his head wearily, sadly. "But enough about all that. How're things going with you, son?"

Jake shrugged noncommittally as, with a pair of chopsticks, he dug into the steaming moo goo gai pan his cardboard carton contained. "I have good days and bad ones, Remy, just like everybody else."

"Everybody else hasn't been through what you have, Jake," the big black man observed quietly. "You look exhausted, like you haven't slept well in weeks, and your partner, Frank, tells me you been doing the job of ten men on the force."

"Yeah, well, I guess I figure it's better to wind up

dead of a heart attack from overwork than to be discovered some morning in a gutter somewhere, drowned in my own liquor-reeking vomit.''

''None of life's answers will ever be found in a bottle, Jake.''

''No, I know that.''

''Good. I'm real glad to hear it—especially since the last time I came by here, this place looked like the Dumpster in the alley out back of some dive bar.''

''Isabel's death was...rough, Remy.''

''Tell me something I don't know, son. I been there, remember? But it's like I told you before. Life goes on. The loss and the guilt...that's hard. But you *will* get through them, Jake. I know it sounds like a tiresome, old cliché, but time really *does* heal all things. You got your feet set on the right road now. So all you got to do is stick with it, just keep on plugging away at it, day in and day out. It won't be easy, and I 'spect you'll fall off the wagon again a few more times at least before you finally get your bearings for good. But you're going to be all right, son—and when you are, don't blame yourself for it. Trust me. It's what your wife would have wanted.''

Jake laughed shortly, a cynical sound. ''You know what, Remy? Somebody else told me almost the very same thing recently.''

''Is that a fact?'' the other man lifted one eyebrow quizzically. ''Anybody I know?''

''No, just some young, eager-beaver reporter so damned wet behind the ears that she hadn't even done her homework. She showed up here the day...the day of the funerals. I'm afraid I was…pretty hard on her, that I…treated her rather badly."

"And that's still bothering you, is it?"

"Some, yeah." Jake nodded, setting his Chinese food down on the table and running one hand raggedly through his hair. After a moment of internal struggle and doubt, he reluctantly confessed, "The truth is, Remy, that I…I was physically attracted to her."

"I see," Toussaint said soberly as he poked through the open cartons, in search of another egg roll. "And you thought that was wholly unnatural under the circumstances and disrespectful to Isabel's memory?"

"Well, wasn't it?"

"No…no, not really. You see, son, no matter what, we don't really stop living ourselves when loved ones die. And the natural human instinct in the face of loss is to cling to another human being for comfort. When we're children, the person we reach for is generally our mother or father. But when we're adults, it becomes our wife or husband. The only trouble is that in your case, it was your wife who died. Now, I'm no psychiatrist or nothing, but it doesn't seem all that hard to me to believe you might see an attractive woman and be drawn to her, to think, whether you realized it or not, that she might offer the solace you're seeking.

"And actually, that's a compliment to Isabel's memory. If the two of you hadn't had such a good, loving relationship, you wouldn't feel so very alone right now, Jake. You wouldn't be interested in reaching out to another member of the opposite sex. In fact, I 'spect that deep down inside, whether you admitted it to yourself or not, you'd feel a pretty damned, deep sense of relief that Isabel was out of your life forever.

"So if you're asking my opinion, I'd say you got nothing to feel guilty about or ashamed of. And if you're asking my advice, I'd say you need to give yourself some time to grieve and to come to grips with Isabel's death before you think about getting involved in another relationship—just so you can be sure in your own mind that you're absolutely ready to make that kind of commitment again and not simply on the rebound. Because to tell you the truth, son, I just can't picture you with some eager-beaver reporter." As he bit into the last egg roll, which he had finally unearthed in one of the containers, Toussaint's eyes twinkled.

Seeing that, Jake chuckled, and for the first time since his wife's death, the laughter was an easy, natural sound. "How'd you get to be so wise, Remy?"

"Well, if you live long enough and you have any sense at all to start with, you generally try to acquire some more along the way. So I reckon that's what I did. Before I moved up to Homicide, I used to cruise a beat just like you, Jake, and I guess that between the streets and the crime scenes, there just ain't much at all I haven't seen over the years. It's been a real education in the worst of human nature. But I've seen the best, too, son. I wouldn't want you to think otherwise. That's what always gives me hope for mankind, the fact that good can and sometimes does come out of a tragedy."

"That's what that reporter said, too. I told her she was naive."

"You're too young to be so cynical, Jake. And I'm too old to be naive. Whether she realized it consciously or not, your reporter was right. The world has to have hope. It has to have meaning. You ought to know that. You're searching for both at the moment." The other man laid down his chopsticks and pushed away his now-empty carton of beef chow mein. "Well, I got to be on my way. Frances worries about me when she thinks I'm out too late. Oh, I almost forgot. She said to tell you she's glad you enjoyed the lemon meringue pie and that she hopes you like apple, since that's what she's baking this week."

"I do. Please thank her for me, Remy. The both of you've been very kind, the best of friends to me, even though you didn't even know me until that...that terrible night. I want you to know how much I appreciate it. I don't know how I can ever repay you."

"We're just happy we could help, Jake. As for repaying us, well, this is the kind of thing you pass on instead. People were good to me and Frances when we lost our boy. So if, God forbid, you should happen someday to find somebody else in your position, then you can repay us by lending them a helping hand, same as Frances and I have you."

"Yes, I will, Remy." Jake stood to walk Remy to the front door. "You have my word on that. Good night—and thanks for the Chinese food."

"Don't mention it. 'Night, now."

From the doorway, Jake watched to be certain Toussaint got safely in his car, then closed the front door and locked it. With that simple motion, the apartment, which had seemed a pleasant enough place just moments before, suddenly took on a lonely, depressing air. Sighing heavily at the realization that he would no longer have Toussaint's conversation to take his mind off his problems, Jake switched on the television set, then began to clear away all the empty containers that littered the coffee table. One thing Claire Connelly's unexpected visit to him the day of the funerals had done was to jolt him into recognizing what a pigsty the apartment had become—and how much Isabel would have hated that, since she had always worked so hard to keep it neat and clean. So now Jake did his best to do the same.

After tossing the cartons into the trash, emptying the ashtrays, and wiping down the coffee table, Jake washed the glasses he and Toussaint had used, then stacked them in the drainer rack to dry. Flicking off the television, he retired to the spare bedroom he had been sleeping in since Isabel's death, unable to endure even the sight of the room the two of them had shared and where the crib they had bought for the coming baby still stood.

Sooner or later, he would need to sort through Isabel's clothes and other possessions, Jake told himself, and to do something about the crib. The Sanchezes, three apartments down the gallery, were young newlyweds and expecting their first child. Jake knew that as a result, they were barely scraping by. He thought they would be glad and grateful to have the crib and the rest of his dead baby's few things....

He inhaled raggedly as he lay there in the darkness. He was a grown man. He would *not* cry, he insisted to himself. He would *not* give in to temptation, rise from the lonely twin bed, and go into the kitchen to open up the bottle of Captain Morgan he had tucked away in one of the cabinets. He was not the only person in the world who had ever suffered a terrible tragedy, Jake reminded himself. He *would* get through this, somehow, someway. It was just so damned hard to be the survivor, the one left behind, the one who ached unbearably, sleepless and alone, in the wee hours of the night. Resolutely, he blinked back the hot tears that stung his eyes, forcing himself to breathe deeply, to empty his mind of its painful thoughts as he listened to the sounds of the night, the banging of a door somewhere in the apartment complex, the loud blare of someone's television set, the voices that rose from the courtyard below, the wail of a police siren in the distance.

Six

Voices in the Dark

The voice I hear this passing night was heard
In ancient days by emperor and clown:
Perhaps the self-same song that found a path
Through the sad heart of Ruth, when, sick for home,
She stood in tears amid the alien corn;
The same that oft-times hath
Charmed magic casements, opening on the foam
Of perilous seas, in faery lands forlorn.

> *Ode to a Nightingale*
> —John Keats

Manolo Alvarez had felt certain it was only a matter of time before he got himself noticed by the people who ran things on his side of the river, for, from the time he was small, he had been sure he would some-day be such a person of importance and authority himself.

He had never known his father, who might have been any one of the dozens of men whom his mother, a professional prostitute, had slept with; and Manny had not seen his mother herself since he was seven and had run away from home. That evening, his mother had been badly strung out, in dire need of a fix. Bewailing her lot in life, she had blurted out to Manny that the only reason he had ever been born was because the abortion she had attempted to perform on herself had failed. She had never wanted him, she had insisted, screaming her words and boxing his ears savagely, although he had done nothing to earn such punishment.

After fleeing from his mother, Manny had lived on the streets for a while, scavenging in garbage pails for food and sleeping in alleys. But of course, it had been only a matter of time until he had been spotted and picked up by the authorities. After that, he had grown up in a series of foster homes that had offered him refuge, he had felt certain, only because of the state funds his foster parents had received for his upkeep. At every opportunity, Manny had run away from the foster homes, too, until finally nobody had bothered to look for him anymore. But by then, it hadn't mattered. He had joined Las Calaveras, and they had become his family—the only one he had ever really known or needed.

They were the kings of the mean streets, more formidable than any of the other gangs in the ghetto because they had far better connections. Tonight, Manny stood in the dockside office of the foremost of these, Leon Gutierrez, the Latino kingpin of the city. Despite that Manny had bathed and donned his best clothes for this meeting, he nevertheless felt dirty and gauche in his benefactor's presence. The expertly tailored suit of raw silk Gutierrez wore must have cost at least a couple of thousand dollars, Manny estimated. The foulard tie exquisitely knotted at the older man's throat and the color-coordinated handkerchief tucked discreetly into the pocket of his suit jacket were unquestionably the work of some expensive designer, and the shoes on his feet were surely handmade Italian leather. The cigar Gutierrez smoked with obvious enjoyment had, Manny knew, been smuggled in from Havana, and the white wine in the glass that sat on his Honduras-mahogany desk had been purchased privately from a small, exclusive French vintner whose stock was never sold to the public. The older man's silver-grey hair was cut in such a way that Manny felt uncomfortably that his own black, shaggy mane must appear as though he had taken a pair of hedge clippers to it, and he thought that no matter how long and hard he had scrubbed his fingernails, they would never have acquired the buffed gleam produced by his benefactor's manicurist. Almost, Manny hated Gutierrez.

"How long have you worked for me now, Manolito?" the older man asked, employing the diminutive name Manny also despised. "Five or six years? And you have always done your job as instructed and well. Do not think that has gone unnoticed by me. Nor, however, have your little escapades on your own time escaped my attention. No, no. Do not be upset. There is no need to defend yourself, Manolito." Gutierrez raised one elegant hand, waving it languidly to show that Manny's private enterprises were of no importance. "You have done nothing to bring the focus of the police upon my organization, and that is all that matters. Taking the videotape from the security system of that convenience store you robbed some weeks ago demonstrated great foresight—although it would be better in the future if, when you resort to rape, you would protect yourself against disease. AIDS is becoming a worldwide epidemic, and of course, it cannot be cured with a round of penicillin.''

Manny didn't bother to inquire how his benefactor had come to learn about the robbery, much less its unsavory details. There was nothing that happened in the city that Gutierrez didn't know about. Even police officers and city officials were in his pocket, it was rumored, routinely bribed with unmarked envelopes filled with cash, or bought off with other gifts like drugs and women, or with favors that included everything from tampering with ballot boxes at election time to disposing of troublemakers by dumping them in the alligator-infested swamps beyond the city.

"Also," his benefactor continued, "semen provides DNA evidence, something else you would be wise to remember in the future—as well as not to choose a policeman's wife as your next victim. The resulting heat might have proved...most unfortunate for us all."
Gutierrez's eyes were steely; his voice was cool and as sharply edged as a razor, so Manny knew that despite Gutierrez's words earlier, he was, in fact, extremely angry about the convenience-store robbery. Manny quaked in his boots at the realization, glancing surreptitiously at the two henchmen who stood behind him, wondering if they planned to put a bullet through

his head before ferrying him out to the Gulf and tossing his body overboard for the sharks.

"We—we didn't know she was a cop's wife, Don Leon," Manny dared to say in his defense. "And we had to kill her. She'd seen our faces."

"Yes, yes, I realize it was necessary that you dispose of her. Nevertheless, you require discipline, Manolito. The street gang has been a good training ground for you, but now, you need more. You must become a full-fledged member of my organization and cease wasting your time with Las Calaveras. Otherwise, you are of no further use to me. Do you understand?"

"Yes...yes, Don Leon." Manny was stunned to recognize that far from being executed, he was to be given a second chance.

"You will perhaps wonder at this—that I should choose to reward instead of punish you for what might have been a disastrous turn of events. Call it an old man's foolish, sentimental whim, if you will. I was...fond of your mother, and you remind me of myself at your age, Manolito. Like you, I, too, was wild and rebellious, and I made mistakes, just as you have. Still, you see what I have become because I was willing to listen to those older and wiser than I was." Gutierrez indicated his surroundings, proof of his success, his cigar wafting smoke into the air. "So consider this your opportunity for advancement, Manolito—and use it to your advantage."

"Yes...yes, I will, Don Leon." Manny's pulse raced so with excitement that he could scarcely contain himself. This was what he had been waiting for, working toward—a position of power within Gutierrez's organization. His benefactor was middle-aged, closer to sixty than fifty, Manny judged, and must eventually make plans for retirement—provided, of course, that he didn't meet some violent, unfortunate end beforehand. This last must be considered a real possibility, since obviously, Gutierrez was getting soft in his old age, his iron control of his organization slipping. Imagine him having been fond of Manny's mother, that worthless, junkie whore who had probably wound up dead of an overdose in a filthy back alley somewhere! Well, at least she had finally proved good for something.

It had long been Manny's secret ambition to take over Gutierrez's organization. He just hadn't known how to get himself on the inside, in a real position of authority and trust, so he could work his way up to the top. Now, he figured that within ten years, if he were clever and careful, he could accomplish this goal—even if he had to kill his benefactor to do it.

The three of them now had hours and hours of film, at least five times as much as they would probably use in the completed miniseries. But they had wanted to make certain they had more than enough, just in case something went wrong. On very rare occasions, film was bad out of the can. More often, it was ruined in the development process.

"You know, some of this stuff is really pretty damned good—even if I do say so myself," Nash observed with a grin as he, McGuinness, and Claire sat in one of the darkened studios at the university, reviewing their footage. "Now, all we need to do is figure out how we want to edit it. Are you still thinking about a six-part series, Claire?"

"Yes," she confirmed, nodding thoughtfully as she watched the footage roll by. "I don't believe it's very realistic to assume Mr. Kendall will air anything longer than that. With that in mind, I also think we should stick to five minutes per segment—thirty seconds for the lead-in, four minutes of actual story, and another thirty seconds for the wrap. So we're talking about thirty minutes of film, total. I want to start off with Officer Seringo's tragedy, of course, then build from there. The liquor-store holdup second, maybe, since that perpetrator was thought to be high on PCP, followed by the overdose of the hooker."

"But the police still aren't sure whether or not that one was murder, Claire," McGuinness pointed out. "It might have been an accidental death."

"Either way, it doesn't matter, Booker. That poor woman was a victim of crime all the same, used and abused by her pimp, her pushers, and her johns. Who knows what she suffered before she died? No, regardless, she's got to be a part of this series," Claire insisted resolutely. "So now that we've got most of the film, we can get this show on the road, right?"

"Right," Nash agreed. "Still, it's going to take some time, Claire. Unless we want Dr. Younger to withdraw his support, we've got to work our editing around the summer night classes scheduled here in the university's studios. That's going to mean some late hours for me and Booker, at least. Thank God this isn't a breaking story, or we'd really be in a crunch."

"If this were a breaking story, Winston, we wouldn't be covering it at all." Claire smiled ruefully at the realization. "The station would have its best, most-experienced talent on it, and while they got all the credit and glory, the three of us would be fetching coffee and running other mundane errands. Fortunately, this story is timely but not crucial—and if it turns out as well as I believe it's going to, well, maybe other rookies will be getting coffee for us! Oh, jeez. Look at the time. We'd better lock up and call it a night, guys. I promised I'd drop the keys to the studio off at Dr. Younger's office, so I need to go slip them under his door."

"I'll do that, Claire," McGuinness offered, "while Winston walks you out to your car. In case you don't know, there was a rape on campus a couple of weeks ago."

She grimaced at the unpleasant reminder that for all that she might wish otherwise, this side of the city was not immune to crime, either. It just came in different guises. "I heard. A date rape at some drunken fraternity blowout. Still, it's nice to know the two of you are watching out for me."

It was a short drive home from the college for Claire. A few minutes later, she stood on her front porch, retrieving her mail from the box before going inside and flicking on the lamp that sat on the gossip bench in the small foyer. She tossed her key ring down on the table. Then, seeing that the red light was blinking on her telephone answering machine, she pushed the button to replay her messages.

"Claire, hon, it's Mother. Call me when you get in."

"Claire, it's Caitlin." Caitlin was her older sister. "If Mother's called there, do yourself a favor and don't call her back. She just wants to try to arrange another blind date for you...the nephew of one of her bridge-club cronies at the country club, I believe. I know how you hate that, so I just thought I'd warn you ahead of time."

"Claire, hon, it's Mother again. Please call me."

"Oh, Claire, you won't believe it!" the laughter-tinged voice of Chelsea, her younger sister, bubbled breathlessly from the machine. "Mom's found another guy she wants to fix you up with...a dentist—and get this! I've seen him, and he's not half-bad. At any rate, he's not going bald, like the last one was! And just think, Claire. If the two of you should ever wind up getting married and having kids, you won't have to pay for braces! Oh, no, on second thought, he'd have to be an orthodontist for that, right?"

"Claire, hon, don't you even have time to call your own mother these days? Are you free for supper this coming Saturday night? There's someone I'd like you to meet."

"Claire, it's Andrew." Andrew was her stepfather, her mother's third husband. "I'm afraid your mother's up to her usual matchmaking tricks again. I just wanted to tell you I'll do what I can to try to nip it in the bud. I know how much you dislike that sort of thing. But that doesn't mean you aren't more than welcome for supper Saturday night, of course."

At first, paying little or no heed to the voices emanating from the telephone answering machine, except to groan inwardly at her mother's well-meant but thoroughly annoying shenanigans, Claire thought the next message was an obscene phone caller, as there was nothing for a long moment except the sound of ragged breathing. Then she heard a muttered, "Christ," before the caller abruptly disconnected and the resulting dial tone buzzed on her machine. She paused in the act of sorting her mail, her heart beginning to pound with nervous excitement. She couldn't be sure, since she was hardly familiar with his voice, but her gut instinct told her the unknown caller was Jake Seringo. Still, if it were, he had obviously changed his mind at the last minute and decided not to talk to her. Or maybe he was just one of those people uncomfortable speaking to a machine.

Claire wondered what she should do. She glanced down at her wristwatch. It was nearly midnight, too late to be calling anybody, even her family and close friends whom she knew would be up at this hour. Still, curiosity—and concern—gnawed at her. What if Jake had had a change of heart and decided to let her interview him? What if something were wrong, and he were suicidal again? A million questions crowded into her mind.

Finally, kicking off her sandals, she curled up on her gossip bench and lifted the receiver of her telephone. Flipping through her Rolodex, she located Jake's number, which she had entered into her files in case she wanted or needed to get in touch with him again. She punched in his number, then abruptly hung up before the connection was made. What on earth was she going to say to him if he answered? she asked herself. What excuse could she give for calling him so late? She should just tell the truth, Claire decided at last. The odds were that he had returned to duty and was still working the graveyard shift, so he probably wouldn't even answer, anyway. With that thought to bolster her courage, she redialed Jake's number, letting it ring once, twice, three times. She was just preparing to hang up when he answered.

"Hello." His voice was low, husky, as though he might have been asleep.

"Officer Seringo...Jake?"

"Yes."

"It's Claire Connelly. I don't know whether or not you remember me, and I'm terribly sorry to disturb you at this late hour. I realize I've undoubtedly woke you up—"

"No...no, I wasn't asleep yet...just lying here, thinking."

"Oh, good, because I would have felt bad if I'd interrupted your rest. Anyhow, I know you're probably surprised to hear from me—and that I'm also probably the last person in the world that you want to talk to. But I... Oh, I know this is going to sound ridiculous, like something I've just made up to get in touch with you, but the truth is that I—I have the strangest feeling that you called me tonight and then had second thoughts about leaving a message on my answering machine. Did you?"

For a moment, Claire was afraid Jake wasn't going to respond, that he intended to hang up on her. But then, sighing heavily, he inquired, "How did you know it was me?"

"I—I don't know…that is, I wasn't sure. It was just a guess. But I *had* hoped to hear from you. Under the circumstances, I…ah…couldn't help but think of you and wonder how you were doing. So are you…okay?"

"I've been better. Look, Ms. Connelly—"

"Claire, please."

"All right. Claire, then. I'm not sure why I called you, but after I did, I realized it was a mistake, so that's why I hung up—which is what I ought to do right now, too, and would if I had any sense at all. I mean, I haven't changed my mind about an interview, if that's what you were hoping for—"

"No…yes…well, maybe just a little," she confessed reluctantly. "But the main thing was that I wanted to be sure you weren't…well, you know. That you hadn't gone off the deep end again, that you weren't…playing Russian roulette again."

"No, I'm not. I haven't done that since that day you came to my apartment. I was just…" *So lonely that I couldn't manage to shut out the pain tonight,* Jake wanted more than anything to tell her. *So tempted by that bottle of Captain Morgan I've got stashed in my kitchen cabinet that I nearly opened it. I just needed to talk to someone, to hear the sound of another human being's voice, and I simply don't feel comfortable imposing on Toussaint all the time, sharing my innermost thoughts and feelings with him.* "Hell, I don't know what I was," he lied, "why I called you, Ms. Connelly…Claire. But it's like I said before. It was a mistake. I apologize for bothering you."

"No, it's quite all right, no trouble at all," she declared, her mind racing as she tried to think of a way to keep him on the line, thinking that no matter what he had just told her, he had nevertheless had some reason for reaching out to her. "Are you...are you back on duty? I thought that perhaps you were and so wouldn't be home, since you worked the graveyard shift before."

"Yeah, well, I've been assigned to second shift now. I actually haven't been home all that long." Mentally, Jake cursed himself for continuing the conversation.

Still, he made no move to break the connection, no further attempt to cut off their discussion, or to press her to do so. Instead, he settled himself more comfortably on his living-room couch and lit a cigarette, blowing a cloud of smoke into the moonlit darkness. Despite himself, he wanted to talk to somebody, to her. Why, he didn't know, except that he had had a rough night that had culminated in a drive-by shooting conducted by a carload of gangbangers. Fortunately, no one had been seriously injured, the three teenagers who had been the gang's targets suffering only minor wounds. Still, the sight of the youths being carted away in ambulances had upset Jake.

"Well, I'm glad I didn't wake you," Claire said quietly. "I'm glad you're all right."

"Not all right. But I'm managing, just trying to get through one day at a time."

"That's good. That's the best way—and in the end, that's all you can do, really. I don't believe that old cliché about time healing all wounds. But it *does* eventually make the worst of them bearable.'' She didn't know what else to say. The conversation was stilted, awkward, guilt-tinged. He was still grieving and needed more time to come to grips with his loss. Still, something had happened to cause him to get in touch with her. Instinctively, she sensed his night had not gone very well. ''I'd...ah...ask you about your job, but I understand cops don't generally like to talk about their work—except to other cops, that is.''

''Yeah, that's right. It's hard for most people really to comprehend what it's like out there on the streets, seeing the worst of humanity day in and day out.''

''It's terribly depressing, I'm sure. So what helps you keep it all in perspective?''

''Nothing at the moment. Isabel did, but she's... gone now. Toussaint tries. He believes what you told me, by the way, that good sometimes comes out of tragedy. He says he's seen not only the worst, but also the best of human nature.''

''Maybe that's because he's looked for it,'' Claire suggested softly.

''The eternal optimist? The guy with the glass that's half-full instead of half-empty?''

''Does it make things better to think of it as the latter?''

''No...no, I suppose not. But at least it's realistic. You can't go through life perpetually wearing a pair of rose-colored shades, either.''

''No, I agree. Somewhere there's got to be a happy medium.''

''Yeah, and I thought I knew where that was, Claire. But now, I don't know anymore.'' Jake paused, dragging on his cigarette. Then he said, "Well, it's late, and I've kept you long enough. I know you have to work in the morning. I appreciate your calling me back, though."

"Anytime. Just don't be afraid to leave a message next time."

"No, I won't. Good night, Claire."

"Good night, Jake."

For a moment, neither one hung up, as though loath to break the connection. Then at last Claire gently replaced the receiver in the cradle. *What are you doing, Connelly?* she asked herself silently as she sat there in the half light, absorbed in contemplation. *This man has lost his wife. He has a lot of problems right now.* Yet, deep down inside, she somehow knew Jake Seringo was a good, decent man, the kind of man she would like to know better. In time, perhaps that would be possible, she thought. But now was not that time.

Still, a beginning of some sort had been made tonight, and Claire knew she would be lying to herself if she didn't admit Jake interested her, attracted her, intrigued her. She had never before known anyone like him. Perhaps it was because he was older and a Latino, and therefore foreign in many ways. Yet, beneath these outward trappings, she somehow sensed the two of them had much in common. Claire had already learned that although opposites might attract, their very dissimilarities almost invariably wound up driving them apart, that it was best to look for a partner who shared your own traits and interests. Had she and Jake met under different circumstances... But they hadn't. She must remember that.

Still, she was glad she had called Jake. No matter what, she had been worried about him, afraid she would walk into the television station some morning and discover he had killed himself. Now she felt that possibility, at least, had passed, that regardless of whatever else he might be feeling at this moment, Jake was no longer suicidal, no longer deeply off balance emotionally. He had begun to recover his equilibrium. Briefly, she wondered if her miniseries would help or hinder that process. Then, determinedly, she shoved the question from her mind. Since she had shifted the focus of the miniseries, it surely could have no effect upon him one way or another, she reassured herself.

Rising from the gossip bench and bending to retrieve her shoes, Claire headed toward her bedroom, peeling off her clothes as she went. It was now after midnight, and she was tired. Still, she thought she would be unable to sleep, that she would lie awake half the night, thinking about Jake. But she was wrong. She dropped off as soon as her head touched the pillow.

So it hadn't killed him to speak to Claire, Jake reflected as he ground his cigarette out in an ashtray and slowly rose from the sofa. So she hadn't plied him with a ton of reporter-like questions. So she had listened and offered quiet but wise observations, just like Toussaint. *Just like Isabel*—the thought came, unbidden, into his mind. That was one of the things he had always loved most about his wife, her capacity for listening, for keeping life in perspective with her astute observations and her sense of justice and fair play. *So it's only natural that you would seek those character-istics in another woman,* he could almost hear Tous-saint saying. So, since talking with Claire, he felt bet-ter, Jake told himself. So what? It meant nothing in the final analysis.

So why did he feel as though it did, that it meant everything, in fact?

"I—I don't believe you!" Vanessa Hampton cried. She was utterly stricken and horrified as she stared at her cousin Lily D'Angelo, who smiled at her cruelly, coolly contemptuous and maliciously satisfied. "You're lying! You're lying!"

"How on earth can you say that, Vannie?" Lily drawled as though now bored to tears by the entire subject under discussion. Languidly, she stretched out one slender, elegant hand to examine her expertly manicured, bloodred fingernails. "You've seen with your own eyes all the documentation I've assembled. It took me seven years and cost me thousands of dol-lars—but it was worth every second and every penny. Wouldn't you agree, Bruno?" From beneath thick, black lashes, Lily glanced with wicked amusement at her brother, who stood looking as though he had re-ceived a stunning blow that had left him dazed and hurting—as, indeed, he had.

"From the time I was just a child, I knew you were evil, Lily." His voice shook with tortured emotion. "I just never knew how much so until now. If you have falsified all this evidence, you are truly monstrous! And if you haven't—"

"Oh, but I haven't, dear brother, I assure you. It's

all perfectly true, the terrible skeleton in the Hampton family closet. Honestly, I just don't know how Grandmother's managed to keep it hushed up all these years. Unquestionably, she's paid out a lot of money, probably even had a few people killed to keep the dirty, little secret, I would imagine, she's such a hateful, old bitch! And now, you and Vannie are a part of it—whether you like it or not.''

"Oh, God," Vanessa sobbed, tears now streaming down her cheeks. "Oh, God. It can't be true! It just can't!'' Blindly, she stumbled from the small Italian villa she and Bruno had rented together in Tuscany for the summer. She had to get away! Away from Lily and her dreadful lies, her glittering eyes, her supercilious smirk, and Bruno's sick, white face. Outside on the moonlit patio, Vanessa didn't stop, but kept on running, staggering wildly down the terraces that led to the drive below.

"Vanessa! Vanessa!" Bruno called, distraught, as he raced after her, scrambling down the wide steps as hard and fast as he could.

But she paid him no heed, pressing on like a demented woman, scarcely even feeling the pain as she tripped and fell in the darkness, badly scraping her hands and knees. Lurching to her feet, she tore on, the enormity of what she and Bruno had done consuming her. He must not catch her! She must go far away from here, as far away as she could get. She must never see him again. And most of all, she must get rid of the child she carried.

Bruno's bright, red Ferrari Testarosa was parked on the drive, and as she reached it and wrenched open the door, Vanessa saw that his keys were in the ignition. Without thinking, she slid into the luxurious, leather driver's seat and started the powerful engine.

"Vanessa!" Gaining the car, Bruno ripped open the passenger door and jumped in beside her. "Vanessa, please! We need to talk!"

"No, no." She shook her head violently, still weeping uncontrollably. "There's nothing to say. Get out! Leave me alone! I have to get away!"

"No, I can't let you go like this."

At that, before Bruno could stop her, Vanessa threw the Ferrari into Reverse and backed the car into the turnaround. Then, shoving the gearshift into First, she barreled down the drive, not realizing until the towering pine trees closed around her that she had not turned on the headlights. Without slowing, she hit the proper switch, and with a low hum, the lamps tilted into place, casting their bright beams onto the road as she veered recklessly onto it.

"Vanessa, please, at least slow down," Bruno entreated futilely as he fastened his seat belt. "This car has too much power for you to handle it properly. You're not used to it, especially on this dangerous road, and you're hysterical, besides. Please, Vanessa."

"What difference does it make if I kill us both?" she wailed, making him wince when she ground the gears as she shifted them inexpertly and propelled the Ferrari on heedlessly, unable to see clearly through her tears and fishtailing along the dark road, tires squealing. "What have we to live for now, anyway, Bruno? How can we live with what we have done?"

"Look, we didn't know, Vanessa—we *still* don't

know—that what Lily said was true. She's crazy, quite insane! Yes, I see that now. And hideously vindictive, too. She was always extremely jealous and resentful of me, and of you and Veronica, as well. She hates us all. She's crazy, I tell you! She would say anything to hurt us!''

"That doesn't mean she wasn't telling the truth!''

"Vanessa, please—''

Whatever else Bruno might have said was lost as, waiting too late to brake for the hairpin curve ahead, Vanessa lost control of the Ferrari. She screamed and screamed as the car skidded horribly, burning rubber for some yards on the asphalt before rolling over, then striking the metal guardrail and ramming through it to plunge down the steep incline beyond.

A few minutes later, the vehicle hit the ground below, exploding on impact.

Seven

Winds of Change

The One remains, the many change and pass;
Heaven's light forever shines, earth's shadows fly;
Life, like a dome of many-colored glass,
Stains the white radiance of eternity,
Until Death tramples it to fragments.

Adonais
—Percy Bysshe Shelley

One of Claire's jobs at Channel 4 was to monitor the Associated Press feeds, and today she saw that the AP machine had spit out reams of its continuous paper, which now lay in an untidy heap on the floor. Ripping the paper at the sawtoothed cutter, she began to fold it up neatly, scanning the printed material while she worked. Most of the stories were updates on national and global news or articles from other local markets, which had uploaded them to the wire service. But there was one piece, which had been originally filed in Italy, that caught Claire's eye, the name *Hampton* seeming to jump off the page at her. Sitting down in a nearby steno chair, she read the article, shocked by its contents.

[*Associated Press*] FLORENCE, Italy. All of Italy is in mourning at the untimely death of one of its national heroes, 23-year-old champion race-car driver Bruno D'Angelo, ironically killed in a tragic, one-car accident near his summer villa in Tuscany. D'Angelo's cousin, Vanessa Hampton, was driving the vehicle at the time of the fatal crash. Details of the accident are sketchy at this point, but an initial examination of the crash site suggests that Hampton lost control of the car at a dangerous hairpin curve where several other vehicles have, over the years, met similar fates. The car apparently rolled at least once before smashing through the guardrail along the curve and plummeting down the hillside beyond. Upon impact, the vehicle's fuel tank ignited, exploding and killing D'Angelo instantly. Hampton, who was not wearing a seat belt at the time of the crash, was evidently thrown clear when the car struck the guardrail. Suffering multiple injuries, she was transported by private plane to a hospital in Florence, where she remains in critical condition.

There was a good deal more, details about Bruno D'Angelo's racing career, about both the Hampton and the D'Angelo families, but Claire didn't read any further. Instead, leaping to her feet, she tore the article from the rest of the paper and hurried out into the corridor with it. She knew the story was doubtless breaking everywhere, that CNN at the very least must already be on the air with it. Still, since the powerful Hampton family had been residents of the city since the time of the Civil War, local interest would be extremely high.

Claire would have liked to handle the story herself, but she had no illusions that it would be assigned to her. However, she would undoubtedly get to play a minor role, doing research and perhaps some follow-up. She soon discovered this was indeed to be the case, and she spent the rest of the day in the morgue of the local newspaper, the *Gulf Coast Courier,* reviewing old articles about the Hamptons. Everybody in town knew who the Hamptons were, of course, but this was the first time Claire had ever really delved into their history, and she found it utterly fascinating.

The family had immigrated from northern England to the United States during the mid-1800s, before the defiant and ultimately lethal shot that had been fired at Fort Sumter. They had been textile manufacturers in England and had brought their knowledge of that industry with them, establishing one of the few such mills in the South and subsequently growing rich off King Cotton. Unlike most of Dixie, they had profited during the Civil War and afterward had not suffered any scruples when it had come to dealing with the carpetbaggers that had swooped down like vultures to pick the bones of the wounded South. As a result, they had continued to expand their growing textile enterprise, and eventually, more than one Hampton businessman had been lured into the local and national political arenas, as well. By the turn of the century, the family had had their fingers in numerous pies, both businesswise and politically.

During Prohibition, it was rumored that the Hamptons had turned to bootlegging and had, it was claimed, done more than one favor for the Mafia dons with whom they had during those years become connected. World Wars I and II had further increased the family coffers when the Hamptons had been awarded several extremely lucrative government contracts to manufacture uniforms for the U.S. Army. There were tales of various high rollers from the family being involved in casinos in Las Vegas, Monte Carlo, and Havana, and one Hampton male had been notorious in his day for wedding the former moll of a well-known mobster. But if the Hampton family tree were littered with the corrupt and scandalous, it also boasted its fair share of the dedicated and heroic. Generous donations had been periodically made to charities and the arts. Vanessa Hampton's grandfather had achieved the rank of brigadier general during the Korean War, and one of her uncles had thrown himself on a grenade in Vietnam, saving the men under his command and receiving a posthumous Purple Heart to add to the cluster of ribbons and medals he had already been awarded prior to his death.

Still, despite all its prosperity, the Hampton family was rife with other tragedies, as well, Claire learned as she read on, scrolling the microfiche slowly. Vanessa's own parents had been killed in a private-plane crash some years back, and just shortly afterward, her aunt—Bruno D'Angelo's mother—had, while abroad, suffered a nervous breakdown and died of an accidental but fatal combination of alcohol and drugs. Bruno's father, stricken with a degenerative disease, had retired from public life and now lived as a recluse in Italy. Some years back, Vanessa's last, surviving Hampton uncle had been assassinated while on business in South America; and just last year, Vanessa's nephew—the only child of her older twin sister, Veronica, and Veronica's husband, local politician Malcolm Forsythe—had been kidnapped and held for ransom. Despite that the one-million-dollar ransom had been paid, the two-year-old boy had never been returned, and his body had been discovered in a shallow grave a few months after the abduction.

When Claire was finished with all her research, she had a spiral-bound notebook filled with data—enough to write a book about the Hampton family, she thought as she leafed through the material. That would be an interesting project, if she only had the time to devote to it. But her milieu was the camera lens, and she would never get in front of one if she didn't get back to the station with all the background information she had collected. Glancing at her wristwatch, she crammed the notebook into the oversize tote bag in which she carried all her paraphernalia, then headed upstairs to the *Courier's* newsroom.

"Hey, Zoey," she greeted her best friend since kindergarten, who, after they had graduated from college together, had got a job at the newspaper—writing obituaries, mostly—and so who thoroughly understood about wanting to move up the corporate ladder. "Is it all right if I use the Xerox machine? I'll pay for the copies, of course.''

"Sure, Claire. Did you find everything you needed in the morgue?" Zoey Rutledge's short but stylishly cropped, chestnut curls, her heart-shaped face, and her big, amber eyes gave her a decidedly gamin appearance that was emphasized when she smiled, as she did now.

"Yes, I think so. If I didn't, I'm sure Mr. Kendall will let me know about it, and I can come back tomorrow or Monday. You know, until today, I never realized what a history the Hamptons have."

"It's really something, isn't it?" Zoey observed as she rose from her desk to accompany Claire to the copier. "Full of fame and fortune, glamour and tragedy...like something you'd read in a novel. Still, even though they've got all that money, you can't help but feel sorry for them. I don't know how old Mrs. Hampton has borne up under the strain...all her children dead and now this latest, the loss of her only grandson and one of her granddaughters near death....'' Zoey shook her head sadly.

"Is there anything new yet on the granddaughter's condition?"

"Not that I've heard. Last I knew, she was still critical."

"What do you suppose actually happened, Zoey?" Flipping open her notebook, Claire laid it down on the Xerox machine and pressed the button to copy the first page. "I mean, I feel certain, somehow, that nobody's got the real story yet. Why do you think Vanessa was driving Bruno's Ferrari? Why wasn't he driving it himself? He was a champion race-car driver, after all. He must have known that Testarosa was more car than she could safely handle, especially on that treacherous road and at night. I wonder where they were going at that late hour, anyway.''

"Who knows?" Zoey shrugged, but her eyes were speculative. "It might be something worth digging into, Claire. But just how would either of us go about it? We sure don't have the professional clout to go jaunting off to Italy on a mere hunch. And what's more, my gut instinct tells me that old Mrs. Hampton has succeeded in hushing up bigger things than whatever may have led to this accident. So from a news standpoint, this is probably just small potatoes to her. You can bet your bottom dollar that if Vanessa survives, old Mrs. Hampton will whisk her off someplace and make sure she stays secluded until all this blows over.''

"Yeah, you're probably right," Claire agreed as she continued to copy the pages in her notebook. "Still, you never know. Something may eventually come out about it. Old Mrs. Hampton isn't going to live forever—and I don't think Veronica's husband is going to be content in local, or even state, politics, either. My guess is that he's going to run for the House of Representatives or even the Senate one of these days. That's why I want to keep a copy of my notes on file at home.''

"Well, I'll let you know if anything turns up here— provided, of course, that you do the same for me." Zoey grinned. "I don't plan on being stuck writing obituaries forever, you know!"

"No, I know—and you've got a deal." Claire closed her notebook and rummaged in her handbag for the proper payment, while Zoey recorded the number of copies on the log taped to the Xerox machine for that purpose. "Thanks for everything. I'll call you later...let you know how my blind date tomorrow night goes."

"Oh, Lord, Claire. Don't tell me your mother's not only at it again, but that you actually succumbed!"

"'Fraid so. Mother's getting a great deal cleverer about these things, you see. This time, she arranged for us all to have supper together at her house, so I won't be alone with the guy, and if nothing else, I'll get to see my family at least. But don't worry. I'm not holding my breath. I mean, the guy's a dentist, for pity's sake. So I just can't imagine we'll have much in common. But you never know, and the truth is, Zoey, that I'd rather have supper at Mother's than sit home alone another Saturday night."

"I know. But, Claire, you were the one who broke it off with Paul."

Paul Langley was Claire's old boyfriend, whom she had dated all through college. "Yes, and no matter what, I still think it was the right thing to do. He didn't want the responsibilities and commitments of marriage while he was away at law school—and I didn't want to move north on the off chance that he might change his mind. He wouldn't have, Zoey. If, once he's completed his law degree, he comes back here and wants to pick up where we left off, I might consider it. But then again, I might not. We were just opposites in every way, and while that was exciting at first, it had started to cause problems in our relationship even before Paul had left town. At least this way, if he *does* return and wants to see me, the two of us will be sure it's the right thing for us both."

"Yeah, I can understand that. Well, have fun with the dentist!"

"Right. Catch you later, Zoey."

After returning to the station, Claire sat down at her computer to type up neatly the notes she had gathered on the Hampton family. Then she printed them out and turned them in to her boss, Mr. Kendall. Finished with work for the day, she shoved her notebook into her file drawer, then collected her purse and tote bag, heading for her car in the parking lot.

Once home, she checked her telephone answering machine first thing, but much to her disappointment, there were no messages from Jake Seringo.

It was the young, Latino woman who did it—who caused Jake's recently but rigidly imposed self-control to snap. He and his partner, Frank Bollinger, spotted her as they made their nightly rounds in their patrol car. She was lying half in, half out of a dark alley. If not for that, if she had been farther back, nearer the rear wall, they would have missed her completely, and her body probably wouldn't have been discovered for days. As it was, they had no idea how long she had been there, dead. From the way she was dressed, they concluded that she was a hooker. Needle tracks in her arms also indicated she was a dope addict, and the two men speculated that she had got into a fatal argument with either her pimp or a pusher, or maybe even another prostitute.

"What do you think?" Bollinger asked as he knelt over the corpse, shining his flashlight to get a better look at her. "Dead two or three hours at least, maybe more, I'm guessing."

Swallowing hard, Jake tersely nodded his agreement, not certain he could speak. It wasn't the young, unfamiliar woman's face he saw, but that of his murdered wife.

"Jake, are you all right, buddy? Why don't you go radio this in, while I check out the rest of the alley? From the blood trail, it looks as though she was either dragged up here after having been stabbed or else, more likely, that the scum who did this only thought he'd finished her off and she crawled up here, trying to get help."

"If she did, she sure didn't get any, did she? No, it's...all right, Frank. I'm okay," Jake lied, trying to get a grip on his turbulent emotions. A muscle flexed in his set jaw. "It's darker than an oil slick back there, and we don't know what all went down here yet, what else we may find. We should check out the alley together, then call it in. I don't want you covering for me, possibly endangering yourself because of me. This isn't going to be the last body we ever stumble over."

"No, I know. But I...well, with your situation and all— Look, I was just trying to help, Jake."

"I know that, and I appreciate it. So please don't think I don't. But the truth is that, like it or not, I have to get on with my life, Frank. I've just got to work through what happened to Isabel and the baby. Otherwise, I'm never going to be any good at my job, and I for damned sure am not going to be any kind of a dependable partner for you or anybody else. Okay?''

"Okay, buddy." Bollinger nodded understandingly. "Let's go take a look, then."

Revolvers drawn and held at the ready, gleaming flashlights raised, the two men started warily down the alley, carefully picking their way through garbage and other debris. But except for a pitiful, scrawny, stray cat, the alley was empty. Both men breathed a sigh of relief as they returned to the cruiser to radio in the homicide.

Pretty soon, Remy Toussaint and his partner had arrived in their unmarked car, along with backup officers in uniform, the medical examiner, and the Crime Scene Unit.

"No purse anywhere? No ID on the body? Anybody call Vice?" Toussaint asked as he surveyed the corpse, grimacing and shaking his head. "Maybe one of those guys knows her. Check with Narco, too, just for the hell of it. Otherwise, unless we get a missing persons report, she's going down as a Jane Doe."

"This part of town and no ID, my guess is that she's an illegal alien, Remy," Jake said quietly. "Probably got mixed up with the wrong people even before she crossed the border."

"Well, whoever she was, she was certainly running with the wrong crowd tonight," the medical examiner observed. "I count half a dozen stab wounds, all apparently made by the same hand and knife, the latter of which was single-edged—just like the one used on your wife, Jake."

"You think there might be a connection?" Toussaint questioned sharply.

"Hard to tell," the medical examiner replied, peeling off his surgical gloves. "But it's probably at least worth keeping in mind. I'll know more after the autopsy."

"What might tie Isabel and our Jane Doe together, Jake?" Toussaint asked soberly.

"I honestly don't know, Remy. Isabel didn't dispense heroin to addicts, if that's what you're thinking. In fact, the only thing that comes to mind is that maybe this girl was hanging around the convenience store that night. She wouldn't be the first hooker to have dropped by for cigarettes or condoms. Maybe she saw something that night, something she would have been better off not seeing, and instead of coming forward to notify the police, she tried to use what she knew to her advantage."

"Blackmail? Yes, I agree that's a real possibility. I know you're not officially on Isabel's case. But you might want to ask around, see what you can find out about our dead working girl here. No offense, but these Latinos over here—especially the ones who're illegal aliens—are a lot more likely to talk to you than to me, Jake. Hell, some of 'em don't even speak English, and I don't know more than a few words of Spanish. But I'm assuming you can speak it fluently. Can you?"

"Yeah, more or less. It was my parents' native language, and they always used it at home. I'll do what I can. Now that I've really taken a good look at her,

I know I've seen this girl around somewhere before. I just can't place her. But maybe it'll come to me."

"If you don't dwell on it, it probably will. If you remember, give me a call."

"I will, Remy."

"You going to be all right alone tonight, Jake, after this? 'Cause if you're not, you know you're more 'n welcome to stay with me and Frances."

"Yeah, I know. But I'll be fine. Really."

But after he got home, Jake knew he wasn't fine. As he changed out of his uniform into a short-sleeve shirt and chinos, he kept seeing over and over in his mind's eye the face of the young, Latino hooker, and like a painting fading to reveal pentimento, it kept evanescing into the countenance of his dead wife, torturing him. Finally, he could stand it no longer, and despite how determinedly he fought against it, he found himself rummaging through the kitchen cabinets, searching for the bottle of Captain Morgan he had stashed away. He opened it up, took a couple of long swallows, savoring the warm, spicy rum as it slid down his throat. *Drinking alone is one of the things that leads to alcoholism, Jake,* he could almost hear Toussaint chiding severely. "Damn it," Jake swore softly, slamming his hand down hard on the kitchen counter.

Impulsively, he screwed the cap back on the bottle, grabbed his keys and left the apartment, striding swiftly along the gallery and down the steps to his car, which was parked at the curb. He drove aimlessly, not wanting to go where anyone knew him. Before he realized it, he was across the river and on his old stomping grounds around the university, where he had got his administration of justice degree. He pulled into the small parking lot of his once-favorite haunt, a little hole-in-the-wall bar called the Why Not?, which was just off campus. Because it was summer, the place wasn't nearly as crowded as it would be in the fall, and it was unlikely anybody here would remember him, anyway. Further, since students in night classes tended to be older, he wouldn't stand out as an anomaly, either.

The place was as dark and smoky inside as he remembered, with candles stuck in old wine bottles on the tables providing most of the light, the rest spilling from the faux-stained-glass fixtures that hung low over the two pool tables to one side. In one corner, on a small platform, a lone blues guitarist sat on a high bar stool, oblivious of his meager audience as he plucked out "Stormy Monday." Jake slid into a chair at the rear, ordering a Cuba Libre and, since he hadn't eaten, a shrimp po' boy from the waitress who sauntered over from the bar to serve him.

He ought to feel some sort of hope at tonight's events, Jake told himself, at the idea that maybe the knife that had been used to murder Isabel had also been employed to kill the young hooker in the alley. It might represent a fresh lead, a break in his wife's case—especially if he could remember where he had seen the prostitute before. But much to his frustration, no matter how he racked his brain, the memory eluded him. Toussaint was right: He needed to stop dwelling on it. Then maybe it would come to him.

Hungrily, Jake ate the po' boy and the red beans

and rice that had come with it. He drank the Cuba Libre and ordered a second one, then a third. He didn't want to think anymore, but to slide into a sweet, numb oblivion where he was no longer haunted by his personal tragedy, where he no longer felt any pain or loneliness. But tonight even the alcohol couldn't seem to fill up the terrible emptiness inside him.

At last, Jake rose a trifle unsteadily, the liquor and his tiredness momentarily wreaking havoc on his equilibrium. After fumbling in his wallet, he tossed enough money down on the table to cover his bill and the waitress's tip, then walked outside to the parking lot, the bluesy strains of the acoustic guitar accompanying him into the night until the bar door slowly swung shut behind him. After the coolness of the air-conditioned bar, the humidity outside struck him mercilessly, like a blast of steam. In seconds, it felt as though his shirt was soaked through, although Jake knew that was only an illusion.

He probably oughtn't to be driving, he mused dully as he got into his car and fastened his seat belt. For a long moment, he just sat there, shaking his head as though to clear it, before he finally turned the key in the ignition. It was late, and he should be getting home—except that there was no longer anything for him there now, no reason to hurry back to the apartment, no one there to worry that if he didn't show up soon, he had been killed in the line of duty.

He just couldn't return to the apartment tonight, Jake thought suddenly. He couldn't face it, not after the dead hooker whose face kept fading into Isabel's.

He would go crazy if he went home, maybe haul out his revolver instead of the bottle of Captain Morgan.

Without even realizing he did so, Jake headed his vehicle along the streets around the college, making a right at the intersection where Claire had directed him to turn when he had driven her home some weeks ago.

Claire wasn't asleep. She had got home late from her mother's, having found the dentist, Brett Deauville, a surprisingly pleasant and entertaining dinner partner. Although he hadn't been her type physically and she didn't want to date him, she had liked him well enough to think he might at least become a friend. Like her, he was ambitious, having informed her at supper that within the next ten years, he planned to become "the dentist to the city's elite." That had made her laugh at her own naiveté, because she had not previously considered that dentists might have aspirations that went beyond just fighting cavities.

Finally, sometime after midnight, Claire had thanked Brett and her family for a delightful evening, then had driven home alone, softly singing along with the car radio, which she had tuned to an adult-contemporary station. She hadn't been able to remember having such a good time since Paul had gone away to law school, leaving her alone and disheartened after their breakup, although she had been the one to initiate it. Except for the blind dates her mother kept arranging for her, Claire hadn't gone out much since Paul had left. Early on in high school, she had learned that her combination of good looks, intelligence, and determination was intimidating to most men. They either assumed she was already committed to a relationship, or else they figured they didn't stand a chance with her, so she actually didn't get asked out on a lot of dates and spent a lot of evenings sitting home alone, studying the anchors and reporters on CNN and planning how to further her career. It had been nice to while away a Saturday night in such good company for a change.

After returning to her bungalow, she had undressed and slipped into her nightgown. Now, as her doorbell rang, Claire hurriedly drew on her robe, wondering who could be calling on her at this late hour and worrying that there had been some mishap with regard to her family.

"Who is it?" she asked anxiously through the closed door.

"Jake...Jake Seringo."

Breathing a sigh of relief, her curiosity piqued, she unlocked the bolts and opened the door a crack to peek out. Much to her surprise, it was indeed Jake who stood there in the soft glow of the lamplight spilling down on her front porch.

"I...ah...I'm sorry. I just happened to be in the neighborhood, and I thought I saw lights on inside, that you were still up. But now, I realize I was mistaken and that you had already gone to bed," Jake muttered as his gaze took in her attire. Then, running one hand raggedly through his hair, he swore softly. "Christ! I don't know what in the hell I'm doing here, anyway."

"No, it's all right," Claire insisted hastily as he turned to go, her heart pounding. One hand tightened on the edges of her robe, which she clutched at her breast. "You weren't wrong. I wasn't asleep. I had just got home, in fact. Won't you...won't you come in?" Moving back into the foyer, she slowly swung open the door to admit him, and after a long moment, Jake stepped inside.

Eight

Grains of Sand

Listen! you hear the grating roar
Of pebbles which the waves draw back, and fling,
At their return, up the high strand,
Begin, and cease, and then again begin,
With tremulous cadence slow, and bring
The eternal note of sadness in.

Dover Beach
—Matthew Arnold

Claire closed the front door and locked it, following Jake into the living room off the foyer. He was as big and tall as she remembered, powerfully but lithely built, like a whipcord. As he stood there, illuminated by the light from the single lamp that burned on an end table, he seemed to dwarf her small bungalow, in a way her old boyfriend, Paul, never had.

"I...don't know why I came here," Jake reiterated lamely as he glanced around, noting absently the simple Victorian furnishings, how neat and clean everything was, how the woodwork gleamed and smelled faintly of lemons. He guessed that on her entry-level salary, the furniture was mostly secondhand, with perhaps a few family heirlooms mixed in.

"Won't you sit down? Can I...get you some coffee? A Coke?" Claire didn't offer him anything with alcohol in it, certain Jake had already had more than a few drinks prior to his arrival. Why she was so sure about this, she didn't know. He wasn't slurring his words; he hadn't staggered his way inside. He didn't appear to be threatening, violent, or out of control, the way he had that day at his apartment. Still, she somehow knew instinctively that no matter how well he appeared to be holding his liquor tonight, he was perhaps drunk and certainly in the throes of some emotional torment.

"No, nothing for me, thank you," he answered tersely. "Look, this was a mistake—"

"Jake, if you want to talk to somebody, I'm more than willing to listen," Claire said gently. "I wasn't planning on turning in right away. I usually read a while before going to bed, and as I mentioned before, I had just got home."

"Of course. I should have realized. It's Saturday...date night. I...ah...didn't interrupt anything, did I?"

"No. I had a blind date earlier, and we had supper at my mother's house. But I came home alone, if that's what you're asking. Is it?"

"Yeah, I guess so." Jake was surprised to discover that the idea of Claire Connelly out on a date, in the arms of some unknown man, disturbed him, ignited within him a flame of jealousy—and a sense of satisfaction that her date hadn't returned here with her. "I suppose things must not have gone very well. I mean, since you came home all by your lonesome self."

"Actually, he was a nice guy, and I hope we'll become friends," Claire declared. "He just wasn't my type physically, that's all. You know? Pheromones and all that jazz. The chemistry just wasn't there. Sometimes it is, and sometimes it isn't—and I think you always know right from the start whether you share it with someone or you don't. At least, I always do. How about you?" Anything to keep him talking to her, she thought. He needed somebody, whether he recognized that fact or not—or just refused to admit it.

"Yeah, I guess I always know." Jake could, in fact, feel the chemistry under discussion even now, he realized, surging between the two of them so powerfully that it was almost tangible. He was vividly conscious of her, of her long, blond hair spilling like silken skeins of silver-gold over her shoulders and haloed by the moonlight filtering in through the plantation blinds at the front windows. Of the filminess of her long, lacy, white robe and nightgown, of the fact that at most, she was wearing only a pair of panties beneath. Of the curve of her soft, round breasts, of the way that her nipples hardened when she became aware of how his eyes raked her assessingly. "I've had too much to drink," he confessed suddenly. "It's late, and I should be going."

"Back to what, Jake?" Claire asked quietly, her

gaze falling beneath his and a blush creeping up to stain her cheeks as she realized how her nipples strained against the thin material of her nightclothes. Her hands trembling a little, she drew her robe more closely around her, the pulse at the hollow of her throat fluttering wildly. "Back to your empty apartment? Your bottle of Captain Morgan? Your revolver? I don't think you really want to go home to any of that. I've got a spare bedroom. You're welcome to stay here tonight, if you wish. You're probably not actually in any real shape to drive, anyway. Come on. I'll show you where you can sleep."

Her robe and nightgown whispered around her long, bare legs as she slipped past him, her feet padding softly on the hardwood floor. The fragrant scent of her...gardenias...wafted to Jake's nostrils, causing his groin to tighten with desire. He wanted her, he realized. Deep down inside, he thought that perhaps that was why he had come here in the first place, to drive away the demons that tortured him in his heart and mind, to forget everything but the feel of Claire Connelly as he buried himself inside her, knowing only that moment of sweet, blind release and nothing more.

Wordlessly then, Jake followed her from the living room into a short, narrow hall that gave way to two bedrooms and a bathroom. Turning right, Claire flicked the switch on the wall, and one of the tall hurricane lamps that sat on the twin, cherry-wood, marble-topped nightstands filled the bedroom with a low, soft, pinkish glow born of the light's fragile, glass shade, which was hand-painted with cabbage roses. Dominating the room was a matching, cherry-wood, tester bed with a white, lace canopy and dust ruffle. A white, eyelet duvet embroidered with delicate, spring flowers in a multitude of colors covered the bed. At its foot was an old-fashioned, cedar hope chest. Against one wall stood a cherry-wood, bow-front dresser, also marble-topped and which apparently served as her vanity, as well, since to one side sat an Abigail Walker chair upholstered in a deep rose velvet. The wooden blades of the overhead fan turned languidly against the ceiling, stirring the air pleasantly.

Jake gave a low whistle of appreciation. Far from making him feel uncomfortable, the room's heavy, ornately carved furniture—in sharp contrast to its delicate, feminine touches—appealed to his masculinity. "Some guest room," he observed from where he stood in the doorway. "I feel as though I were somehow just transported back in time, that I'm trespassing in some Southern belle's boudoir."

"Hardly that," Claire replied, smiling as she turned down the quilt and sheet, and plumped up the lacy, sham-encased pillows. "This is my room. Cars at sixteen, my sisters and I had to work for. But Mother said every woman should have a beautiful, restful bedroom in which to retreat from the day's hustle and bustle, and she gave each of us girls a bedroom suite when we graduated from high school. The guest room only has a twin bed, and given how tall you are, I thought you'd be more comfortable in here, since this set has a queen-size bed. I'll sleep across the hall."

"No, I can't let you do that," Jake protested, disturbed by the idea of displacing her from her room. "I'm already imposing on you as it is, and I wouldn't feel right about turning you out of your own bed. The guest room will be fine for me, I assure you."

"Don't be silly. You won't get any good rest at all, sleeping in that small of a bed." Finished fussing with the covers and knowing there was no other reasonable excuse for her to remain, Claire started toward him. "The bathroom's right next door. I'll just get you some fresh towels. Since tomorrow's Sunday, I don't have to work. So please feel free to sleep as late as you like—unless, of course, you have to get up for Mass or something. If so, there's an alarm clock beside the bed."

"Are you usually so generous about opening your home to men you hardly even know, Claire?" Like some predator stalking its prey, Jake moved into the room, coming to stand before her, blocking her path to the hall beyond. "Are you always so trusting? I mean, my behavior toward you at our last meeting was scarcely of a kind to inspire confidence."

"No, it wasn't—and no, I'm not in the habit of offering a bed to men who are practically strangers to me. But you weren't yourself that day we met," she pointed out, her heart thudding so loudly in her breast at his proximity that she thought he must surely hear it. "And you were terribly drunk, besides."

"I'm drunk now," he insisted, his voice low, husky. "Otherwise, I wouldn't still be here. I wouldn't even have come here to begin with. But you were right. I just couldn't face going back to my empty apartment tonight." Without warning, he reached out, slipping one hand gently beneath the edges of her robe, drawing his fingers lightly along her collarbone before trailing them up her throat to cup her chin. "So why am I different from the other men you hardly know, Claire? Why did you take me in? Pity?" His mouth twisted mockingly as he spoke the word.

"I suppose that was a part of it," she admitted softly, after a long moment in which she seemed to struggle for breath. "But mostly, it was because I know what it's like to be alone. I lost someone recently, too. Oh, not in the same way as you did. He didn't die, and there was nothing tragic about his leaving—except that it was hard for me to know he went without me, even though I was the one who sent him away."

"Were you in love with him?"

"At the time, I thought I was. But I'm not so sure anymore. I only know there's an emptiness inside me now, Jake, that even my work doesn't fill up. I think that's the way you feel, too, that that's why you sought me out this evening. And as strange as it may sound to you, despite that we scarcely know each other, I somehow feel as though I've known you all my life, even so. It's curious and inexplicable, but there it is all the same. I guess that's why I was drawn to you despite your behavior to me that day we first met, why I said you could stay here tonight."

Claire paused for an instant, gathering her thoughts, her courage. Then she continued.

"I think that perhaps sometimes two people, for whatever their reasons, just need each other, Jake, if only for a moment out of time, that they're like those grains of sand that, despite that there're millions of them, compose what is still a bleak and lonely beach.

You don't have to pretend with me, you know. I'm not asking you for anything. I'm not expecting any more from you than you're capable of giving right now. Nor am I offering you any more than that myself. I'm here for you if that's what you want—no strings attached. That's all I'm trying to tell you.''

At that, he murmured, ''I want very much to kiss you, Claire. God forgive me, but I think I've wanted that from the first moment I ever saw you. I've tried to fight my feelings for you. They've eaten me alive with guilt. They go against everything within me that is decent and moral—not because of anything to do with you, but because they came at the wrong time and for all the wrong reasons. Do you understand that? But still, they just won't be suppressed—at least, not tonight, anyway. That's where I am right now emotionally, for whatever that's worth. So I hope you meant what you said, Claire, because I want to be honest with you—and the truth is that I just can't promise you anything...except this....'' Then, before she realized what he intended, his hands tunneled through her hair on either side of her face, and he lowered his head to hers, claiming her mouth with his own.

His kiss was tentative, tender, at first, as though he were unsure of himself, or of her. As lightly as the gossamer wings of a butterfly flicked against the petals of a flower, his lips brushed hers, once, twice, before capturing them completely. But when she did not demur, made no effort to pull away from him, the pressure of his mouth gradually increased, growing less restrained, more insistent, as though he had broken through some emotional barrier deep within himself and there were no turning back now. His tongue traced the outline of her lips, then inexorably insinuated itself between them, plunging deep, touching, tasting, making Claire shudder irresistibly with a sudden surge of longing. She swayed against him, steadying herself by placing her palms flat against his chest. She could not remember ever being kissed in quite this way before, as though a man had all the time in the world to savor her—and fully intended to do so, kissing her endlessly, shattering and scattering her senses.

Of their own volition, her arms crept up bit by bit to fasten around Jake's neck. Her hands burrowed through his thick, glossy, black hair, tightening into fists as his tongue continued to explore her moist, parted mouth, twining with her own tongue. His breath had begun to come more harshly now; she could feel it warm against her skin as his lips slid across her cheek to her temple, the strands of her hair. His tongue caressed her ear; his teeth nibbled her lobe, sending an electric thrill coursing through her. She was intensely aware of how her nipples stiffened at the sensation, tautening again beneath her nightclothes. Jake was highly cognizant of it, too. His hand glided down to cup one breast, his thumb rotating deliberately, sensuously, across the engorged peak, causing Claire's breath to catch in her throat.

"Tell me to stop, Claire," he muttered hoarsely, his eyes like twin flames beneath hooded lids as he gazed down at her, seeming to rivet her where she stood. "Tell me to stop, or I'm going to make love to you. You know that now, don't you?"

"Yes," she whispered, and in response, she slowly shrugged her robe from her shoulders, so it trailed down her back to puddle at her feet on the hardwood floor. He had promised her nothing except this—and right or wrong, she wanted him. Perhaps tomorrow, she would regret that—and what was to come, even more. But in this moment, it didn't matter if there would never be anything more than this night between them.

The long nightgown she still wore was like a diaphanous cobweb delicately woven around her, so she appeared to Jake like some sylvan nymph as she stood there before him, gauzy, white folds stirred gently by the turning fan, her blond hair gleaming like fiery, golden streamers shot from a midnight sun, her pale, creamy skin bathed with a soft, rosy glow from the low light cast by the hurricane lamp. Her body was beautifully proportioned, her long, graceful legs making her seem taller than she really was. Through the translucent material of her nightgown, Jake could see her full, round breasts tipped with their dusky-rose nipples, her slender waist that flared into narrow hips with dainty hollows on the sides, revealed by the lacy, white, French-cut panties she wore. He was mesmerized, tantalized.

The likes of her were, in all truth, beyond his realm of experience. Growing up in the barrio as he had, he had known mainly Latino women, dark of skin, hair, and eyes. In college, he had already been married, and faithful to his wedding vows, he had never even considered sampling any of the wide variety of females who had made plain the fact that they found him attractive. Dimly, it occurred to him as he looked at Claire that none of those barriers existed for him now, that with her, he was stepping into a different world from the one he had inhabited before, the world that lay across the river—yet might as well have been a light-year away in this moment. That perhaps there would be no going back afterward was an idea that never even entered his mind.

He half thought he must be dreaming as Claire's slender, artistic hands, fumbling a little, revealing her own nervousness, began to undo the buttons of his shirt one by one, then tugged it from him, folding it neatly and laying it on the nearby chair—to buy time, Jake realized as he watched how she took several deep breaths, struggling for composure, to conquer her uncertainty and perhaps her misgivings. He understood then that she had not lied to him, that unlike so many other women of her ilk, she was not, in fact, given to one-night stands or casual affairs, that those were beyond her own experience, as well. Perhaps he himself, too, was different from any other man in her past. Almost, guilt that he was taking advantage of her gnawing at him, Jake turned to leave. But then she was standing there before him once more—and he discovered that no matter what, he could not bring himself to go.

Like a dragonfly skimming the still waters of a summer pond, creating ripples that disturbed and incited the surface, Claire's fingertips drew tiny circles amid the crisp, black hair that matted his broad chest, causing his bronze flesh to tingle, his sex to grow hard and heavy with desire. With a tortured groan born of his internal conflict, Jake pulled her into his strong arms, his hands gliding down her back to her hips, hauling her against him so she could feel the evidence of his yearning, would know how much he wanted her. Perhaps he thought to frighten her with the force of his need, to make her stop what he could not seem to halt himself. But if so, he failed, for instead of pulling away from him, Claire settled into the curve of his embrace, laying her head against his chest, trembling with the strength of her emotions, her rising passion. Heat pooled at the core of her being, then flooded her entire body as she felt his maleness against her, bold, taunting, and promising.

"Do you always wear this?" she inquired curiously, touching the gold crucifix that hung around his neck, playing idly with the chain.

"Yeah." Jake stroked her silky, blond hair, eased one cap sleeve of her nightgown from her shoulder to plant tiny kisses there, his mouth finding the curve of her neck, tongue and teeth wreaking havoc on the sensitive spot at its base, making her shiver in his arms, her breasts burgeon against him. "My mother gave it to me not long before she died, while I was getting my administration of justice degree. She thought it would keep me safe once I became a cop. She was a woman of great faith."

"And you're a man of equally little faith?"

"Let's just say that I wouldn't necessarily choose a crucifix over a bullet-proof vest."

Then, deliberately, Jake silenced anything else Claire might have said by kissing her mouth again thoroughly, his tongue delving deep into its innermost secrets, wreathing her own tongue, his hands roaming over her body in ways that aroused and excited her, intensifying the desire he had wakened within her, and which now built steadily with each demanding kiss, each intoxicating caress, making her heart race in her breast, her blood sing in her ears. Her breath came quickly, shallowly, as though she had run a very long way and now had no air left in her lungs. All her bones appeared to be dissolving inside her, so she felt weak in her knees, as fluid as quicksilver, his to mold and shape as he willed—and did.

Claire had no sense of time's passing. She did not know how long they stood there, locked in each other's arms, kissing and touching, getting to know each other in ways only lovers can, becoming familiar with scents and tastes and textures. She knew only that she had never before felt so vividly alive, as though she had somehow been transported to a place out of time, a place where every sensation was heightened, expanded. Jake seemed instinctively to know what would fan the flames of her ardor. She didn't demur when he slowly drew the sleeves of her nightgown down her arms, momentarily imprisoning her and baring her to the waist, so her swollen breasts with their flushed, rigid nipples were fully revealed to him, thrust against him as though begging to be fondled. He inhaled sharply at the sight before one long, elegant hand tangled in her hair, bending her head back. His lips sought her throat, searing its length as his other hand caressed her breasts, squeezing and kneading them, stimulating their nipples. His mouth seized one cherry-ripe bud, sucking hotly, greedily, sending waves of pleasure radiating through her whole body. She moaned low in her throat, an impassioned sound that inflamed him, spurring him on.

He dragged away her nightgown so it dropped to the floor. His hand stole inside her panties to cup her downy mound, fingers tangling in damp curls, parting tender folds, stroking the mellifluous cleft of her. Claire's breath came even faster, tiny gasps for air that mingled with Jake's own in the otherwise silent room. Sweat beaded her upper lip, trickled down the valley between her breasts. Lingeringly, he licked it away, then kissed her mouth again, his tongue twining with hers as he grasped her hips and lifted her in his arms to lay her crossways on the bed, so that her legs hung over the side. He nudged them apart, his lips covering her breasts once more, tongue laving her nipples before licking her flat belly and probing her navel. Then, kneeling on the floor before her, he unhurriedly drew Claire's panties down her legs until at last she was totally naked.

Her pearlescent skin was like sun-touched cream on a summer's morning, Jake thought as his eyes devoured her, taking in her disheveled hair, her generous, tremulous mouth slightly bruised from his kisses, her pouting breasts with their pebbled nipples, her slack, quivering thighs. She was open and wet for him, an unfurled rosebud, delicate petals glistening. Watching her face, he caressed her mound once more, a quick, light touch that sent a shudder rippling through her. Unable to go on meeting his avid gaze, Claire averted her eyes, her throat working with emotion. At the sight of her sprawled there, exposed to him, his for the taking, another spasm of desire ripped through Jake's groin. He wanted to make her come until she begged him for mercy, he realized dimly, in some dark corner of his mind. He reached out again and, taking his time, deliberately prolonging the action, pushed one finger fully inside the slick, welcoming heat of her, only to withdraw it just as torturously, wringing a mewl of distress and need from her lips.

"You want that, Claire?" he asked, his voice low and thick.

"Yes...please..." she breathed.

This time, in response, he penetrated her with two fingers, stretching and opening her even more as he began to thrust them deeply in and out of her, causing her body to tremble uncontrollably, her thighs to spread even wider for his invasion. His thumb found the tiny, hidden nub that was the key to her delight, adroitly manipulating it until it was as hard and taut as her nipples, aching for release. Still, he did not give it to her, but continued to bring her to the brink, only to leave her unsated, driving her wild. Her head thrashed, and her nails dug into the sheets as she pleaded with him for fulfillment; and when finally he let her come, intensifying her orgasm with his skillful fingers and thumb, the waves that broke inside her were so powerful that Jake could feel them, too. As she rode the surging crest, he thrust his fingers into her as deeply as possible one last time, then slowly withdrew them, leaving her gasping raggedly and pulsating vibrantly in the aftermath of her orgasm.

"Did you like that, Claire?"

"Yes...yes..." she whispered brokenly.

"Good...because I'm going to do that to you all night long—until neither one of us can think anymore, until there are only you and me in this bed together, breathless and exhausted," he insisted determinedly, kissing and stroking the insides of her quivering thighs, the sensitive places behind her knees, before at last he rose and stripped away the remainder of his clothes.

Naked, Jake towered over her, looking in the half light like some barbaric conqueror of old, Claire thought, his tall, bronze body as supple and muscled as that of some sleek predator. His dark eyes glittered as they appraised her, his nostrils flaring slightly at the gardenia fragrance of her, mingled with her own musky scent. Feeling suddenly vulnerable and helpless against him, Claire sat up on the edge of the bed, then stood on shaky legs, laying her palms against his chest, as though to hold him at bay. But he only ensnared her tangled hair, compelling her head up to take her mouth again with his own, his tongue shooting deep while he drew her against him, so his tumid sex pressed into her belly, a potent portent. Then, taking her hand in his, Jake wrapped it around his erection, wordlessly teaching her what pleased him best.

"Yes...like that," he murmured as she continued the motion on her own.

He was powerful, beautiful, and sensual, Claire thought as she stroked him, like no other man she had ever before known. She reveled in the taste of his lips on hers, the smoky, masculine scent of him, the warmth of his breath against her skin, the touch of his hands upon her breasts, fingers teasing her nipples, the feel of his arousal, hard and throbbing as she caressed him, explored him, tracing ridges and contours.

"Take me in your mouth, Claire," Jake urged hoarsely in her ear.

In response, she sank to her knees before him, clutching his taut, firm buttocks for balance, kissing his flat, corrugated belly and hard, corded thighs, tasting the salty sweat that sheened his skin. His indrawn breath was a serrated rasp that set a shiver chasing down her spine when she finally found him with her lips, enveloping him. Jake groaned as her eager, untutored mouth sheathed him with its softness and wetness, so he felt as though he had become a mass of pure sensation. Involuntarily, his hands caught hold of her head, tightened in her hair, and unable to restrain himself, he pushed into her again and again, quivering with desire as her tongue taunted him, licking, swirling, eliciting low sounds of both pleasure and torment from his throat.

"Oh, God, Claire, you don't know what you're doing to me." He couldn't believe the carnal delight that pervaded his body as she worked her sweet magic on him, her lips and hands exciting him until he was afraid he wouldn't be able to hold back any longer. With another anguished groan, he abruptly tugged her away, lifting her to her feet and shoving her back upon the bed, his mouth pressing feverish kisses to her breasts, her belly, the hollows of her hips, the inside of her thighs.

Rougher now in his passion and need, Jake spread her legs wide and lapped her with his tongue, rekindling the fire he had ignited in her earlier, making her burn fervidly anew for assuagement. Claire writhed frantically beneath him, straining exigently against his lips, reaching for him desperately; and at last, he poised himself above her, the muscles bunching and rippling in his strong arms as the tip of his maleness sought and pierced her. He drove deep, burying himself inside her, causing her to gasp and then cry out. Her climax came almost immediately, seizing her with such unexpected force that she arched violently against him. Gripping her hips tightly, Jake moved on her then, thrusting into her deeply again and again, harder and faster as the blinding spasms rocked her. His own release followed close on the heels of hers, savagely racking the length of his body and leaving him collapsed and panting for air atop her, his heart hammering furiously against hers.

"Dios mio," he muttered after a long moment.

"You can say that again," Claire said softly.

"No, I'm going to *do* that to you again—just as soon as I recover." Jake smiled down at her, brushing her damp, snarled hair from her eyes.

"Is that a promise?"

"Yeah, it is. All night long—remember?" He kissed her mouth gently, then slowly withdrew from her to roll over onto his back, his breathing still harsh and labored. He ran one hand through his own tousled hair, then wiped the sweat from his chest before pulling Claire into his embrace, cradling her head tenderly against his shoulder. With one hand, he reached for his chinos lying on the floor, taking a lighter and a half-crumpled pack of Marlboros from one pocket. Shaking a cigarette from the pack, he lit up, exhaling a stream of smoke into the air. "Okay if I use this as an ashtray?" He pointed to a small, cut-glass dish that sat on her night table, and at her nod, proceeded to flick ashes into it. "You were wonderful," he told her quietly.

"So were you."

"Good. I'm glad I pleased you."

"You did." Despite herself, Claire was slightly surprised he cared about her feelings, about whether or not she had enjoyed their lovemaking. Paul, her only other lover, had never been so considerate. Most of the time, she had not even climaxed with him; she had only faked orgasms so his fragile male ego wouldn't be deflated—along with his erection. Afterward, having satisfied himself, he had almost always promptly fallen asleep, seldom holding her, making small talk with her, as Jake did now, making her feel safe and appreciated. Relatively inexperienced herself, Claire had given little or no consideration to the fact that sex with another man could and would be different, that she was capable herself of responding as she had to Jake, with a passion and lack of inhibition to match his own.

I could fall in love with him so easily. The thought came, unbidden, into her mind, startling and dismaying her. She had promised him she would expect no attachments, no commitments from him. Yet she was even now lying here beside him, envisioning a future with him. That would never do. He wasn't ready for that. He had made that quite clear, had been brutally honest about the fact that he could offer her nothing other than what he had already given her.

"A penny for your thoughts, Claire." Jake's low voice spoke drowsily in her ear.

"They're not worth even that much," she told him, making an attempt at lightness. But he must have sensed something in her voice all the same.

"Regrets, Claire?" he asked quietly, his hand abruptly stilling upon her hair.

"No...no," she reassured him hastily. "It's just that I...I never knew before that it could be the way it was for us, Jake. I—I...really haven't been around all that much—"

"Is that right?" He feigned surprise, his lips curving into a smile that didn't quite conceal the concern in his eyes as she glanced up at him worriedly.

"Was it...that obvious?" she inquired, flushing with embarrassment.

"No. I just knew, Claire."

"How? Was it something I did? Something I didn't do?"

"No, don't worry. It was nothing like that. Really. You did everything right...better than right, in fact. It's just something I sensed, that's all."

"Oh, Jake, are you sure?" she asked anxiously.

"Yeah, I'm sure. So forget about it now—and answer me this. Are you sorry you asked me to stay here tonight with you?"

"No. I just...I would like to think we can at least be friends. I don't want you to wake up in the morning regretting this and hating the very sight of me."

"I may regret it, Claire," he conceded slowly, "but I promise I won't hate you—that is, just as long as you don't try to interview me over breakfast!"

She felt a sharp stab of guilt at that. As hard as it was for her to believe, she had tonight forgotten all about the miniseries she, Winston, and Booker were working on in their spare hours, taking their time with the editing process and even shooting some additional scenes and reshooting others to try to get every inch of film as perfect as possible so that their boss, Mr. Kendall, would be impressed enough to air the six segments. Involuntarily, as she remembered the miniseries, Claire tensed, thinking that despite that she had shifted its focus, Jake would surely be angry at having his own personal tragedy anchoring her work. She ought to tell him about it now, at once, while she had an ideal opportunity, she thought, dismayed. Lying here with her, satiated, he would perhaps be more understanding at this moment than any other. But somehow she couldn't bring herself to destroy their interlude of closeness with what would, to him, be an unpleasant revelation; and Jake, who might otherwise have felt the brief tightening of her body and questioned it, had been engrossed in grinding out his cigarette in the cut-glass dish on the nightstand, so he was unaware of her troublesome contemplations.

When he turned back to her, it was to take her in his arms once more, to cover her mouth with his own possessively. As, sighing, she gave herself up to him completely, felt her desire for him start to roil again like a riptide surging and swirling within her, Claire thought that perhaps it was better if she said nothing to him about the miniseries, after all.

After a few minutes, as his lips and tongue and hands worked their feverish will on her, she ceased to think at all.

Nine

Come Morning

For Lycidas your sorrow is not dead,
Sunk though he be beneath the watery floor;
So sinks the day-star in the ocean bed;
And yet anon repairs his drooping head,
And tricks his beams, and with new-spangled ore
Flames in the forehead of the morning sky.

Lycidas
—John Milton

Claire awoke the following morning with Jake atop her, inside her, a part of her again, filling her fully. Her body tingled afresh as he thrust in and out of her slowly, lazily, taking his time, so her desire for him stirred and then began to swell within her fervently. More than once, he paused to kiss her mouth lingeringly and to caress her breasts languidly, allowing the frantic throbbing at the molten core of her to ebb and nearly die away before he moved on her once more, so it burgeoned inside her again even more hotly and urgently than before. At last, just when Claire thought she could endure no more, he slipped one hand between their slick, sweat-sheened bodies, his fingers seeking and then finding the secret heart of her, stroking hard and quickly as he pushed into her, bringing her swiftly to her peak.

She cried out, bucking against him as the powerful, uncontrollable tremors exploded within her, shattering her, leaving her shaking and pulsing beneath him as, just as fiercely, he came inside her, the heated juices of him rushing into her, his heart hammering against her own.

Afterward, Jake continued to lie atop her, supporting his weight on his strong forearms, his sex still a part of her. "Good morning," he murmured, his dark eyes gleaming drowsily with satisfaction as he gazed down at her from beneath lazy lids, a smile curving his lips before he brushed them against her own.

"Good morning," Claire managed to whisper before he captured her mouth with his completely, his tongue delving deep, sampling, savoring, sliding around her own tongue skillfully. He was insatiable, she thought, for true to his word, he had indeed made love to her all night long, taking her in ways beyond her previous experience, making her come again and again. She had never before known such exhilarating pleasure, such uninhibited intimacy with a man, and she had been utterly exhausted and replete when Jake had finally permitted her to sleep.

Now, as though last night and the minutes just past were not enough for him, he refused to allow her desire for him to abate, as though he could not bear to withdraw from her and so must bring her satisfaction yet again to remain inside her. Claire wanted to tell him that wasn't so, that her bed was big enough for two, and that to leave her physically didn't necessarily mean he would be alone again emotionally afterward. She sensed instinctively that Jake equated sex with closeness and intimacy, and that even if he himself did not consciously realize it, it was these as much as pleasure that he sought from her. Nor was she herself eager for their interlude to end. Despite everything, she had in the space of a single night formed an attachment to him that was as emotional as it was physical. Silently, she had cursed herself as a fool for it, but there it was all the same.

So Claire said nothing to him of her thoughts as he kissed and caressed her, but gave herself up to him instead, luxuriating in the sensations he wakened within her. She could feel his warm breath against her skin, the movements of his chest as he inhaled raggedly, the steady, thudding beat of his heart against her own. Boldly, his tongue plundered her mouth, a heady experience that dizzied her and left her gasping, her body quivering, pliantly molding itself to his. He intoxicated her, overwhelmed her with tastes, scents, and textures. His flesh, coated with a thin layer of sweat, had the tang of salt when she kissed him and smelled the musky, masculine aroma of him. His beard stubble was coarse against her skin, in sharp contrast to the fine, black hair that feathered his chest and that was like silk beneath her palms and against the sensitive tips of her breasts as she explored him, touching him everywhere she could reach, discovering afresh every plane and angle she had charted last night in hot, blind passion, every curve of muscle and sinew.

Bracing himself on one arm, Jake cupped her breast, pressing it high, his thumb and forefinger taking hold of her nipple, tugging, rolling, and teasing it into a hard, flushed nub that sizzled with arousal, sending electric waves coursing through her body. Slowly, he lowered his head to her breast, capturing her nipple with his teeth, which nibbled it gently, then held it in place for the laving of his tongue. Warmth and delight stabbed her there, and she arched against him, whimpering in her throat. The sounds she made, the taste and feel of her incited Jake. Claire knew that without asking or being told as she felt him grow big and hard inside her again, stretching her, pervading her, beginning to push in and out of her once more.

She was wet and heated and sheathed him like a tight fist, Jake thought, a perfect fit for him, and he reveled in the feel of her enveloping him, the soft, supple walls of her gripping and massaging him. He could feel the tension that coiled in her body as she neared her climax, and then the spasms that erupted within her as she came, her breath catching in her throat. She went rigid beneath him, and Jake rode her until his own orgasm racked him, leaving him spent and gasping against her.

After a long moment, he rolled off her, reaching for a cigarette from his pack on the nightstand. He lit up, blowing a cloud of smoke, while one hand idly played with her long, blond hair that spilled across the pillows. Outside, the sun had risen and filtered through the plantation blinds at the bedroom windows, making her hair look as though it were strands of fiery gold and giving her creamy skin a gilded luster, the crests of her breasts a rosy glow. She was beautiful, Jake thought, and she had given of herself more than he had ever imagined. He had never in his life before felt so sexually satiated. Isabel had been a good Catholic girl, a virgin when he had married her, timid and inhibited, and although he had tried to teach her otherwise, she had resisted anything that in her mind had smacked of sinful pleasure. Sex was for purposes of procreation, she had insisted sternly. It had been the major bone of contention between them, and for a minute, Jake felt guilty and disloyal to his wife's memory for having taken such delight in Claire's body.

But then he reminded himself grimly that Isabel was dead, that nothing could bring her back, and that he had to get on with his life. Asking nothing in return, Claire had opened her home and herself to him at a time when he had desperately needed closeness and comfort. That he had received much more from her than he had ever expected was a gift he should treasure, not reproach himself for. Wrapping his hand in her hair, he tilted her face up to his and kissed her mouth again thoroughly.

"Hmm. You know, I think a man could get addicted to you." His voice was low, husky. "How was it that your boyfriend managed to let you get away?"

"After he'd got his bachelor's degree, he wanted to go on to law school, which was going to take him two more years at least—and he didn't want to get married until he had completed his studies,'' Claire explained quietly.

"Yeah, under the circumstances, I can understand that. Still, wasn't he afraid some other guy would come along and snatch you up in his absence?"

"If he was, he concealed it, because his career took precedence, even though I told him I wouldn't wait for him, that I intended to date other men. That's why I broke it off with him, why I sent him on his way without me. I thought that if he loved me, he'd have married me and taken me with him, and he thought that if I loved him, I'd be content to stay behind here and wait for him to return. Eventually, I saw that either way, we weren't going to have a happy ending, so I made what I felt was the right decision at the time."

"And now? Are you sorry?" Taking a long, last drag off his cigarette, Jake ground it out in the cut-glass dish on the night table.

"I don't know. Sometimes, I guess—mainly when my mother manages to scrounge up another blind date for me." Claire laughed ruefully.

"Does she do that a lot?"

"More than I'd like. But she means well. She's from that old southern school of thought that says a woman isn't complete unless she has a husband."

"And you're not?" Jake inquired.

"No. I'd like to get married and have children someday, but I don't believe I'm not a whole person without that. I have my home, my work, my friends. It's a full life."

"Yet, last night, you knew what it was to be lonely and empty inside. You didn't have to take me in,

Claire—or to go to bed with me, either. But you did, and I know you don't make a habit of having casual affairs, besides. So I want *you* to know that last night meant something to me, that I didn't take it lightly. I'd like to take you to breakfast.''

''You don't have to do that, Jake,'' she protested gently, remembering her promise to him that last night would have no strings attached.

''I know, but I want to. So why don't we take a shower together and then get dressed? I seem to remember a little hole-in-the-wall café at Lafitte's Quay, where they had the most marvelous beignets and coffee....''

''Yes, the Café Chantilly. It's still there.''

''Good. Let's go, then.''

Claire's bathroom had Victorian fixtures and thus boasted an old, claw-foot tub with a shower curtain that wrapped around an oval hoop suspended from the ceiling.

''Well, that's no good,'' Jake announced wryly upon spying it.

''Why? What's wrong with it?'' Claire asked as she retrieved fresh towels from the linen closet, along with a new toothbrush and a disposable razor from the supply she had previously kept on hand for Paul. Setting everything down on the pedestal sink, she turned on the taps in the bathtub.

''No shower wall,'' Jake replied. ''Nothing to press you up against so I can make love to you again.''

She flushed rosily at that, suddenly and intensely aware that they were both stark naked and that Jake's gleaming eyes were running over her unabashedly.

"Haven't you had enough already?" she queried tartly.

"I don't know. What do you think?"

Inadvertently, her gaze strayed to his maleness, which caused her blush to deepen as she spied the evidence of his desire for her. "You're incorrigible...insatiable," she accused.

"You appear to have that effect on me...yeah."

She drew back the shower curtain and turned the knob so the shower head sprayed steaming water into the bathtub. "I believe you're right. I don't think we can manage that in here," she declared a trifle breathlessly, unable to meet his eyes.

"We'll manage," he said.

They took turns lathering each other with the new bar of oatmeal soap Claire had unwrapped from the big basket in which she stored her bath essentials, "because I know you don't want to leave here smelling like lavender or roses," she had told Jake.

"You're right," he'd agreed. "The guys at the station would have a heyday with that one—not that I have to work tonight, you understand. But the scent might linger despite my own deodorant soap at home. Then my fellow officers would be bound to tease me, I'm afraid, and ask questions, and I just don't think I'm ready for any of that quite yet."

But he was certainly ready for her again, she knew, as he soaped her breasts, running his slick, foamy palms over her hard nipples and between her soft thighs. "I've figured out how we can manage this," he murmured wickedly in her ear. Parting the shower curtain on the far side, he turned her to face the lace-draped window there, which looked out over the side of her lawn and the blank wall that was her next-door neighbor's garage. He placed her hands on the sill to brace her, then thrust into the warm core of her from behind, making her gasp as one hand slipped around her hip to stimulate the tiny bud hidden in the tender folds of her.

The warm water sprayed down upon them, heightening sensations as he drove into her, one strong, corded arm supporting her so her trembling legs held her upright, despite the spiraling excitement that gripped her. When Claire came, whimpering with it, Jake sank his teeth lightly into her shoulder, intensifying the climax that burst inside her even as his own orgasm seized him, his life forces jetting into her.

Afterward, he rinsed her off under the shower head, kissing her mouth lingeringly and cupping and fondling her breasts. Then he turned off the water and toweled her dry, leaving her tingling and flushed with a rosy glow.

"Get your clothes on," he told her, "before I'm dead of exhaustion. I'm going to shave."

From the dresser in her bedroom, Claire withdrew a set of lacy underwear, and from the closet, a simple, flowered sundress and a pair of sandals. She dressed quickly, wanting to have enough time to do her hair and makeup before Jake was through in the bathroom. By the time he emerged, she was ready, her hair plaited into a neat French braid, her face lightly accentuated with the natural-toned cosmetics she preferred.

"You look just like one of those lovely, fragile women in flower gardens painted by old masters," Jake observed as he pulled on his own clothes, tucking in his shirttails and buckling his belt. "There's something simultaneously ethereal and earthy about you, Claire. I think that's what drew me to you from the start. Shall we go?"

The stretch of beach that was known as Lafitte's Quay wasn't far from the university, and as a result, it was a popular area, particularly on weekends. It was an old, historical part of the city, situated along the waterfront and filled with small shops, cafés, artists' stalls, boardwalks, and wharves. It was a gorgeous day outside, so that after reaching the Café Chantilly, Claire and Jake opted to eat in its tiny, brick courtyard, at one of the forest-green, wrought-iron tables. They ordered beignets, fruit, and hot, black coffee, and although the meal was simple, Claire thought she had never tasted anything so good, sitting there with the warm, buttery sunlight streaming down on them, the Gulf breeze taking the edge from the heat.

Throughout, she and Jake conversed easily, seeming instinctively to steer clear of sensitive topics, as though each of them was determined that nothing should spoil their morning together. After they had finished eating, Jake suggested they take a stroll around the Quay, and Claire nodded her agreement, not wanting her day with him to end. She kept telling herself how foolish she was being, that he was only spending time with her to be polite because she had shared her bed with him last night. But it didn't help.

The longer she was in his company, the more attracted to him she grew.

She discovered as they talked that he was an educated and well-read man who shared many of her own interests in art, history, literature, music, and philosophy. Unlike her two cameramen, Winston Nash and Booker McGuinness, Jake knew *The Brothers Karamazov* was a novel by Dostoevsky and *not* the latest rap group and that "Take Five" was a jazz hit by Dave Bruebeck and his band and *not* an instruction to a news anchor. Such things mattered to her, Claire realized slowly as she and Jake meandered along the boardwalks. That was one of the reasons why, despite the fact that she and Paul Langley had been opposites in personality, she had been attracted to him—but not to Nash or McGuinness, who had never been more than just her friends, despite how closely she had worked together with them in college and still did on the job.

Claire and Jake had reached the piers now, where numerous boats were moored in the slips. "I used to come down here when I was in college," he said, "and wonder what it would be like to live aboard one of those." He pointed to an attractive houseboat. "To be able just to cast off the mooring lines and take to the sea whenever you wanted. I guess the idea represented my dream of getting out of the barrio someday, of moving to this side of the river. Now, I can't feel anything but guilt and horror that Isabel's death should have put me in the position, financially, of making that possible. We both had life insurance policies—not huge ones, of course, but still, enough that with the benefit money I received, I could leave the barrio now, make a down payment on a houseboat like that and invest the rest to cover the payments. I've played the stock market for a long time in my head, learning how it works and watching a number of companies, so that when the day came that I ever had any extra funds to invest, I'd know what to do. So far, I'm ahead of the game—on paper, anyway. But Jesus, I hate like hell to think I should profit from Isabel's murder!''

It was the first time since his arrival on her doorstep last night that Jake had mentioned his dead wife, and Claire wasn't sure what to say. "I'm probably not the best person to advise you, Jake," she finally replied slowly, "but if you're asking my opinion, I don't think Isabel would see it that way. I know I wouldn't. I'd see my life-insurance payoff as…well…my last gift to my husband, I guess—and if it helped his dreams to come true, I'd be glad beyond all measure. Besides, maybe you should get away from your memories, make a clean break with the past. Sometimes, a sharp, swift cut is a kindness in the long run.''

"Yeah, that's what I've been thinking. That's what I believe in my heart that Isabel would have said. But still, it bothers me, you know?''

"Of course. You're a decent man, Jake, and you loved your wife. But she loved you, too, so I can't imagine she would grudge you a houseboat, an escape from the barrio. We only want the best from life for the people we love, the things that will keep them safe and make them happy.''

"I didn't do a very good job of keeping *her* safe.'' Jake's voice was tinged with bitterness and regret.

"Yes...yes, you did, Jake. You had warned her more than once to drive straight home after work. But Isabel was an adult, and she made her own decisions. It wasn't your fault she stopped at that convenience store that night. And whatever else you did, I feel certain somehow that you *did* make her happy. Now, you need to stop blaming yourself and let her go," Claire said gently. "You shouldn't forget her—ever—and I know you won't. But it's all right to let yourself heal."

"Yeah...deep down inside, I know that's true. Remy's told me the same thing. So what do you say? Do you want to go into that boat shop over there with me? Find out what one of these houseboats costs?"

"Yes...yes, if you're sure that's what you really want."

"It is. I'm sure."

So they went into the boat shop, to be greeted by a salesman who, much to Claire's relief, proved to be a sensible, good-natured man rather than a pushy, obnoxious sort. He and Jake talked, while Claire wandered around, amusing herself by looking at the various boats on display. Finally, Jake rejoined her.

"Come on. New houseboats are a little out of my league, I'm afraid. But Mr. Allen has a used one he's going to show us. It's only about four years old, but it needs some work. Apparently, it belonged to a couple of spoiled-rich, fraternity boys who used it primarily for parties on the weekends. But they graduated from college earlier this year, and so they didn't need it anymore, which is why it's on the market. It's moored in one of the slips."

Once they reached it, it was obvious the houseboat

had doubtless indeed been employed for drunken orgies. Clearing his throat, Mr. Allen apologized.

"Like I said before, Mr. Seringo, I only got her in a few days ago, and I haven't had time yet to get her all cleaned up. The engine itself is in excellent condition, however. Those boys were only interested in taking her out far enough that their dates would have to swim back to shore if they weren't agreeable. But as you can see, there's been some damage to the interior."

"Yeah." Jake nodded as they moved through the houseboat, inspecting its two bedrooms, the head, the galley, and the living quarters. "Still, a man who was skilled with his hands and tools and wanted to spend the time doing it could fix her up. What do you think, Claire?"

At first, she thought Jake was asking her opinion merely as a courtesy. But then, slowly, she realized he was unaccustomed to making this type of decision without a woman's advice, that Isabel had no doubt chosen and furnished their apartment, and that as a result, he was unsure of himself in this milieu.

"Can you repair all the damage yourself?"

"Yeah, I think so. It would take me a while, but I'd get it all done eventually."

"Then, if it's what you want and the price is right for you, I think you should buy her. She has a lot of potential, Jake. The layout is nice and convenient, and the windows afford a great view—not to mention good cross breezes, I'll bet, when they're open. Plus, you can tell all the brass and woodwork were gorgeous at one time.... Oh, Jake—I only just thought to ask. You don't get seasick, do you?''

He laughed at that. "No, I don't. Well, Mr. Allen, I'm interested, so could we take her out, see how she runs?''

"Sure thing, Mr. Seringo.''

So they fired up the houseboat and took her out into the Gulf. As Mr. Allen had said, the engine was in excellent condition, and the houseboat itself handled well enough on the water, although, unlike a yacht, it wasn't built for either speed or lengthy ocean voyages. Still, standing on the deck beyond the living quarters, Claire could see the attraction. It would be pleasant just to be able to take off in one's house, cruise out into the Gulf, and weigh anchor for a little sunbathing and fishing.

"I think I'm sold," Jake whispered in her ear as he came up behind her. "But don't tell Mr. Allen. I want to see if I can get a little better price out of him.''

"And if you can?''

"Then I'm going to buy her.''

"I don't think you'll regret your decision, Jake.''

"No, neither do I. And fixing her up will give me something besides being a cop to keep my mind occupied, something to strive toward, to make a fresh start with. I've always loved the sea, but I never saw too much of it, growing up in the barrio. I think I could be content, living at Lafitte's Quay." Jake didn't add that the Quay wasn't far from Claire's house, either, although the thought had crossed his mind. He already knew that right or wrong, ready or not, he wanted to see her again if she'd let him, that he wanted more from her than just a one-night stand, although he wasn't sure just yet about what it was that he did want.

He knew only that last night with her had been incredible, that for the first time since Isabel's death, he had felt a spark of life flare within himself once more. It reminded him now of something Albert Schweitzer had once said, about a person's light sometimes going out, but being blown again into flame by an encounter with another human being. Whether she knew it or not, that was what Claire had done for him—she had rekindled his inner light. He owed her something for that, he thought.

Once they had returned to the Quay, Jake sat down in Mr. Allen's office with him to hammer out the details of buying the houseboat. A short while later, Jake and Claire left the boat shop, Jake the proud, new owner of the *Sea Gypsy,* as he had decided to christen the houseboat. He insisted on taking Claire into one of the bars on the waterfront, for a glass of champagne to celebrate. Then, finally, he drove her home.

After walking her to the front door, he kissed her, then said, "I'll call you, Claire."

"No, please don't say that—at least, not unless you mean it, Jake. Otherwise, I'd just rather remember that we had a perfect night and day together, and leave it at that."

"I do mean it. I'm serious. I wouldn't have said it if I weren't. I don't want to lead you on, to make promises to you that I can't keep, and I don't know where we're going together from here, you and I. But I do know this. I don't want us to end right here and now. I want to go out with you again, Claire, to go to

bed with you again. So if that's not what *you* want,
tell me now.''

''No, I *do* want that. It's just that I wasn't expecting
anything more.''

''No, I know you weren't, that you said last night
that there were no strings attached. But we can take
things slowly, play them by ear, can't we?''

''Yes…yes, I'd like that very much.''

''Good. Then, like I said before, I'll call you.'' After that, whistling, his hands tucked into his pockets,
Jake strode down her sidewalk to his car.

Claire watched him go, waving to him as he drove
away. Then she slowly turned and went inside, her
heart pounding with joy. She must be going crazy, she
thought. She was head over heels about a man who
had only recently lost his wife, a man she hardly even
knew, a man she had met only once in her entire life
before she had taken him into her bed. That was just
wholly out of character for her. What was she thinking
of? What would her family and friends say if they
knew?

Yet, even as these thoughts occurred to her, Claire
recognized that she didn't care if she had gone totally
mad, if everyone she knew would be totally shocked
by her behavior. Something deep down inside her had
connected on every level with Jake—physically, mentally, and emotionally. She had not lied last night
when she had told him she felt as though she had
known him forever, that she always knew upon first
meeting a man whether or not there was chemistry
between them. Despite everything, she had been attracted to Jake from the very first moment she had ever

seen him standing in the doorway of his apartment—drunken, disheveled, and dangerous. Why he had appealed to her so powerfully, so irresistibly, Claire didn't know. She had never before believed in love at first sight, in the Greek myth of souls divided at creation and who spent the rest of eternity searching for their other halves. Yet she could not deny that it was these things that filled her mind when she thought of Jake.

Laying her key ring down on the gossip bench in her foyer, she glanced down at the telephone. He would call her, he had said. Did she dare believe that, trust in it, hope for it? Was he a man of his word or not?

He was.

Ten

Interlude

He passed the flaming bounds of place and time:
The living throne, the sapphire-blaze,
Where angels tremble, while they gaze,
He saw; but blasted with excess of light,
Closed his eyes in endless night.

The Progress of Poesy
—Thomas Gray

Those days that followed would, to Claire, seem forever like an interlude out of time, with an unreal, dreamlike quality to them, as though whenever she looked back on them, she saw them not through a glass darkly, but through a silver mirror blasted with some unearthly, radiant light that softened and diffused the otherwise sharp and painful edges of her memories.

Jake did call, and after that, they saw each other steadily, at least two or three times a week or more. She helped him clean out his apartment, sorting through Isabel's possessions and deciding what to do with them. At first, Claire had thought this was a task Jake would want to undertake alone. But in the end, he had told her it was too hard for him emotionally to endure in solitude and, moreover, that he wasn't sure how best to distribute his dead wife's belongings. So Claire assisted him, separating things into piles for the Catholic church Isabel had faithfully attended—although Jake had gone only sporadically—and for Isabel's parents and various neighbors in the apartment complex, with a few mementos set aside, as well, for Jake's ailing father.

Other items, such as Jake and Isabel's wedding pictures, taken at the time by their parents and friends, Claire carefully boxed up, knowing that despite his insistence that he would never be able to bear looking at any of them again, a day would, in fact, come when Jake would want to see them once more, to remember his dead wife when her face had begun to grow misty in his mind. Jake assumed Claire gave the wedding pictures and other such things to Isabel's parents. But instead, she took that particular box home with her and stored it away in the back of her bedroom closet so it would be there for him, undisturbed, when he needed it. It was not that she didn't trust that Isabel's parents would take care of it. But they were an older couple who had eight other grown children and, as a result, countless grandchildren who got into everything, according to Jake. The box would be safe with Claire.

After almost everything in the apartment had been separated and dispersed, Frank Bollinger, Remy Toussaint, and a couple of other officers from the station came around one weekend with a pickup truck to help Jake move his furniture to the houseboat. He invited Claire to join them that day, but she sensed instinctively that this ought to be an all-male get-together, especially when she saw that Jake had bought a couple of six-packs of beer for the occasion. Besides which, she thought Jake would be more comfortable if he didn't have to introduce her to his friends. His wife had, after all, been dead only a few months. At the very least, his friends would no doubt think it was too soon for him to have become involved with someone else. Not that she and Jake *were* involved, precisely, Claire insisted to herself.

After all, their relationship was without commitments. Jake had not asked her not to date other men. Nor had he said anything to suggest he had formed a serious attachment to her. Rather, he had made it clear he wanted to take things slowly, one day at a time; and for the moment, Claire was content with that, because she sensed that at this point, to push him would be to lose him. And she didn't want that. Even just the thought of it was painful to her, because despite everything, she knew that if she hadn't already foolishly done so, she was in significant danger of losing her heart to him.

For that reason, she worried constantly about the miniseries and Jake's reaction to it when he found out about it. Time and again, Claire told herself she should make a clean breast of it. But she feared he would feel as though she had deceived him and that his anger would be such that he wouldn't want to see her any-more. She wished she had never started the project with Nash and McGuinness. But there was nothing she could do about it now. Her two cameramen had invested too many hours of their spare time in the mini-series for her to tell them she no longer wanted to continue with it. So at this point, all she could hope for was that when the project was finally completed, Mr. Kendall wouldn't think enough of it to air it. Then Jake need never know about it.

That if Mr. Kendall didn't like the miniseries and, worse, thought she and her two cameramen had demonstrated presumption rather than initiative in under-taking such a project, she would probably have sabo-taged not only her own career, but also those of Nash and McGuinness, was a notion upon which Claire refused to let her mind dwell. But deep down inside, she believed she would rather have Jake than her job—and that realization frightened her. She had worked so hard to get her bachelor's degree, to graduate among the top ten percent of her class; and she had put in many long hours, not only at Channel 4, but also on the miniseries she, Nash, and McGuinness had developed. She thought she must be mad to be willing to throw all that away for a man who wasn't even in love with her.

Still, when Jake made love to her, Claire believed he *did* care about her, even if he wasn't yet at a point emotionally where he could acknowledge that fact. That he was, in a sense, a man on the rebound, griev-ing and in need of comfort, was something she preferred not to think about too deeply, for she felt that if that even had not been the case, she and Jake would still have been attracted to each other, would still have found common ground.

So Claire determinedly pushed her own nagging doubts aside, and each day that passed, whether she was willing to admit it to herself or not, Jake crept more surely and securely into her heart.

"So what do you think about this latest development concerning Vanessa Hampton?" Zoey Rutledge asked as she settled into her wicker chair at Le Bistro, which was a popular restaurant downtown, where she and Claire were meeting for lunch. "They're calling it a complete nervous breakdown, but I'm wondering if maybe she suffered some kind of brain damage or something during that car crash."

"I just don't know." Claire opened her menu and glanced at its contents. "But whatever's happened since they took her off the critical list at that Florence hospital and said she could come home to the States, it must be serious if the family's going to commit her to a sanatorium here locally." She thought about the AP feed she had read earlier this morning.

[Associated Press] FLORENCE, Italy, Ms. Vanessa Hampton, who has been hospitalized since a fatal car accident in Tuscany, which claimed the life of her cousin, champion race-car driver Bruno D'Angelo, will be flown home to the United States within the next few days. Al-

though Hampton was removed from the critical list some time ago and her physical condition upgraded to stable, doctors have announced that the shock of learning about her cousin's death has affected her mentally, resulting in a complete nervous breakdown. A spokesperson for the Hampton family has stated that plans have been made for Hampton to recuperate at a private sanatorium in her hometown, located on the Gulf Coast, where her family principally resides. It is not yet known at this time whether or not Hampton is expected to make a full recovery.

After ripping the wire from the chattering printer, Claire had carefully copied on the station's Xerox machine that portion containing the Hampton story. Then she had tucked the copy into her handbag to take home with her that evening to add to her growing file on the family. Why she had become so interested in the Hamptons, she didn't know, except that from a news standpoint, she thought they bore watching. In years gone by, it had been generally agreed locally that at least one of the Hampton men would wind up in the White House. Now that hope seemed permanently dashed. Still, there was Veronica Hampton's husband, Malcolm Forsythe, who was politically ambitious and who could go far with the Hampton riches and connections behind him.

"Well, it wouldn't surprise me if Vanessa Hampton's gone totally off her rocker," Zoey declared stoutly as she laid down her menu. "I never have thought that entire family was very stable mentally. I mean, in the old days, all those upper-crust families like that...well, they intermarried a lot to keep their bloodlines pure before scientists discovered the results of inbreeding and most states passed laws against wedding your relatives. But it's still legal to marry your first cousin in a few southern states—and Bruno D'Angelo was one handsome guy.''

"You think he and Vanessa were having an affair?'' Claire asked curiously, the wheels in her mind churning speculatively at the idea.

Zoey shrugged. "I don't know, but something funny must have been going on. Why else would the two of them have been out on that road at such a late hour—with Vanessa driving that Ferrari instead of Bruno being at the wheel? After all, he'd grown up in Italy and spent most of his summers in Tuscany. He must have known how dangerous that hairpin curve was, and you can bet he probably wouldn't have lost control of the car, the way she did, either. From all reports, she was going far too fast—and he must have known that, Claire.''

"So what do you think? That they were arguing...having a lovers' quarrel?''

"Maybe.''

"Or maybe they were both just high or intoxicated,'' Claire suggested thoughtfully as she tore open a packet of sugar and stirred its contents into the glass of iced tea she had ordered earlier from the waiter. "The reports said they'd been drinking.''

"Yeah, but neither one was legally drunk, and no

evidence of any drugs at all was found. Besides which, Bruno, at least, couldn't afford to be a doper, Claire. He couldn't have driven those high-powered race cars if he'd been an addict—or even a casual user. I mean, they test drivers for drugs, don't they, just like they do other athletes?''

"I suppose so, but I couldn't say for sure, Zoey. To tell you the truth, I've never been much of a race-car fan, and I don't know anything at all about the sport in Europe. But didn't Bruno win the Grand Prix or some other well-known race over there?''

"Yeah, I think so...one of the youngest drivers ever to do so or something like that. It's really sad about what happened to him and Vanessa, both. That entire Hampton family is just cursed, if you ask me.''

"I've heard that before, but really, Zoey, do you actually believe it?''

"I don't know...sort of, I guess. Because you've got to admit it's pretty damned eerie how tragedy seems to have stalked that family ever since the eighteen hundreds, when the quadroon mistress of one of the Hampton men got mad about him casting her aside and worked some kind of voodoo spell on him, by which means she cursed not only him, but also all his descendants for all time—or so the story goes.''

Despite the bright, yellow sunlight streaming in through the wide windows of Le Bistro and the fact that she had always been well grounded in reality, Claire shivered involuntarily. "This is the twentieth century, Zoey," she stated firmly. "The purview of modern technology and surfing the Internet. Nobody really takes that voodoo stuff seriously anymore, do they?''

"You'd be surprised." Zoey lowered her voice and glanced around the restaurant warily, as though afraid of being overheard. "Voodoo's still got quite a large following, Claire, especially here in the South, in places like New Orleans, for example. I've seen footage of voodoo ceremonies, and it's always struck me that *something* powerful is definitely happening to those people involved, whether it's spirits taking them over or whatever. So let's just say that I wouldn't want to know anybody was sticking pins into a little doll with *my* hair and nail clippings attached to it!''

"Oh, Zoey." Claire shook her head skeptically, a rueful smile curving her lips. "Sometimes, I really do think you let your imagination run away with you. I mean, when was the last time you read a news article about somebody dying because an effigy of them had been stabbed through the heart?''

"Go ahead and scoff if you want, Claire. But I'm telling you...there's something to all that voodoo magic—because if there isn't, how do you explain what all's happened to the Hampton family over the decades? Even you can't deny they've had more than their fair share of tragedy and adversity.''

"Perhaps not," Claire agreed slowly. "But still, I'm more inclined to believe they're just accident-prone or the victims of bad luck. There're just some people who seem to have been singled out by misfortune, for whatever unknown reasons. It happens all the time to perfectly ordinary persons or families. We're just more aware of it where the Hamptons are concerned, I think, because they're so wealthy and prominent.''

"Well, maybe you're right. But even so, if I were them, I'd be looking for somebody who knew how to remove an ancient voodoo hex!'' Zoey insisted resolutely, her eyes wide. "You'd think that with all their money and connections, that wouldn't be a problem for them. But enough about the Hamptons.'' She dismissed the current topic of conversation airily. "I didn't call you for lunch to talk about them. What I really want to hear about is this new man in your life. So how about your telling me all about him over a bowl of gumbo?''

One of Leon Gutierrez's more legitimate businesses was a place called Flamingo Landing. It was located on the right side of the river that divided the city, at a point where the land jutted into the water, forming a small peninsula, and from where rice and cotton had used to be shipped to faraway ports from the plantation that had once occupied this area just north of the municipal limits. The acres of rich land previously devoted to farming no longer lay beyond the city's boundaries. But now, instead of boasting crops, the region had, as the municipality had grown over the years, gradually pushing northward, been given over to sprawling, modern developments, many of which required space the original city had lacked, its founders never having envisioned the likes of what the future was to hold. Among these results of twentieth-century progress were the airport, a coliseum and exhibition hall, horse and greyhound racetracks, an amusement park, a yacht club, and a series of shops, restaurants, hotels, and nightclubs.

Of all these last, despite that it was the most isolated, being the only edifice actually situated on the tiny peninsula itself, Gutierrez's place, Flamingo Landing, was the most exclusive and popular with the city's upscale residents. It had not always been so. Many of these very same people, when Gutierrez had first expressed an interest in buying the property, had attempted to block his acquisition of it, fearing he intended to tear down the old, antebellum mansion that stood at the peninsula's heart and which had, through neglect, somehow escaped being designated as a historical building. But Gutierrez had been all smiles and charm, smoothly insisting that the thought of destroying such a splendid—however then currently dilapidated—example of Greek Revival architecture had never even occurred to him. Of course he not only agreed the mansion must be placed on the historical register, but he also fully intended to restore it to all its former glory, he had declared.

In the end, his apparent affability and numerous bribes under the table to the city officials who had counted most had ensured not only the success of his purchase, but also of the changes in the zoning restrictions he had required in order to bring his grand plans to fruition. Thus Flamingo Landing had been born. True to his word, Gutierrez had spent quite a considerable sum renovating the antebellum mansion—well aware that the most skillful and difficult lies to detect were always those mixed in with the truth. Besides which, it suited his own purposes to have as respectable a front as possible to cover up what he intended to carry on behind closed doors. Thus, to all outward appearances, the mansion now seemed to be a small, exclusive hotel and supper club, its former outbuildings a series of shops dedicated to antiques, objets d'art, designer clothing, and jewelry.

Only those in the know were aware that in certain back rooms off-limits to ignorant guests, high-stakes, illegal gambling was the vogue of the evening, and that not only smuggled Cuban cigars, but also marijuana and cocaine were discreetly offered for sale to customers who could afford to pay for such vices. And if a gentleman wished to rent a bedroom upstairs for a few hours, the type of woman necessary to accommodate his every desire was available for a price, as well.

To safeguard this elite, nefarious enterprise, Gutierrez had installed in the mansion and on its grounds an elaborate, although wholly unobtrusive, security system that was a masterpiece of technology, and further—quite unbeknown to both the elderly, genteel ladies and their younger, more militant counterparts who made it their mission to protect old buildings of historical interest and value—steel doors that could seal off the mansion's back rooms at the touch of a button. Additionally, during the reconstruction process, Gutierrez had discovered secret, bricked-off, underground passages leading to the former stables and the landing itself—old escape routes for the plantation

owners in case of slave uprisings, he had surmised—
and these he had reopened and shored up, as well. In
the former stables, he kept housed a small, private
plane, which had access to an old, dirt track that had
been carefully cleared and lengthened to make a take-
off possible, if necessary; and at the wharf, he kept
moored a high-speed motorboat.

Thus assured of making his own getaway should
anything of a disastrous nature ever occur at Flamingo
Landing, Gutierrez roamed the mansion and mingled
with its guests in complete confidence that he was so
much smarter and more foresighted than anyone else
around him that he would never be caught, tried, convicted, and put into prison, as so many of his less
astute colleagues had been over the years. Nor did he
worry very much about being assassinated by anybody
within the ranks of his organization. He handpicked
his own, personal bodyguards from among only the
most trusted of his longtime associates, and the sole
person whom he had made an exception to this rule
was Manolo Alvarez, his illegitimate son.

As he gazed at Manny now across the mansion's
oak-paneled library, which housed the roulette and
craps tables, Gutierrez sighed heavily. He wished he
had known sooner about Manny's existence, because
he had indeed been genuinely fond of Manny's
mother, had, he supposed, loved her in his fashion, as
much as he were capable of loving anyone. She, however, had loathed him, seeing only the ignorant brute
he had been twenty years ago; and eventually, she had
run away from him. Had such a thing happened today,

he would have no difficulty in locating and retrieving her. But back then, he had been a mere nobody, with few resources at his disposal. So she had escaped from him, and he had never learned about their child until much later, when he had expanded his operations to make use of Las Calaveras and various other Latino gangs that had sprung up in the barrio.

For a while, Gutierrez had simply kept tabs on Manny, in order to determine his character. But after the incident at the convenience store, the older man had realized that if he wanted a blood relative to inherit the empire he had built, he needed to take his son into his organization and begin teaching him how to become something other than an uneducated thug. When it came to crime, Manny had demonstrated both potential and cleverness. But these were overshadowed by his impulsiveness, passions, and lack of sophistication—the same faults Gutierrez himself had possessed until he had learned how to control his hot temper and volatile emotions, and had acquired a sufficient amount of knowledge and refinement to distinguish between a Renoir and a Rembrandt. That Manny was the proverbial sow's ear, there was no doubt; whether he could be turned into a silk purse was another matter entirely. For now, however, Gutierrez was willing to make the attempt.

Life on the mean streets had given Manolo Alvarez the same kind of wariness that a dog regularly beaten by its master possesses. Thus he was vividly aware of his surroundings, of the high-rolling customers crowded around the roulette and craps tables, of the brawny bodyguards-cum-bouncers who stood around the library, on the lookout for potential trouble, and of Gutierrez in one corner, watching him surreptitiously. It made Manny distinctly uneasy, the way his bene-factor was always spying on him from beneath hooded lids. He felt as though the older man could somehow see right into his very soul, knew his every waking thought and sleeping dream, that he was always one step behind Gutierrez instead of ahead.

That would never do—because then it would be im-possible for Manny to take over Gutierrez's operation, and this had become the younger man's burning am-bition. He didn't realize he was, in fact, being groomed for precisely that responsibility, that he was his benefactor's illegitimate son. The older man had not shared any of that information with him, knowing instinctively that at this point in his life, Manny would use it to take advantage, manipulating it to his own ends. So it was that in blissful ignorance, Manny plot-ted and planned how he would acquire Gutierrez's em-pire.

Now, with that single, all-consuming goal in mind, Manny surveyed the library as watchfully as his father, nothing escaping the dark, narrowed eyes in his shrewd, thin, ratlike face. He had already taken the first step in accomplishing his aim, he told himself. For the first time in his entire life, he was being paid a regular and livable wage—one that had enabled him to buy a decent suit. It didn't begin to compare in material and craftsmanship to those worn by Gutierrez, but it was the closest an off-the-rack suit could come to an Armani. Manny had also had his hair cut and styled by a hairdresser instead of taking a pair of scissors to it himself, and had had his nails manicured, too. As he gazed around the library, he thought with satisfaction that he could hold his own with anybody present, and he prided himself that more than one of the females gathered around the roulette and craps tables had given him the eye.

He had never before seen such women...dressed to the nines and loaded with jewelry. Many of them, Manny knew, were prostitutes who worked for his benefactor. It was their job to lure important customers to the bedrooms upstairs, in which Gutierrez had video cameras installed to film those men whom he wanted to blackmail. Manny thought that perhaps he would avail himself of one of the hooker's services later. He didn't mind being captured on tape, screwing some whore; he would show Gutierrez how it was done. The notion made Manny smile smugly to himself before his eyes focused on the man who had just entered the library.

It was Councilman Malcolm Forsythe. Manny had seen him at Flamingo Landing a couple of times before and thought the councilman bore watching as someone who might be useful to him in the future. Forsythe had expensive tastes and habits...Cuban cigars, a little marijuana and cocaine, the best-looking prostitutes. Most of all, he liked to gamble. He could afford it, of course, since he was married to Veronica Hampton, one of the richest women around. Nor had his own family been poor, by any means. Still, a man like Forsythe would most likely eventually dig himself into a pit too deep to escape from. Manny surmised that somewhere his benefactor already had film stored away of the councilman making a drug buy or banging a couple of hookers. No doubt Gutierrez was just biding his time, waiting until Forsythe became a much-bigger fish in a much-bigger pond, since it was rumored that the councilman had political aspirations that involved being ensconced on Capitol Hill.

Gutierrez hadn't got where he was by being a fool. He didn't need money, so he wouldn't be tempted by the thought of trying to milk the Forsythe and Hampton family coffers dry. No, the sort of blackmail he engaged in was a great deal cleverer and more insidious than that. Having a congressman or senator in his pocket would be quite a coup. But Manny was learning, too, that patience had its rewards, and he figured that by the time the councilman was entitled to call himself Senator Forsythe, he, Manny, would be in charge of Gutierrez's operation—and pulling Forsythe's strings himself.

"Do you know where you are, dearie?" the middle-aged head nurse at the Seabreeze Sanatorium, Mrs. Netherfield, asked kindly as she studied her new patient.

"Of course...a small, exclusive hotel on the Riviera," Vanessa Hampton announced quietly as she gazed around blankly at her surroundings. "Is that where I check in...over there?" She pointed to the admissions desk. "I'll just go sign the register now. Oh, I do hope I have a suite with a view of the ocean. I've always loved the sea."

"I feel certain that can be arranged, Vannie." Veronica Hampton Forsythe took her twin sister's arm gently as Vanessa started toward the admissions desk. Once there, the younger, more fragile twin picked up a pen attached by a chain to the counter, and spying a piece of paper lying next to it, she carefully signed a name...Veronica Hampton Forsythe. "Vannie, you've written my name down there." Veronica's brow was knitted with concern as she glanced at her twin.

"No, of course I haven't. Why ever would I want to do that, Vannie?" Vanessa's own face betrayed puzzlement as she looked at her older twin sister.

"Perhaps because it was a game we used to play together," Veronica suggested. "You remember, don't you? How we used to trade places to tease our family and friends? But we're not playing that game now, Vannie, and you've just got to know who you are."

"I *do* know who I am." A tiny note of anger and coldness had crept into Vanessa's tone now, and her wide, sapphire-blue eyes narrowed slightly. "It's *you* who are confused, Vannie. I don't know why you're trying to trick me like this, but it's wicked and cruel, and you ought to be ashamed of yourself! You know I haven't been at all well lately...." Her voice trailing away, Vanessa pressed one hand to her temple, as though her head hurt.

"Mrs. Hampton Forsythe." Carrying a file, Dr. Kyle Logan, the head of the sanatorium, turned from the conversation he had been conducting with the twins' grandmother, Nadine Hampton, and Nurse Netherfield, to draw Veronica aside. He spoke to her softly. "There's no use in attempting to force your sister to try to recall her past. The trauma of the car accident, coupled with the shock of learning of your cousin Bruno's death, has simply proved too much for her. I understand that she was never what one would have referred to as a strong, independent woman, but, rather, highly sensitive and vulnerable. This confusion of identities on her part is therefore no doubt a subconscious attempt to equate herself with someone whom she perceived as capable and assured—in this case, you, her older twin. I see no harm at this point in permitting her to indulge that fantasy, particularly if it helps her to cope with the terrible blows that she has recently endured."

"Yes, of course. I understand, and I apologize, Dr. Logan." Veronica's hands tightened involuntarily on her Gucci clutch bag as she glanced again worriedly at her twin sister. "It's just that we've always been so close, and it's…so hard to see her like this. Do you—do you believe she'll ever make a full recovery?"

Dr. Logan shook his head noncommittally. "I'm afraid that's very difficult to predict right now, Mrs. Hampton Forsythe. Your sister may abruptly come to her senses tomorrow—or she may go on for years believing that she is you and that you are her. There's just no way to tell until I've had a chance both to interview her and to observe her at some length. But please rest assured that she is in excellent hands here at Seabreeze and that we will do everything in our power to restore her to you.''

''Thank you. Thank you very much, Dr. Logan. I'm sure my grandmother has already told you how much we appreciate the assistance of both you and your staff in this matter, how grateful we are for all the fine care Vannie will receive here.''

''Yes, indeed. Your grandmother has been...most generous.''

Finally, after chatting for a few more minutes, Dr. Logan and Nurse Netherfield led Vanessa away to the private suite that, during an earlier visit to the sanatorium, Nadine Hampton had approved for her granddaughter.

''Come along, Veronica,'' Nadine now ordered briskly. ''There's nothing further that we can do here at this point in time. Kyle Logan's sanatorium is the best in the city. Vanessa will be quite comfortable here and well taken care of until she is able to return home.''

''Yes, I know you're right, Grandmother. Still, I can't help being anxious about her. She's so pale and...and so utterly bewildered.''

''Yes, well, it is my understanding that a trauma to the brain, particularly when combined with a severe shock, may result in unpredictable behavior. Therefore, it is only to be expected that Vanessa is not herself at the moment. Give me your arm, Veronica. I'm afraid all this has tired me out far more than I believed it would, and my hips are acting up again...damned arthritis!"

Leaning heavily on both her cane and her granddaughter's arm, Nadine Hampton made her way slowly toward the front doors of the sanatorium. Once outside, she and Veronica stood at the curb until Wilkes, Nadine's chauffeur, had pulled their long, black car around and got out to open the rear door. Settled comfortably upon the vehicle's plush, leather seat, Nadine pressed the button that rolled up the glass partition inside, so Wilkes could not hear her and Veronica conversing as he drove.

"Have you learned anything further at all from Lily about what occurred that night at the villa in Tuscany, Veronica?" the elderly woman inquired.

"No. She still insists she doesn't know what happened, that she was upstairs when Vannie and Bruno began quarreling, and that she doesn't have a clue as to what they argued about. She said she heard raised voices and that then Vannie and Bruno both ran out of the villa, with Bruno shouting, and that they took off in the Ferrari, with Vannie at the wheel. Lily claims that the next thing she knew, the Italian police were standing on the doorstep, informing her that there'd been a terrible accident."

Nadine sighed heavily. "Yes, that's pretty much the same story Lily gave me, as well. Still, my gut instinct tells me there's much more to it than that, that Lily knows a great deal more than she's told us."

"Yes, that's what I think, too, Grandmother. But I don't know what Lily could be hiding—except perhaps the fact that Vannie was having an affair with someone who was totally unsuitable. Maybe, when Vannie found out she was pregnant, she went to Bruno for help and he blew his top when he learned the identity of the baby's father.''

''That's certainly one possibility,'' Nadine conceded reluctantly. ''Still, somehow, I can't help feeling there's more to it than that. However, be that as it may, it's surely a blessing under the circumstances that Vanessa miscarried the child and that the father, whoever he may have been, is obviously not coming forward. I will not have scandal attached to the Hampton family name, Veronica. We are a proud, distinguished, old family—one of the foremost in the state. Perhaps that's why we've suffered so many tragedies over the years—because we have always triumphed over adversity—and we will get through this ordeal, as well. I have lost my only grandson, and one of my granddaughters may never recover, may never be her former self again. But I still have you, Veronica.''

''And Lily,'' the younger woman added.

''I wonder,'' Nadine said.

Having returned to Italy following the admission of Vanessa into the Seabreeze Sanatorium, Lily D'Angelo now sat outside on the balcony of her luxurious apartment in Rome, sipping a cup of cappuccino. The effects of the bombshell she had dropped on Vanessa and Bruno that night at the villa in Tuscany had proved even more devastating than she had ever dared to hope. Her brother, Bruno, was dead, and her cousin

Vanessa was now a complete mental case; and although both her grandmother and her cousin Veronica had high hopes for Vanessa's eventual recovery, Lily felt certain in her heart that Vanessa would never leave the sanatorium, that she would remain ensconced there for the rest of her life. Vanessa had always, ever since childhood, been a fragile, high-strung girl—and the blow she had received would have felled even a strong, stable woman. No, Vanessa was no longer a player in the deadly game Lily had embarked upon ever since she had learned exactly who and what she was.

Since that time, clever and patient, she had laid her plans carefully, taking advantage of every chance. One by one, her opponents had been eliminated—and she had never once been suspected of having had a hand in their demise. Now only Veronica and Malcolm stood in her way. It was too soon to move against either one of them at the moment. But eventually, Lily's opportunity would come, she knew.

Until then, she could afford to bide her time and wait. After all, there were millions of dollars at stake.

"Gee, what in the hell's wrong, Claire?" Winston Nash asked, frowning, his eyes filled with puzzlement, as he studied her pale face. "This is what we've worked so damned hard for—so I thought you'd be ecstatic about Mr. Kendall's decision. Instead, you look as though your best friend just died!"

"I'm…sorry. I guess I'm just totally surprised and overwhelmed," Claire said slowly. "To tell you the truth, as much as I had hoped otherwise, I just don't think I ever truly believed Mr. Kendall would think enough of our miniseries to actually air it. That he's going to is just, well...wholly unexpected, that's all.'' In reality, Claire had felt sick inside, not glad, about Mr. Kendall's announcement, his enthusiasm for the miniseries she, Nash, and McGuinness had worked so long and hard on. Despite how she had attempted to talk both her cameramen into downplaying Jake's tragedy during the editing process, it was still the undeniable anchor of the six segments, both opening and closing the miniseries; and now she could not help but be upset at the realization of how angry and hurt Jake would be when he viewed the film. He would surely feel as though she had betrayed him, Claire thought, that she had used her relationship with him to further her career.

After leaving the station for the evening, she drove home in a daze, her entire body pervaded with an uneasy sense of fear and doom, her mind working overtime. She should inform Jake about the miniseries at once, she told herself over and over. Instead, afraid of his reaction, she said nothing to him that evening, thinking that perhaps he would somehow miss seeing the film, would never know what she had done.

That hope lasted exactly a week, until one morning while she and Jake were eating breakfast in her kitchen and watching the local news on television, Channel 4 ran a promotional trailer for Claire's miniseries. A close-up of Jake's figure, seated on the stoop of the convenience store, his head buried with grief in his hands as his dead wife's corpse was carried outside in a body bag, filled the screen, while Claire's voice-over announced, "The Great American Dream...The Great American Tragedy."

In that moment, except for the sound coming from the television set—ironically, some stupid commercial for a painkiller, Claire realized dully—silence reigned supreme in the kitchen. Seeing the trailer, Jake had gone utterly still, his thick, spiky, black lashes sweeping down to conceal his thoughts, his fork poised half between his plate and his mouth. Now, after what seemed to Claire like an eternity, he slowly laid his fork down and pushed his chair back from the table. Without a single word, he rose and went into her bedroom, where she heard him moving around, gathering his things. A few minutes later, he came back out, carrying his black-leather, overnight bag. He paused in the living room, glancing at her frozen figure still sitting there in the kitchen.

"You can't have any real kind of an intimate relationship that isn't founded on trust and commitment, Claire," he insisted quietly, dispassionately, only the muscle flexing turbulently in his set jaw revealing the true state of his emotions. "I trusted you—and you let me down. So I'm leaving now, and I won't be back. Being a gentleman, I suppose that before I go, I should thank you for the ride—but somehow, I just can't help but feel the price was too high."

He didn't slam the front door behind him. Instead, he just pulled it shut firmly with a finality that rang in Claire's ears like a death knell. She wanted to call after him, to run after him, to apologize profusely and beg him to return. But somehow she seemed to be rooted to her chair, unable to breathe, so big was the lump that had risen to her throat, choking her. Tears streamed silently down her cheeks.

After a very long moment, she slowly stood and, walking blindly to the kitchen sink, poured the last of her coffee down the drain.

Book Two

Riptide

Where thou perhaps under the whelming tide
Visit'st the bottom of the monstrous world.

Lycidas
—John Milton

Eleven

Casualties of Sin

Cromwell, I charge thee, fling away ambition:
By that sin fell the angels.

> *Henry VIII*
> —William Shakespeare

A Small City, The Gulf Coast, Six Months Ago

She hadn't even struggled.

That was what had surprised him most of all. He had come fully prepared with a pack of lies he would have spoken smoothly to allay her sudden suspicions, a clean, white handkerchief with which to gag her in case she had begun to cry out when she had grasped what he intended, and a pair of long, silk scarves with which to bind her wrists and ankles in the event that she had fought him desperately at the end, the horrifying realization that he meant to murder her giving her a strength that her small, too-thin body would normally have lacked.

And she hadn't even struggled, hadn't even screamed, however faintly. If she had had even an inkling of what was happening to her, she had been too drunk, too drugged, and too incredulous to try to help herself.

Now, as Senator Malcolm Forsythe gazed down at the woman's dead body, he shook his head both with disbelief at her naiveté and with a great deal of contempt at her stupidity. She had been his mistress for the past three months, but he had never enjoyed making love to her—at least, not until this evening. Tonight had excited him because he had known it would be the last time, that he would kill her afterward. Otherwise, he had found no pleasure whatsoever in her brassy, dyed-blond hair, her slutty makeup, and her bony body. She had dressed in cheap, trashy clothes from discount stores, lingerie from Frederick's of Hollywood, and had gone braless all the time, as though she were still a teenager, when, in reality, she would never see forty again. She'd had small, pathetic breasts, besides—and a brain to match. He doubted that she had ever cracked open a book since leaving high school.

The poor, trusting fool, he thought, his lips twisting into a faint, unconscious sneer.

Despite his relief that the woman's infatuation with him had made her so very easy to kill, he was genuinely sorry she hadn't fought him. It wouldn't have prevented him from murdering her, but it would at least have made him respect her as having been worthy of the time and money he had lavished on her. As it was, he felt his great talents had been wasted on a wholly ignorant and unappreciative victim.

Still, she had done what he'd asked of her, and he felt he owed her something for that. As he stared down at her, he made a mental note to himself to send flowers anonymously to her funeral—nothing ostentatious, of course, which would undoubtedly provoke comment, but a small, inexpensive wreath befitting her memory.

After all, he believed in paying his debts.

He continued to stand there, motionless, for several minutes, his head cocked, listening intently for any sound that would tell him his murder of the woman had been detected, that the police were even now en route to her apartment. But he heard nothing except the frantic hammering of his heart, the blood roaring in his ears as adrenaline pumped furiously through his big, strong, handsome body. Deliberately, he forced himself to remain still, to take several deep breaths in order to recapture his calm. Panic, just like stupidity and hubris, caused a person to get sloppy, to make mistakes. That was why killers got caught. They acted out of fear or foolishness or arrogance. He would not commit any of those errors. He had made it his business to learn how the police operated. So he was aware that nine times out of ten, they only got their man because he had slipped up in some fashion or somebody else had ratted on him. That was why he had not hired a second party to do his dirty work for him— because he knew the chances of a really clever, careful criminal being arrested were virtually nil.

Forsythe had ensured that there was absolutely

nothing to connect him to the woman whom he had just murdered. Her name was Patsy Traynor, and she was a mere nobody. She had worked for the Metro Cleaning Company, scrubbing toilets for a living, so she had not even begun to move in the same circles as he. He had never told her his true name, and he had disguised his appearance every time he had been with her, covering his greying temples with a temporary hair dye, applying a false mustache to his upper lip, and wearing a pair of nonprescription glasses. Fortunately, Patsy—the stereotypical bimbo of dumb-blond jokes—had never taken any interest whatsoever in politics, so that to her, Senator Malcolm Forsythe had been nothing more than a faceless name she sometimes heard about on TV. She had known Forsythe himself as Dean Jeffreys and had never once questioned his identity. He had picked her up in a sleazy bar, to which he had followed her after she had got off work one evening.

Exuding smooth talk and charm, he had declared that he was a professional photographer and that she would be a perfect model, flattering her into thinking she was the next Claudia Schiffer. The thick-headed bitch had fallen for it hook, line, and sinker, Forsythe thought now, remembering. Before more than a couple of hours had passed, he had worked his way into her confidence, apartment, and panties. After that, he had dated her regularly—he had even taken some pictures of her to bolster his false claim of being a professional photographer. Eventually, it had been easy enough to convince the gullible Patsy to let him into one of the offices she cleaned nights...that of Brett Deauville, D.D.S.

After screwing her in one of the dental chairs, then escorting her to the bathrooms and leaving her to clean herself up—not that her personal hygiene had been anything to write home about—Forsythe had used the time alone to rifle the office's dental files, stealing several of them at random, but specifically including those of his wife, Veronica, and his sister-in-law, Vanessa. He had tossed them into the canvas duffel bag in which he had carried several pieces of photographic equipment, having told Patsy that he had come to her directly following a location shoot. She had never had a clue.

But afterward, she had become a loose end, and of course, he couldn't afford to have any of those.

"Thank God you were such a stupid slut, Patsy," Forsythe muttered now as he stood over her corpse. "You sure made my job a hell of a lot easier." He had got her drunk on the cheap wine she had preferred, her low-rent palate not having known the difference between Moët and Chandon and Mogan-David. It had been easy enough, when she wasn't looking, to pour the contents of his own glass into hers so he would stay stone-cold sober—and easier still to insist that he be the one to go out into the kitchen and open up the second bottle of wine once they had polished off the first, to dump the overdose of barbiturate pills into her glass and wait until they had dissolved before taking it in to her.

When Patsy had started to moan that she didn't feel

well, he had silenced her with kisses until she had finally slipped into unconsciousness and then died.

Now Forsythe began to move, mentally checking off all he needed to do before vacating her apartment. First, he donned surgical gloves, then flushed down the toilet the condoms he had used to avoid leaving any traces of his semen in Patsy's body. Then, being careful not to disturb her corpse too much—since this could be detected through lividity—he washed her off, then changed the sheets on her bed in an attempt to ensure that none of his body hair remained behind for the police to collect in case they should decide her death was suspicious. He bundled up the dirty sheets and stuffed them into his canvas duffel bag for disposal later.

He had been careful not to touch the first wine bottle, and he had wrapped a towel around the second one so he wouldn't leave any fingerprints on it. Now he carefully positioned one wine bottle on Patsy's nightstand, along with an empty prescription bottle that lacked a label and into which he dropped a couple of barbiturate capsules, so it would appear as though she had obtained the pills illegally and the police would have no idea how many capsules had originally been in the container. The second wine bottle he tossed on the floor, as though she had knocked it off the night table in her drunken stupor.

At Patsy's kitchen sink, Forsythe thoroughly washed the glass he had used, placing it back in her cabinet. Returning to the bedroom, he wrapped her lifeless hand around her own glass several times, then laid it on the floor, as though it had slipped from her grasp. That she was stark naked was a real plus, since most women stripped to commit suicide. It was mostly men who dressed in their best clothes for the deed. Finally, Forsythe conducted a complete search of her apartment, just to be certain nothing incriminating remained. Just before he left, he turned her thermostat down several notches, so the cooler temperature in the apartment would help to make it difficult for the medical examiner to determine the exact time of her death.

Making sure he was unobserved, he slipped from Patsy's run-down apartment complex to the cracked sidewalk beyond. Keeping in the shadows cast by the old, soughing trees that lined the deserted street, he strode down several blocks to the bus stop. His timing was perfect; the bus was just pulling to a halt. Adopting a shuffling gait and keeping his head ducked low to avoid attracting attention, Forsythe followed a hooker and a bag lady aboard, making two transfers before getting off the last bus to walk an additional few blocks to the secluded place where he had parked his car. Along the way, he tossed the duffel bag into a Dumpster. Everything had gone off like clockwork, he assured himself smugly as he started his vehicle and drove away.

Lily would be extremely pleased.

Twelve

Reunion

It is only the dead who do not return.

Speech
—Bertrand Barère de Vieuzac

"The victim's name was Patsy Traynor, aged forty-three. She worked as a maid for the Metro Cleaning Company—but she apparently hasn't been on the job for at least a week," Jake reported as his partner, Remy Toussaint, joined him in the bedroom of Patsy's apartment.

"A week?" Toussaint's eyebrows flew up in surprise. "Would you please explain to me just exactly how in the hell you could skip work for a week and nobody know about it, Jake?"

"Well, the company cleans a number of different offices, each of which, depending on its size, is assigned to one or more maids who do the job after normal business hours. Each maid receives her schedule, cleaning supplies, etcetera, at the beginning of the week, and then reports directly to her job site each evening. She's generally let in by security, although a few trusted, longtime employees have keys to some offices. Mostly, however, there's a relatively high turnover rate among these maids. For the most part, they're cheap labor—uneducated, unskilled workers, welfare and blue-collar backgrounds, single mothers trying to get off food stamps and the public dole...probably a lot of them are illegal aliens, if the INS ever bothered to check into it.'' Jake grimaced wryly. ''At any rate, the company charges each office a set fee, while the maids themselves are paid a minimum wage based on the number of hours the company estimates it takes them to clean any given office.

''Traynor hadn't been on the job long...about six months,'' he continued, flipping the pages of his notepad to read back the information he had collected from the uniformed officers on the scene. ''Before that, she worked as a stripper at the Kit-Kat Klub. It seems, however, that despite the fact that the Kit-Kat is the bottom of the barrel, the manager had decided her dubious assets were turning his customers off instead of on, and he fired her. After that, I guess she figured it was either hit the streets or find some other line of work—and evidently, she decided scrubbing toilets for a living was better than doing back-alley blow jobs and stand-up quickies, although that's not to say she didn't supplement her income by turning a few tricks on the side. Still, from various comments made by her co-workers, it appears she had a sometime boyfriend, at least...first name Dean, surname currently unknown. He's supposed to be some kind of a photographer—probably the type you wouldn't take your mother to for a family portrait.'' Jake's voice was tinged with irony.

"However, we haven't as yet turned up anything to suggest he ever really even existed. He may just have been a figment of Traynor's imagination, somebody she made up to impress upon her co-workers the fact that she was still capable of getting a man. It wouldn't be the first time a woman's ever done something like that. Or it could be that he recently dumped her. From the looks of the place and the body itself, it appears as though Traynor either killed herself or else was too drunk to keep track of the number of barbiturate capsules she had consumed with the booze. The M.E. will know more after the postmortem.

"In any event, since she mostly worked alone, at small offices that could be handled by a single maid, there was no reason for anybody to know she had gone AWOL. Most of Metro's clients' offices to which she was assigned just assumed she had skimped on the cleaning on their particular night. A few didn't even notice their trash cans hadn't been emptied or their floors vacuumed. Only one customer was upset enough to complain…a dentist, Dr. Brett Deauville. Apparently, she hadn't done too good of a job of cleaning his office the previous week, and he had decided she hadn't shown up at all this week, so he checked with his building's security, then called Metro. Seems he flosses the teeth of the city's rich and shameless, so he's real persnickety about how his office looks.''

"God forbid that his clients should spit in a dirty

sink, is that it?'' Toussaint inquired dryly. ''Well, I reckon we ought to be grateful Dr. Deauville's a clean freak, or else there's no telling how long poor Ms. Traynor there might have lain undiscovered, huh? How long's the M.E. say she's been dead? Two, three, four days?''

''Yeah, somewhere in there. It's hard to tell at this point. She had her thermostat set much lower than normal...sixty-five degrees, so the place was like a cooler when the apartment manager opened it up for the two uniforms first on the scene. The woman who owns Metro had called Traynor in as a possible missing person, since she didn't believe Traynor would have walked off the job without at least collecting her paycheck first.''

''Instead, it looks like Traynor figured she wouldn't be needing the money, so why bother?'' Toussaint observed as he glanced at the corpse. ''Still, that's interesting about the temperature.''

''No, not really. The M.E. claims it's not unusual for women who're going through the change of life—having hot flashes, you know?—to crank their thermostats way down. He says his own wife damned near froze him to death when she hit menopause.''

Toussaint rolled his eyes disbelievingly at this revelation. ''Lord, I sure hope Frances doesn't do anything like that when she gets to that stage. On the other hand, our electric bill's already so high I can hardly afford it.''

''Gotta pay for the Accident-Waiting-to-Happen, don't you know, Remy?'' Jake referred sarcastically to the wholly unpopular nuclear plant that had been constructed by the electric company—over most of its customers' protests—and that, despite the company's claims that the plant had been direly needed or else blackouts would result, had never run at more than a third of its capacity.

"Yeah, right," Toussaint replied, his own voice equally derisive. Then he got back to the business at hand. "So what've we got here with the Traynor woman? Any suspicions of foul play whatsoever? Or were the two of us called out here on a wild-goose chase?"

"Probably the latter At the moment, the M.E. says suicide or accidental overdose. I say we let him bag her and tag her, and that we get the hell out of here. We might try to get a make on the alleged boyfriend, just as a precaution. But my guess is that we're going to turn up *nada* on the guy. None of the neighbors ever saw him coming or going, at any rate. I think we can chalk this one up as a lonely, aging, lower-class female hitting the skids and deciding to end it all with whatever little dignity she had left."

"Yeah…it's sad, but it happens. Did she have any relatives?"

"A couple of grown kids. The daughter was estranged from her and, according to the uniforms, didn't appear too broken up about her death. The son's in the federal pen—grand theft auto. The ex-husband vamoosed over a decade ago, and nobody's seen him since."

"Christ, what a family." Toussaint shook his head, disgusted. "All right, then. Tell Forensics and the

M.E. to wrap it up, and then let's get the hell out of here.''

"Right." Jake closed his notepad, tucking it and his pen into the inside pocket of his suit jacket.

During his ten years on the police force, Jake had worked hard to become a homicide detective and, at Toussaint's request, had been assigned as the big, black man's new partner when his old one had retired. Over the past few years, Jake and Toussaint had formed a good, close, respectful working relationship that had resulted in the number of investigations they conducted having a high percentage of successful arrests and convictions. Toussaint was experienced and methodical, while Jake had developed a sixth sense that was uncanny when it came to crime.

Now, despite his assurances to his partner that Patsy Traynor had almost certainly committed suicide, there was something about her death that bothered Jake, a tiny, nagging doubt that refused to be quelled, but that he could not put his finger on. There was no way of telling whether or not her apartment had been ransacked in some fashion, whether or not there was anything missing, the place was such a pigsty. Nor was there anything unusual in the fact that Patsy's corpse was naked, since women commonly stripped to kill themselves. The sheets were clean; there was apparently no trace of semen in the body. There was only one glass—which had slipped from the victim's hand—on the floor, and it appeared to contain traces of the wine and barbiturates on the nightstand. But still, as he gazed at the tableau, something unsettled Jake.

He felt somehow as though he were looking at a theater set, as though everything he saw were artificial and had in some way been carefully staged. But as he could not determine any possible motive for a perpetrator to have done such a thing—there were no signs that the corpse had been forcibly violated or the apartment broken into and robbed, for example—he was at last forced to dismiss his suspicions as the product of his imagination.

Still, as he followed Toussaint from Patsy's bedroom, Jake called back over his shoulder to the medical examiner, "Let us know if you happen to turn up anything out of the ordinary."

Outside on the front stoop of Patsy's apartment, Jake paused to withdraw a pack of Marlboros from one of the pockets of his suit jacket. Shaking out a cigarette, he lit up, inhaling deeply, then blowing a cloud of smoke into the sunny, spring air. Every time he saw the corpse of a lone woman, he was transported back in time—back to the convenience store where his wife had been murdered, back to the dark alley where the young, Latino hooker who had been vaguely familiar to him had been stabbed to death. Despite how he still occasionally dwelled on the latter's identity, Jake had never remembered the circumstances under which he had seen her previously. He felt certain that if only he could recall that time, he would know not only who had killed her, but had also murdered his wife. But every time he felt he was getting close, would at long last be able to connect the prostitute's countenance with that of another person, the image faded maddeningly away, as though the harlot's face were evanescing, until all that was left in his mind was her fleshless skull. As a result, Isabel's murderer had never been caught and punished, and now, after ten years, it was extremely unlikely an arrest would ever be made in the case. Jake considered it his one failure, and it haunted him endlessly.

With a start, he drew himself back to the present, to the matter at hand. Toussaint had wandered away, examining the layout of the apartment complex, occasionally stopping and poking into the blooming bushes and vines, so that although Remy had said nothing to the contrary, Jake knew his partner, too, was bothered in some indefinable way by Traynor's death.

Serial killers sometimes passed themselves off as photographers to lure unsuspecting females—usually women who fancied themselves as would-be models—into their clutches, Jake knew. But Patsy's death didn't have any of the earmarks of that type of crime, either. He sighed heavily. It was a puzzle—or maybe it wasn't. Maybe it was just as it appeared and he was making too much of it. But then, there was Toussaint, down on his hands and knees to search the grounds beneath the windows of Patsy's apartment. A half smile curved Jake's mouth at the sight. There were many in the department who referred to Toussaint as "plodding." But Jake knew he had learned more from Toussaint than he had while obtaining his administration of justice degree at the university or from anybody else while on the job.

Jake started to join his partner, then suddenly halted in his tracks as he spied the woman coming briskly along the sidewalk of the apartment complex. For a moment, blinded by the bright, yellow, spring sunlight streaming down through the branches of the greening trees, he thought he was somehow still lost in the past, that a decade had not come and gone since the first time he had ever seen her, leaving him older, wiser, and harder. He thought he was still twenty-eight years old, grieving, alone, and desperately in need of some kind of connection with another human being.

Adding to his strange sense of disembodied time was the fact that he could have sworn she herself had not aged a single day, that she was still the same, young, fresh-faced, gilt-haired nymph who had stood on the gallery beyond his front door that day of his family's funerals, with the sunlight casting a halo around her head. But then, as she noticed him standing there, blocking her path, her step visibly faltered, and she abruptly came to a stop beneath the shade of a moss-draped tree, so he could see her face clearly.

The years had been kind to her, he observed, leaving her beautiful, oval countenance only faintly marked by time, so it was her eyes alone that gave testimony to the ways in which the past decade had scarred her soul, causing her to be forever changed. They haunted him…those eyes—wide, heavily lashed, as sea-green and fathomless as the ocean, and touched by knowledge and shadows that were somehow painful to him to observe. He had heard it said more than once in the city that it was her remarkable eyes that had catapulted her to the top of her field. Now, seeing them live, up close and personal, instead of just looking out at him from a television screen, Jake could believe that was true.

"Hello, Claire," he said, his voice low and, despite himself, husky with sudden emotion.

"Hello, Jake," she replied quietly.

For so many years, Claire had dreamed of this meeting. Long ago, she had used to drive down to Lafitte's Quay, just to see if his houseboat was still moored there and hoping to catch a glimpse of him. Then, when common sense had finally prevailed, she had never gone there again, not even to shop, in case she should accidentally run into him. But still, deep down inside, she had thought of him and dreamed. Yet, now that Jake was actually standing here before her, Claire found that, perversely, she did not want to face him, after all.

She had not realized how just the sight of him would affect her, would still have the power to take her breath away. It seemed only yesterday that the two of them had shared a bed; she could still feel his hard, whipcord body pressing her down, making her respond in ways she had not known were possible, wringing soft, little cries of entreaty and pleasure from her lips. Despite the fact that a decade had come and gone since then, that strong, physical attraction still stretched between them like a tangible thing. She could feel it, setting her skin to tingling, her heart to hammering, her body to trembling, turning her knees to quicksilver, so she was vaguely surprised they didn't give out from beneath her.

He was, if possible, even more handsome than before, Claire thought, the years having honed and re-

fined his features, smoothing away the last traces of
youth, leaving in their place a man wise in the ways
of the world—and one who had grown hard and cynical as a result. There was nothing grief stricken or
vulnerable about this Jake who stood before her now.
He didn't look as though he needed anyone; rather,
here was a man who could take care of himself. That
thought was confirmed for her a moment later when,
motioning toward her two cameramen busily unload-
ing their equipment from the media van parked at the
curb, he drawled, "Still chasing ambulances, I see."

"That's hardly fair, Jake," Claire insisted defen-
sively, her chin lifting, her eyes flashing in a way that
reminded him of the sky over the Gulf, just before a
summer storm.

He felt like kicking himself. He hadn't meant to say
that. She was right: It wasn't a fair assessment of her
work. The six-part miniseries she had been the driving
force behind all those years ago had ultimately done
a lot of good. As a result of her efforts, there were
several places in the ghetto that were now free of
crime, where the citizens had taken back their neighborhoods, formed Watch programs, developed youth
centers, and cleaned up their streets, calling the police
to drug dealers and crack houses, pimps and prostitutes, mobsters and gangs. Jake's old neighborhood
was one such haven...too late for Isabel, of course.
But perhaps now, because of his wife's death and
Claire's dedication, there were young women living in
the barrio who could safely stop at the convenience
store on the way home.

"I'm sorry," he told her. "I thought I'd got over

what you did to me all those years ago. But I guess it somehow still has the power to wound, after all.''

"I never meant to hurt you, Jake. I never meant to betray your trust."

"No, maybe not," he conceded, his mouth twisting dryly. "But the fact remains that that's what you did. You lied to me all along about being a full-fledged reporter, and you used me, Claire, to launch your career. Now, I suppose you're here to put the life of that poor, dead woman inside that apartment there on display for your morbid viewers. Haven't you learned anything since last I saw you?''

"Haven't you?" she retorted hotly, stung. "It's safe these days to walk the streets in your old neighborhood. Or are you so far removed from the barrio now that you don't even know that?''

"No, I know it," he answered tersely, a muscle throbbing in his taut jaw.

"Then maybe you ought to ask yourself whether you're still angry at me because I put a tragic part of your life on film—or whether it's because by doing so, I managed to accomplish something you couldn't, despite your being a cop! Now, step aside and let me pass.''

For a moment, Jake had a wild, savage urge to grab her roughly instead, to fling her down in the grass, to shove up her skirt, and to make her beg him to take her. He thought he must be mad. The sweet, heady scent of her...gardenias, he remembered...wafted to his nostrils. He recalled the fragrance of it clinging to her smooth, satiny skin, saturating the silky, blond strands of her hair. He wanted to reach out and yank the pins from the classic, sophisticated French twist in which her hair was upswept, to see the shining mass tumbling around her shoulders, to feel it wrapped around his throat, his wrists.

Instead, he moved out of her way. Her head held high, Claire swept past him, her cheeks flushed heatedly, her eyes filled with both sparks and sorrow. It was the latter that suddenly made Jake feel very small and ashamed of himself. When he had been in anguish, she had offered him solace; but he had extended her only pain, not even his condolences.

"Claire, I'm...I'm sorry about your husband," Jake muttered contritely to her retreating back.

She paused in midstep, her graceful shoulders squaring. She did not glance back at him as she responded very quickly, "Thank you," then walked on. But a moment later, without warning, she suddenly stopped and resolutely pivoted on her heel, striding back toward him, her faced naked with determination and earnest emotion. "No...no, that won't do. I promised myself a long time ago that if by some chance I ever saw you again, I would never lie to you, that I would be completely honest with you. So I don't want you to imagine, like everyone else, that I'm a grieving widow. If I'm sad, it's for all the bright dreams of youth that are lost because you let the moment when you could have made them come true pass by, and you can never go back and recapture it. If I'm heartbroken, it's for all the lovers who hope for so much from each other, only to destroy piece by piece whatever it was they shared in the beginning, until in the end, there's nothing left but regret—and a profound sense of relief that it's finally over. As cruel and ironic as it sounds, in a way, you were one of the lucky ones, Jake. In your mind, Isabel will be forever on a pedestal. But Paul...well...he had fallen off so many times that I was planning to divorce him—and the night he was killed, he was kidnapping our daughter, Gillian. He was going to take her across the state line, to make sure I never saw her again. So don't be sorry for me, Jake—because if there's one person's pity that I don't want in this city, it's yours."

Then, without waiting for him to reply, Claire turned and walked swiftly on, leaving Jake standing there dumbly, staring after her—and thinking that no matter what she had just said, she was hurting deeply inside. Now, vividly, he recalled the sharp blade of pain that had lanced through him when he had heard some years back that she was going to marry her old boyfriend, Paul Langley. Jake had told himself then that it didn't matter that all he had apparently ever been to her was a means to an end—while Langley had been the man whom she had loved. When she had given birth to Langley's daughter, Jake had determinedly thrust from his mind the realization that, under different circumstances, the child could have been his own and Claire's. And when, six months ago, Langley had, while driving drunk, smashed his fancy Mercedes-Benz into a bridge, killing himself and leaving his seven-year-old daughter hospitalized in critical condition, Jake had somewhere deep within himself genuinely grieved for Claire. More than once, he had picked up a telephone receiver to call her then, only to hang up before he had finished dialing her number, feeling strangely like both a fool and a cad.

In the end, he had done nothing, deciding it was best to let sleeping dogs lie. Even now, he cursed himself as an idiot and a bastard for the terrible twinge of satisfaction he had felt at learning she had been going to divorce Langley, that her old boyfriend had not, after all, proved to be the man of her dreams. Hard on its heels, Jake now experienced guilt that he should have had such an uncharitable thought. Whether she wanted it or not, Claire merited his pity; whatever she had done in the past, she had not deserved a failed marriage and a dead husband.

"Just forget it, Jake!" he growled fiercely to himself, in an attempt to rid himself of his feelings of compassion toward her and his own self-reproach. "She's nothing to you now, and you sure as hell were never anything to her." Taking a final, unsteady drag off his cigarette, he dropped the butt onto the sidewalk, crushing it deliberately beneath his boot as he went to join Toussaint.

Thirteen

Gently Awful Stirrings

There is, one knows not what sweet mystery
about this sea, whose gently awful stirrings seem
to speak of some hidden soul beneath; like those
fabled undulations of the Ephesian sod over the
buried Evangelist St. John. And meet it is, that
over these sea pastures, wide-rolling watery
prairies and Potters' Fields of all four continents,
the waves should rise and fall, and ebb and flow
unceasingly; for here, millions of mixed shades
and shadows, drowned dreams, somnambulisms,
reveries; all that we call lives and souls, lie
dreaming, dreaming, still; tossing like slumber-
ers in their beds; the ever-rolling waves but
made so by their restlessness.

Moby Dick
—Herman Melville

Claire was startled and angry to realize she was shaking violently following her unexpected encounter with

Jake. Somehow in the past decade, she had managed to avoid running into him at a crime scene, finding out from uniformed officers if there were homicide detectives present or en route and the identities of same. That way, she had at least been prepared, had been able to gauge her timing so she had never inadvertently connected with Jake. She had been careless today, thinking it was doubtful he and Toussaint would be assigned to this case, since it probably did not involve a murder.

Under normal circumstances, the suicide or accidental overdose of a former stripper in a low-rent part of the city was unlikely to prove very newsworthy. Claire wouldn't even have been here at the apartment complex had not the debut of Demi Moore's new movie, in which the star played a stripper, made a segment on the profession locally seem like a natural, especially as there were constant battles in the city with regard to whether or not strip joints should be regulated or shut down entirely.

Claire had already interviewed both a young woman who was paying her way through college by working as a stripper, and a single mother who was just trying to make ends meet the same way. When Claire had learned the dead female at the apartment complex was a former stripper, she had thought film of the scene, accompanied by her voice-over, would make a good addition to her segment.

The last person she had ever expected to see at the apartment complex was Jake Seringo. Now, leaning against the trunk of a tree for support, she forced herself to take several long, deep breaths in an effort to try to regain her composure. She felt like a complete idiot. What in the hell had ever made her blurt out her personal life's story like that to Jake? No one except her attorney and Zoey, her best friend, knew the intimate details of her marriage to Paul Langley, the fact that she had been on the verge of divorcing him when he had cracked his car up on the White Strand Bridge.

Claire firmly believed it was in the best interests of all broadcast journalists to report the news—not to become stories themselves. On too many occasions, the results of the latter had proved detrimental to broadcast careers... Claire didn't want to wind up as one of the jokes on late-night TV or as a target for notorious radio talk-show hosts. As a widow, she was an object of sympathy. But if the true state of her marriage and the fact that Paul had been in the process of abducting their daughter the night he had been killed ever became known, Claire knew she would find herself an object of scandal instead...a newsmaker instead of a newsbreaker. More than one of her jealous, highly competitive colleagues would like to get their hands on a story that would cast her in a bad light so she would be booted out of Channel 4's door, making way for the ambitious, eager beavers following in her footsteps.

Now she wondered anxiously what Jake would do with the knowledge to which she had made him privy, whether or not he would use it to his advantage. Given the history between the two of them, another man in his place would see the inside information as a means of gaining revenge, and the Jake she had seen today had certainly appeared capable of that, not a man whom one would want to cross lightly. If it were only herself whom Claire had to worry about, she wouldn't be so upset. But while she knew she could endure anything that might be directed at her, she was also highly cognizant of the fact that her daughter, Gillian, could not.

Traumatized by her ordeal, Gillian was still in a fragile state. In his drunken stupor that night of the accident, Paul had shouted all kinds of terrible things at the poor, unsuspecting child, making her aware that he was stealing her away from her mother, and that since he was a lawyer, he would make sure Claire never saw Gillian again. Crying hysterically, the terrified child had pleaded desperately with her father to slow down, to let her out of the car. But her tearful entreaties had only enraged Paul all the more, causing him to accuse Gillian of siding with Claire against him. A few moments later, barreling along the road like a complete maniac, he had lost control of the vehicle, smashing into the side of the White Strand Bridge.

As long as she lived, Claire would never forget that dreadful night. She blamed herself for having earlier that day, during an argument over the telephone, told Paul she intended to divorce him. She had that morning, by accident, discovered he was having an affair— and in an attempt to save her troubled marriage, she had already forgiven him for two previous ones, and she and Paul had gone for counseling. But she knew now that he had never wanted to be helped, that, following his return to the city after obtaining his law degree, the only reason he had ever asked her to marry him was because her own career had been flourishing, and he had seen her as a status symbol, a showpiece to flash around at bar-association galas and assist him in getting high-powered, high-paying clients for his new law practice.

He had used her—in exactly the same way Jake thought she had used him.

"Claire…are you all right?" Nash inquired, concerned, as he and McGuinness came up the sidewalk, camera gear in hand.

"Yes, I…just suddenly felt a little sick for a moment, that's all…too much shrimp at lunch, I guess," she lied.

"You want some Tums?" McGuinness offered her the roll of antacid tablets he always carried in his pocket.

"No, thank you." Claire shook her head. "Let's just get on with this, and then I think I'll go on home afterward…maybe lie down for a while."

"Jeez, Claire, you don't suppose it's food poisoning or something, do you?" Nash grimaced at the notion.

"No, nothing like that. I probably just ate too much. Don't worry. I'll be fine."

But fine was far from how Claire felt when she drove home later to The Breakers, the secluded neighborhood into which she and Gillian had moved after Paul's death, Claire feeling a change of scenery would be best for them both. The house she had bought was wholly different from anything in which she had ever before lived, a sweeping, one-story contemporary at the isolated far end of the neighborhood, all white-wood siding and huge windows that afforded spectacular views of the Gulf. It was both an awesome and peaceful site, and like Claire, Gillian had fallen in love with it at first glance. Inside were big, airy, high-ceilinged rooms with pastel-painted walls that flowed seamlessly into one another, tied together by ceiling fans, white-woodwork trim, and dark, hardwood floors throughout. To her eclectic mixture of English, French, and Spanish furniture from the Victorian era, Claire had added overstuffed couches and chairs, creating a beautiful, tasteful blend that was both surprising and unique. Unlike Paul, she wanted her house to say something about herself— not about the decorator she might hire.

The high-tech furnishings Paul had brought to their marriage and that Claire had always despised, finding them cold and hideous, she had sold after his death, glad to be rid of them.

"You're home early today for a change, *señora*," the housekeeper, Ana Maria, observed brightly as Claire entered the kitchen from the garage. "Gillian will be so pleased."

"Where is she, Ana Maria?" Claire asked as she laid her keys, handbag, and portfolio down on the counter.

"On the beach…where else?" the housekeeper replied with a laugh as she kneaded dough for homemade bread. "She loves the sea, that one does."

After changing into an old, oversized shirt and a pair of leggings, Claire joined her daughter on the beach, the foamy breakers swirling around her ankles, the wet sand squishing between the toes of her bare feet as she strolled toward Gillian. Variously shaped, bright-colored, plastic buckets scattered around her, a small, plastic shovel in hand, Gillian sat on the beach, painstakingly building a sand castle. Lopsided and half crumbling away in places, the sand structure sprawled before the child like some kind of an odd mountain range, so it took Claire a moment to realize her daughter was attempting to create a replica of their house. She smiled tenderly, her heart filled with both love and pain as she watched Gillian at work. The child was so earnest, concentrating so hard on her task, her tongue caught between her teeth, her hands and legs grubby with damp sand. Beside her, their cat, Mr. Whiskers, lounged, the flick of his tail making it clear he was not at all happy about being so close to water.

"Want some help, sweetheart?" Claire queried.

"Mommy!" Gillian's lovely, little face broke into a rare smile. "You're home early! Yes, come see! Come see what I'm making! What do you think it is?"

"Well, if I had to guess, I'd say it's our house."

"That's right. See? Here's your bedroom, and here's mine, and this is Ana Maria's. Here." As Claire sat down in the sand, Gillian handed her one of the plastic buckets. "You can make the kitchen if you like. I'm afraid Mr. Whiskers hasn't been much help at all. He tried to use the great room as a potty box, so I'm quite cross with him at the moment." Gillian frowned reprovingly at the big, fat cat, who merely yawned in response, then began to wash one paw. "Emma was helping, but she had to go home for her piano lesson." Emma was Gillian's best friend and lived next door.

"Well, I'll help now." Claire began shoveling wet

sand into her bucket, packing it down firmly. "Did you practice for your own piano lesson?"

"Yes, twenty minutes. Ana Maria set the timer, so I'd know how long I had to practice."

"And how did your day at school go?"

"Okay," Gillian said, some of her cheerfulness dissipating. She hadn't been doing well in school even before the accident, and now she was having to make up for the lost time she had spent in the hospital, recovering. But since Paul was out of the picture permanently, her grades were slowly but steadily improving. Claire knew the constant arguments between her and Paul had put a strain on their child, making it difficult for her to concentrate on her homework. So although Claire now went out of her way to help and encourage her daughter where school was concerned, she tried not to push her too hard. Fortunately, Gillian attended a private academy that was not only understanding and sympathetic, but also willing to work with the child so she could realize her full potential as a student. "We made papier-mâché animals in art class today, and that was fun," Gillian continued, "and I got a B on the science test I took on Monday."

"Oh, honey, that's wonderful! I'm so proud of you!"

"You are?" Gillian's face brightened again.

"Of course. I think that calls for something special this evening—and I just happen to know Ana Maria has a key-lime pie put back in the freezer."

"Really?" Key-lime pie was Gillian's favorite dessert.

"Really." Claire nodded stoutly. "So what do you

say we brush ourselves off here, gather up all your toys, and go inside and ask Ana Maria to set that pie out to thaw so it will be ready for us to eat after supper?''

"That sounds real good, Mommy."

Together, Claire and Gillian collected all the various pails, small shovels, rakes, and hoes, and assorted sand molds, and loaded them into the big, red, plastic muck bucket in which the child stored her beach toys. Then, each of them grasping one of the rope handles on either side, they carried the bucket between them back to the house and put it away in the storage cabinet on the wooden deck. Claire turned on the outside faucet, and she and Gillian hosed off their feet before going inside, Mr. Whiskers dashing in ahead of them, obviously afraid his paws were in danger of being washed off, as well.

"Why don't we get your homework done early tonight, darling?" Claire suggested. "Then once we finish our pie after supper, we can play cards or a board game together."

"Gee, that would be wonderful, Mommy! I'll go get my backpack."

Claire sat down at the kitchen table, accepting gratefully the cup of hot, green tea Ana Maria handed her wordlessly. The housekeeper was a great believer in natural remedies, in herbs, teas, organically grown fruits and vegetables, and homemade foods like fresh bread. She also read the tabloids regularly—and, despite being a devout Catholic, believed at least half of what she read therein. More than once, Ana Maria had been known to point out the lights of a plane in the sky, mutter something darkly about a UFO, and cross herself hastily. But she was an excellent housekeeper, with an extremely kind heart, and Claire didn't know what she would do without her.

"Thank you for the tea, Ana Maria. It's just what I needed. Would you mind very much also taking that key-lime pie out of the freezer to thaw? Gillian got a B on her science test, so I thought we'd have a little celebration after supper."

"*Sí, señora.* I will do it right now. It is a good thing for the child to have a treat now and then, especially to reward her improvement in school. She is doing much better these days in many ways."

"Yes, I think so, too." Claire smiled gently as, having fetched the backpack, Gillian joined her at the kitchen table.

Unzipping the backpack, the child pulled forth her schoolbooks and assignment notebook. "I don't have a whole lot, Mommy, mostly English and math questions."

"Well, then, it shouldn't take us very long tonight. Have you got a sharp pencil? Good. All right, let's get started."

For the next hour, Claire worked with her child, more than once reaching out to lay her hand on Gillian's soft, blond hair, to reassure herself that her daughter was actually alive and sitting there beside her. She had come so close to losing her forever. So many times, Claire had asked herself what on earth had been in Paul's mind that awful night, that he should have been driving drunk, with Gillian in the car, bent on stealing her. As an attorney, he must have known the law, that he would never get away with such a thing.

As usual, Claire could only think Paul had made such a financial shambles of his law practice that he had just gone totally off the deep end and panicked when he had learned she intended to divorce him. Without Claire's income, he would have been in a very bad way financially, would probably have been forced to declare bankruptcy. But what had he done with all his money? Some of it had gone to pay bills, of course. However, there had been numerous large, cash withdrawals that still, six months later, remained unaccounted for. Had he spent all his funds on his extramarital affairs? Had he gambled? Used drugs?

Claire didn't know—and she wasn't sure how to find out, either. She could hire a private detective, of course. But what if the fact that she had done so leaked out somehow and her colleagues learned about it? Worse still, what if Paul had been up to something truly terrible? That was her real fear, the one that preyed constantly on her mind.

Jake would know how to investigate the matter.

The thought came, unbidden, into Claire's mind—only to be swiftly dismissed. She couldn't go to Jake. If he had ever felt anything for her at all, she had destroyed it with the miniseries she, Nash, and McGuinness had assembled all those years ago. Jake couldn't have made his contempt for her any plainer earlier today. Even if she had the courage to ask him for his help, he would probably just laugh in her face and tell her to get lost.

No, Jake Seringo was the last person in the world she could turn to.

He hadn't been able to stop thinking about her all day. Surely, that was a clear sign he was under too much stress on the job and was now losing his mind as a result. What else could it be? Jake asked himself, annoyed. Still, she haunted him. Claire Connelly, the ice queen of the media, the grieving widow who hadn't looked at another man since her husband had been killed. Except that she wasn't grieving at all—at least, not in the way everybody in the city supposed. What he couldn't do with *that* particular information, Jake told himself as he sipped the Cuba Libre he had just now finished mixing. It would serve her right to find herself plastered all over the six o'clock news— from the other side of the camera for a change!

But even as the thought occurred to him, Jake knew he would do nothing with what he had learned today. Such a vengeful act would be cruel and vindictive, and he wasn't that sort of a man. He wished he had never seen her again. Even now, he refused to admit to himself how many times he had watched her on television, his hand poised on his remote control, somehow unable to push the button that would change the channel and wipe her cool, lovely face from the screen. It was funny, he mused absently, how Isabel's countenance had grown blurred and dim in his mind over the years, while Claire's image had remained sharp and vivid.

"Why don't you just 'fess up, Jake?" he muttered heatedly to himself. "The truth is that you not only saw her again—but you wanted her just as much as you ever did before. After a decade, you'd think you would have got her out of your system. But somehow, she managed to get her hooks in you so deep that the barbs are still there, poisoning you so badly that she's in your blood like some kind of a fever, damn her!''

Thumping his drink down on the coffee table, Jake abruptly rose from the couch to wander outside onto the deck. There were no memories of Isabel here at the houseboat. Only Claire's face tormented him here. He remembered her standing at the deck's railing, gazing up at the summer stars in the night sky, the breeze off the Gulf rippling the strands of her hair and the dark waves below the houseboat, rocking the hull gently. She had momentarily lost her balance and stumbled into his arms, and he had made love to her here on the deck, laying her down on cushions he had pulled from the lounge chairs.

Despite himself, Jake wondered what Claire was doing now, at this very moment, if she thought of him as he did her. In his mind, he pictured her seated at her kitchen table, where they had so often sat together. He imagined a small replica of her—her daughter— beside her, homework spread over the table, blond heads bent close together. The fantasy he conjured up filled him with both yearning and pain. Isabel and his own child were long dead, and Jake was alone, without any family except for his father, who had retired a few years ago and stubbornly refused to budge from his tiny apartment in the barrio, where he played cards and swapped war stories with his old cronies all day. Jake dutifully visited him at least once a week. But much to his sorrow, without his mother and Isabel to bind them together, he and his father had drifted further and further apart over the passing years. Jake had moved up and on in the world. He wasn't stuck in the barrio and a time warp, the way his father and his father's friends were, dwelling on the old days and the old ways in Puerto Rico and Cuba, Mexico and Colombia.

Jake didn't even remember San Juan, where he had been born. In his mind, he was an American citizen and Spanish was a second language he often went for days without speaking. When talking to his father, he sometimes struggled to find the right words, causing the old man to grow angry and disgusted with him, to wave him away with a curt, impatient gesture.

He could, Jake realized, have married again, had children. But somehow in the past decade, there had been no one capable of taking Isabel's place, of blotting Claire's face from his memories. More than once over the years, he had experienced a strange, disturbing dream in which he stood again in the small, Catholic church where he and Isabel had been married and watched her walk slowly down the aisle toward him, then kneel beside him before the priest. But when at last the wedding ceremony had ended and he lifted her gossamer, white veil to kiss her, it was Claire's beautiful countenance that gazed back at him, Claire who had become his wife.

Once at a crime scene in one of the red-light districts, an unknown quadroon woman had approached him, her dark, liquid eyes hypnotic and filled with mystery, her low, smoky voice sending a chill up his spine as she had laid one hand on his arm and spoken.

"Your wife's spirit is restless," the quadroon had told him huskily. "She wants you to let her go, to know that all you blame yourself for is forgiven and forgotten. It was never your fault, but her own destiny. Yours lies elsewhere—and always has. You must learn to accept the will of the spirits, Detective, for it is like the sea…all-powerful. Do you know Shelley?" she had asked. Then, seeing his puzzled expression, she had quoted softly:

> "Full fathom five thy father lies;
> Of his bones are coral made:
> Those are pearls that were his eyes:
> Nothing of him that doth fade,
> But doth suffer a sea-change
> Into something rich and strange."

"What in the hell is all that supposed to mean?" Jake had questioned sharply, unsettled despite himself by the peculiarly compelling woman and her cryptic words.

"You will know when the time comes. There are dark forces at work around you, Detective. I can feel them…violent, unseen currents that are like a treacherous riptide, waiting to pull under the unsuspecting, the unwary. You are neither, but you must learn to have faith and put right the wrong. When the betrayer offers trust, believe in it, and you will not falter, for despite what you thought, the heart was ever constant."

"Look, I don't know who you are or what you're after," Jake had begun, only to be momentarily distracted by some discovery of the Crime Scene Unit. He could have sworn his attention had strayed for no more than an instant. Yet when he once more turned back to the enigmatic quadroon, she had disappeared, and he had not been able to locate a trace of her anywhere. When he had made inquiries of the officers at the crime scene about her, no one had remembered seeing her—although she had been a remarkable woman who would not have been easy to miss or forget—and she was nowhere to be found on the witness list that had been compiled at the scene. It was as though she had never existed.

Afterward, Toussaint had teased Jake about having seen a ghost. To this day, Jake half believed he had.

Now, sighing heavily, he took a last drag off the cigarette he had lit a few minutes ago, then pitched the butt into the water that lapped gently at the houseboat's hull. With a small hiss, the orange-glowing tip winked into darkness. Nothing more than flotsam now, the butt floated away in the silence broken only by the forlorn cry of some restless seabird winging its way across the night sky, casting a solitary shadow against the face of the moon.

Fourteen

The Vesture of Decay

Sit, Jessica: look, how the floor of heaven
Is thick inlaid with patines of bright gold:
There's not the smallest orb which thou behold'st
But in his motion like an angel sings,
Still quiring to the young-eyed cherubins.
Such harmony is in immortal souls;
But, whilst this muddy vesture of decay
Doth grossly close it in, we cannot hear it.

The Merchant of Venice
—William Shakespeare

No one observing the two people sitting in the beautiful conservatory of the Hampton family mansion would have suspected they were lovers—and had been for quite some time. Knowing what all hinged on the absolute secrecy of their illicit relationship, they had been inordinately careful to ensure that nobody had learned about their torrid affair, not even so much as a trusted servant.

Thus, puffing contently on one of his smuggled, Cuban cigars, Senator Malcolm Forsythe barely glanced up as his cousin-in-law, Lily D'Angelo, joined him at the large, white, wrought-iron table at which the Hampton family frequently ate breakfast, the bright sunlight and exotic plants that filled the conservatory making it a pleasant place to begin the day. It was not until the young, Hispanic maid had finished pouring hot coffee into a china cup for Lily and retreated from the conservatory that Forsythe, certain he would not be overheard, actually spoke.

"All is well, darling. The paper's buried the story on one of its back pages, and the medical examiner has ruled Traynor's death a suicide."

"But of course," Lily replied calmly, having expected nothing less. "Didn't I tell you no one would give a damn about what happened to an aging, former stripper turned cleaning woman? Such persons are the dregs of humanity, Malcolm. Nobody cares what becomes of them. They are meaningless in the grand scheme of the universe, mere flotsam on the waves. They make up a worldwide sea of pathetic human beings who will never amount to anything in their entire lives, living in poverty, filth, and disease, starving and dying, and in between breeding more of their wretched kind."

"But, darling, somebody has to do the world's dirty work, the shit jobs nobody else wants to undertake," Forsythe pointed out logically.

"But that's just it, Malcolm," Lily protested as she buttered a fresh croissant. "They're *not* doing them. They're doing drugs instead, committing crimes, spilling over their boundaries into elegant, old neighborhoods that have been in existence since before the War Between the States. Let me tell you, Malcolm, the world was much better off when people of that ilk knew their place—and kept to it! They don't want to haul themselves up from the muck. They want to drag the rest of us down into it! I just don't know why Ronnie can't understand that. My God. We'll both be lucky if there's any of the Hampton fortune left at the rate she's going...food banks, mission kitchens, youth centers, homeless shelters, hospital wings...there's just no end to her list of so-called good deeds. I tell you, she's another Eleanor Roosevelt.

"Good grief. Nobody in this country even knew black people existed until good, old Eleanor made them her personal crusade—and only look what came of that! Decades of welfare and food stamps funded by hardworking, taxpaying citizens, while uppity white trash and niggers sat at home on their fat, lazy asses, watching color TVs, driving Cadillacs all over town, and having another little bastard every nine months in order to make more money off the public dole! Well, thank God they aren't going to be able to do that anymore, at least, since welfare reform. When I get my hands on all of Grandmother's fortune, I'm going to buy an island someplace and tell the U.S. government to shove its stupid federal income tax and bleeding-heart social programs where the sun don't shine!"

"That's not going to be very practical, Lily, considering that I'm planning on being this country's president one of these days," Forsythe stated coolly, annoyed.

"Oh, of course, darling, you're right," Lily conceded, flashing him a practiced smile meant to soothe and placate. "How foolish and thoughtless of me. It's just that I get so angry sometimes at the unfairness of it all." She paused for a moment, then continued. "We've got to proceed even more carefully now, Malcolm. We can't afford a single slipup. Are you sure Ronnie doesn't suspect about us?" Lily's calculating, blue eyes narrowed thoughtfully.

"No, she hasn't a clue," Forsythe replied. "She's probably aware that there's someone else, even though I'm discreet. She's dropped a few hints, even threatened a couple of times to divorce me—the stupid bitch! As though I would ever tolerate anything that would prove detrimental to my political career. So far, however, duty compels her to turn a blind eye...to be the perfect political wife, don't you know? She doesn't want to besmirch the Hampton family name and upset that haughty old bat, Nadine."

"Yes, it's unbelievable, isn't it, how Grandmother should be so very proper? It's because she's only a Hampton by marriage. She wasn't born to it, so she's always felt as though she had to out-Hampton the Hamptons. Only Ronnie, Vannie, and I are purebloods, Hamptons through and through," Lily insisted, in her eyes a strange, far-off glow, on her lips a peculiar, little half smile.

"What're you talking about, Lily?" Forsythe asked, frowning as he tapped the ash from his cigar and folded up his newspaper. "I swear. Sometimes, I don't understand you at all. Ronnie and Vannie's mother was an Endicott, for crying out loud, and your father is a D'Angelo with a dubious Italian title!''

''Well, after we've carried out our little scheme, I won't have to worry about him anymore, will I? The crippled, old fool! I'll be Veronica Hampton Forsythe, your wife—and Lily D'Angelo will be dead and buried forever. Oh, Malcolm, it gives me such a thrill just thinking about it! Only imagine, darling! Soon...very soon now...we'll be together forever and ever, with the entire Hampton fortune at our disposal!'' Lily glanced at Forsythe in a way that made his sex grow hard.

As he had learned over the past months, there was nothing she wouldn't do in bed. He had never before known a female so uninhibited, who took such enjoyment in the act. Compared to her, his wife, Veronica, was a pale imitation. Yet it was impossible to tell the two women apart. Physically, ever since childhood, seeing Veronica, Vanessa, and Lily standing next to one another, a person would have said they were triplets rather than a pair of identical twins and a first cousin. As they had grown older, the remarkable resemblance among them had only been enhanced by subtle plastic surgery. Everything the twins had done, Lily had done, also. It was as though she had known all along that it would someday be important to her, as though for years she had planned to take Veronica's place.

The plot he and Lily had concocted was foolproof, Forsythe thought smugly. First, they would switch the twins, removing Vanessa from the Seabreeze Sanatorium where she had resided for the last ten years, and leaving Veronica there in her place. It would not matter if Veronica attempted to tell anyone the truth. No one would believe her, since to this very day, Vanessa continued to suffer her identity crisis, to believe herself her older twin sister. Once Vanessa was out of the sanatorium, it would then be a simple matter for Lily to switch places with her, passing herself off as Veronica. Afterward, each of the twins would, of course, suffer a fatal accident. That was why he and Lily had needed the dental files from Dr. Brett Deauville's office, so that if any suspicions arose, there would be no means of positively identifying any of the three women. They had never been fingerprinted, and without dental records, Forsythe and Lily could say anything, and people would be forced to accept their word.

It was perfect, Forsythe told himself again. He would get rid of Veronica and gain Lily in the process—and nobody would ever be any wiser. He would never wind up the subject of a messy divorce and scandal that would certainly ruin his political career, and he would keep the Hampton fortune that would come to Veronica at Nadine's death. Unfortunately, gambling, booze, marijuana and cocaine, whores, and a number of bad investments had depleted Forsythe's own riches considerably; and although that bastard Manolo Alvarez never wanted money, the favors he blackmailed the senator into performing for him frequently cost thousands of dollars' worth of bribes—all of which came out Forsythe's own pocket.

He would like to get rid of Alvarez, too. But so far,

the senator hadn't figured out how to accomplish the deed. People who crossed Alvarez had a nasty habit of disappearing, never to be seen alive again. Only a few years ago, Leon Gutierrez, the former Latino kingpin and whom everyone had thought invincible, had vanished without a trace. His body had never been found. It had been rumored in the city that he had been cut up into bloody chunks and tossed overboard into the Gulf, as chum for the sharks. No one had ever been arrested in the case—and Alvarez had stepped without challenge in Gutierrez's shoes. Forsythe would have liked to just hire somebody to bump Alvarez off. But he was smart enough to know he would only be exchanging one blackmailing devil for another. He would have to set the problem posed by Alvarez aside for the time being.

"When do you want to make the first switch, Lily?"

"We need to wait a little while, darling…just to be sure there won't be any connection made between Traynor's death, the missing dental files, and our plan."

"You're right, of course." From the sterling-silver coffeepot on the table, Malcolm poured more of the dark, rich, hot beverage into his china cup.

Of course, Lily thought superciliously. She was always right. She had never in her life known anyone even half so clever as herself—and certainly not Senator Malcolm Forsythe. What a pompous, arrogant fool he was! Another womanizing Jack Kennedy. If he ever became president, he would no doubt be banging women in the Oval Office. Bill Clinton's White-water and Travelgate scandals would be nothing compared to the kinds of messes Forsythe would create. He had already proved stupid enough to place himself in Manolo Alvarez's power, and if he ever got control of the Hampton fortune, he would fritter it away in the same manner as he had done much of his own wealth. Lily had never known a single man who didn't let sex make all his decisions for him, and she hadn't plotted and schemed for years to achieve her own ends, only to share all her hard-earned riches with Forsythe.

When the time came, she would get rid of him, too. But for now, she needed him. Reaching for the newspaper, she unfolded it to read the back-page article on Traynor's death. While she scanned the story's contents, Lily eased one feathery slipper off, then placed her foot on Forsythe's crotch, beginning to massage him under the table.

A few minutes later, he grabbed her foot and worked himself with it until he climaxed. Smiling with satisfaction, Lily folded the newspaper back up and poured more coffee into her cup. "Why, Malcolm, darling, you're all sweaty and flushed. Perhaps you should move your chair out of the morning sunlight."

Fifteen

Unexpected Encounter

I want to tell you now about the insects to whom God gave "sensual lust."…I am that insect, brother, and it is said of me especially. All we Karamazovs are such insects, and, angel as you are, that insect lives in you too, and will stir a tempest in your blood. Tempests, because sensual lust is a tempest—worst than a tempest! Beauty is a terrible and awful thing! It is terrible because it has not been fathomed, for God sets us nothing but riddles. Here the boundaries meet and all contradictions exist side by side.

The Brothers Karamazov
—Fëdor Mikhailovich Dostoevsky

It was as though seeing Jake once more had opened some hitherto closed and peculiar, unfathomable gate in reality that, after that day, would not be shut back up again. Whereas before, Claire's path had not once crossed his in the last ten years, now, as the weeks passed, it seemed she was as likely to run into him as not. Part of this, she knew, was because having once got that initial confrontation out of the way, she no longer took any precautions to avoid him. But the rest she could only attribute to some horribly ironic cosmic force that, had she been asked, she would have labeled kismet or karma. Sometimes she and Jake spoke to each other, and sometimes they said nothing. But always, Claire could feel between them the powerful, electric current of attraction that had drawn them together a decade ago.

It unnerved her to realize that despite everything, she was still consumed with lust, at least, for Jake. That other, deeper feelings for him also still lurked within her was something she refused to admit herself. Whatever she had once shared with Jake was long over, and as she learned from her marriage to Paul, there was no going back to try to recapture what had been lost. It was like a broken, clay pot from centuries of old; unearthed, its fragments could be carefully glued back together to re-create the whole—but still, the cracks showed always afterward. The pot was never again what it had once been.

Claire knew that. So she did not make the mistake of deluding herself into thinking there could ever again be anything between her and Jake, other than that strange, magnetic attraction and the grievous memories that made being in his presence like walking a tightrope, so she felt as though if she even once looked down, she would lose her balance and fall a very long way. His contempt for her was clear. She was as dead to him as though she had never been a part of his life, had never shared his bed. That this realization should even now have the power to wound her made Claire recognize how vulnerable she still was to him, so that whenever she saw him, she did her best to keep her distance from him both physically and mentally, outwardly coolly aloof, although she was a mass of tumultuous emotions inwardly.

Of the fact that she was not alone in her feelings, Claire remained painfully ignorant. She would have been astonished and disbelieving to learn Jake's own emotions toward her were equally ambivalent. But they were.

He never once saw her that he didn't feel as though he were being torn in half by the strong, turbulent feelings that gripped him. He wanted to make love to her again. He wanted to strangle her with his bare hands. Not even for Isabel had he ever experienced such violent, equivocal emotions, blowing hot and cold, so he felt like some bizarre but highly volatile mixture of fire and ice inside.

Now, wandering through the farmer's market at Lafitte's Quay, filling a brown paper sack with fresh fruits and vegetables, Jake stopped dead in his tracks as, at one of the courtyard tables of the Café Chantilly where he and Claire had used to come now and then for breakfast so long ago, he spied her. It was, he mused in some dim corner of his mind, almost as though he had wished her there. Then, abruptly, he realized she was not alone, and a hard, painful lump of emotion rose to lodge in his throat, nearly choking him.

The little girl was a miniature replica of Claire herself, an ethereal fairy child, all golden, silky hair and pale, luminescent skin touched with a delicate, rosy glow born of the sun's rays. He did not even need to ask to know this was Claire's daughter.

She might have been your daughter, too, Jake. The thought echoed achingly in his mind, so he closed his eyes for a moment from the deep and unexpected pain of it. Involuntarily, he leaned against a wooden display stall stacked high with oranges as, without warning, the loss of his own baby, the son who had never even had a chance to be born, swept over him with such force and anguish that it was as though the child had died anew instead of lying dead and buried in the grave these past ten years. For a horrible instant, time seemed to stop, and Jake felt frozen where he stood, as though he couldn't get his breath, were having a heart attack right there in the farmer's market. But then the awful, alarming sensation passed; air rushed into his lungs, and time slipped back into focus.

Rattled, he almost set his brown paper bag filled with produce down, thinking to come back and do his grocery shopping another day, that right now, all he wanted to do was to return to the houseboat and drown his sorrows in a quart of Captain Morgan. But he had long ago learned that down that road lay madness, that there was no real solace to be found in a bottle, only a slow, terrible slide into a dark and demon-filled abyss. Besides, even more powerful was the peculiar, driving compulsion he felt to sit with Claire again at a courtyard table at the Café Chantilly, to see her daughter—who might have been his own, as well.

Fumbling for his wallet, Jake paid for the contents of his brown paper sack, then strode toward the Café

Chantilly. The courtyard was bounded by a low, iron-lace railing, with gates set into each end. Swinging open one gate, he made his way through the crowded tables to the one occupied by Claire and her daughter. He felt like a total fool, unable to understand the irresistible force that seemed to have propelled him here and not knowing what in the hell he was even going to say. The two of them had their heads bent close together, smiling and whispering to each other, so they didn't notice him at first, and he almost turned away. But then Claire glanced up and saw him, her eyes widening and the smile dying on her lips, and it was too late then for Jake to make good his escape.

"I realize it's probably a real imposition, but do you mind if I sit down?" he asked, indicating the jam-packed courtyard. "There don't seem to be any other tables, and I don't know anybody else here."

At first, Jake thought Claire was going to refuse permission for him to join her. But then, finally, she said, "Of course, please do sit down. Gillian and I were just about to order lunch. Gillian is my daughter. This is Jake Seringo, honey," she told the child, whose big, blue eyes were filled with both wariness and curiosity. "He's a homicide detective on the police force."

"Are you going to arrest my mommy?" Gillian inquired soberly as he put his brown paper bag down on the brick courtyard and pulled out a chair.

"Now, why would I want to do that?" Jake's tone was deliberately light. He had not failed to observe the anxiety in Claire's eyes where her child was concerned.

Gillian shrugged in response to Jake's question. "I

don't know…but isn't that what detectives do? Arrest people?''

''Yes, but only people who've committed crimes— and I don't think your mommy's one of those.'' Reaching for one of the menus lying on the table, Jake opened it up and perused its contents. ''What're the two of you having?''

''Jambalaya,'' Gillian announced.

''That sounds good to me, too.'' Jake closed the menu and laid it aside. ''How about a stack of flour tortillas on the side? Do you like those?''

''Uh-huh.'' Gillian nodded. ''Ana Maria—she's our housekeeper—makes them for us at home a lot. I put butter on mine.''

''Then we'll be sure to get some of that, too,'' Jake said.

Despite herself and her confusion as to why Jake had joined them at the table, Claire had to admit he was good with Gillian, that he had somehow succeeded in drawing the child out. Usually, Gillian was shy and reticent around strangers, and she had grown even more so after the night of the car accident and Paul's death, clinging to her mother and trusting no one else but Ana Maria. But Jake seemed to have a knack for making conversation with the child. Claire decided that maybe learning how to deal with children had been part of his police training. But she also had to consider the fact that perhaps he was just naturally good with kids.

For the first time, she thought to wonder what kind of father he would have been had tragedy not intervened in his life, had his wife not been killed, had his baby had a chance to be born and to grow up. The boy would have been ten years old now. Claire remembered the long, frantic hours she had spent, praying desperately at St. Anthony Hospital the night of the car accident, when Paul had been killed and she had not known whether Gillian was going to live or die; and in that moment, her heart broke anew for Jake and his loss. It must surely be hard for him, sitting there talking to Gillian, knowing she was only a few years younger than his own son would have been had the boy survived.

But if so, nothing of this showed on Jake's face as he conversed easily with Gillian, who appeared fascinated by the fact that he was a real, live homicide detective. When the waitress finally arrived at their table, it was Jake who gave her the order, just as he would have if the three of them had been on an outing together. The realization brought back memories for Claire, of the times when she and Jake had come here a decade ago. More than once, they had sat at this same, exact table in the corner of the courtyard, where a mimosa tree grew, its wispy, pink flowers in full bloom, its brittle pods scattered heedlessly upon the brick floor.

"Claire, do you want more iced tea?" Jake queried, startling her from her reverie.

"What? Oh, yes…yes, please."

They waited until the waitress had poured more tea all around. Then Jake observed, "So, Claire, you must be very happy with your job at *Inside Story*. It's what you've dreamed of ever since college."

"You knew Mommy when she was in college?" Gillian's eyes widened with surprise.

"Well, not exactly," Jake explained, hesitating for

a moment before smoothly continuing. "I met her shortly after she'd graduated, when she first started to work for Channel Four."

"Jake was a...friend, sweetheart, just like Winston and Booker," Claire said hastily, not knowing what other questions her daughter might be tempted to ask and not wanting her to inadvertently touch on painful memories of that time, to reopen old wounds for Jake. "Yes, I'm very proud to be a part of *Inside Story*," Claire responded to Jake's question as the jambalaya arrived. "It's a great format—somewhat on the order of the old *P.M. Magazine*, really, so there's sometimes an opportunity for national exposure. As a result, I've been fortunate to have more than one of my stories seen all across the country."

"And yet despite that, you're still here in the city," Jake noted, buttering a steaming tortilla for Gillian before digging into his own food. "Why is that, Claire, I wonder? You could have gone anywhere, surely...to New York, Los Angeles, Washington, D.C....become another Barbara Walters or Diane Sawyer."

"I suppose the truth is that I just don't want that kind of a life, that sort of constant pressure and cut-throat competition," Claire answered slowly as she analyzed her reasons for never having moved to a larger market. "It's bad enough here. I like the fact that my schedule is fairly reasonable and predictable, so I'm able to be home most nights with Gillian, to take her to school most mornings. I like the fact that despite its being a city, this place still has something of a small-town atmosphere about it, that decisions can be reached here relatively swiftly, programs enacted, and goals accomplished. That's just not true for many of the major markets. Washington, D.C., especially, is a nightmare. I feel as though I can make a positive difference here—and that's important to me. It always has been.''

''Yeah…it's important to me, too. I guess we just have wholly dissimilar ideas as to how to go about that.'' Jake's words revealed he had not changed his mind about Claire's career or how she had employed it over the years.

''Each of us has to fight our own battles in our own ways, Jake,'' Claire pointed out quietly, ''to make the best decisions we can at the time we make them, and always, our actions are colored by our age and experience, our emotions and values. If we could see into the future, we'd know the answers to all our questions. But we can't, so we don't. We can only look back on the past and recognize what we'd do differently if we had it all to do over again. That's both the merit and the deficiency of hindsight. It highlights our failures rather than our triumphs. Hopefully, however, we learn from our past mistakes, grow into better human beings for them.''

Jake didn't know what to say to that. Deep down inside, he knew Claire was right, that she was even, in her own way, apologizing again to him for what had happened between them a decade ago. He felt it was petty and churlish of him to hold a grudge. Nevertheless, the memory of her betrayal still had the power to hurt him. If he were honest with himself, he knew he would admit that was because she had meant far more to him than he had ever permitted himself to acknowledge. Even now, he looked at her—and he wanted her still. But the past ten years had hardened him, wiped away his illusions about humankind, and left him a cynic. How could he ever trust her again? He didn't want to be only Claire's friend and not her lover—and it wasn't within him to be her lover without also being her friend. It seemed he was at an impasse where she was concerned.

"Usually, if you're even halfway intelligent, Claire, the main thing you learn from your past mistakes is not to make them again." Jake paused, then abruptly changed the subject. "Do you want some dessert, either one of you? How about some ice cream or something, Gillian, after we've finished our jambalaya?"

"I like key-lime pie," the child offered shyly, smiling in a sadly tentative way that did something funny to Jake's heartstrings.

For the first time in a very long while, a small face that was a mixture of his own and Isabel's filled his mind—the image he had envisioned for his son who had never had a chance to live. With difficulty, Jake fought for control of his emotions. "Key-lime pie it is, then. Claire, do you want some coffee with yours?"

"Yes, please. Coffee sounds wonderful."

So after the jambalaya and tortillas had been polished off, the three of them had pie all the way around, and Claire and Jake each had a cup of strong, black coffee, which they sipped in silence, lost in memories. As she consumed her dessert, Gillian chattered on like a little squirrel about nothing in particular, as though she sensed the tension between her mother and Jake, and sought instinctively to lessen the awkwardness.

At last, the waitress brought the bill to their table, and Jake reached for it over Claire's protests, insisting on taking care of it himself. "I'm not a poor boy from the barrio anymore, Claire,'' he asserted firmly, a serrated edge creeping into his voice. "And I'm not the kind of man who lets a woman pay his way, either. So don't let's argue about this. You shared your table. I'm buying lunch. That's all there is to it."

"Well, all right, since you put it that way—"

"I do."

"Thank you for lunch, Detective Seringo." Gillian spoke up quickly again, as though she had had a lot of practice at intervening to prevent a quarrel—a fact that disturbed Jake for both her sake and Claire's. He discovered he didn't much like thinking about what their lives had been like with Paul Langley in the picture, what had put the faint, purplish-blue, crescent shadows beneath Claire's sea-green eyes and the timidity and anxiety in Gillian's china-blue ones. "It was very nice meeting you."

"It was very nice meeting you, too, Gillian," Jake replied, smiling gently to reassure the child that an argument wasn't about to break out. "I hope I'll see you again sometime. Claire, I'm sure we'll run into each other again in the future."

"Yes, it certainly seems as though our paths have crossed several times lately," she observed as he pushed his chair back from the table and stood. "Goodbye, Jake. Thanks for lunch."

"Don't mention it. *Hasta la vista.*" Collecting his brown paper sack, Jake strode from the brick courtyard of the Café Chantilly, haunted by the strange, unsettling feeling that in doing so, he was somehow losing a wife and child all over again.

Sixteen

A Dreadful Trade

How fearful
And dizzy 'tis to cast one's eyes so low!
The crows and choughs that wing the midway air
Show scarce so gross as beetles; halfway down
Hangs one that gathers samphire, dreadful trade!

King Lear
—William Shakespeare

When she awoke, Veronica Hampton Forsythe felt groggy, disoriented, and sick to her stomach, as though she might vomit. At first, she thought she had suffered a terrible dream, a hideous nightmare. But then, much to her horror, as her eyes gradually began to focus, her mind to clear, she recognized that she was lying in the bed of her twin sister Vanessa's suite at the Seabreeze Sanatorium. Dazed and stricken, Veronica attempted to rise, her head swimming, her stomach protesting instantly by making its queasiness felt with a vengeance, so she was quickly forced back down into a fetal position, her arms locked around her cramping abdomen. With difficulty, she fought down the gorge that rose to her throat.

Drugged. She had been given some kind of drug, she realized dimly, suddenly seeing in her mind's eye a syringe coming at her, stabbing into her, piercing her skin. Vaguely, she remembered that she had stumbled after that, her surroundings seeming to spin around her all of a sudden, making her feel ill and faint. Someone had caught her...who? Malcolm? Lily? Yes, they had been with her. The three of them had come to the sanatorium to visit Vanessa. They often did that. On Vanessa's more lucid days, they would stay all afternoon or evening, playing bridge in her suite, so it seemed almost like old times, when they were younger and the curse that haunted the Hamptons had not yet stretched out its awful tentacles to victimize any of them, leaving tragedy in its wake.

There had been nothing different about this particular visit, Veronica reflected, except that in retrospect, she saw that neither Malcolm nor Lily had been themselves. Malcolm's temper had been short, his tone snappish. More than once, he had apologized and claimed to be exhausted and under stress from his constant travels between Washington, D.C., and home, the demands of his senatorial office. Lily, on the other hand, had seemed abnormally excited, as though keyed up by some wild, unknown secret. Her blue eyes had positively glowed, and her cheeks had been flushed, as though she had just completed a strenuous workout at the gym. Veronica herself had been subdued, her emotions conflicted. She both anticipated and dreaded her visits to her younger twin sister, never certain what kind of a mood Vanessa would be in. Invariably, even when things went well, Veronica left the sanatorium feeling as though half of her were remaining behind. She had felt Vanessa's absence keenly ever since the terrible accident that had claimed the life of her cousin Bruno and turned Vanessa into a vapid and confused stranger.

What had happened today? Veronica asked herself now, trying hard to think instead of to panic. Obviously, something horrible had occurred. Little by little, bits and pieces began to come back to her. Lily...*Lily* had wielded the syringe, on her face a malicious triumph and satisfaction that had been truly gruesome to witness. It had been as though Lily had suddenly gone insane, as berserk as a rabid dog as she had jammed the needle into Veronica's flesh. At the swift and wholly unexpected attack, Vanessa had leaped to her feet, her countenance draining of color, her mouth opening to scream. Malcolm had caught hold of her roughly, one big hand clamping over her nose and lips, momentarily suffocating her and silencing any sound she might have made. After a few minutes, Vanessa had gone limp in his arms.

Veronica recalled briefly staggering around the room herself before Lily had caught her and dragged her ruthlessly to Vanessa's bed. There, Lily had methodically began to strip off Veronica's clothes, smiling malevolently and speaking to her viciously all the while. What had Lily said?

"Don't struggle, Ronnie darling. The drug I've injected you with is extremely powerful, a mixture of several different chemicals. It's so new that it hasn't even really hit the market yet. Malcolm got it from a Latino gangster. All we really know about it is that it won't kill you, so you don't have to worry about that. You're just going on a little trip, Ronnie, that's all. And when you wake up, you'll have taken Vannie's place here at the sanatorium. You really shouldn't have threatened to divorce Malcolm, you know. He was sure you weren't really serious, that you wouldn't actually go so far as that, considering his career and the scandal it would have involved the Hamptons in. But we just couldn't take that chance. Did you know I was the one he was having the affair with all along? I often wondered about that...whether you were cleverer than we ever gave you credit for. But it doesn't matter now. You're never going to get out of here, Ronnie darling. We'll see to that, you know. And of course, eventually, we'll take care of Vannie, too. Then I'll be Veronica Hampton Forsythe, and Malcolm and I will have all the Hampton millions, and no one will ever know what really happened to either you or Vannie." Lily had paused after slipping off Veronica's blouse and then her bra, baring her to the waist.

"What beautiful breasts you have, Ronnie darling, not as good as my own, of course. But still, they're quite nice, truly."

Now, horror and nausea assailing her anew, Veronica recalled how she had lain helplessly on the bed, powerless to protest or move, while Lily had deliberately fondled her. To her utter shame and mortification, Veronica remembered that the effects of the potent, unknown drug had been such that she had been unable to prevent herself from responding to Lily's taunting caresses. How Lily had laughed at that, a low, throaty purr of spiteful glee.

"I was the one who set poor Vannie off that night of the accident, you know," Lily had continued, tugging off Veronica's sandals and silk stockings. "I told her all about the nasty, little skeleton in the Hampton family closet—and since she was sleeping with Bruno, was carrying his child, the shock of it proved far too much for her, just as I'd known it would, although dear Bruno actually took it much better than I'd thought he would. But that didn't matter, because in the end, it destroyed them both, just as I'd intended.

"Ever since childhood, I've always hated you and Vannie, both. You never did know that before, did you Ronnie darling? But it's true. The two of you were Hamptons, while I was only a D'Angelo, the child of an Italian playboy with a dubious title. It didn't matter that my mother had been a Hampton. Grandmother always loathed Mother. I used to wonder why—until I found out the answer. And then I knew everything...how I'd been cheated of my rightful place in the family. It wasn't fair. It just wasn't fair at all. So that's when I decided to get even, to get rid of you and Vannie, both—no matter what I had to do to accomplish it."

Finished removing Veronica's clothes, Lily had finally risen from the bed. "She's all yours now, Malcolm darling," she had said, smiling in a way that had sent a chill up Veronica's spine. "Why don't you give your dear wife something to remember you by, while I get Vannie properly dressed."

As she hazily recalled what had happened next, unable to fight off any longer the nausea that roiled inside her, Veronica abruptly lurched from the sanatorium bed and stumbled into the adjoining bathroom, doubling up over the toilet as the violent retching seized her.

Malcolm had raped her. Right there on Vanessa's bed, with Lily watching and laughing, goading him on. Veronica couldn't believe it, told herself again that, surely, she was suffering some grotesque nightmare. But it wasn't so.

After Malcolm had finished, Lily had bent over to whisper cruelly in Veronica's ear. ''What a pity it is you couldn't have any more children after the birth of your son, Drew, Ronnie darling, and how terribly sad for you that the poor, little boy was kidnapped and killed—because otherwise, Malcolm might not have wanted to be shed of you. But a senator needs a family, you know, an heir to carry on his name—and so I knew he wouldn't want you anymore if something were to happen to his only child.''

Now, as she clutched the cold, porcelain toilet bowl in Vanessa's bathroom, Veronica knew with horrific certainty that somehow Lily had been behind Drew's abduction and murder.

For a very long time afterward, Veronica huddled on the hard, tile, bathroom floor of her twin sister's suite in the sanatorium, shivering and weeping uncontrollably for her two-year-old son, dead and buried now for more than a decade. She had never got over his loss. After his tiny body had been discovered in a shallow grave, she had thrown herself into endless charity work, as though she could somehow single-handedly right all the wrongs in the world—for Drew's sake, for every mother's child's sake. And she had managed somehow to soldier on, to present to the world the courageous face and determinedly squared shoulders with which the Hamptons had always endured their tragedies.

Malcolm just couldn't know Lily had kidnapped and killed Drew—which meant he was as deceived by her as the rest of the Hampton family had been over the years. No doubt, when all her evil plans were finally brought completely to fruition, Lily intended somehow to be rid of him, as well. It would serve him right, Veronica thought now. He deserved whatever happened to him. She just couldn't believe she had been married to him for so many years—and yet had never truly known him at all, what he was capable of. He was as sick and deranged as Lily, gone mad with ambition and his quest for political glory.

Maybe it all had, in fact, started with Drew's abduction and murder, because Malcolm had never been the same after that. He had begun gambling and drinking, even taking drugs, Veronica had suspected, and she knew he had cheated on her more than once, finding comfort in the arms of whores when she herself had had none to offer. He hadn't realized how deeply she was grieving herself at having lost her son, her only child—and knowing she could never bring him back, was denied even the solace of ever having another baby. Yes, perhaps Drew's death had unhinged Malcolm's mind, had driven him to the lengths he had gone to be rid of her, to set Lily in her place.

After a great while, Veronica at last managed to haul herself upright, cringing at the dull ache between her thighs, where Malcolm had assaulted her. She was shocked to see her reflection in the mirror over the sink. Her hair, coiffed by Fabrizio himself just that morning, was now in a state of dishevelment resembling Vanessa's usual, vaguely unkempt style, and she was dressed in Vanessa's casual, comfortable clothes, designed without buttons or straps or anything else that might conceivably be used to inflict injury on one's self. Looking into the mirror was like seeing Vanessa staring back at her.

Her hands shaking, Veronica rinsed her mouth out in the sink, then went back into the bedroom and finally the small sitting room. The door leading to the corridor beyond was locked, and after a moment, she was compelled to ring for a nurse.

"Mrs....Netherfield." Having difficulty focusing her memory, Veronica read the woman's name off the badge pinned to her tidy, white uniform when she finally appeared in the doorway. "I have to talk to someone in authority at once. I...I know this is going to be incredible for you to believe, but while Mr. Forsythe and Ms. D'Angelo were here today, they administered some kind of a drug to me, then switched me with my twin sister, Vanessa. I'm Veronica Hampton Forsythe."

"Now, now, dearie," Mrs. Netherfield said calmly, "you're just having one of your bad days, is all. If I've heard that story once, I've heard it a thousand times over the years. You're Vanessa Hampton, dearie, and you've been a patient here at Seabreeze

Sanatorium for the past decade. You had a bad accident right before you came here, and you've been confused ever since. So you come on, now. Let's get you into bed, and then I'll have one of the orderlies bring you a nice tray from the kitchen. You missed supper, but Ms. D'Angelo said you were tired and not feeling well, that you'd been worse than usual this afternoon, and just to let you sleep.''

"No…no, you don't understand, Mrs. Netherfield. Ms. D'Angelo is quite insane, and switching me with my twin sister is part of some hideous plot she has to get rid of us both, so she can get her hands on all of our grandmother's money. You must let me speak to Dr. Logan at once.'' Veronica realized with dismay that her voice had risen shrilly, that she was trembling all over, and that she probably appeared as crazy as her twin sister in one of her distraught, irrational spells. With difficulty, she struggled for composure.

"Now, Vanessa.'' The nurse's tone had grown stern. "I don't want to hear any more of that nonsense. You get right into your bed, or else I'm afraid I'll be forced to have you sedated.''

Of course, Veronica recognized now, her twin sister was on a daily regimen of drugs to keep her docile, since she was prone to the bewildered outbursts, one of which the nurse obviously believed was taking place at this moment. More than once over the years, Vanessa had also attempted to run away from the sanatorium. When captured, she had been unable to explain where she had been going.

All at once, Veronica grasped the utter hopelessness of her situation. Lily had been right: No one at the sanatorium was going to be convinced by her story. It was just too ludicrous to be believed. Veronica had to admit to herself that if she hadn't known better, even *she* wouldn't have thought it the truth; it sounded so crazy and far-fetched. No, until she could figure out some means of escape, she was stuck here at the sanatorium. She would have to do everything that was asked of her, she told herself now, so she could attempt to avoid being medicated with drugs that would undoubtedly leave her mind clouded and her body lethargic.

After a moment, turning away from Mrs. Netherfield, Veronica walked dully back into the bedroom and forced herself to get into the bed where Malcolm had so brutally raped her. She could have sworn she heard Lily's wicked laughter ringing in her ears—and at that, the first of the doubts that were to plague her in the coming days with regard to her own sanity surfaced, leaving her to wonder if perhaps she weren't really Vanessa Hampton, after all, living in a nightmare in her own mind and only imagining she were Veronica Hampton Forsythe, cruelly drugged and deliberately left here by her husband and her cousin.

"Claire, the bad news is that I'm afraid we're going to have to take new X rays this appointment, even though you and Gillian weren't originally scheduled for that," Dr. Brett Deauville explained, his demeanor a trifle embarrassed. "The good news is that I'm not going to charge you for them as, unfortunately, my office is in the rather disconcerting position of having mislaid both your files, which of course had all the

X rays of your teeth in them and your dental histories.''

"Well, I suppose such things happen in even the best of offices, Brett," Claire said, smiling teasingly as she glanced up from the dental chair at her one-time blind date who had become not only her dentist, but also a friend. "But don't worry. I won't tell any of your other patients or broadcast it on *Inside Story*.''

"No, I didn't think you would. Some of my other patients already know, anyway, since their files have disappeared, too. It's the damnedest thing, Claire. We've torn this whole office apart, and we just can't seem to find those missing files anywhere. I'm beginning to think they were accidentally thrown away or something...maybe knocked off one of the receptionists' desks into a garbage can, and nobody ever noticed it. The cleaning lady wouldn't have known any better, would probably just have thought they were old files we were dumping. I'd ask her about it, but unfortunately, she didn't turn up for work one week, and when I phoned the agency to complain, the woman who owns it got all upset and called the police to make a missing person's report. Turned out that my cleaning lady had gone home one night and killed herself...OD'd or something.''

"Oh, yes, I know the case you're talking about." Claire was surprised at this unexpected connection between her dentist and her work. "Her name was Patsy Traynor, and she was a former stripper, down on her luck. I did a short piece on her as part of a segment on real-life strippers. There was an interest because of the new Demi Moore film.''

"Yes, that's the woman—except that, believe me, I had no idea what Ms. Traynor had done for a living before becoming a cleaning lady. But you know how it is these days…good help is just so hard to find. At any rate, those missing files have sure created havoc for me, what with my having to tell various patients their charts have taken a hike. Sorry yours had to be one of them. Be that as it may, one of my hygienists will be in shortly to take the new X rays of your teeth, and then I'll be back in myself to check on you. In the meantime, Gillian's right next door."

"I know. I can hear her." Claire smiled.

Brett Deauville's office had an interesting interior design. It was constructed so that the examination rooms were on three sides of the perimeter. They all faced ceiling-to-floor windows that looked out on a small, stucco-walled garden filled with bird feeders, which Brett's assistants kept well supplied with seed to attract birds. Birdhouses also hung from the branches of the ornamental trees in the garden, so there was always constant activity in the garden to entertain patients. The examination rooms themselves were separated by walls that extended only slightly beyond the full length of the dental chairs, so that while patients had privacy, the rooms were actually open to one another at the windows end. That was why Claire could hear Gillian chatting to herself and singing along with the piped-in music as the child waited to have her teeth examined.

"She sounds pretty happy today," Brett observed quietly. "I take it that she's doing a lot better, then?"

"Yes, much." Claire nodded. "It was hard for her,

after the accident...hard for both of us, actually. It was as though Paul had that night suddenly turned out to be...well, a complete stranger to us, Brett, someone whom we'd never really known, if that makes any sense to you. And because he was killed in the crash, we didn't have a chance to come to terms with that side of Paul. So we've just had to deal with everything as best we could under the circumstances. And of course, since Gillian was nearly killed herself in the accident, she's had a long recovery physically, too. But she was able to go back to school this past spring, and I've been working with her in the evenings to try to help her get all caught up academically.''

"Good. I'm glad to know you're both doing well, Claire. I'll return shortly."

After Brett had gone, Claire thought to herself how pleasant he was, how nice it was that at least one of the blind dates her mother had arranged for her over the years had turned out so well—although not in the way her mother had hoped. But if Claire had been interested, she could perhaps have married Brett. Instead, she had chosen to renew her relationship with Paul Langley and eventually to wed him—with ultimately disastrous results. She sighed heavily. Given what had happened with Paul and Jake both, it would seem she didn't have a very good track record where men were concerned, that she lacked judgment when it came to her personal relationships with them.

Claire thought that perhaps she would not try again. She was thirty-one years old. She had Gillian and a flourishing career.

It was enough, she told herself. There were worse

things than being alone—as anyone who had ever been in an unhappy relationship knew.

Vanessa Hampton was not only horribly bewildered, but also utterly miserable and thoroughly frightened. She wasn't even marginally safe anymore. That was the one thing that was clear and paramount in her mind.

Lily was here—and wherever Lily was, Vanessa was not safe.

Lily wanted to destroy her—the way that she had destroyed Bruno. Lily had told them both terrible things...things that had caused Vanessa to run away so she could escape from the sound of Lily's malicious voice, of Lily's malevolent laughter. Tortured by both, Vanessa had pressed her foot down on the accelerator of the Ferrari harder and harder, so the car had gone faster and faster. But still, she hadn't been able to get away. Even Bruno's voice, pleading desperately with her to slow down, had not been able to drown out the echo of Lily's laughter in Vanessa's ears. The awful sound had got louder and louder, until it had turned into a long, hideous shriek as the vehicle had skidded on the pavement, then smashed into the guardrail.

Having failed to buckle her seat belt, Vanessa had been thrown clear of the Ferrari before it had plunged over the side of the road to tumble down the steep embankment beyond, exploding on impact, lighting up the night sky in a way that had made Vanessa think dimly of the fires of hell before she had lost consciousness and known nothing more until waking up in a hospital in Florence to learn that Bruno had been killed.

All this was now, at long last, coming back to her in bits and pieces, flashes of memory that confused and unsettled her, making her increasingly frantic. She kept trying to tell herself she wasn't Vanessa Hampton, that she was Veronica Hampton Forsythe, and that everything that had occurred in Italy had really happened to her younger twin sister, who was shut up in the Seabreeze Sanatorium.

But now dreadful things were taking place again.

Every night, Malcolm, her husband, would remind her she was ill and would inform her that it was time for her medicine. Then he would prepare a syringe full of some unknown drug and inject her with it. Afterward, while Vanessa lay dazed and helpless, Malcolm and Lily would make love beside her on the bed and talk about their plans to do away with her after they had taken care of her twin sister.

The next day, ill and petrified, Vanessa would keep to her suite, frantically plotting and planning, knowing only that she had to get away from Lily, as she had escaped from her once before. She had to attempt to gather her wits, to think what she should do, Vanessa told herself now. She had been relatively safe at the Seabreeze Hotel on the Riviera, daring to check herself out only periodically to search for Bruno. Somehow she must get herself back there. Even now, Bruno might be waiting there for her. Malcolm and Lily had gone out for the day. Vanessa knew that because before leaving, they had come to her suite—not with a syringe, but with a paper cup in which there had been two capsules, drugs she had recognized that she had often received at the sanatorium to make her sleep. As she had on several occasions to fool Nurse Netherfield, Vanessa had only pretended to swallow the capsules. Then, after Malcolm and Lily had left, she had spit them out and flushed them down the toilet so they wouldn't be discovered later on.

Now, forcing herself to keep moving, despite how dazed and sick to her stomach she felt, Vanessa slowly dressed herself, fumbling with buttons long unfamiliar now to her fingers. Her hands trembled so badly as she combed her hair and applied makeup that she made a crimson slash of her mouth and had to wash off the lipstick and try again. But finally, she felt as though she looked all right.

She tried the bedroom door, unsurprised to discover that it was locked. But that posed little difficulty. After ten years at the sanatorium and numerous attempts at escape in order to find Bruno, Vanessa had grown adept at picking door locks. Fetching a hairpin from the bathroom, she set to work. Once she was free, she crept downstairs on stockinged feet, carrying her shoes. Malcolm and Lily had disconnected the telephone in her suite so it was useless. But there was bound to be a telephone she could use somewhere else in this place, to call a taxi. Vanessa only hoped she wouldn't have to explain to the desk clerk at the Seabreeze Hotel why she didn't have any luggage.

As Jake had surmised, Patsy Traynor's supposed boyfriend, Dean, the unknown photographer, had proved as elusive as his last name and could not be located.

"He was probably never anything more than a figment of her imagination, just exactly like you originally suspected, Jake," Toussaint declared as he withdrew from his desk a jelly doughnut that he had saved from breakfast. Carefully, he removed it from the paper napkin in which he had wrapped it earlier and bit into it, chewing slowly.

"Yeah, you're probably right, Remy," Jake agreed, grimacing as, picking up his heavy, ceramic mug, he sipped the thick, black liquid that passed for coffee in the squad room. "But still, I can't get out of my mind the fact that there's something wrong somewhere with regard to Traynor's death."

"Uh-huh…you and me both, partner. But the M.E. has spoken. The verdict was suicide, and officially, the case is now closed. And if Captain Nichols finds out you and I have been wasting our time, trying to track down a nonexistent photographer, he's going to be pissed as hell at us both."

"Yeah, I know all that. But when was the last time we let a little something like that stop us when instinct told us that there was more to a case than what appeared on the surface?"

"Never. But…well, look, Jake. What if it's just that we've both been on the job for so long now that we've grown suspicious of everyone and everything? What if there simply *isn't* any more to Traynor's death than what the M.E. decided?"

"You don't believe that, Remy—not in your heart, anyway—and neither do I. I just don't know where else to look to try to uncover any new evidence with which to get the case reopened."

Toussaint sighed heavily. "It happens, Jake. Sometimes, no matter how much we hate even the very idea, the bad guys get away.''

Left unspoken, but echoing in both Jake's and Toussaint's minds, were the words: *Just like they did after murdering Isabel.*

"Ronnie?" Vanessa spoke tentatively after Nurse Netherfield had exited the suite at the sanatorium and closed the door behind her. "Ronnie, is that you? Is that *really* you? I have to know...I have to be *sure*— because Lily's so very clever.... You could be *her*—"

"No...no, Vannie, I'm not." Slowly, Veronica rose from the couch in the sitting room, her heart pounding with sudden excitement at her younger twin sister's unexpected reappearance. For days now, Veronica had attempted to think of a way to free herself from the sanatorium, from the nightmare that her life had become. But so far, she had failed, unable to convince anyone of her true identity and often unsuccessful at avoiding being compelled to take the drugs that were a part of Vanessa's daily regimen at the sanatorium. "Vannie, it *is* me...Ronnie. I'm not Lily, I swear. She's the reason why I'm in here, in your place. She and Malcolm, they switched us. Do you remember that, Vannie? Is that why you've come back here?"

"I—I don't know. I'm—I'm so confused. Frightening things have been...happening to me lately. Or maybe I only dreamed them. I'm not sure. I only know I'm not safe where I am now, that I'm afraid...so afraid of Lily. She's evil...my evil twin. She wants to destroy me. That's why I have to know—to be certain—you're my good twin...."

"I am, Vannie. I'm your *only* twin."

"No." Vanessa shook her head vigorously in denial. "No, you're not. That's why I have to know for *sure*. Prove to me you're my good twin, Ronnie, and then I'll know I'm safe again—or at least, as safe as I can ever be anywhere, so long as Lily exists in this world. She's a descending angel, you know, who's sworn vengeance on us for the sins of our fathers and mothers...."

"What sins, Vannie? What're you talking about?" Veronica asked, puzzled but thinking that somehow this must be the key to Lily's madness. Or maybe it was only a product of Vanessa's own, some wild imagining of her frail, befuddled mind.

"If you don't know, then I can't tell you, Ronnie," Vanessa said. "It would destroy you, the same way it almost destroyed me. It killed Bruno, you know, and now, he's a ghost, wandering around in search of me, to warn me. I hear him all the time, telling me to slow down. Maybe you *do* know all this, in fact—and that's why you can't prove to me that you're my good twin—" Vanessa's voice had risen to a hysterical level that was alarming and was sure to attract Nurse Netherfield's attention if not quieted right away.

"Yes, I *can* prove it," Veronica insisted quickly, realizing that for all that her twin sister appeared suddenly to have recalled who she was, she was still extremely mixed up and largely out of touch with reality. "Double swear. Double swear, Vannie. Do you remember?" Veronica held up two fingers. "It was our special secret, known only to us and nobody else. We never shared it, not even with Lily. Never. That way, no matter how much she looked like us, she could never pass herself off as one of us, unbeknown to the other.'' Softly, in a singsong voice, as Vanessa pressed two fingers against her own, Veronica began to chant their childhood pledge:

> ''Spirits' brew, boil and bubble,
> Cauldron full of toil and trouble,
> Curse me if I'm not your double.

> ''Voodoo night, as black as sin,
> Into a doll, just stick a pin,
> And curse me if I'm not your twin.''

''You're her...you're Ronnie.'' Vanessa's face and tone both were filled with enormous relief. ''Lily never did know that poem we made up together. It was our secret—ours alone—just like you said. Oh, Ronnie, what're we going to do?''

''Don't worry, Vannie. You're safe now, here at the sanatorium. Just remember that, and don't try to run away from here anymore.''

''I was only trying to find Bruno...to apologize for running away that night, for not being stronger. It wasn't his fault, what happened between us. He didn't know the truth any more than I did. I wanted him to know I understood that, that I never blamed him.''

''Bruno's dead, Vannie,'' Veronica reminded her twin sister gently. ''He's been dead a very long time now.''

''Yes, that's what that stern-faced, fat woman in the white cap keeps telling me. I try to remember...only, it's so hard sometimes that my head aches—and then I know I don't really want to think about anything that occurred that dreadful night. It's easier that way. And then sometimes when I *do* recall, I know it never would have taken place at all if I had been you instead of me. You were always the strong one of us, Ronnie. You would have known what to do that night. You would have found some means of shutting Lily up instead of running away, the way I did. And when I think of that, I pretend it *was* you that night, and then I get all mixed up in my mind...because it just *hurts* me so bad to remember...."

"I know, Vannie. I know. Don't think about it anymore now. Get undressed. We'll have to change clothes so I can get back to the house right away, before Malcolm and Lily find out you're gone."

"They won't be back for a while yet. They went to some luncheon...something to do with politics, I think. They locked me in my room, but I used a hairpin to open the door. I was real careful. Nobody saw me leave. I called a taxi to bring me here. I just had to get away. I wasn't safe there, in that house to which they took me."

Tears started in Veronica's eyes. She reached out and took Vanessa's hands in hers, squeezing them tightly. "Oh, Vannie. I'm sorry...so very sorry. But I promise you this. They'll be punished for what they've done...both of them! I swear it! I swear it with all my heart that I won't rest until somehow, someway, they've both been made to pay!"

Seventeen

The Seabreeze Sanatorium

About, about, in reel and rout
The death fires danced at night.

The Ancient Mariner
—Samuel Taylor Coleridge

The fire that had swept through the Seabreeze Sanatorium, ravaging one wing, resulting in its now being a pile of blackened, still-smoking, wet debris, and killing at least three people, had definitely been deliberately set, Jake was informed by one of the officers from Arson. As nearly as could be determined, a mixture of flammable chemicals from one of the storerooms had been used to start the blaze, and the wing had fallen prey to the flames because the sanatorium's sprinkler system had been damaged beforehand.

"Was it a professional job?" Jake asked as he examined the charred ruins.

Deavers, the arson expert, shook his head. "It's

hard to know at this point. There are some aspects about this whole case that are just downright troubling. On the one hand, it looks as though somebody in a hurry simply splashed the chemicals every which way, which generally indicates an amateur. On the other hand, whoever did it had the foresight to ensure that the sprinkler system wouldn't be operational—at least, not in this particular wing. A pro would have thought of that...an amateur, maybe, but then again, maybe not.''

''Any ideas as to a motive?''

''I might be able to help with that,'' Toussaint declared as he joined the two men. ''Dr. Logan, the head of the sanatorium, has informed me that one of the patients in this wing was something of a firebug... suspected of burning up his parents twenty years ago for the inheritance—although nothing was ever proved against him. But if he somehow managed to escape last night, he could conceivably have been capable of torching the place and might have done so. He's one of the missing patients, by the way.''

''One of the crispies, maybe,'' Jake observed as he stepped gingerly through the cinders and rubble of the wing. ''We're up to three of them so far and still taking a body count.''

''A lunatic pyromaniac could fit the profile of the arsonist we may be dealing with here,'' Deavers confirmed. ''That would explain the absence of any particular pattern to the chemicals, as well as the haphazard sabotage of the sprinkler system.''

''Great,'' Jake growled. ''Our best suspect at the moment is a crazed inmate who may have killed not only himself in the blaze, but also the rest of those patients in this wing. I thought the people being treated here weren't supposed to be dangerous.''

"Yeah, well, I guess that if you've got enough money, you can get the right psychiatrists to sign off on just about anything.'' Toussaint grimaced wryly. "Not that Oxbridge—that's our firebug inmate—was ever considered a menace. Apparently, he was on a regimen of medications that kept him pretty mellow, and of course, he wasn't given access to anything with which he might have ignited a fire.''

"Anybody else have a motive?'' Jake inquired.

"Not that we've been able to determine right offhand,'' Toussaint replied. "However, it's entirely possible, I suppose, that Dr. Logan is addicted to gambling, up to his ears in debt, owes a bundle to a loan shark who isn't too happy about not being paid, and decided to solve all his problems by torching his sanatorium. Still, I wouldn't count on it. A place like this...it ain't cheap, Jake, no way. They don't take just anybody here...got to have a family or friends with a hefty bank account to get a room in this joint. And Dr. Logan strikes me as the kind who's got tax lawyers, stockbrokers, accountants, and financial planners out the ying-yang. Probably lives over in Bayview and has a Porsche, a Mercedes, and a speedboat sitting in his three-car garage.''

Jake sighed as he considered the fact that this was undoubtedly the truth. "Well, what about the rest of the staff? Maybe one of them just got sick and tired of taking care of rich nutcases all day...decided to reduce their number accordingly.''

"Yeah, we're running background checks on all of them," Toussaint reported, "and all the patients, too. Could be that one of the latter has a relative who isn't too happy about continuing support for an insane member of the family. But meanwhile, our best bet still looks to be the missing Oxbridge. The water in his parents' house was shut off at the main, by the way, when the place went up in smoke twenty years ago. Could be the same type of MO."

"It's certainly similar," Deavers agreed, "an attempt to prevent water from being readily available to fight the blaze. The only reason the flames didn't spread here, didn't do even more damage, was because the fire extinguishers were still in place. Our inmate Oxbridge might not have thought about that. It would be consistent with the fact that twenty years ago, there wasn't the market for residential smoke alarms and fire extinguishers that there is today. His parents probably didn't have them in the house."

"Okay, so we have the M.E. concentrate on finding out if one of the crispies is Oxbridge—or whether we have a lunatic pyromaniac on the loose." Jake scribbled some more notes to himself in his pad, then flipped it closed and slipped it and his pen into his suit jacket.

"One more thing," Toussaint added, "Captain Nichols wants this investigation run as quietly and efficiently as possible...no leaks to the media."

"Oh? Not that I personally plan on talking to the media, but why's the lid being clamped down tight on this one?" Jake queried, curious.

"One of the patients unaccounted for is Vanessa Hampton."

They had murdered her younger twin sister. Veronica Hampton Forsythe knew that as surely as she knew her own name. Somehow, someway, Malcolm and Lily had killed Vanessa. They had visited the sanatorium earlier last evening—and then, afterward, the building had caught fire. In her mind, Veronica imagined how they had carried out the crime, Lily distracting the guard from the security cameras, while Malcolm had let Oxbridge out of his suite and into the storeroom in Vanessa's wing. No doubt Lily had some time ago managed to filch a set of keys to all the rooms at the sanatorium. Ever since childhood, she had always stolen things; in their teens, she had got a thrill out of shoplifting, despite her having had more than one credit card and the ability to pay for the items she had taken.

And poor Billy Oxbridge. He, too, had died in the fire—just as Vanessa had. What a perfect scapegoat he had been for Malcolm and Lily. They had known all about his history, of course, why he was at the Seabreeze Sanatorium. Over the years, Vanessa had learned the details of the lives of all her fellow inmates—although she had referred to them as other "guests" at the "hotel." Oxbridge had been one of her favorites, and she had talked about him on many occasions. It wouldn't have been all that hard for Malcolm himself to have poured the chemicals around Vanessa's wing of the sanatorium, damaged the sprinkler system, and then to have unlocked Oxbridge's door and given him a book of matches or a lighter, anything with which to start a fire in the storeroom. No doubt if that plan had failed, Malcolm and Lily had had another wicked scheme up their sleeves, anything to avoid having suspicion fall upon themselves.

Even Veronica herself, had she not known better, would have been fooled by the act they were putting on for the two homicide detectives who had come to the Hampton family mansion to inform them that Vanessa had been identified as one of the corpses in the aftermath of the blaze at the sanatorium. Apparently, she had not been as badly burned as some of the other patients who had died, and Dr. Logan had made the identification, based on the location of her body and the pieces of jewelry she had been wearing at the time of her death.

Lily was weeping copious crocodile tears in the wing chair in which she sat in the elegant living room of the family mansion. Malcolm himself was seated next to Veronica on the couch, patting her arm comfortingly.

Veronica wanted to scream, to leap to her feet, and to expose their terrible charade. But then Malcolm and Lily would know she was alive, that it really *was* Vanessa who had been killed in the fire—because of course, they believed it had been her, Veronica, who had died. They didn't know Vanessa had made her way back to the sanatorium, to switch places once more with her older twin sister. And despite her certainty that Malcolm and Lily had murdered Vanessa, Veronica knew she had no means of proving that— worse, that if she made such a seemingly wild accusation, with no evidence whatsoever of its veracity, she would be playing right into the hands of Malcolm and Lily, providing them with a reason to declare that she had lost her mind and to commit her to some institution—where a fate like the one Vanessa had suffered last night would surely befall her.

No, she must be patient, Veronica told herself sternly; she must bide her time and wait. She must be cleverer than Malcolm and Lily if she were to get even with them. Still, Veronica's nerves were so on edge with fear, anger, and sorrow that after a moment, she realized she was digging her fingernails so hard into her palms that she had drawn blood. With great effort, she forced herself to take several deep breaths, to uncurl her fingers. Hot tears stung her eyes. But that was all right, she thought. It would have been natural, under the circumstances, for Vanessa to cry for her. Still, Veronica blinked back her tears of anguish determinedly, striving for the same stoic expression that her grandmother displayed.

"We're terribly sorry for your loss, Mrs. Hampton," Jake reiterated to the elderly woman, who had so far throughout the interview demonstrated little, if any, emotion, instead sitting so straight and still in her chair that he half thought she must be carved from stone.

Now, however, she inclined her stylishly coiffed, grey-streaked head ever so slightly in acknowledgment of his words. "Thank you, Detective Seringo. We appreciate the kindness you and Mr. Toussaint have demonstrated in delivering the news to us about Vanessa's pitiful, untimely death. It cannot be an easy chore for you, being the bearer of such sad tidings to people, informing them of their grievous loss. However, as I'm sure you are aware, the Hamptons have faced many trials and tragedies through the years, and we will endure this one, as well. I feel certain Dr. Logan and his entire staff at the Seabreeze Sanatorium had taken every precaution to ensure that Mr. Oxbridge was properly medicated and secured. If, as you suspect, he was indeed the culprit responsible for setting the fire, then I know it can have been nothing more than a horrible accident." Nadine paused for a moment, then continued.

"Veronica, dear, would you mind lighting me a cigarette, please? My poor hands are worse than usual today." She turned back to Jake and Toussaint. "One of the tribulations of old age, I'm afraid. I suffer with arthritis, which is aggravated by our humid climate. But of course, I would never even consider moving to a dryer region. There have been Hamptons here for generations, since the time of the War Between the States." She employed the euphemism common in the South to refer to the Civil War. "You'll forgive me for smoking, gentlemen. A bad habit—but one I continue to indulge. Age *does* have its prerogatives as well as its afflictions. Should either of you be equally inclined, please feel free to join me."

"Thank you, ma'am, I believe I will." Jake withdrew his pack of Marlboros from the inner pocket of his suit jacket. Courteously, he offered one to Veronica, but she shook her head, reaching instead for the alligator-skin cigarette case that lay on the coffee table before her.

Opening it up, she took out the brand-new pack of Virginia Slims 120s inside, pulled off the wrapper, then tore off the entire top of the box that contained the cigarettes.

"Do you always do that?" Jake asked, slightly bemused by her unusual action.

"What? Oh, yes, it makes it easier to get the cigarettes out of the box when they're inside the case," Veronica explained, laying her hand on his to steady it as she bent forward, the long cigarette she now held between two fingers poised for the lighter he had ignited for her.

She lit up, then handed the cigarette to her grandmother, her gaze meeting Nadine's own. Deep within the sapphire-blue eyes that the elderly woman had bequeathed to all her granddaughters, flames hotter than the orange-glowing tip of the cigarette burned. Despite her grief at Vanessa's death, Nadine was furious. She alone of all the household, Veronica had taken into her confidence, knowing her grandmother would believe, help, and protect her. Nadine had always been suspicious of the part Lily had played the night of the fatal car crash in Tuscany, which had left Bruno dead and Vanessa traumatized beyond recovery; and after Veronica's revelations upon returning home from the sanatorium, her grandmother had at long last shared with her the skeleton hidden away in the Hampton family closet, the terrible secret Lily had somehow uncovered. Like Vanessa, Veronica had been shocked and horrified. Even now, her mind reeled whenever she thought of it. But she was not mentally frail, as her younger twin sister had been. Somehow she would cope with the devastating knowledge.

Now, as she looked into Nadine's eyes, Veronica knew her grandmother, too, believed Malcolm and Lily had in some way been responsible for the dreadful fire at the sanatorium, which had resulted in Vanessa's death. But as Veronica herself did, Nadine, also, realized there was no concrete proof with which to bring Malcolm and Lily to justice. Her grandmother's eyes warned Veronica of that, to keep silent, not to reveal anything to the two homicide detectives that would arouse their suspicions.

"You must understand that the fact that Mr. Oxbridge started the fire is only a theory at the moment," Toussaint was saying as Veronica forced her thoughts back to the conversation at hand. "There are perhaps other possibilities that have yet to be determined. You yourselves visited the sanatorium last evening, did you not, Mr. and Mrs. Forsythe?"

"Yes," Malcolm answered quickly, before Veronica could reply—because of course, it had been Lily who had accompanied him, pretending to be Veronica, whom they had believed safely drugged and left behind in Lily's suite.

But Veronica had got adept at avoiding swallowing the sedatives they attempted to ply her with, and afterward, her grandmother—who possessed the keys to every room in the family mansion—had come to Lily's suite, where the two of them had tried to plan what they must do. Since Veronica had returned home after switching places with Vanessa, Nadine had pretended to be ill and insisted that no one but Veronica attend her, so that most evenings, Veronica had been able to avoid Malcolm and Lily, the body- and mind-numbing drug with which they would otherwise have injected her, the horrible assaults to which they would have subjected her, spending her nights instead in her grandmother's room. Nadine had been adamant that Veronica should not suffer such abuse—besides which, the two women had felt that it would be only a short while before Malcolm and Lily made their next move. That it should result in Vanessa's death had taken the two women by surprise.

They had expected Malcolm and Lily to strike first against Veronica—believing her to be Vanessa and thinking she had to be got out of the way before their substitution of the younger twin for the older was discovered. Now, Veronica realized that with their miscalculation, she and her grandmother had indirectly caused Vanessa's death. That thought was torment. It was all Veronica could do to restrain herself as her husband continued.

"Vanessa often spoke about Mr. Oxbridge and the fact that he wasn't allowed to have anything to do with matches, lighters, or the like," Malcolm was saying. "I can only assume that despite all the sanatorium's precautions, he somehow gained access to something like that last night. We didn't see him, however. I presume he was in his room during our visit. We only dropped by to play cards for a while with Vanessa. We frequently did so in the afternoons or evenings when here in the city. My wife was quite devoted to her twin sister." The senator made a show of patting

Veronica's hand comfortingly. "Weren't you, my dear?"

"Yes," Veronica managed to choke out woodenly, knowing her husband still believed her to be Vanessa and under the influence of the sedatives he had administered to her earlier that day, watching to be sure she had swallowed them. But instead, Veronica had fooled him, only pretending to take them, in reality keeping them concealed under her tongue until he had left the room. Then she had spat them out and flushed them down the toilet.

Now, with difficulty, she resisted the urge to slap the supercilious expression of concern from his face. It was hard for her to believe she had ever once loved this man. At this moment, she hated him with a passion that had her trembling where she sat. But Malcolm, she knew, would only attribute that to the fact that after the fatal car crash in Tuscany, Vanessa had always been uneasy around men, cringing from their touch.

"Well, I guess that's all we need for now," Jake declared, crushing his cigarette out in an ashtray and getting to his feet. "Again, we're deeply sorry for your family's loss. We'll let you know when the M.E. has finished with the autopsy, so arrangements can be made to release Ms. Hampton's body to you. In the meanwhile, Mr. and Mrs. Forsythe, if you happen to remember anything—anything at all, no matter how small or seemingly unimportant a detail—that struck you as unusual about last evening, we'd appreciate it if you'd give us a call at this number." Jake handed the senator a business card.

"Of course, Detective," Forsythe responded. "Whatever we can do to be of assistance."

As though by magic, the maid who had earlier admitted Jake and Toussaint to the Hampton family mansion now reappeared to walk them to the front door, closing it firmly behind them. The two men got into their unmarked car and drove slowly down the winding drive to the gates that, triggered by an electronic eye, opened automatically to let them out.

"So...what did you think, Remy?" Jake inquired as he pulled out into the street, scowling darkly at the media vans parked out front, the Channel 4 logo prominent on one of them. *Trust Claire to be Johnny-on-the-spot,* he thought irritably, knowing she was waiting to interview the Hamptons for *Inside Story,* and recalling how she had looked earlier that morning outside the sanatorium, her long, blond hair swept up into the customary French twist she had adopted as her signature style, her svelte body encased in a deep rose, linen suit. At least she had had sense enough not to shove her microphone into *his* face—because he would have told her to eat it, Jake insisted stoutly to himself, despite his knowing deep down inside that that was a lie, that because it was her, he would only have snarled, "No comment," and strode on through the crush of reporters who had flocked to the crime scene.

"What do you mean? 'What do I think?'" Toussaint replied, cranking down his window to let out the heat that had accumulated inside their locked vehicle while they were interviewing the Hamptons. "Good grief, Jake. What'd you have in your coffee this morn-

ing? You think the senator and his wife torched the
Seabreeze Sanatorium last night or something?''

"No, I suppose not," Jake admitted reluctantly.
"The idea *does* seem a little far-fetched. Still, we can't
discount the fact that Mrs. Hampton Forsythe's share
of the family fortune must be substantially increased
now that her twin sister is no longer alive to be an
heir.''

"Yeah, but why wait until now to do the deed?
Vanessa Hampton's been a patient there for the last
decade. Besides, the same thing could no doubt be said
of that other one, too—the cousin, Lily D'Angelo.
Surely, she had as much to gain as Mrs. Hampton
Forsythe.''

"Probably. But *she* wasn't at the sanatorium last
night—besides which, she seemed pretty broken up
about her cousin Vanessa's death, and you just can't
say the same about Mrs. Hampton Forsythe.''

"Oh, I don't know, Jake. People grieve in different
ways," Toussaint asserted firmly. "You ought to
know that by now.''

"Yeah, I guess I do. Still, there's something bothering me about this case, Remy. I just can't put my
finger on what it is. I feel as though we're overlooking
something, somehow.''

"Well, if we are, we'll probably find out about it
sooner or later. In the meanwhile, I still say our best
bet as a suspect is the inmate Oxbridge. The man was
a known firebug, Jake.''

"No." Jake shook his head. "The man was only
suspected of being a firebug. There's a hell of a lot of
difference. Nothing was ever proved against him with

regard to his parents, and it may be that because he was never right in the head to begin with, he made a convenient scapegoat for somebody else.''

"Possibly—except that Homicide never was able to determine that anybody else was really in a position to benefit from his parents' deaths monetarily the way he was, Jake. That's why everything pointed to Oxbridge right from the start."

"If that's the case, then Vanessa Hampton and the rest of the patients in the sanatorium wing that burned last night were just the unfortunate victims of a crazed inmate who somehow managed to escape from his suite and set the fire. I don't know, Remy. Maybe it's just the fact that the entire Hampton family has been stricken by one tragic accident after another over the years that has me all hot and bothered by suspicion. But you have to admit it's strange, the way one after another of them keeps biting the dust."

"Yeah, but there's no pattern to any of it, Jake, nothing to get a handle on that would point to any one particular family member as systematically doing away with the others. Besides, everybody in this city knows the Hamptons are cursed—and have been for more than a century."

"Oh, come on, Remy. Don't tell me even you believe all that nonsense!"

Toussaint grinned. "Hey, I wasn't the one who saw the quadroon ghost that time at the crime scene, Jake," he needled good-naturedly.

"She wasn't a ghost," Jake muttered, annoyed.

"Uh-huh. You just keep right on telling yourself that, partner. Me...I know better."

Eighteen

The Matchbook

And now the matchless deed's achieved,
Determined, dared, and done.

A Song to David
—Christopher Smart

It had taken every ounce of courage Claire possessed to come here, and now, as she sat in her parked car at Lafitte's Quay, she almost restarted the engine and drove away. Her nerves were so badly on edge that she felt as though she were going to jump clean out of her skin, and the quickness and shallowness of her breathing made her wonder half fearfully if she were in the process of hyperventilating.

"This is stupid, Connelly," she told herself resolutely. "The worst thing the man can do is slam his door in your face—and God knows, that won't be anything compared to his walking out on you all those years ago." But if Jake did, in fact, refuse to see her now, it would still hurt, she acknowledged as she at last forced herself to get out of her vehicle, to trek slowly down the wharf to the slip where his houseboat, the *Sea Gypsy,* was moored.

She half wished he wouldn't be at home, but that hope was in vain, she realized as she spied the lights that glowed at his windows, diffused by the curtains that hung at the panes. He was inside; she could tell as one of the lamps was suddenly shadowed by his tall figure moving in front of it. Her hammering heart seemed to lodge in her throat, and it was all she could do to prevent herself from turning around and running back down the pier in the direction she had come. Instead, she compelled herself to continue onward, swaying a little unsteadily on the gangway as she made the brief transition from the wooden dock to the houseboat. Raising her fist, she knocked gently at Jake's door, and after a moment, he opened it.

"Claire!" He was obviously startled to see her.

"If I'm interrupting anything, if my timing is bad, I can go away…come back at another time," she said quickly, remembering the very first occasion when she had ever stood at his front door.

"No, I'm just…surprised by your being here, that's all. Won't you…won't you come inside?" He stepped back to permit her entry, and she realized he was holding his gun. "Just a precaution," he announced at her inquiring glance. "You can't play Russian roulette with an automatic pistol."

"Yes, I suppose that's true."

He shoved the weapon back into his shoulder holster, which hung on a peg near the door, then motioned toward the built-in couch. "Sit down. Can I fix you something to drink?"

"No, nothing, thank you. I feel quite certain that when you find out why I'm here, you'll be showing me the door at the very least—maybe even pitching me overboard." She strove to keep her tone light as she tentatively took a seat on the couch.

Much to her confusion, Jake actually smiled mockingly at that. "I'll admit I wasn't expecting you to show up on my doorstep, so I was a little slow on the uptake. But I *do* think I've got it all figured out now, Claire. You're here because you want the inside scoop on the arsonous fire at the Seabreeze Sanatorium."

"You're—you're not angry?"

"Oh, yes, very. You of all people know how much I don't like being used in that way. However, like it or not, I'll confess there's a part of me that actually admires your grit and determination. It must have taken a lot of...courage for you to come here."

"Or foolishness? Or desperation?" she suggested, her hands fidgeting nervously.

"I didn't say that."

"No—but you thought it all the same," Claire insisted, then thought better of her words. "Or perhaps I'm just being presumptuous," she said by way of apology.

"No," he replied tersely after a moment. "You still have an uncanny way of being able to read my mind." Going into the galley, he reached beneath the counter that divided it from the living quarters, producing a bottle of red wine, apparently having decided that despite her refusing his offer, she looked as though she could use a drink. Uncorking the bottle, he poured burgundy liquid into two glasses, then, returning to the living quarters, handed one to her. "Did you really think I would answer your questions about this case, Claire?"

"To be honest? No, not really. But I seem to be stymied at every other avenue of approach, so I didn't think it would matter if you turned me down flat, too. You were a last resort—worth a shot, at least. But I didn't have any great expectations, other than that you'd probably toss me out on my ear. You must know I wouldn't have come on my own, Jake. But…well, *Inside Story* is always particularly interested in anything involving the Hamptons, and since I'm the local reporter on the scene in this case, they're counting on me for coverage."

"Yeah, I figured it had to be something more than just Channel Four breathing down your neck to bring you here. But the truth is that there's really nothing to tell, Claire. Our primary suspect, as you're doubtless already aware, was a patient himself at the sanatorium…one Billy Oxbridge, a probable firebug. Unfortunately, since he also perished in the blaze, we aren't able to question him, so we don't even know what motive may have been in his crazed mind, how he was able to escape from his suite at the sanatorium, how he got into the storeroom to gain access to the chemicals used to cause the fire, where he might have obtained the matches with which the flames were ignited."

"I see."

"Sorry to disappoint you, but that's how it is.

Sometimes people die...and we never know why, never catch the perpetrators of the crime.'' Jake stared down into his wineglass, swirling its dark red contents before lifting it to his mouth and taking a long swallow.

Claire knew he hadn't been talking about the patients who had been killed at the sanatorium at all, but, rather, about his dead wife, Isabel.

"You never got any leads in her case, did you?'' she inquired quietly.

"No.'' Jake was unsurprised by Claire's perception. "But that's all water under the bridge now—just like so many other things.''

And that, too, she understood...that their own relationship was over a long time ago, that there was nothing left between them now—nothing except the powerful undercurrent of physical attraction that had always pulled them to each other. "I never saw the houseboat after you finished fixing it up,'' she remarked, striving for safer ground as she glanced around, taking stock of her surroundings. "You did a wonderful job. One would never know what it looked like before. You must be very pleased with it.''

"Yeah, it suits my needs. You were right all those years ago about my making a clean break from the barrio, from the past. So...how about you? Is that what you did after your husband died? Moved? Started all over again?''

Sipping her wine, Claire nodded in confirmation. "Gillian and I have a house out at The Breakers now, so we spend a lot of our time on the beach and sometimes here at Lafitte's Quay. Gillian loves the shops here, the places like Café Chantilly. I never did get a chance to thank you for how kind you were to her that day at lunch. She's had a hard time since Paul died, and I appreciated your thoughtfulness and understanding."

"It was nothing. She's a beautiful little girl. I'm sure you're very proud of her, Claire."

"I am. But more than that, I'm just grateful she's alive and getting better every day." Claire set her wineglass down on the old steamer trunk that served as Jake's coffee table. "Well, I'm sure you've got things you need to be doing, and I've taken up enough of your time, so I guess I'll be going now. But before I leave, there is one more thing I'd like to thank you for, Jake, and that's for not saying anything to anybody about...well, what I told you about that day with regard to the state of my marriage, the fact that I was going to divorce Paul. It was bad enough that he had been drinking that night—without everyone in this city learning he was also abducting Gillian because I intended to file for a divorce from him the following morning."

"You must have known I'm not the kind of man to have used something like that against you, Claire. There was nothing for me personally to gain from it— at least, nothing any decent-minded man would find satisfactory—and nothing good that would have come from it as a whole. But I suppose that having learned what I know about your marriage, I *am* curious about it. To be frank, I was...surprised when you wed Paul Langley. I had thought you didn't love him anymore."

"I didn't think I did. But then he came back to this

city, law degree and engagement ring in hand, and I...changed my mind." Claire didn't add that once Jake had gone out of her life, it had been as though some light inside her had been extinguished, as well, never to be reignited; that she had settled for contentment with Paul because the utter happiness she had experienced with Jake had seemed to her like something that came only once in a lifetime, never to be recaptured once lost. "I don't know. Maybe it was me. Maybe it was Paul. Or maybe it was the both of us...the fact that we just weren't right for each other in the end. He started drinking, having affairs, and he gambled heavily, I think. There were several large, cash withdrawals from his account, but I never have found out where all the money went."

"No clues at all?" Jake queried, his detective instincts aroused by this piece of information.

Claire shook her head. "No, none—except that I did find this in one of his suit jackets later, when I was sorting through all his things after his death." Reaching into her handbag, she drew forth a matchbook. It was black and glossy, like Japanese lacquer. Stamped into the front, in gold, was a wharf stretching into water that somehow gave the impression that treachery lurked beneath the waves, in the form of an unseen riptide. There was nothing else, no name or monogram printed anywhere on the cover, no other form of advertising inside or out.

Abruptly reaching out, Jake grasped Claire's outstretched hand so tightly in his that she winced, feeling as though he were crushing her very bones. "Do you know where this came from?" he asked harshly, his dark eyes narrowed, gleaming with both suspicion and excitement as he stared at the matchbook.

"No, why?"

"Because the charred remains of a matchbook just exactly like this one were found in the ruins of the wing at the Seabreeze Sanatorium. It's one of the things we haven't released to the media."

Book Three

Glory Seekers

Oh heart! oh blood that freezes, blood that burns!
    Earth's returns
For whole centuries of folly, noise and sin!
    Shut them in,
With their triumphs and their glories and the rest!
    Love is best!

    Love Among the Ruins
    —Robert Browning

Nineteen

Diamonds Are Forever

O Diamond! Diamond! thou
little knowest the mischief done!

> *Said to a pet dog who knocked over a
> candle and set fire to his papers*
> —Sir Isaac Newton

A Small City, The Gulf Coast, The Present

The medical examiner and his assistants had now finished zipping Veronica Hampton Forsythe's sodden, bloated corpse into a body bag and loaded it onto a gurney for transportation to the morgue, where an autopsy would be performed to ensure that there was nothing suspicious about the way in which the victim had drowned.

In the meantime, the police dive team had arrived and were currently in the process of examining every inch of the Olympic-sized swimming pool at the Hampton family mansion. The evening shoe that, after

the drowning, had come off Veronica's foot, falling to
the bottom of the pool, had already been retrieved,
along with the expensive, elaborately designed, diamond necklace she had also been wearing last night
at the private fund-raising bash for her husband Senator Malcolm Forsythe's re-election campaign. Apparently, the necklace's ornate catch had broken when her
corpse had begun to swell in the water and the summer
heat, the morning sun beating down on her accelerat-
ing the rate of putrefaction of the body.

In addition to the inspection of its interior, the pool
was being backwashed, the runoff filtered through a
cloth to collect hair fibers and other minute debris that
might prove of value in determining just what had
occurred last night.

Off to one side, Jake stood silently, smoking a cigarette and watching the proceedings, while Toussaint
continued to conduct interviews, questioning both the
Hampton family and the staff who worked at the mansion.

"Hey, Detective Seringo," one of the dive-team
members called as he surfaced and pushed up his face
mask, swimming over to the edge of the pool. "Found
something here that might be of interest."

Striding over to the pool's rim, Jake knelt on the
pebbled deck to examine the object the dive-team
member now held out to him. It was a twenty-four-
karat-gold cuff link—engraved with the initials *MF*.
Malcolm Forsythe. "Well, well, well," Jake murmured thoughtfully, the wheels in his mind churning.
"I wonder what kind of an explanation the senator will

have for this? Not quite the thing one wears for a midnight dip, is it? Good work, Padilla.''

''Thanks, Detective.''

With one hand, Jake motioned to a member of the Crime Scene Unit to bring him one of the plastic bags in which evidence was collected. He dropped the cuff link into the bag. ''See that that's properly tagged, will you, Morrow? I've got a strange feeling that maybe our drowning victim didn't accidentally take a tumble into the pool, after all—which means that contusion on her head may have been caused by a deliberate blow. Check around. My guess at this point is that something like a small, smooth stone—which would mimic the rim of the pool and the rocks employed to construct the waterfall—was used to strike Mrs. Hampton Forsythe down before she was shoved into the pool.''

A quarter of an hour later, Jake's suspicion was proved potentially correct when a stone in one of the big, wooden, planter boxes scattered around the pool was discovered to have traces of what looked to be blood on it.

''What's going on?'' Toussaint inquired as, his interviews complete, he joined his partner at the poolside. ''I thought the M.E. figured this to be an accidental drowning.''

''Yeah, well, it appears as though he may have figured wrong. Here. Have a look at this.'' Jake handed over the bags containing the cuff link and the stone. ''I think we ought to ask the senator to take a little ride with us down to the station for further questioning, don't you?''

"It certainly seems that way, doesn't it?" Toussaint agreed after examining the evidence. "I reckon we'd better start looking for a motive, partner—just in case."

"You got that right, Remy. I told you this entire damned family was way too frigging accident-prone for my liking. Makes me wonder now whether Billy Oxbridge was really to blame for that fire at the Seabreeze Sanatorium. With both twins out of the picture, I imagine Lily D'Angelo's got quite a substantial inheritance coming whenever old Mrs. Hampton finally kicks the bucket. It may be that the cousin and the senator had a little something going on the side together...saw a way of cashing in on it all."

"Maybe. But I have to tell you, Jake—that scenario's more than a tad difficult for me to swallow. I mean, it's kind of like trading your brand-new Jaguar in for a brand-new Jaguar, if you get my drift. You've seen the twins and their cousin. Look like three peas in a pod. You couldn't even tell them apart, so what's the difference? Man don't trade in one rich, gorgeous, redheaded wife for a poorer mirror image—'specially if he's running for re-election. Don't make any sense, that, no. Besides which, D'Angelo didn't visit the sanatorium the evening of the fire, and further, old Mrs. Hampton swears her arthritis was kicking up again last night, that she left the party at a relatively early hour, and that D'Angelo accompanied her to her room to assist her, since most of the staff were busy catering to the guests. So if you're right, either D'Angelo made damned certain she covered her ass, or else the senator acted entirely on his own—and we don't even know that the two of them were having an affair.''

"It's only one possibility, Remy. I didn't say there weren't at least a couple of others.'' Jake grimaced sourly at his partner. "For all we know, old Mrs. Hampton intends now to leave all her money to a home for orphans, and D'Angelo's not even in the picture. But the senator definitely *is*. That cuff link didn't just take a dive into the pool all by its lonesome self—and I'd be willing to bet my last dollar that it's one of a pair the senator was wearing last night.''

"Well, let's go get him and find out.''

Claire was startled to say the least when she saw the wrought-iron gates of the Hampton family mansion swing open to reveal Jake and Toussaint escorting Senator Malcolm Forsythe from the premises. Whatever she had expected, it was certainly not this. Like the rest of the media present, she rushed forward, microphone in hand, hoping to get at least one question answered as Nash and McGuinness jostled for positions with their cameras. Shouting orders, the uniformed officers on the scene spread their arms wide in an attempt to hold back the press of the media as Jake and Toussaint hustled the senator down the street, toward their unmarked car. Across the way, the high-strung cockapoo belonging to one of the onlooking neighbors at last managed to wriggle free of its owner's frail grasp.

"Honey-bun, you naughty girl! Come back here right now,'' the elderly but spry woman cried as she chased after her errant little dog. Ignoring her, it in-

stead raced excitedly across the street, weaving among
a crowd of legs somehow to emerge at the senator's
heels, yapping shrilly and nipping fiercely at his cus-
tom-tailored trousers. Then, snarling furiously, the pre-
cocious animal abruptly caught hold of one of Forsythe's pant legs, obstinately refusing to let go, despite
how the senator swore and attempted to shake free.

"Scat! Scat, you!" Toussaint demanded, stamping
his foot in a futile effort to chase the frenzied, growling dog off, then nervously backing away when it
seemed as though the tiny but fierce animal would
charge him, too.

"My God, Nash! Tell me...you're getting all
this...on film," Claire gasped out as she struggled to
retain her footing amid the surging throng, torn between mortification and hysterics at the unfolding
spectacle and seeing national exposure for herself
again on *Inside Story.*

"I'm getting it! I'm getting it!" Nash's face was
positively gleeful.

Cursing mightily at how the situation had spiraled
out of control, Jake bent and scooped up the small,
snapping dog, forcibly tearing it away from Forsythe's
trousers and thrusting it into the arms of one of the
patrolmen attempting to be of assistance. But the delay
had given the media time to become something of a
mob, and now they broke through the phalanx of uniformed officers, pushing microphones and cameras at
Jake, Toussaint, and Forsythe—whose face had turned
an alarming shade of red with fury and embarrassment.

Separated from Nash and McGuinness, carried helplessly along in the maddened crowd's wake, Claire

tripped and, before she could regain her balance, was knocked down. Suddenly, what had just moments before had her fighting to restrain laughter now caused her heart to leap to her throat as she realized she was in grave danger of being trampled underfoot. She cried out, wincing as, without warning, a strong, steely hand wrapped bruisingly around her upper arm, jerking her upright and hauling her from the close, lunging press of bodies.

"You damned fool!" Jake's voice snarled in her ear as he dragged her along so roughly that she stumbled repeatedly, only keeping her feet because he held on to her so tightly. "What in the hell do you think you're doing? Trying to get yourself killed?" She had no chance to reply as they reached the unmarked car and he ripped open the door. "Get in, Senator," he ordered curtly, then pushed Claire into the vehicle's back seat, too, before climbing in beside her and yanking the door shut with a bang. Up front, Toussaint slid into the driver's seat and started the engine, pulling away from the curb, then guiding the car gingerly through the mass that attempted to surround it.

"Jesus Christ!" Jake muttered heatedly. "We'll be lucky if we get out of here in one piece. Damned vultures!" He glowered at the media swarming the vehicle before turning to glare at Claire, a muscle working violently in his set jaw. "And you, Claire—you're the worst of the whole fucking lot!" Jake knew that as long as he lived, he would never forget that moment when he had seen her fall to the ground and heard her cry out, watched her trying desperately to shield herself from the throng that had swept over her, nearly crushing her beneath their feet. His heart had seemed to stop in that instant, frozen with fear, before it had lurched again into motion. Instinct and dread had propelled him forward, his arm reaching out for her.

Strands of silky hair had escaped from Claire's previously neatly wrapped French twist. There was a smudge of dirt on her cheek and blood on her lip from a cut resulting from her ordeal. Grass stains soiled her linen skirt. Her knees were scraped, and her hose had run in more than one place. She was still shaking in the aftermath of the close call. Jake's hands curled into tight fists. He wanted to strangle her. He wanted to enfold her in his arms and make feverish love to her, to protect her forever from the crimes and cruelties of the world.

"I didn't ask you to rescue me," she choked out in a very small voice, "although, of course, I'm glad you did."

"Well, thank you so much for your gratitude, sweetheart!" Jake retorted sarcastically. If they'd been alone in the car, he would have kissed her until she was breathless and aching for him, he thought, enraged. She wouldn't have been so uppity then. But instead, withdrawing a clean, white handkerchief from his pocket, he reached out, his fingers tangling in her hair to hold her still as he carefully wiped the blood from her lower lip. "Damned stupid woman!"

"Would the two of you like me to sit up front?" Forsythe inquired insolently.

"It would behoove you to be quiet, Senator," Jake warned tersely, "that is, unless you're planning to confess to your wife's murder en route to the station."

"Veronica's death was an accident. She'd had far too much to drink last night, and she drowned," Forsythe insisted firmly. "It's that simple. And the only reason I agreed to being questioned at the station was to spare her family from further grief and torment. I've nothing to hide—and even if I did, my attorneys will make mincemeat out of you, Detective."

"We'll see," Jake shot back shortly.

"Then you're not officially under arrest, Senator?" Claire asked, realizing abruptly that Jake's unexpected action to save her life had also handed her an ideal opportunity to garner an exclusive interview with Veronica Hampton Forsythe's husband.

"I'll ask the questions, Claire," Jake growled angrily, "that is, unless you want me to cram this handkerchief in your mouth to shut you up. You're only here because you would have been trampled to death, otherwise. So don't go getting any bright ideas about how to turn this situation to your advantage. There's no way that's going to happen—not on my watch."

Claire would have argued with him, but the manner in which Jake was scowling at her made her think he wasn't above actually gagging her, as he had threatened. So instead, she forced herself to remain silent, vividly conscious of his proximity, of the way in which the two of them were crowded together in the close quarters of the back seat. His arm was draped along the top of the back seat and so rested almost casually on her shoulders. His thigh was pressed hard against her own, stirring old memories best forgotten.

Still, they crept into her mind...visions of his powerful body covering her own weaker one, weighing her down, compelling her to respond to him again and again, driving her to heights of rapture she had never even dreamed of, leaving her trembling with pleasure and exhaustion, and gasping for breath. Even now, as Claire remembered those days and nights spent in Jake's embrace, an electric thrill of desire shot through her, making her feel heated and flushed. Perspiration sheened her creamy skin.

"Doesn't the air conditioner work in this car?" she queried agitatedly, fanning herself with her hand.

"Not so's you'd notice," Jake replied laconically. However, now that they were free of the media and speeding along the city streets toward the police station, he cranked down his window to let in whatever breeze was available. It didn't help much. The interior of the vehicle was still hot and muggy. He could feel the warm dampness of Claire's body pressed against him, reminding him of how she had felt lying naked in his arms, covered with sweat from their lovemaking. His groin tightened at the memory, desire igniting within him. He swore under his breath, jerking at his collar and tie as though they were too tight, although he had loosened them earlier that morning.

He had never felt so relieved in his life as he did when Toussaint pulled their unmarked car into the parking garage of the station. Jake got out, then assisted Claire from the vehicle in such an abrupt fashion that he caused her to stagger against him. For a moment, he clasped her close against him to steady her, his hard, muscular body pressed against the length of her own soft, voluptuous one, making her painfully aware of the fact that he was aroused by her.

"Yeah...you still have that effect upon me," he confessed irately in her ear before he released her to shrug on his suit jacket. Then, his hand gripping her arm, he propelled her toward the station, Toussaint escorting Forsythe ahead of them.

"You're hurting me, Jake," Claire managed to get out breathlessly as she made vain attempts to keep up with his long, determined stride.

"I'd like to do a hell of a lot more than that to you!" he snapped heedlessly, taking a perverse, savage satisfaction in the small gasp that issued from her throat at his intentional double entendre. "Captain Nichols is going to hit the roof when he finds out Remy and I have not only brought Senator Forsythe in for questioning, but dragged a damned reporter along with us, too!" But despite his wrathful words, Jake slowed his pace and loosened his viselike grasp on Claire's arm slightly.

Even so, she knew she would still have bruises there later, and she was outraged by his manhandling her, his barbaric behavior toward her, and the coarse words he had spoken to her just moments ago. Equally unnerving was the realization that only volatile, emotional duress drove Jake to such brutal extremes. He wouldn't be treating her in such a fashion if he didn't still have deep feelings where she was concerned, didn't still want her—if only in his bed. Claire felt a shiver of both fear and perverse excitement at the thought—coupled with shame and mortification at the recognition that if he were suddenly to haul her into a broom closet inside the precinct and roughly shove up her skirt to take her in a fit of rage and passion, she wouldn't do anything to stop him.

But instead, once they had reached the Homicide Division inside the station, Jake pushed her down into an uncomfortable, straight-backed, tubular-steel-and-vinyl chair beside his desk. Then he yanked off his mirrored, aviator sunglasses and tossed them onto the green blotter that covered most of his old, metal desk. His dark, smoldering eyes raked her hotly, causing her cheeks to flame.

"Sit there, and don't move a muscle until I get back!" he demanded harshly.

"Am I—am I under arrest, Jake?"

"No. But you *will* be, Claire, if you don't do exactly what I tell you—charged with hindering a police investigation, for a start, and anything else I can think of. Do you understand me?"

"Yes."

"Good. Then let's hope you have sense enough not to cross me this time!" With that Parthian shot, he strode away, disappearing down a corridor Claire surmised must lead to the interrogation rooms of the precinct.

Of course, Jake would have to take care of business first, since clearly, Senator Malcolm Forsythe was not a person to be left cooling his heels at the whim of the local police. Even as this thought occurred to her, Claire saw several men in well-tailored suits enter the squad room, some of whom she recognized as the senator's aides; two others were prominent, local attorneys, and one was the top-ranking assistant district attorney. Plainly, Forsythe had requested that his lawyers be present during the interrogation. Still, that didn't necessarily mean he had anything to hide, she told herself. Given his status, it would be the natural precaution under the circumstances. But surely, the senator wouldn't even have been brought in for further questioning if the police didn't suspect him of having had something to do with his wife's untimely death.

The wheels in Claire's mind churned furiously as she considered that fact. If it turned out that Forsythe had actually murdered his wife, it would be one of the biggest news stories of the decade. Warily, she looked around the squad room. Except for an occasional, curious glance in her direction, no one was paying any attention to her. As unobtrusively as possible, she reached for the telephone on Jake's desk and drew it toward her. Cradling the receiver against her ear, she punched one of the buttons for an outside line to dial the number of Nash's cellular telephone.

"Nash, here," he answered on the first ring.

"Winston—"

"Claire! Jesus Christ! Where in the hell are you? The shit's hit the fan at the station—big-time! One of the biggest news stories of the decade is breaking even as we speak, and you're nowhere to be found! Kendall's having a conniption fit...nearly tore my and Booker's heads off when we called in to report that you'd gone missing! He said if anything had happened to you, it was all our damned fault! That there was no way you would have just disappeared for no good reason from a live remote—"

"Winston...Winston!" Claire hissed sharply, afraid of being overheard. "If you'll just listen to me for a minute, I'll explain. When the media went overboard and all that chaos outside the Hampton family mansion ensued, I was knocked down and nearly trampled. One of the homicide detectives grabbed me up, and with everything that was happening, he didn't see any other choice except to push me into his unmarked car, along with the senator. I'm down at the police station even as we speak. Tell me what you've managed to learn. Why did they bring Forsythe in for questioning?''

''Apparently, he had a major blowup with his wife last night at the gala affair, and the rumor is that the police found something in the swimming pool that gave them cause to believe her death might not be an accidental drowning, as they'd originally thought.''

''No wonder all those aides and attorneys hustled themselves down here, then.''

''Yeah...Booker and I are in the media van, en route to the precinct ourselves—along with every other reporter in the city, I might add. Where's the senator now? We want to try to get film of him on the precinct steps.''

''The homicide detectives have him back in one of the interrogation rooms. I tried to interview him on the way here, but I'm afraid the detective who rescued me took great exception to that, said his captain was going to be mad enough as it was at the whole debacle.''

''Yeah, I can imagine.'' Nash chuckled at the image her words had conjured up for him. ''But that doesn't matter. Claire, do you realize what this means? Even though you didn't manage to get an interview, we've still got an angle to this story that nobody else in the entire city has! Jeez, I can't wait to tell Kendall! He'll be dancing a jig!''

"Winston, tell him I'll try again to speak with the senator after he gets out of the interrogation room. But I don't know how good my chances of success are. This detective who rescued me...well, he's something of a barracuda, if you know what I mean, and he's not likely to let me get close to the senator.''

"Well, then, interview the detective instead. Take whatever he says to you, and use it.''

"I—I can't, Winston. It's extremely doubtful he'd tell me anything of value, anyway, and even if he did, I—I just couldn't use it, that's all. I can't explain why. You'll just have to trust me on this one. But there are other detectives here, as well as the senator's aides and attorneys and A.D.A. Unruh. So don't worry. I'll get something—even if it's only my own impressions of what's taken place here at the station. And of course, I'll try to arrange a formal interview with old Mrs. Hampton and her remaining granddaughter, Lily D'Angelo. I think they'll see me. Mrs. Hampton sent me a note, you know, right after my coverage of the fire at the Seabreeze Sanatorium, thanking me for the manner in which I'd handled the story. She was grateful I hadn't sensationalized her granddaughter's life and death, but had concentrated on the lovely, fragile woman Vanessa was. At any rate...oops...I've got to go, Winston. I'll talk to you later.''

Without waiting for a reply, Claire quickly hung up the receiver as she spied Jake emerging from the corridor leading from the interrogation rooms. Despite everything, the sight of him still made her stomach do flip-flops. He was, she thought, the most handsome man she had ever seen. He was also only marginally less steamed than he had been earlier. She could tell that by the resolute thrust of his jaw, the muscle that flexed there.

After pouring himself a cup of coffee, he sat down at his desk, grabbing his telephone and moving it to one side, setting it down with a violent thump. "I should have known the minute I left you alone here, you'd be calling in to Channel Four, in an attempt to scoop your competition," he remarked dryly. "How maddening it must be for you, Claire, actually to be present here in the precinct—and not permitted to witness the senator's interrogation."

"Is that what it was? An interrogation? I thought he was only here for questioning."

"Off the record, my every gut instinct tells me that cocky son of a bitch whacked his wife on the head with a rock last night and then shoved her into the Hamptons' pool to drown. But proving it's another matter entirely, so the insolent bastard's walking out of here free and clear for the moment. God, I hate politics. If Malcolm Forsythe were Joe Blow down the block, he'd be sitting in a jail cell right now."

"May I quote you on that?"

"No, you may not, Claire." Jake rocked back in his chair, lighting a cigarette and eyeing her in a way that left her feeling as though she had just been strip-searched. "So...what do you think I ought to do with you? Take you home—or lock you up for making such a damned, interfering pest out of yourself?"

"What's that supposed to be? A trick question?"

"Very funny, Claire. You keep on like that, and I'll put you in the holding tank."

"Right. Are we all through here, Jake? Because I've got a job to do, too, you know."

"A job that nearly got you killed today."

"It's not usually so dangerous. Things don't generally get out of hand like that."

"No? You forget. I've seen it all before, Claire. It's like a damned feeding frenzy."

"Senator Forsythe and his wife are big news. What makes you think he killed her?"

"Nice try, but huh-uh. We're not releasing that information at present. So give it up. You'll get nothing from me. You see, when it comes to handling the media, I've had experience that most of my colleagues lack. I know how you operate, Claire."

"No, you know how a young girl fresh out of college and eager to try and change the world did her job, Jake. But you don't know anything about how I work these days."

"I know I didn't see you hanging back today."

"Would it have made a difference if I had? The story was going to be told one way or another, anyway. Wasn't it better for me to try to report it in a fair, objective manner? What if you're wrong, and the senator is innocent, simply an unfortunate victim of circumstance? Doesn't he deserve his say? Isn't his dead wife entitled to a voice, as well? You see, Jake, these are questions to which you haven't any answers that would support your own viewpoint. I'm not denying that the media sometimes go overboard. But on the other hand, I don't condemn the entire police force just because I know there're corrupt cops on the streets, either."

"Point well taken," Jake said, after a moment.

"Just like everybody else, I'm afraid that for good or ill, my own perceptions are colored by my experiences—and those haven't been particularly pleasant where the media are concerned."

"I've tried more than once to apologize for what I did to you all those years ago," Claire asserted quietly. "It's you who can't forgive or forget it, Jake. Now, if there's nothing else, I'd like to leave here and get back to work."

"I'll drive you," he offered.

"Thanks, but my cameramen, Winston and Booker, are on their way here. So there's no need for you to put yourself out. I'm certain you're already in enough trouble as it is for having brought me here in the first place."

"Yeah, Captain Nichols isn't too happy about it, that's for sure. But don't worry. He'll get over it. He always does. My arrest record goes a long way toward keeping his temper in check."

"I'm glad. I'd hate to think that your having rescued me caused a real problem for you." Gathering up her purse, Claire stood. "Thanks again for hauling me out from under that mob. I realize I might have been seriously hurt or even killed if it weren't for your help."

"Don't mention it. Just do me a favor and try to be more careful in the future."

"Right, I will." Settling the wide strap of her handbag over her shoulder, Claire left the squad room. She didn't look back, but even so, she was vividly aware that Jake's gaze followed her every step of the way.

Twenty

Perfume Elysian

> But who is this, what thing of sea or land?
> Female of sex it seems,
> That so bedecked, ornate, and gay,
> Comes this way sailing
> Like a stately ship
> Of Tarsus, bound for th' isles
> Of Javan or Gadire,
> With all her bravery on, and tackle trim,
> Sails filled, and streamers waving,
> Courted by all the winds that hold them play;
> An amber scent of odorous perfume
> Her harbinger?
>
> *Samson Agonistes*
> —John Milton

In the days that followed, it became clear to Claire as she covered unfolding events that whatever had occurred during Senator Forsythe's interrogation at the precinct, his answers to the questions put to him by the police had apparently proved unsatisfactory. Although the medical examiner had initially labeled Veronica Hampton Forsythe's death an accidental drowning, as a result of the autopsy in conjunction with an analysis of the evidence at the scene, his ultimate conclusion was that she had, in reality, been murdered; and despite the attempts of all the senator's spin doctors at damage control, it was plain he was the primary suspect.

What seemed to be lacking in the case, however, was a motive. Since old Mrs. Hampton was still alive, the senator appeared to have nothing to gain and everything to lose from his wife's death. Veronica's own money was all tied up in a trust fund that could only pass to blood relatives, so he would not benefit from it; and old Mrs. Hampton, it was presumed, would now change her will, leaving the bulk of the Hampton fortune to her only surviving grandchild, Lily D'Angelo.

If Forsythe and D'Angelo had had a relationship, a motive could have been established. But so far, there seemed to be nothing that would link them together, although, now, as she sat in the living room of the Hampton family mansion, conducting an exclusive interview, Claire thought she detected a strain of tension between the two of them. Despite the senator's attempt to appear honest and open, a man with nothing to hide and genuinely grieved by his wife's death, Claire nevertheless believed him to be deeply furious and agitated—emotions that puzzled her greatly. A man guilty of murdering his wife might indeed be nervous, fearful of discovery, but angry? That did not seem to fit at all.

Of course, Veronica's death had thrown a real monkey wrench into Forsythe's plans for re-election and focused upon him the kind of media attention that public figures generally went out of their way to avoid, which might, in fact, be the source of his ire. But it also diminished any motive he might have had for killing his wife—for surely, had he indeed done so, he would have waited until after his re-election, Claire speculated.

"Senator, it's a well-known fact that the morning following your wife's death, the police also found, in the swimming pool where she drowned, one of a pair of gold cuff links that you were wearing the night before. How do you account for that?"

"It's quite simple, really, as I explained to the police. Veronica and I had argued earlier that evening— a silly, stupid quarrel, in retrospect. I felt she had been working too hard since the death of her younger twin sister, Vanessa. As you know, my wife was not only very involved in my own re-election campaign, but she devoted time to a number of charities, besides. That evening of my fund-raiser was supposed to be a party, of course—yet Veronica couldn't seem to relax and enjoy herself, as I had wished. We exchanged words over it, a fact that I've never denied and which I now deeply regret, and at one point, she grabbed my wrist, insisting that I was making a scene. I can only assume that my cuff link came off in her hand at that time, and that she was too upset to notice. Certainly,

I wasn't aware of its loss until the following morning, when it was discovered in the pool.''

Although Claire knew Forsythe must have rehearsed his answer countless times with his attorneys and public-relations personnel, she was still impressed by how smoothly and reasonably he delivered it, making it appear wholly credible. No wonder the police had held off arresting him, lacking any believable motive and with nothing but circumstantial evidence to make their case. The senator's lawyers would have had a heyday with that, making the D.A.'s office look ridiculous, as though they had rushed to judgment without sufficient cause and preparation.

''And what about the stone that was also found, Senator, and that is rumored to have traces of your wife's blood on it?'' Claire inquired.

''I don't believe even the police have been able to determine how or when that stone might have got the blood on it—or even that it's positively my wife's blood, since she did have a twin sister whom she occasionally brought here to visit and who, as I'm sure you're aware, hadn't been mentally stable for the last decade or more. In fact, Vanessa was prone to bouts of severe depression during which she made more than one attempt to injure herself.''

''I see. Well, thank you very much, Senator.'' Turning to Nash and McGuinness, Claire said, ''Okay, guys, I think that's a wrap.'' Instantly, the living room became a hive of activity, with Forsythe's attorneys and spin doctors hustling him away, while the two cameramen began breaking down the lights they had set up for the exclusive interview and collecting the rest of their equipment.

"Ms. Connelly, would you care to join my granddaughter and me in the conservatory for a glass of lemonade?" Nadine Hampton leaned heavily on her omnipresent cane as, with difficulty, she rose from the wing chair she had occupied during the interview. Despite that she was as exquisitely groomed as always, she did not look well, as though the strain of the past few months had been too much even for her determined spirit.

"Yes, thank you, I would." Claire did her best to restrain her enthusiasm for the idea of a private tête-à-tête. With her coverage of Vanessa Hampton's death in the arsonous fire at the Seabreeze Sanatorium, she had, it seemed, made quite an impression on old Mrs. Hampton, the result of which was the interview just conducted and now the opportunity for a private conversation with the two remaining Hampton women. "Your conservatory is lovely," she commented as they entered the glassed-in room filled with every kind of plant imaginable.

"How kind of you to say so." Nadine indicated that they should be seated at a wrought-iron table and chairs, while instructing a Latino maid to bring a pitcher of lemonade and three glasses. "My late husband was particularly fond of it. Botany was a hobby of his. It was he who collected many of the more exotic specimens you see here."

Claire sat down at the table. "I want to thank you again, Mrs. Hampton, for agreeing to allow me to interview you, the senator, and Ms. D'Angelo this afternoon. I know the past few months can't have been easy for any of you."

"No, they haven't been. Still, we'll manage to get through this, just as we have all the other tragedies that have afflicted the Hampton family. Despite everything, I still have Lily, and she is a great comfort to me now that the twins are…no more." Reaching out, the older woman patted her granddaughter's hand, smiling at her tremulously. "We're all each other has now, aren't we, dear?"

"Yes, Grandmother." Lily nodded, her big, sapphire-blue eyes filled with love, sadness, and concern as she gazed at the older woman.

"But what about the senator?" Claire queried as she sipped the icy lemonade the maid had brought and poured into tall, frosted glasses. "Where does he fit into all this? Or doesn't he?"

Nadine and Lily exchanged a meaningful glance. Then, after clearing her throat, the older woman spoke. "Obviously, until we know for certain what actually happened that night of the fund-raiser, there are… difficulties where Malcolm is concerned."

"Are you…are you telling me that you believe the senator is guilty of having murdered your granddaughter, Mrs. Hampton?" Claire was extremely startled and intrigued to learn this piece of information.

"Off the record, Ms. Connelly?" One of Nadine's elegantly penciled eyebrows arched quizzically. "I don't know. Despite that Malcolm has frequently been hailed as the man who would bring back the era of Camelot to the White House, his and Veronica's marriage was hardly the fairy-tale romance the media have portrayed it as being. Although Malcolm has persevered in the political arena, the truth is that ever since his and Veronica's little boy, Drew, was kidnapped and killed, he has been a changed man…a man driven by demons.''

"Changed to the point that he was capable of knocking his inebriated wife in the head and shoving her into your pool to drown?'' Claire asked bluntly, her face knitted in a puzzled, curious frown. "But what possible motive could he have had for doing such a thing? And in the midst of his re-election campaign, besides? He must have known it would be political suicide, that if even a hint of suspicion arose that her death wasn't accidental, that if he wound up a primary suspect in the crime, his career would be finished.''

"Yes, but then, who ever really knows what goes on in somebody else's mind?'' Lily swirled her tall glass so the chunks of ice clinked and the thin lemon slices floated to the top. "It may be that Malcolm's hubris is such that he believed Veronica's drowning would, in fact, be labeled as nothing more than another tragic accident in the Hampton family. As for whatever motive he may have had, if there was anyone Veronica confided in with regard to her marriage, it was her hairdresser, Fabrizio. Why don't you ask him?''

Claire was so stunned by being casually handed this news that for a moment, she couldn't speak. It dawned on her, suddenly, that the two remaining Hampton women not only believed the senator had murdered his wife, but they also suspected what his motive for doing so had been and were giving her the means to

expose it. They were using her—either because they
were uncertain about their suspicions, or else because
people like the Hamptons simply didn't become involved with the police and had chosen her as their
intermediary.

"Yes, I believe I will ask Fabrizio," Claire replied
slowly, setting down her nearly empty glass of lemonade and pushing back her chair to get to her feet.
As she did so, the wrought-iron legs of the chair
caught on the inlaid, rough, brick floor of the conservatory, causing her to lurch forward and accidentally
knock over her glass. Much to her relief, it fell into
her lap instead of smashing upon the floor, the ice,
lemon slices, and dregs of lemonade spilling onto her
linen skirt. "Oh, I'm so terribly sorry!" Claire cried
softly as she swiftly scooped the glass's contents back
into it and carefully placed it back on the table. "How
stupidly clumsy of me! I almost broke your glass."
She shuddered at the realization, having a fairly good
idea that it was an expensive piece of either Baccarat
or Lalique that had nearly met its demise on the inlaid
bricks.

"The glass is not important." Lily dismissed it with
a nonchalant wave of her hand, then pulled a lacy,
white handkerchief from the bodice of her sundress.
"But I fear your skirt may be permanently stained if
we don't blot that up quickly."

"I doubt it. It's only lemonade, after all, and my
dry cleaner has got out worse, I assure you—one of
the hazards of the job, I'm afraid. Coffee, tea, wine,
rain, saltwater…my clothes have seen it all over the
years. But I do appreciate your assistance," Claire in-

sisted as she dabbed ruefully with Lily's handkerchief at the damp, lemonade stain on her skirt. "I'm just glad the only damage done was to me. And now, I'd better go before I commit some other faux pas. I've still got work to do at the station, so I'll need to run home and change clothes. Thank you both again so much for agreeing to the interview this afternoon. I promise you, you won't regret it."

"No, Ms. Connelly, I don't believe we will." Nadine inclined her head graciously. "Teresa will show you out." As though by magic, the same Latino maid who had earlier served the lemonade now reappeared to escort Claire to the front door of the Hampton family mansion.

She was so surprised by all the information she had received that afternoon, so rattled by the near disaster with the costly glass, that it was not until Claire had returned home that she realized that after blotting up the spilled lemonade, she had inadvertently tucked Lily D'Angelo's handkerchief into the pocket of her linen skirt. Now, mortified that she had unwittingly taken it, she slowly withdrew the delicate square of lacy, white lawn embroidered with equally dainty, white flowers in one corner. Claire didn't own any handkerchiefs herself, but the one she held in her hand was no less than she would have expected a woman from an old-money family in the South to possess.

It was sadly wrinkled from being crumpled up in the pocket of Claire's skirt, but even that couldn't disguise its fineness. Nor did the faint, citrus scent of lemonade detract from the rich, heady fragrance of flowers and musk that emanated from its folds. As she inhaled the redolence that permeated the handkerchief, a slight frown knitted Claire's brow. There was something about it that touched a strange chord in her memory, something she couldn't quite put her finger on. She could have sworn she had smelled this particular perfume before. It was not, she thought, anything on the market, however; rather, it was an expensive, custom scent, a signature fragrance especially blended. For some inexplicable reason, she believed the perfume to be important, and after a moment, she guiltily decided against cleaning and returning the handkerchief. Instead, she carefully folded it up in a piece of tissue paper and tucked it into her handbag, telling herself that Lily D'Angelo probably had dozens more just like it at home and so wouldn't miss this one.

Twenty-One

Revelations

The Book of Life begins with
a man and a woman in a garden.
It ends with Revelations.

A Woman of No Importance
—Oscar Wilde

The likes of Fabrizio on a regular basis were beyond Claire's own pocketbook. However, after hearing what she had to tell him, Mr. Kendall had agreed that under the circumstances, Channel 4 should spring for her to be coiffed by the hairdresser to the city's rich and shameless. Even so, Claire had to wait nearly two weeks for an appointment, "because no matter who you are, Ms. Connelly, we just can't possibly work you in before then," the salon's receptionist had haughtily informed her. "We simply have to give preference to our customers with standing appointments."

Although Claire was impatient at the delay, there was nothing she could do about it. So she wisely used the time to collate and type up all the information she had ever amassed about the Hampton family over the years of her career, including additional material that Zoey sent over from the morgue of the *Gulf Coast Courier.* As she worked, Claire cross-referenced her own records with Channel 4's archives, dutifully noting what the station had film of, in preparation for what she knew was evolving into a news story that would continue to receive media coverage for weeks to come, at least. *Inside Story* had already aired nationally her first segments on the drowning of Veronica Hampton Forsythe and the police's interrogation of Senator Malcolm Forsythe in connection with his wife's untimely death. If the senator were eventually to be arrested and tried for Veronica's murder, the story had the potential to become as big as O. J. Simpson's "trial of the century." And Claire would have not only a ringside seat, but also an inside track that everyone else in the media would lack.

As she reviewed her files on the Hamptons, Claire was reminded of her conversation with her best friend years ago at the *Courier,* when Lily D'Angelo's brother, Bruno, had been killed in the fatal car crash in Tuscany, and Zoey's suspicions that there had been more to that night than had ever been released to the media, a story old Mrs. Hampton had succeeded in hushing up to avoid a scandal. As Claire read on, sorting and chronicling, she was struck by a strange, growing sensation that what she was looking at was, in reality, a big, interlocking picture puzzle—with several pieces missing. The more she dwelled on that notion, the more convinced she became that it was indeed correct, that she could identify the shapes of the missing pieces if only she tried.

It had all started with that inexplicable car accident, Claire thought, or maybe even long before then; and now, her gut instinct told her that that night in Tuscany a decade ago was somehow inextricably linked to the past few months' events, the arsonous fire at the Seabreeze Sanatorium, the drowning of Veronica Hampton Forsythe in her family's Olympic-sized swimming pool. But…how? Bruno had long lain in his grave, and now Vanessa and Veronica were dead, too. That left only Lily to inherit the Hampton fortune.

Claire wondered why the police had not investigated Lily, why they were instead concentrating the majority of their efforts on Forsythe. What if the senator were innocent of the heinous crime of murdering his wife—and being cleverly framed by his cousin-in-law? That was certainly an idea worth delving into, Claire told herself slowly, contemplating the facts at hand. She would begin there, then, she decided resolutely, with Lily D'Angelo.

Claire's international flight to Rome had gone fairly smoothly, for which—being a white-knuckles flier—she was inordinately grateful. Much to her surprise, she had even managed to sleep for much of the trip across the Atlantic Ocean, so she was able temporarily to fight off most of the effects of transatlantic jet lag as she disembarked from the 747 and made her way through the airport to the taxi stands out front. Accustomed to traveling light and knowing she wouldn't be

in Italy long, she hadn't checked any baggage, but had
made do with her carry-on luggage.

After hailing a cab, Claire settled into its back seat
for the ride to the hotel where Channel 4, in conjunction with *Inside Story*, had made arrangements for her
to stay during her sojourn in Rome. Due to a combination of charm, determination, and persistence, she
had succeeded in being granted an extremely rare interview with Lily D'Angelo's father, Eduardo, the
count of San Paolo, who, suffering from a degenerative disease, had years ago retired from any public life.
As a result, no one had seen him for ages, so the interview was quite a coup. Claire was to visit him tomorrow at his villa, and she was both anxious about
and eager for their meeting. She felt somehow that the
count was privy to many of the Hampton family secrets, if only he chose to reveal them. But whether he
would or not was another matter entirely.

In his salad days, Eduardo D'Angelo had been a
wild, dissolute, jet-setting playboy, his title dubious at
best, his income erratic and of an uncertain nature,
besides. Mostly, he had been a gambler and a gigolo
until he had married old Mrs. Hampton's daughter,
Autumn. She had been named that for her flaming-red
hair—which she had bequeathed to her own daughter,
Lily, as well as to her twin nieces, Veronica and Vanessa—and she had possessed a temperament to
match. Even so, why the Hamptons had ever permitted
Autumn to wed a man like the count was still, after
more than thirty years, a mystery. It was inconceivable
that they hadn't known what he was, as well as the
fact that his principal interest in marrying Autumn had

been to acquire her share of the Hampton fortune. Still, the family had paid for the wedding and accepted D'Angelo with every appearance of being satisfied with him as a husband for Autumn.

Within a year of the marriage, Lily had been born, followed after a time by her younger brother, Bruno. But despite the fact that the D'Angelos had lived a luxurious lifestyle that most people would have envied, it had soon become clear that there was trouble in paradise. Rather than being settled by their marriage and children, Autumn and Eduardo had grown even wilder, partying until the wee hours with other, equally jaded, young jet-setters. Rumors of drinking binges, drugs, affairs, and orgies had abounded. Eventually, Autumn had been found dead one morning; her autopsy had revealed a lethal combination of alcohol and narcotics, which the coroner had ruled an accidental overdose.

Oddly, instead of blaming the handsome but decadent count for their daughter's death and taking his two children away from him, the Hamptons had continued to support him financially and, as far as Claire could determine, still did. They had also established trust funds for Lily and Bruno, although these had not been nearly as generous as those set up for the twins, whose own father had been the eldest Hampton son and therefore the primary heir. Despite its being the twentieth century, the family had continued to follow the archaic traditions associated with primogeniture, which had succeeded in keeping the bulk of their fortune intact throughout the decades.

Claire found it all very antiquated and unfair to the

younger Hamptons, but she had to admit there was a certain cold, hard practicality to it, which ensured the financial well-being of the family.

Once ensconced in her hotel room, she unpacked, washed her face and hands, and then fell into bed, knowing her biological clock was now out of sync with her current time zone and that, regardless of the fact that she had slept on the plane, she needed to be fresh and alert for her interview tomorrow morning. It didn't matter that she wasn't going to be able to capture it on film, since the count had expressly forbidden her to have any cameras or even a tape recorder present. It was enough that she had been granted the interview, that perhaps she would learn something that would help her piece together the jigsaw puzzle that was the Hampton family. And she could always do an on-camera report later, using whatever information she received from Eduardo. He had not declared the interview off the record, although there was always the chance that he might when she arrived at his villa, or even that he would announce that he had changed his mind and didn't want to talk to her, after all.

That was Claire's major worry, that she would have come all this way only to be refused admittance at the count's villa tomorrow. But much to her relief, that proved not to be the case when, the following morning, she hired a car and driver to take her out into the countryside beyond Rome, to Eduardo D'Angelo's small, secluded villa.

The maid who answered her knock at the front door escorted her through the wide, tiled foyer and living room to the terrace beyond, where the count sat in a wheelchair, looking as though he dozed in the morning sunlight beating down on the patio. Because there had been no film or photographs of him available for several years, Claire was unprepared for and shocked by his appearance. Her image of him had been that of a dark, handsome playboy. Instead, Eduardo was silver-haired and aged by illness almost beyond recognition, a pitiful, wasted shell of a man.

"Signora Connelly." An attendant she had not noticed before stepped from the shadows of the terrace. "I am Alfredo, the count's caretaker. If you will please be seated." He indicated a wrought-iron table and chairs to one side. "May I get you some coffee?"

"Yes, thank you."

From a serving cart, he filled a china cup with rich, black coffee and handed it to her. Then he wheeled the count close to the table, nodded politely to them both, and departed from the patio, leaving the two of them alone together. It was only then that Eduardo spoke, his voice low, his speech slow and a little slurred, so that at first, Claire had difficulty understanding him and would have thought he was drunk had she not known otherwise.

"Please...forgive me for not getting up to greet you, Signora Connelly," he said, with a small, casual wave of his hand and what she realized to her astonishment was a decided touch of his former charm, however now dissipated by illness. "But as you can plainly see, the years have exacted their toll in a way that has not been kind...punishment for the sins of my youth, I have always presumed." He paused for a moment, gathering breath. Then he continued. "Doubtless you are wondering why, after so many years away from the limelight, I decided to grant you this interview."

"Yes, I confess it's made me more than a little curious."

"It is a long tale—and one I have been well paid over the years to keep silent about. So perhaps it is unchivalrous of me not to take my secrets to the grave. But I no longer care, for in the end, I have lost far more than I ever gained. My silence cost me the life of my son, Bruno, and now that I know I am at long last dying, I intend to exact my revenge."

Then, with that pronouncement, Eduardo D'Angelo proceeded to tell Claire a story that shocked her to the very core of her being.

The last person Claire ever expected to see as she disembarked from the 727-Stretch on which she had made the last leg of her journey homeward was Jake Seringo. She had known it would be very late when her plane finally landed, so she had planned to take a taxi home from the airport and thus wasn't looking to be met. But as she walked from the jetway into the gate, the first person she saw was Jake, leaning casually against the far wall of the corridor beyond, clearly waiting for her, since there was nobody else around.

Despite herself, Claire's heart began to pound uncontrollably at the sight of him. She was always struck by his physical appearance, how tall, lean, and muscular he was, the suppleness of his whipcord body, the length of his corded legs, the provocative thrust of his hips that accentuated his predatory stance, his pantherish, black hair and swarthy skin, his glittering, dark-brown eyes alert beneath deceptively lazy lids. Seeing that she had spied him, he sauntered toward her, reaching for her carryall and slinging the leather strap easily over his shoulder before she could protest.

"What are you doing here, Jake?" Claire asked, not knowing what to make of his presence at the airport.

"To be perfectly frank, I'm checking up on you, Claire." He took her arm proprietarily, and when he touched her, it was as though an electric shock jolted through her as he began to propel her down the wide, red-carpeted corridor toward the main terminal. "It's probably just my cop's instinct working overtime, but somehow, when I learned you had jaunted off to Rome to meet with Eduardo D'Angelo, I got the strangest sensation that you weren't just after a story, that you were maybe playing detective."

"I'm sure I don't know why you should have thought that, Jake," she declared, although she was unable to prevent the betraying blush that stained her cheeks, and her guilty gaze fell beneath his own piercing one.

"Uh-huh," he drawled laconically as he stared down at her. "It couldn't possibly be because you've been digging extensively into the Hamptons' background, or because Senator Forsythe, old Mrs. Hampton, and Lily D'Angelo had you out to the mansion for a little tête-à-tête after Veronica's murder, or because after that, you just out of the blue made an appointment with Veronica's hairdresser, Fabrizio, or because Lily's father, Eduardo, the count of San Paolo—who hasn't granted an interview in years—

suddenly decided to see you following the deaths of his twin nieces. No, it couldn't be any of that, could it, Claire?''

''Maybe I'm just a good broadcast journalist who's thorough and efficient on the job.''

''Oh, you are that, I'll grant you. But you forget. I know you a little better than that, however much you might like to think otherwise.'' And from beneath his hooded lids, he looked at her in a way that abruptly made her breath catch in her throat, caused her to recall vividly the feel of his hard body pressing her down, quickening fiercely against her own soft one. She knew from how his dark eyes smoldered like twin flames that he remembered, too, that despite everything, he still wanted her. ''I don't know what you think you're up to, Claire. But I warn you. If I find out you're withholding information, that you're in any fashion impeding a police investigation, I'll have you down at the precinct and slapped with charges so fast that it'll make your head spin.''

Her head was already spinning, Claire thought, insisting to herself that it was only the result of her long, exhausting, international flight and had nothing whatsoever to do with the way Jake's eyes continued to rake her hungrily, even while he threatened her. She swallowed hard.

''I will tell you anything I believe to be relevant to the case, Jake, of course,'' she said. ''But this is hardly the time or place. I've been on one plane or another for the last twelve hours or so, and I'm very tired. But maybe you counted on that,'' she reasoned aloud slowly, as some inkling of understanding dawned.

"Maybe you thought you'd catch me off guard, that after a long, transatlantic flight, I wouldn't be thinking as fast on my feet as I normally would. You see, Jake, I know you a little better than perhaps you would like to believe, too."

A mocking half smile curved his full, sensual mouth, and his eyes gleamed as he glanced down at her intently. "How do you know *that* wasn't what I was really counting on, Claire?" he inquired softly, insolently, making her blush again hotly.

Abruptly changing the subject, she announced, "I don't have any luggage, so I don't need to stop at the baggage claim, and you don't need to drive me home, either, if that's what you intend, Jake. I can catch a cab out front."

"No, we're going to talk, Claire. We can do it on the way to your house, or we can do it down at the station, whichever you prefer."

"Fine. Have it your way. Take me home, then."

A low laugh emanated from Jake's lips at that, echoing in the nearly deserted terminal, and Claire blushed yet a third time as she grasped the inadvertent double entendre of her words. "I don't know what's got into you tonight, Jake, but I'm not sure I like it," she hissed furiously, her pulse racing, for she felt as though he played some sort of cat-and-mouse game with her, a game in which he knew all the rules and so held the upper hand, and she didn't.

For the first time, Claire thought to wonder how Jake knew so much about her recent activities. It occurred to her that whatever his reasons for doing so, he must have been keeping close tabs on her. She did

not know what to make of that; nor did she make the
mistake of underestimating him. He was extremely
clever and determined. Even had she not known him
as well as she did, his arrest record alone would have
told her that. He knew that as a broadcast journalist,
she had access to resources that he himself lacked, and
clearly, he intended to make use of those. She would
walk a delicate tightrope, trying to decide how much
to tell him, how much to keep to herself in the hope
of scooping her competition—and because of their history together, Jake would be wise to that fact, and
intensely watchful. He was not a man to be made a
fool of a second time. Nor had he demonstrated any
reluctance in employing his badge to apply pressure
upon her.

Claire grimaced at that thought, realizing that none
of her colleagues covering the murder of Veronica
Hampton Forsythe was likely to have a homicide detective breathing down his or her neck. If Jake were
on her case, he would greatly hamper her investigation. Still, at this point, she didn't know what she
could do about it. As he ushered her through the
heavy, glass, automatic doors of the terminal, she wondered what he would do if she suddenly broke away
from him and made a dash for one of the taxis lined
up out front. But even as that thought crossed her
mind, Jake deliberately tightened his grip on her arm.

"Don't even think about it, Claire," he warned as
he strode toward the short-term parking lot, hauling
her along in his wake. Upon reaching his classic Mustang convertible, he tossed her carryall into the back,
then opened the passenger door for her. "Get in," he

ordered tersely, and as she obediently settled herself inside, he went around the vehicle to slide in beside her. After starting the car, Jake cruised slowly through the parking lot to the exit, where he paid the attendant before pulling out onto the access road that led to the main highway.

Wearily, Claire laid her head back against the back of the leather seat, closing her eyes and relishing the feel of the cool, Gulf breeze against her face as the Mustang swept forward into the darkness, the stars in the night sky glittering like diamonds above them.

"Don't go to sleep, Claire," Jake admonished as he guided the convertible up the on-ramp and accelerated into the traffic on the six-lane highway. "I want to know why you went to Rome, why Eduardo D'Angelo agreed to see you."

Instead of answering directly, Claire queried, "Why do you think that has any bearing on your case?"

"I don't know that it does. But still, it's so out of character for the count that until I know otherwise, I'd be a fool if I didn't assume some connection between your interview with him and Veronica Hampton Forsythe's murder."

"I guess that's fair enough, but I don't know that there *is* a connection, Jake."

"Why don't you tell me what he revealed to you in your interview with him, and let me be the judge of that."

Claire hesitated for a moment, then said, "Eduardo—Eduardo D'Angelo is dying. That's the only reason why he ever agreed to meet with me...that and his desire for revenge on the Hamptons for the death of his son. He told me—he told me such a shocking, sordid story, Jake, that even now, I have a hard time believing it's all true, although I know it must be. He showed me documentation as proof of all his allegations...Autumn Hampton D'Angelo's diary, letters of testimony and signed affidavits from those involved in the terrible secret, birth certificates— He never trusted the Hamptons and so collected evidence to use against them in case it should ever become necessary.''

"In case he ever decided to blackmail them, you mean. As far as I've been able to determine, old Mrs. Hampton has supported him financially all these years.''

"With good reason. The twins and Lily...they weren't cousins, Jake. They were triplets, the product of—of incest, born to Autumn and her oldest brother, Spencer. Spencer's wife, Katherine, couldn't have any children, which is how they managed to persuade her not only to keep the dirty skeleton locked away in the Hampton family closet, but also to pass Veronica and Vanessa off as her own—that and a considerable amount of hush money, I suppose. At any rate, that's why Katherine and Autumn went away together to Italy that year more than three decades ago, so the two of them could switch identities, and no one would ever know it was Autumn and not Katherine who was really pregnant. Everything went as planned, except that the youngest triplet, Lily, was so puny at birth that she wasn't expected to live. That's why Katherine returned home with only Veronica and Vanessa. But somehow, Lily managed to survive, and of course, the Hamptons couldn't just suddenly produce a third baby.

"Autumn had stayed on in Italy. Old Mrs. Hampton had blamed her for the incestuous relationship with her brother and told her never to darken the family door again. So when Lily didn't die as expected, old Mrs. Hampton arranged for Eduardo to marry Autumn and pass Lily off as his own child. Lily was still so small and frail that it was easy enough for them to get away with the deception, and in the end, nobody ever suspected a thing. If any of it had ever got out, it would have ruined all of Spencer's political aspirations, of course, not to mention what it would have done to the family name here in the South—which must have been the Hamptons' biggest fear. You know what it's like here, Jake, how in some ways, traditions that have existed since before the Civil War have still managed to prevail."

"Yeah, I know. What I don't yet understand is why, even though he's dying, the count has decided to expose all this now, what it has to do with Bruno's death."

"Because Bruno was indirectly killed as a result of it all. Somehow, several years ago, Lily managed to unearth the truth about her real parentage, and that night at Bruno's villa in Tuscany, she chose to tell him and Vanessa that instead of being just first cousins, as they had always believed, they were, in fact, half brother and half sister, Autumn being the true mother of them both. Vanessa was horrified, as she and Bruno were having an affair, and she was carrying his child. You know what happened next. Vanessa ran out of the villa, with Bruno hard on her heels, and got into his Ferrari, ultimately crashing it on that dangerous, hairpin curve below Bruno's villa, killing him, and then suffering a nervous breakdown as well as a miscarriage, from which she never recovered.

"Now, what, if anything, all this may have to do with Veronica's murder, Jake, I don't know—except that it shows what Lily was capable of doing to her half brother and her sister. I know things don't look good for Senator Forsythe, that he's your primary suspect. But, well, what if—what if it were Lily who actually killed Veronica that night and then framed the senator? After all, it's Lily who's undoubtedly profited from Veronica's death—and Vanessa's, too, when you get right down to it. I mean…I know it might sound really far-fetched, but what if Lily has somehow systematically destroyed everyone who ever stood between her and the Hampton family fortune? The count believes her to be fully capable of it. He thinks she's quite insane and that she was maniacally jealous of Veronica and Vanessa, who spent their lives basking in the adoration of old Mrs. Hampton, while Lily, who ought to have shared equally in their good fortune, was instead left to grow up under the aegis of an ailing, degenerate stepfather with a dubious title and a life-style dependent upon remaining in old Mrs. Hampton's good graces."

"Claire, I see what you're driving at," Jake stated as he stepped on the accelerator to pass a slower-moving car in front of them. "But there are major flaws in your theory. After all, Lily wasn't at the wheel of Bruno's Ferrari that night in Tuscany. She wasn't at the Seabreeze Sanatorium before the arsonous fire.

She wasn't poolside at the senator's big fund-raising bash."

"I—I guess I hadn't thought about any of that," Claire admitted dejectedly, all the elation she had felt at possibly uncovering the news story of the century abruptly dissipating in the face of his cool logic.

"However, it's still a shocking, scandalous tale— so I feel quite certain you can make good use of it somehow to send *Inside Story's* Nielsen ratings sky-rocketing," Jake continued, his tone now tinged with bitterness and sarcasm.

Claire flinched at that. "I suppose it would surprise you to learn that I—that I haven't yet decided what, if anything, to do with all the count told me."

"Yeah, that would indeed surprise me." Jake shot her a wry, disbelieving glance that spoke volumes.

"Nevertheless, it's true," she insisted resolutely. "If any of it has bearing on Veronica's murder, on the senator's innocence or lack of it, that's one thing. But otherwise, I do not see that there is anything useful to be gained by broadcasting such shocking and sordid revelations. The Hamptons have surely suffered more than their fair share of tragedies over the decades, and there is nothing in this particular secret that affects the public welfare."

"I see. There are limits, after all, to how you will pander to the public, then."

"Perhaps there always were. Or perhaps I have grown...wiser over the years."

"Have you, indeed?"

"Yes, I have. But this is an old quarrel, Jake—and I'm too tired to have it again with you tonight. It no longer matters whether or not you believe me. It is enough that I know it myself.''

After that, instead of asking her about the time she had spent with the Hamptons or about her appointment with Fabrizio, Jake fell strangely silent, his concentration seemingly focused on weaving the Mustang in and out of the traffic that swept briskly along the six-lane highway into the city, amber-glowing streetlights and white-shining headlights streaking the asphalt still steaming with the day's heat and making it shimmer. But Claire knew him too well to suppose he had given up so easily. She might have halted his onslaught temporarily. But he would be after her again for information if he thought it would help his case. He hadn't become one of the department's top homicide detectives by not being as tenacious as a bulldog.

Still, she was relieved he hadn't persisted, for what she had told him was true: She didn't want to argue with him. So she said nothing further, but settled herself more comfortably into her seat and, from beneath her thick, sooty lashes, studied Jake surreptitiously. Like many Latinos, his Spanish blood was pronounced in his hawkish features—the raven-black hair, the bronze skin, the high cheekbones, the strongly chiseled nose, the sensual mouth—so he resembled some bold, arrogant conquistador of old. The wind streamed through his sleek hair. The neon signs of the hotels and restaurants that lined the highway alternately illuminated, then cast into shadow, his dark, handsome visage. His hands, grasping the steering wheel, were long and deceptively elegant, for she knew their power, recalled the feel of them moving over her body feverishly and possessively, leaving in their wake faint bruises born of passion upon her delicate skin.

Even now at the memory, a slow-burning heat pooled at the core of Claire's being to gradually suffuse her entire body, stirring her senses and desire, leaving her molten and aching. She should be used to it by now, she thought dimly—to this strange, exciting, irresistible effect he had always had upon her. Yet, somehow, the strength of the attraction never ceased to startle her. She had never felt it for anyone but Jake. It was as though all those years ago, when he had opened his front door to her, pinned her to the floor of his apartment, he had marked her in some way as his. Deep down inside, she knew that despite the fact that she had married Paul Langley, some treacherous part of her had always still belonged to Jake. Paul had sensed that, too, because although he had never known about Jake, he had nevertheless always accused her of withholding some vital piece of herself from him. It was just one more thing for which Paul had ultimately come to hate and resent her.

Claire wondered what Jake was thinking, but knew it would prove fruitless to ask. She had given up that right a decade ago. Now, she had nothing but her memories of what they had once shared together, and the want and need that were like a fever in her blood, disturbing and arousing her, no matter how hard she strove against them. Except that tonight she was too weary to fight her feelings. So she sat there in the silence and darkness, letting them wash over her, engulf her like the waves of a maddening sea. Eventually, her eyes drifted shut, and she slept—and

dreamed, the nightmare in which she was caught by
the deadly riptide, being pulled under and drowned.

She awoke to find herself wrapped in Jake's strong
arms. He was stroking her hair gently and speaking
quietly, soothingly, to her. But for a moment, disoriented, Claire didn't understand that and struggled
against him wildly, mistakenly thinking she was being
dragged down to the bottom of the ocean and her panic
only increasing as he tightened his grip upon her.

"Claire...Claire! It's Jake, baby. For God's sake,
stop fighting me, damn you, and hush! You'll wake
up the entire neighborhood!"

She realized then that the sobbing cries she had
heard, which had wakened her, were coming from her
own throat, and that she wasn't headed for Davy
Jones's locker, or even in her own bed, but was sitting
in Jake's Mustang, which was now parked in front of
her house. Slowly, she ceased to whimper and strive
against him, merely gasping a little for breath as she
stared up into his dark-brown eyes, his face just inches
from her own.

"I'm—I'm sorry," she choked out, suddenly all too
aware of his proximity, the way her heart was racing,
how adrenaline pumped wildly through her body. "I—
I must have fallen asleep. I was...dreaming."

"More like a nightmare, I'd say." To her surprise,
Jake's gaze was filled with concern as he studied her,
noting the faint lines of strain that now etched her
countenance, pale in the moonlight. "Do you have it
often, Claire?"

She nodded, biting her lower lip with embarrassment, then managed a short, quiet laugh. "I feel so

silly…like a child afraid of the dark. It's nothing, really."

"Do you want to tell me about it? I've heard it said that if you describe your nightmare to someone, you'll never have it again."

"I'd be glad if that were so, because to be honest, it…it really frightens me, Jake. In my dream, I'm—I'm caught in a terrible riptide, and it's dragging me under, so I know I'm going to drown. I keep struggling to break free, but there's no air in my lungs, and every time I try to get my breath, I swallow big gulps of saltwater. It's dark and cold, and I can feel my whole body getting numb, and the shore's so far away that I can't reach it. Then, out of nowhere, this shadowy figure appears on the beach. I never see him—at least, I think it's a he—clearly, only his hand, which he's stretching out to me. If I take hold of it, I'll be saved. But somehow, I'm as afraid of the hand—of the man it belongs to—as I am of drowning. And so in the end, I always hesitate, and then I'm lost, and I—I go under for the last time. That's when I invariably awaken in a panic. I know it's just a ridiculous dream, but—"

"I don't think it's ridiculous at all…not if it scares you, Claire." Jake's voice was low and curiously gentle, his breath warm against her face, as he continued to stroke her hair, her arms, making her skin tingle. "But dreams, even nightmares, can be controlled. It's called directed dreaming, I believe, or something like that. Anyway, have you ever tried forcing yourself to take hold of the hand, just to see what happens?"

"No. Do you think I should?"

"Yeah. You never know. It might change the whole ending of your nightmare."

Wordlessly, Claire contemplated that idea. She had dwelled on it many times before, but she had somehow always lacked the courage to carry it through. Perhaps now, having shared her dream, she would remember this conversation when the nightmare came to her again, and she would be able to alter it. It was worth a try, she thought. Then, after a moment, despite how it had upset her, she ceased to think of her dream at all as she slowly became aware of how Jake continued to hold her in his arms.

Her cheek was pressed against his broad chest. She could hear the steady beat of his heart, reassuring somehow in the wake of her nightmare. She could feel the heat of his hard, lean body seeping into her own softer, slender one, mingling with the humidity of the night air and with the steam that still rose from the asphalt of the street. A thin coat of perspiration sheened her skin, beading her upper lip and trickling from her temples and down the valley between her breasts. Deep down inside her, emotions and sensations Claire had thought long buried—or even dead—were stirring to life again, roused in a way that only Jake had ever been able to do.

She wondered if he felt the same, if he were even now remembering all the times he had cradled her against himself like this in the past, had kissed her, had made feverish love to her. She suspected that maybe he was, for he had suddenly become very still, as though he could see into her mind, knew what she was thinking. He had always known. Some things, it seemed, hadn't changed. His sharply indrawn breath rasped in her ear. In some dark corner of her brain was the thought that she should disentangle herself from his embrace before something untoward occurred.

But she couldn't seem to force herself to move away from him, not even when she felt his hand at her throat, fingers tightening there briefly in a strangely erotic, possessive gesture before sensuously sliding up to cup her chin, deliberately compelling her face up to his own.

"Witch," he muttered before, without further warning, his mouth swooped to capture hers, hard and hungry, his tongue parting her lips and plunging deep.

In her fantasies, Claire had imagined just such a moment as this so many times over the past ten years that now, at first, she thought she must still be asleep and dreaming, that this couldn't possibly be happening, that no matter how much he might still want her, Jake would never give in to his desire for her after what she had done to him so long ago.

Yet his mouth felt undeniably real, moving demandingly, savagely, on hers, as though the tide of passion he had so carefully mastered and dammed within himself the past decade had suddenly swollen and burst uncontrollably through its barriers, sweeping him along as ruthlessly in its wake as he now swept her, swallowing her breath and leaving her senses reeling. Dimly, Claire realized that the little whimpers and moans she heard came from her own throat as she melted helplessly against him, her hands creeping up of their own volition to fasten themselves around his neck, to draw him even nearer, her lips yielding pliantly to his onslaught.

At her response, his fingers tangled roughly in her hair, yanking impatiently at the pins that secured it in its French twist, so the heavy mass tumbled around her shoulders. His hands tightened in it, hurting her, but she didn't feel the pain. She was lost, drowning in a sea of sensation that was as deceptive and dangerous as the riptide of her nightmare. For there could be nothing between her and Jake now—nothing, except this. She knew that even before he abruptly tore his mouth from hers, his breath harsh and labored, his eyes glittering not only with desire, but also with anger and self-contempt. A muscle flexed in his taut jaw as he fought for control of the turbulent emotions running rampant within him.

"Damn you!" he grated, his voice low and throbbing with feeling—as though what had just occurred had somehow been all her fault. "I promised myself I would never fall under your spell again. But there's just something about you, Claire, that makes me want to make love to you, to protect you and to take care of you, and to do you some violence all at the same time!" Suddenly realizing he still had his fists wrapped in her hair, Jake released her. Then he flung wide his car door and slid out, grabbing her carryall before striding around the Mustang to open her own door. "Get out," he ordered tersely, running one hand raggedly through his hair. "Now—before I do something we might both regret afterward."

As, slowly, she eased herself from the vehicle and stood, Claire discovered that she was trembling from the emotions and passion he had wakened inside her. Her knees were weak and nearly gave way beneath her, so Jake's arm shot out to take hold of her, steadying her. He swore under his breath, practically dragging her up the walk to her front door, so that before they reached the porch, she stumbled more than once, causing him to curse again. But she knew from experience that deep down inside, he was actually furious at himself, not her.

"Where's your key?" he asked curtly.

Still shaking, she fumbled in her purse for it. "You—you don't need to see me inside, Jake. I—I think you've done...more than enough already."

"I deserved that. I know I did. But that doesn't make it any easier to swallow, Claire." He snatched the key from her grasp, then inserted it into the lock and opened her front door. "If it's any gratification to you, however, I blame myself for it as much as I blame you."

"I know. But that doesn't make it any easier for me, either, Jake!" Quickly, Claire stepped across the threshold, punching her security code into the alarm panel to deactivate the alarm before it could sound. Then she switched on the foyer light and turned back to Jake, intending to collect her carryall from him and shut the door. Her heart was still pounding, and she couldn't seem to think straight. Her brain was muddled from jet lag and exhaustion, she told herself. The last thing she had needed on top of it tonight had been to fall asleep in Jake's convertible, suffer her nightmare about the riptide, and then, out of the blue, be fervently kissed by him as though ten years hadn't come and gone since the first time he had ever held her in his arms. And the fact that he had so abruptly broken off the kiss, rejecting her yet again, stung even through the cloud of weariness and arousal that saturated her whole being.

Claire was therefore unnerved to find that he had followed her inside to set her carryall down in the foyer. "I suppose I should thank you for driving me home from the airport. But since you obviously had ulterior motives for doing so, I won't bother," she announced indignantly, making it clear that she wanted Jake to leave. She didn't trust herself—or him—and she didn't know what she would do if he suddenly took her in his arms and kissed her fiercely again. No doubt she would allow him to carry her down the hall to her bedroom, strip off her clothes, and do as he damned well pleased with her, she thought, silently cursing herself for being so weak-willed where he was concerned.

"Yeah, well, you needn't think this is the end of the matter, Claire. You're meddling in things that don't concern you—and like I said before, if I find out you're impeding my investigation, you'll be sorry. I mean that, so don't take me lightly."

"I never did, Jake. Now, if you don't mind, I've had a long day, and I'm very tired. So good night."

"Good night, Claire." For a moment, it seemed as though Jake would say something more. But then he must have decided against it, because instead, he turned on his heel to stride from the house and down the walk out front to his Mustang. There, he paused momentarily to light a cigarette before sliding into the driver's seat, starting the engine, and pulling away from the curb.

His red-glowing taillights disappeared as Claire closed the front door after him and locked it securely, then reactivated her alarm system. It was only tiredness, she told herself later, that caused her to cry herself to sleep that night.

Twenty-Two

Planned Encounters

Though all the winds of doctrine were let loose
to play upon the earth, so Truth be in the field,
we do injuriously, by licensing and prohibiting,
to misdoubt her strength. Let her and Falsehood
grapple; who ever knew Truth put to the worse,
in a free and open encounter?

Areopagitica
—John Milton

Despite Jake's warning to her, in the days that followed, Claire continued to dig into the murder of Veronica Hampton Forsythe, which, because the senator was known to be under investigation by the police for the crime, continued to be a hot news story. It had recently been revealed that some time ago, Forsythe had taken out a multimillion-dollar insurance policy on his wife's life, and this information had appeared to supply a motive for him that had previously been lacking. Even so, he had not as yet been arrested, and the rumor was that despite this new revelation, the D.A. still did not feel that the evidence against the senator was strong enough to build an airtight case against him. It was further gossiped that the D.A. was moving slowly because he didn't intend to embark on a trial that might turn into a complete fiasco resulting in an acquittal that left him with egg all over his face. "This isn't L.A.," he had snapped during one stressful, heated interview. However, none of this prevented jokes from circulating around the city—not the least of which ended with Forsythe making his escape in a white Ford Bronco, cruising casually down the Gulf Coast highway.

Like the rest of her colleagues in the media, Claire dutifully filed her own reports, doing what she could to keep them fresh and current so the public wouldn't lose interest in the story. But realistically speaking, there was little breaking news until the day of her hair appointment with Fabrizio.

The hairdresser was a flamboyant, critically opinionated homosexual, so Claire knew there was little use in flirting with him in an attempt to gain information from him. He wasn't going to prove susceptible to her sensual charms—only to her flattery and wit. So those were what she employed in an effort to get him to open up about his dead client, Veronica Hampton Forsythe.

"Poor Ronnie." Fabrizio sighed as he snipped expertly with his scissors at Claire's hair. "She wasn't just one of my regulars, you know. She was a friend. That was why I insisted on doing her hair for her funeral, even though they had to have a closed casket because she had drowned. Such a terrible way to die, I'm told—although I suppose she was unconscious through it all and so didn't feel a thing, thank heavens. At any rate, I'm just positive that husband of hers killed her. He was never any good. I tried to tell Ronnie that when she married him. But of course, she was young and in love then, and she wouldn't hear a word against him. She changed her tune later, though.''

"Oh, why was that?'' Claire inquired, careful not to display too much eagerness in the answer.

Fabrizio shrugged carelessly, rolling his eyes. "You know, the usual. When it came to other women, Forsythe just couldn't keep his trousers zipped. I daresay Ronnie would have ignored a casual fling or two. Most political wives do for the sake of their husbands' careers. But she said that this last time, the senator had gone too far, that she'd had it, and that she wasn't going to turn a blind eye any longer.''

"What are you saying...that she was going to divorce him?''

"That's what she told me—that, and that she was going to ruin his career with the scandal in the process. Of course, I didn't take her seriously at the time. Old Mrs. Hampton would have pitched a fit if Ronnie had caused the family to become fodder for the tabloids— not that they aren't currently, thanks to all this mess— and since Ronnie loved her grandmother, she would never have done anything to upset her.''

"But now, you think maybe Ronnie was actually serious about the divorce?''

"Well, it certainly looks that way, doesn't it? Obviously, Forsythe wouldn't have got a penny of the

Hampton fortune if Ronnie had divorced him—and I suppose it's possible his little bit on the side could conceivably have been such that exposure of the affair would indeed have proved ruinous."

"Still, the senator's got money of his own," Claire remarked as she reflected upon the hairdresser's words, "and accusations of infidelity on the part of politicians have been ignored by the public as often as they've been taken seriously. Do you know who Forsythe was allegedly fooling around with?"

"No, Ronnie wouldn't say. And I wouldn't be too sure the senator's pockets are still as deep as hers were. He has a lot of other vices besides women... gambling, drugs, alcohol. Sooner or later, those things take their toll, you know, and I've heard through the grapevine that he's a high roller in Manolo Alvarez's private rooms out at the Flamingo Landing. Everybody who's anybody in this city knows all about the gambling and prostitution going on at that place, even though the police never seem to be able to catch anyone in the act there. Besides which, I'd be willing to bet that Forsythe's hands are none too clean politically, either."

"Have you told the police about any of this, Fabrizio?"

"Yes—for all the good it did me. It's all hearsay evidence, rumor, and speculation, you see, so they can't use any of it without corroboration. But perhaps if you mention it on *Inside Story,* it'll put the pressure on the police to substantiate it."

Claire was tactful enough not to point out that perhaps there was nothing to confirm, that people like

Fabrizio routinely dealt in gossip and innuendo, that it was part and parcel of their trade, employed to shock and titillate their clientele and keep them coming back for more. Just because all that was so didn't mean that what the hairdresser had told her didn't have a grain of truth in it, all the same. She would do some more checking of her own to find out.

She left the salon with her hair slightly shorter and sleeker than when she had come in, swinging freely around her shoulders, parted on one side, and hanging sensuously over her right eye. She wondered idly if Channel 4 and *Inside Story* would think their money had been well spent. She hadn't worn her hair this way in years, thinking it made her look like some sex kitten in a porno movie rather than a serious broadcast journalist.

"So that's what a couple of hundred bucks and a day at Fabrizio's does for one, is it?"

In the salon's parking lot, Claire drew up short at the sight of Jake leaning casually against the side of her snappy, red Beamer, his suit jacket tossed over one shoulder, his eyes concealed by mirrored, aviator sunglasses, a lit cigarette dangling from one corner of his carnal mouth, his shirtsleeves rolled up to reveal his muscular forearms, damp in the summer heat.

"Is this what's known as police harassment, Jake?" she inquired tartly, both confused and stirred by his presence. "You know my schedule. You knew my home address the other night. You appear to be spying on me—and you've certainly made at least one sexual advance toward me. I wonder what Captain Nichols would have to say to all that?"

"I imagine that would depend on what he'd seen on the news that day. He likes reporters just about as much as I do."

"Then why are you following me around?"

"I told you. Because you're meddling, Claire—and I don't want this case blown clear to hell in a handbasket because it was tried in the media before it ever got to a courtroom."

"I'm not trying to wreck your case, Jake. But the public has a right to know whether the man they've elected to the U.S. Senate is a womanizing, drug-and-alcohol-abusing gambler who murdered his wife."

"That's what Fabrizio said to you, is it?"

"Among other things, yes. He also intimated that the police have made little or no effort to corroborate his allegations."

"That's a damned lie," Jake asserted, his nostrils flaring at the insult. "It's just that these things take time. Senator Forsythe's not just some punk off the mean streets. In some circles, he's considered the next JFK, and he's got connections that go all the way to the White House. It's not easy to bring somebody like that down, Claire—which is precisely why I don't want or need your interference in this investigation."

"I've done nothing that could be considered as such, Jake."

"Perhaps not yet. But somehow, I have the strangest feeling that you will. Look, Claire, did you ever stop to consider the fact that you are dealing here with somebody who has already killed once—possibly even twice if Vanessa Hampton is factored into the equation—and that you might wind up as victim number three? Think about that—if not for your own sake, then at least for your daughter's.''

"You don't think I *have* thought about that? I'm not a fool, Jake."

"No, but sometimes, you act like one, anyway, Claire. Perhaps we all do. And the truth is that I...I don't want to get a call on my radio some night and discover you dead in an alley somewhere."

She wished desperately that she could see his eyes then, so she would have some idea what he was thinking, if there were actually still some spark of caring in him for her, after all, as his words would lead her to believe, or if he were only saying them to conceal other, less altruistic motives. It shouldn't have mattered so much to her. She was dismayed to find that it did. "I appreciate your concern. But I've been taking care of myself for a long time now. I imagine I can go on doing so."

"I wonder. Despite the cool, competent image you project, deep down inside, you're very vulnerable, I think...perhaps even more than you realize since your husband died. No matter what, that has to have been hard for you. I've been there. I know."

"It...wasn't the same for me as it was for you, Jake. I told you that."

"Yeah, but it still had to hurt." Taking a last, long drag off his cigarette, he dropped the butt on the pavement and ground it out with his boot. "I like your hair that way," he said before he strolled from the parking lot, leaving her standing there staring after him, wholly bewildered and yet oddly intrigued by his contradictory behavior toward her.

She would have been quite surprised to learn that Jake was equally puzzled by and conflicted about his actions where she was concerned.

"Get a grip, Jake," he growled irately to himself as he reached his Mustang, parked at the curb, and wrenched open the door on the driver's side. "Either you want her, or you don't."

The trouble was that he thought he did.

He had tried to tell himself otherwise, to fight his feelings for Claire. Even so, he couldn't stop thinking about her, finding reasons to see her—excuses that sounded lame even to his own ears. In reality, Claire had been right: What he was doing to her actually *did* verge on police harassment. If she decided to make an issue of it, he could conceivably wind up with the Internal Affairs Division breathing down his neck, conducting a full-scale investigation into his police activities to determine if and how else he might have abused the privileges that had come with his badge. But even that thought had not deterred him.

Jake could still taste Claire's mouth, sweet and tremulous beneath his own after he had driven her home from the airport the other night, smell the heady, gardenia scent of her, her signature fragrance, the only perfume he would ever recognize instantly anywhere. Standing in her foyer after dropping her off, it had been all he could do not to drag her down the hallway beyond, kicking open doors until he found the one that led to her bedroom. More than once, he had called himself a fool, despised himself for his weakness where Claire was concerned. But still, every time he saw her, old memories and desires stirred within him, wreaking havoc on his senses and making him behave in ways for which he would have censured another detective.

Jamming his foot down on the accelerator, he sped along the sunlit streets, cursing himself yet again for his reckless disregard of police regulations and Captain Nichols's orders to avoid all contact with the media. Jake knew he was walking a fine line.

The only thing he wasn't sure of was where it was leading him.

Twenty-Three

Flamingo Landing

There is no disguise which can for long conceal
love where it exists or simulate it where it does not.

> *Reflections; or, Sentences and Moral Maxims.*
> *Epigraph*
> —François, Duc de La Rochefoucauld

Upon further reflection of all she had learned, it appeared to Claire that perhaps she had been on the wrong track about Lily D'Angelo, after all, that Jake was right, and it was really the senator who had murdered Veronica Hampton Forsythe. Certainly, Claire had to take into account the fact that old Mrs. Hampton and Lily themselves had obviously privately believed the senator to be guilty, regardless of how they continued to support him publicly. Further, there were Fabrizio's allegations to consider. If the senator's own financial resources had indeed dwindled to any great extent over the years due to womanizing, gambling, drugs and alcohol, or even just plain, old bad investments, then he might have become dependent on his wife's money. He might have grown desperate if he had discovered she was planning to divorce him.

The whole scenario was, in fact, not all that much different from what had happened in her own marriage, Claire realized slowly, except that Paul hadn't decided to conk her over the head and shove her into a swimming pool to drown. He had simply attempted to run away, to escape instead, and had tried to take Gillian with him in the process.

Now, as she gazed down at all the materials spread on the coffee table before her, Claire focused on the glossy, black matchbook she had found amid Paul's possessions after his death. She had stuck it into her file on the Hamptons because of Jake's informing her that an identical matchbook had been found in the debris that had resulted from the arsonous fire at the Seabreeze Sanatorium. Somehow, there had to be a connection, she thought—only she just couldn't see it. From where had the matchbook originally come? If Jake knew, he had not enlightened her about it. But staring at the wharf etched in gold on the cover of the matchbook, some more of the pieces of the puzzle abruptly fell into place for Claire as she realized what the dock actually represented—a landing—and she recalled Fabrizio's words to her about Manolo Alvarez's private rooms for gambling and prostitution at the Flamingo Landing.

Was that where Paul had gone, how he had somehow run through so much money? Was Senator Forsythe, too, somehow mixed up with the Latino kingpin? If so, the senator might indeed have been driven to murder, for being in the media, Claire perhaps knew better than most Alvarez's dubious background and unsavory reputation. Despite numerous police investigations, nothing had ever been proved against him, as any charges that had resulted in his being arrested invariably wound up being dismissed for insufficient evidence. It was uncanny how vital proof would mysteriously disappear from the property room or how witnesses recanted statements against him or simply vanished, never to be seen again. It was bandied about that Alvarez had not only city officials, but also those at state and federal levels in his back pocket—which probably explained how those rumored private rooms at the Flamingo Landing continued to operate. Maybe the matchbook—otherwise unmarked save for the pier—was some kind of passport to those rooms, Claire thought suddenly, her heart beginning to pound with excitement. Maybe there was a possibility that with it, she could get herself on the inside of Alvarez's operation, find out what, if any, his connection to Senator Forsythe was.

If one surfaced, it seemed likely to her that the senator, and not some deranged inmate, had torched the Seabreeze Sanatorium, as well as murdering Veronica Hampton Forsythe. But for what reason, Claire was as yet unable to guess. It was really far-fetched to think Forsythe had had his sister-in-law's life insured, in addition to his wife's. Still, somehow there must be a relationship between the arsonous fire that had killed Vanessa Hampton and her twin sister's drowning in the Hampton family's Olympic-sized swimming pool. Certainly, Jake appeared to believe there was—and whatever else he might be, he was a damned fine homicide detective with extremely keen instincts.

And he was on her trail like a relentless bloodhound, Claire reminded herself grimly.

She was going to need some sort of disguise. She had one of the most recognizable faces in the city, anyway, so it was stupid to think Alvarez was simply going to let her, a broadcast journalist, walk right into his private rooms, in any event. She'd call Fabrizio, Claire decided, have him send over a wig, and she'd get some glasses with tinted, nonprescriptive lenses. She'd do her makeup differently, too, and wear something she'd otherwise not be caught dead in... something tastefully flamboyant—if there was such a thing—that would be bound to attract Alvarez's attention. If she could get him talking, maybe he would make some slip, inadvertently reveal something he ought not have. The idea that if by some miracle he actually did and realized his mistake, her own life would undoubtedly be in jeopardy, Claire resolutely shoved from her mind, along with Jake's warning that her meddling might get her killed. She would be careful, and besides, Alvarez could hardly drag her away from such a crowded establishment as the Flamingo Landing without people noticing what was happening to her.

It had proved more difficult than anticipated for the police to uncover Senator Malcolm Forsythe's financial dealings, as he had safeguarded himself by means of several different corporate entities, some of which were legitimate and others of which were little more than shell companies. Since the same was also true of Manolo Alvarez, finding a connection between the two men was a time-consuming and painstaking task. Nevertheless, Jake felt certain there *was* some relationship between them—although he had nothing more to go on than a matchbook found in the ashes of the arsonous fire at the Seabreeze Sanatorium and his gut instinct that if the senator had murdered his own wife, he had also, for whatever as-yet-unknown reason, somehow been involved in setting the blaze that had taken the life of her younger twin sister.

Because of all this, Jake had recently made it his practice to drive out to the Flamingo Landing for supper at least two or three times a week. Besides the fact that he wanted to unsettle Alvarez, the food at the hotel was superb, and Jake could afford it. Over the years, with the exception of his houseboat, the classic Mustang, and a couple of good suits, he had spent relatively little on himself, investing his money instead. These days, he actually made a great deal more income from playing the stock market than he earned as a homicide detective.

Only once had he ever attempted—casually—to stroll back to what he knew without a doubt were Alvarez's private rooms devoted to gambling and prostitution. He had been politely but firmly halted in his tracks by one of the Latino kingpin's henchmen, and within moments, Alvarez himself had appeared.

"My apologies, Detective Seringo. But the rooms beyond this hallway are where the offices of the hotel are housed, and they are strictly off-limits to guests," Manny had declared with a wolfish, mocking smile that had let Jake know that far from being unnerved by having a homicide detective present at the Flamingo Landing, the Latino kingpin was actually highly amused by the cat-and-mouse game he and Jake had embarked upon. "Unless, of course, you have a search warrant...?" One of Manny's brows had lifted inquiringly before he had shrugged carelessly. "What a pity for you to be so frustrated by superiors who do not share your intellect."

"Yeah, it's enough to make a man long to take the law into his own hands," Jake had replied with seeming indifference, intimating that he might be a cop who had reached the point where he had become corruptible. When he had seen the interest and speculation flare in Alvarez's eyes, Jake had known his shot had not missed.

But, "Indeed," was all the Latino kingpin had said.

Since then, Alvarez had watched Jake as closely but surreptitiously as he had watched the Latino kingpin. But tonight, as Jake's dark-brown eyes flicked alertly, however covertly, around the hotel, his attention was attracted not by Alvarez, but by a woman he was sure he had never seen at the Flamingo Landing before— or anywhere else, for that matter. But despite that fact, she nevertheless appeared oddly familiar to him. There was, he realized after a moment, something about her proud, elegant carriage, her unconsciously seductive, self-assured walk, her firm, rounded derrière, and her long, racy legs that reminded him of Claire. This woman, however, had a mass of curly, dark-brown hair that framed a pair of striking, tortoiseshell, tinted glasses adorning her face and long, gold earrings that dangled from her lobes to dust her bare shoulders. She was wearing a short, tightly molded, midnight-black, halter dress that made it clear there was one hell of a body underneath.

Much to his surprise, as he looked at her, Jake felt his groin tighten with a sudden desire that flared as hotly for the unknown woman as it did for Claire herself. He was momentarily thrown for a loop by the unexpected impact of the sensation, because until now, he had not thought any female could stir him as quickly and deeply as Claire Connelly. The woman disappeared into the bar, and after an instant, Jake rose from his table in the dining room, where he had just finished eating a later supper, to follow her.

She had seated herself on one of the high stools at the long, hand-carved, Honduras-mahogany bar with its gleaming, brass foot rail and had ordered a Tom Collins, the perfect drink, he decided, for a long, cool woman in a black dress. Casually, he sat down beside her, asking the bartender for a Scotch. Then he lit up a cigarette, surveying the woman appreciatively from beneath hooded lids. Much of her profile was concealed from him by her riotous mass of curls and her tortoiseshell, tinted glasses, but he liked what he did see...the long, thick, black lashes, the delicately chiseled nose, the full, sulky mouth colored with rich, burgundy lipstick. But as he studied the woman, Jake found he couldn't stop thinking about how much even her profile reminded him of Claire. That was why she had appealed to him so, he realized.

She reached for her Tom Collins, and for the first time, he observed how her hand trembled ever so slightly, the way in which the pulse at her throat fluttered wildly. She practically drained her drink in one nervous gulp. Clearly, she was highly agitated about something—but what? After a moment, she reached into her handbag, withdrawing several dollar bills that she tossed on the bar to pay for the Tom Collins. Then, without glancing even once his direction, she slid off the high stool and headed for the glass bar doors.

As her swift movement stirred the air, the sweet, intoxicating scent of her wafted to Jake's nostrils...gardenias. He would know that fragrance anywhere; even in this dimly lighted, smoke-filled bar, it couldn't elude him. It was a perfume that was especially blended in New Orleans. Claire had told him years ago that, like her bedroom suite, it had been something her mother had insisted on, that each of the Connelly daughters should have her own, signature scent. Thumping his empty glass down violently on the bar top, Jake spat a very foul curse, knowing now the cause of his powerful reaction to the previously unknown but hauntingly familiar woman. Then he paid for the smoky Scotch he had drunk and, his detective instincts and more aroused, went after her, raw, primitive emotions now thoroughly raging within him.

Oh, God, Claire thought, horrified, as, in the mirrors hanging throughout the bar, she spied Jake coming after her, his dark visage looking like a thundercloud. He had figured out who she was; she knew that without a shadow of a doubt, and it was all she could do to restrain herself from running toward the doors.

She had nearly died when he had come into the bar

and sat down beside her. Of all she had imagined might happen at the Flamingo Landing, that scenario had never even crossed her mind. She hadn't even known that Jake came here. But now a multitude of thoughts and emotions crowded into her brain, nearly overwhelming her. The foremost of these was fear. Jake was almost surely here because, like her, he had connected the matchbook to the hotel, and having recognized her, he could only think she had totally disregarded all his warnings to her about interfering with his investigation. He would be livid about that, and there was no telling what he would do when he caught her—especially if she had somehow inadvertently blown a big, undercover operation. For all she knew, he might be on the premises in conjunction with Vice and Narcotics. The police might have been watching the Flamingo Landing for days, weeks, or even months, hoping to carry out a successful sting and to arrest Manolo Alvarez on charges that would finally stick. It occurred to her that if she had unwittingly screwed up a police operation, Jake would have every right to be angry with her.

Mingled with these ideas, however, were others that said perhaps she was wildly jumping to conclusions that had no basis in reality. Maybe Jake was only here for supper and then to pick up some female for the evening in the bar afterward. Despite herself, Claire was both piqued and strangely, deeply, hurt by that thought. Of course she knew Jake hadn't lived the past ten years like a monk. He was a virile, macho, Latino male, single and perfectly free to pursue whomever he wanted. Still, it had been a real shock to her senses to see him cruising the bar and then choosing to sit down beside her—because he had not recognized her at first. She felt certain about that. What in the hell had given her away to him? She didn't know. She didn't plan on sticking around to find out as she pushed through the glass bar doors and hurried through the lobby beyond, toward what she hoped were Alvarez's private rooms.

But much to Claire's dismay, she hadn't got far before she was roughly grabbed from behind and shoved up against the nearest wall, between two huge, potted palms in giant, brass containers. There was no way for her to escape. Jake made sure of that, crowding her against the wall and pinioning her arms behind her back before she even realized what he intended. He was so furious that he was actually shaking from the force of his emotions.

"Damn you, Claire!" he snarled at her, his voice low but lethal as he gave her another rough shake. "What in the hell do you think you're playing at, coming here to this hotel, decked out in that getup? Are you just deliberately trying to get yourself killed?"

"N-n-no," she managed to choke out, trembling herself with fright at his rage, her face white and her eyes huge. "Now, let me go. Whatever I'm doing here and however I'm dressed are none of your damned business!"

"I'm making it my business," he ground out tersely. "So help me God, Claire, if you don't tell me what you're up to—as though I don't already have a fairly good idea—I'll haul you down to the station right now and charge you with...with prostitution!"

"You—you wouldn't!"

"Oh, wouldn't I? You just give me a reason—and I'll make it stick, too, believe me. It'll be your word against mine, and the way you're tricked out, you won't stand a chance when I report that you solicited me, offered me sexual favors in return for a price. Especially after I leak the news of your arrest to your fellow colleagues!"

He might actually be mad enough to do as he'd threatened, Claire thought anxiously, her pulse racing wildly. He'd had at least one Scotch in the bar... maybe more beforehand, at supper; and she already knew from experience that his black temper and alcohol were a volatile combination. "If you must know, I didn't want anyone here to recognize me," she finally said sulkily, with ill grace. "I wanted to get into Alvarez's private rooms—and he was hardly likely to admit Claire Connelly, Channel Four's broadcast journalist, now, was he?"

"No. But for God's sake, you stupid, little fool! Did you think about what might happen to you if by some miracle you managed to get inside and then your disguise were penetrated?"

"Yes. I figured...I figured Alvarez would probably try to kill me."

"And you actually believed a frigging news story was worth that risk? Goddamn it, Claire! I ought to throttle you myself!" Jake's eyes smoldered dangerously as they raked her, terrifying thoughts of her body washing up somewhere on the shore beyond the landing having pushed his temper to the breaking point.

"Excuse me. Is there a problem here, *señorita?* Is this man bothering you?" Manolo Alvarez's cool, faintly amused voice intruded upon them, causing Jake to stiffen and then glance warily over his shoulder at the Latino kingpin and the two henchmen standing just behind him.

"Yes...yes, he is," Claire answered quickly, before Jake could respond. "I—I think he's drunk. He followed me out of the bar, and then he—he grabbed me and threw me up against the wall and—and tried to put his hand up my dress. However erroneously, he appears to believe I'm a—a hooker—"

"Detective Seringo, I'm very surprised at you." Alvarez shook his head with feigned sadness, making a *tsk*ing sound with his mouth. "What would your superiors say if they knew? Now, why don't you be a good boy, and let the lady go? Gentlemen—" he turned to his two brawny bouncers "—please see that the detective is escorted from the premises. You understand, don't you, Detective? It's nothing personal, I assure you, just strictly business. I can't have a drunken police officer insulting and assaulting guests at my hotel."

The muscle that throbbed in Jake's set jaw was the only visible sign of his fury as the two henchmen unobtrusively but firmly took hold of him, one of them, Claire saw to her horror, surreptitiously pressing the barrel of an automatic pistol threateningly into Jake's side. Since he didn't appear too concerned about this, however, she could only assume he somehow knew they didn't intend to take him out into the parking lot and shoot him. Most likely, even Alvarez was prudent enough not to kill a cop. Still, her heart pounded with a fright stronger than any she had ever before known, and she would have objected, started screaming in panic, if she hadn't seen Jake's dark, sharp glance, the almost imperceptible shake of his head, warning her to remain silent as the bouncers led him away, leaving her alone with the Latino kingpin.

"My apologies, *señorita,*" Alvarez said smoothly, his black eyes flicking over Claire in a way that reminded her of a reptile preparing to strike and that made her shiver involuntarily as she tried to gather her courage and wits in the face of his scrutiny. "I trust you have suffered no injury to your person?"

"No…no, nothing permanent." Remembering her purpose in coming to the Flamingo Landing in the first place, she swallowed hard and forced herself to smile up at him brightly. "Thank you so much for coming to my rescue."

"It was my pleasure. I don't believe I've ever seen you here before, Señorita…?"

"Saint John," Claire supplied, employing the fictitious name she had finally, after much deliberation, decided to use at the hotel. "Cocoa Saint John. Perhaps you've heard of me? I'm a blues singer. I travel a lot…mainly been working the Gulf Coast circuit for the past couple of years—small clubs, mostly, New Orleans when I can get it."

"And what brings you here to our fair city?"

"I'm trying to broaden my circuit. Plus, a friend of mine suggested I might have a good time here at the Flamingo Landing." Her heart hammering, Claire reached slowly, seductively, into the bodice of her dress to draw forth Paul's glossy, black matchbook with its wharf etched in gold on the cover. "Do you happen to have a cigarette?'' she asked, striving to keep her face and tone all innocence. ''I ran out earlier and forgot to buy some more in the bar.''

His dark, ratlike visage betraying nothing, Alvarez reached into the inner pocket of his impeccably tailored suit jacket to draw forth a gold cigarette case. With a practiced but elegant flick of his wrist, he snapped it open and offered it to Claire. She took one of the cigarettes, then handed him the matchbook, praying that she wouldn't begin coughing up a storm as he lit her cigarette and she inhaled the acrid, unaccustomed smoke into her lungs. Much to her relief, she managed to get by with only a few choked rasps. ''Smoking's bad for my voice, so I've been trying to quit,'' she offered by way of an explanation. ''But you know how that is. One nicotine fit, and you're an addict again.''

''Yes, it is a difficult habit to break. But we all have our little vices. Cigars more often than cigarettes is mine.'' He returned the matchbook to her. ''Would you like to go somewhere more...private, Señorita Saint John?''

''I suppose that depends on what you have in mind. I don't even know your name.''

''Alvarez. Manolo Alvarez. I own the Flamingo Landing. I thought perhaps you'd like a drink—on the house, of course—to make up for your annoying, little encounter with Detective Seringo. His pregnant wife, Isabel, was murdered several years ago during a robbery at a convenience store in the barrio—had her throat cut by what were assumed to be gangbangers after they'd all four raped her—and I'm afraid he's been something of a loose cannon on our police force ever since, prone to hit the booze now and then, and obviously to associate with hookers and no doubt other sundry and ill-assorted lowlifes. I cannot imagine what—other than a Scotch-soaked brain—ever possessed him to rank you among their ilk, however. Are you fond of blackjack, Señorita Saint John?"

"I've been known to play a hand occasionally."

"Then perhaps you would care to try your luck tonight?" the Latino kingpin suggested as he took her arm firmly in his and began to lead her toward the rear of the hotel.

Claire dreamed again that night—the nightmare in which the unseen riptide was inexorably dragging her under, seaweed snarling like thick, confining ropes around her, hauling her down. She struggled desperately against the maddened waves, swallowing bitter saltwater as she gasped frantically for breath. But it was no use. She was doomed, powerless against the monumental force of the riptide; her attempts to save herself were futile. The starry shore was too far away, and she would never reach it before she was towed beneath the dark, frothing sea and drowned. Numb with cold and utterly exhausted, she at last ceased to fight any longer, resigning herself to her terrible but inevitable fate.

And then, as always, the strange, seemingly disembodied hand was there, reaching out to her, offering her hope. Everything within her urged her to take hold of it, but still, she hesitated, uncertain and afraid of the shadowy figure to which the hand belonged and which she could never clearly discern. Her heart thudded horribly in her breast, for she knew from past experience that if she didn't grasp the hand, she would drown, the icy, swirling water closing over her forever, hauling her down to the bottom of the ocean to metamorphose into coral bones.

Dreams—even nightmares—can be controlled. It's called directed dreaming…take hold of the hand…see what happens…. The words rang deep in her memory, and suddenly, with her last ounce of will and strength, Claire forced herself to grasp the strong, proffered hand, felt it close tightly around her own, pulling her from the lethal clutches of the riptide, on to the beach and into arms corded with muscle. She was weeping and shivering violently. But the tall, dark figure of her rescuer embraced her securely, so she knew she was safe on the sands where they stood. His powerful body was hard and lean, but nevertheless comforting, radiating heat that gradually warmed her, and he stroked her hair tenderly, murmuring to her soothingly all the while, until she finally began to calm.

After a long while, she looked up gratefully into the face of her rescuer.

It was Jake.

Without warning, his handsome, bronze visage evanesced into nothingness as Claire abruptly awoke, swirling up from her somnolent state to one of startlement and confusion. For a moment, she thought she had not been dreaming at all, that the riptide and Jake's saving her had been real. Then, slowly, she recognized that she was lying in her own bed, in her own house, and not standing on the shore, as she had believed herself to be just minutes past. She had suffered a nightmare, she realized, the same one that had haunted her for so long. Only this time, because she had taken hold of the disembodied hand, the dream had evolved from a horrifying scenario to one in which she had survived.

Sitting up in bed and switching on the hurricane lamp on her night table, Claire pressed her fingers to her temples, massaging gently. She had a dreadful headache, as though the air pressure outside had started to change, the result of a storm brewing far off in the distance, the beginnings of a squall in the Gulf, perhaps. She was hot, too, drenched in sweat from her nightmare that had this night changed without warning, introducing a new element—*Jake*.

Was that because she had seen him so much lately, because he was so often in her thoughts, because it had been he who had suggested how to conquer the immobilizing fear she experienced in her nightmare? She didn't know. She knew only that no matter what, she couldn't seem to put him from her mind. Earlier tonight, when Alvarez's henchmen had stuck a gun in Jake's ribs, the fear she had felt had been almost overwhelming; the thought of him dying, disappearing from her world forever, had been agonizing. Deep down inside, Claire knew that if she were honest with herself, she must admit that no matter what, some part of her had never stopped loving him.

She had been widowed now for nearly a year, and in all that time, she had not even gone out with another man, much less taken one to her empty bed. Tonight, restless and disturbed by her dream, she felt that lack keenly of a sudden, remembered all too vividly the way in which Jake had kissed her so feverishly that night he had driven her home from the airport.

Manolo Alvarez had kissed her, too. At the end of the evening, he had lifted her hand to his lips. But instead of kissing its back, Continental fashion, as Claire had expected, he had turned it over, pressing his mouth to her palm, his tongue darting forth like a snake's to stab her there, quickly and hotly. It had been all she could do not to jerk her hand away, so strongly had she felt as though she had somehow been intimately violated.

But at least the evening had not been a total loss. In the private rooms to which the Latino kingpin had escorted her, Claire had spied not only Senator Malcolm Forsythe, gambling heavily, but also more than one city and state official, men and women she had hitherto believed to be staunch pillars of the community. She had been deeply shocked to grasp the extent of the political corruption, the adulterous affairs, and the drugs and alcohol consumption going on around her in the city she had grown up in and that she had until tonight believed had largely escaped the decadence and decay that permeated others of its ilk. She had felt as though she had been living and working in a complete fog, so focused on the trees that she hadn't ever before actually viewed the entire forest. How she had ever managed to get through the evening, Claire didn't know, and at the end of it, she had made her escape as swiftly as possible, breathless from her wildly beating pulse as she had thanked Alvarez for his hospitality—while praying desperately that he weren't about to haul her upstairs to one of the hotel's suites and brutally force himself on her. It had occurred to her that if he did, her disguise would be undone, and he would ensure that she never left the Flamingo Landing alive.

It was only then that, despite all of Jake's urgent warnings to her, the prospect of being murdered for her meddling had loomed large and terrifyingly real in her mind. Fortunately, much to her relief, the Latino kingpin had done nothing further untoward after kissing her hand in so disturbing a fashion, but had simply bid her good-night, ordering one of his henchmen to walk her outside to her car.

Claire had more than half expected to discover Jake waiting for her in the hotel's parking lot—or at least sitting on some deserted side lane down the road a piece, from where he might follow her home. However, he had been nowhere to be found. That realization had worried her so much that she had swung by Lafitte's Quay on the way home, to see if his Mustang was parked near the slip where his houseboat was moored. But the classic convertible had not been anywhere in sight. She had been sorely tempted to contact the police, but remembering Jake's warning glance to her at the hotel, she had hesitated. If there were nothing wrong, she didn't want to be responsible for causing him to get in trouble on the job.

She knew there had been more than a grain of truth in Alvarez's accusation that Jake was something of a loose cannon on the police force. It was entirely possible, she had recognized, that whatever he was doing out at the Flamingo Landing was not sanctioned by his superiors. So in the end, Claire had followed what she had considered to be the only sensible course of action: she had telephoned Remy Toussaint, explaining briefly what had happened and asking to be notified one way or another with regard to Jake's well-being. Much to her relief, Toussaint had called back within moments to let her know his missing partner was, in fact, quite all right.

After that, Claire had gone to bed—and dreamed of the riptide.

Now, untangling herself from her twisted, sweat-sodden sheets and rising, she went to stand at the French doors that led to the deck beyond her bedroom. But she could see nothing on the horizon to herald a storm, no telltale flashes of lightning; nor did she hear any muffled rumbles of thunder. If there were indeed a squall coming, it was as yet too distant for her to know it. Still, she sensed the change in the air pressure—and experience had taught her just how rapidly a tempest could sweep inland from the Gulf.

Deactivating the alarm system, Claire opened the doors wide and stepped outside, the muggy night air hitting her with its full force, although a slight, cooling breeze blowing in from the Gulf mitigated the worst of the summer heat. In the night sky hung a moon silver and full, surrounded by countless stars that glittered like the diamonds of a strand that had been carelessly broken and scattered to the four winds—as the diamond necklace Veronica Hampton Forsythe had worn the evening she had been murdered had broken to fall from her throat.

Above the dark waves some yards distant from

Claire's beachfront house, a seabird winged its way across the firmament, its low cry piercing and forlorn—like the sudden ache deep in her heart, in her very soul.

Twenty-Four

Full Circle

That sunny dome! those caves of ice!
And all who heard should see them there,
And all should cry, Beware! Beware!
His flashing eyes, his floating hair!
Weave a circle round him thrice,
And close your eyes with holy dread,
For he on honeydew hath fed,
And drunk the milk of Paradise.

Kubla Khan
—Samuel Taylor Coleridge

If Claire had not eventually come out of the Flamingo Landing, Jake knew he would have gone barging back into the hotel—and to hell with all the legalities and ramifications to his career. But at the end of the evening, she *had* left the place, looking none the worse for wear than when she had first entered it—except that her face had been paler than usual in the moonlight, and her body filled with a tension that perhaps only he, who had once possessed her so intimately and often, would have recognized.

So skillfully and unobtrusively that she had been oblivious of his actions, Jake had followed her home—not only to make sure she arrived there safely, but also to satisfy himself that Alvarez had not seen through her disguise, that none of the Latino kingpin's henchmen was tailing her, intent on causing her to have a fatal accident on the road, or worse. That Claire's well-being mattered so desperately to him had at long last forced Jake into a deeper examination of his feelings toward her—which he had hitherto avoided at all costs—and he had been compelled to admit to himself that it wasn't simply an overwhelming lust he felt for her, that what drove him where she was concerned wasn't something he could just slake and then be done with. It went deeper than that—much deeper. And bound up with it was a chilling, mind-numbing fear that he would prove unable to protect her, as he had failed to safeguard Isabel, who had ultimately not heeded his warnings to her, either—at the tragic cost of her young life and that of their unborn child. Whatever it took, Jake was determined not to allow that to happen to Claire, even if she *were* hellbent on being her own worst enemy!

He knew that regardless of what she had told him, she really didn't, in fact, have any idea of the way in which she had possibly imperiled herself. She wasn't out on the mean streets day after day, looking at an endless string of corpses and seeing at close hand what human beings were capable of doing to one another. To her, crimes were something that happened to other people, events that she reported on *Inside Story*. Despite everything, their reality hadn't ever become anything up close and personal—the way it had for Jake. Even her husband Paul's abduction of her daughter would have seemed to Claire only a terrible extension of marital discord, the effect upon her quite different from what she would have experienced had Gillian been kidnapped by a total stranger.

As a result, Claire had been recklessly playing dress-up this evening, thinking only of scooping her competition, probably counting for protection on the fact that Manolo Alvarez would hardly attempt to do away with her in the midst of a hotel crowded with guests. She didn't truly understand how criminals like the Latino kingpin operated, that they didn't play by any rules whatsoever, they didn't have the kind of morals and scruples that other people did. One word from Alvarez tonight, and Jake knew he would have wound up fighting for his life in some dark, isolated spot beyond the Flamingo Landing. It was only because the Latino kingpin was smarter than that that he hadn't. And now that Alvarez had seen him with Claire, she was doubtless in even more danger than if the Latino kingpin had merely believed her to be some snooping reporter—which was why, when he had reached her neighborhood, The Breakers, he had flashed his badge to get past the guard at the gatehouse of the fashionable, upscale enclave, then cruised the quiet, well-lit streets until turning on to the one on which Claire lived.

Her spacious, contemporary house was located at the far end of the neighborhood, on a secluded strand that guaranteed her privacy since there was nothing beyond except the sea and a small, wildly overgrown plot that would never be developed. Claire had bought that land, too, when she had purchased the house, Jake knew from delving into her business affairs in an attempt to learn what her husband had been up to, if the matchbook she had found meant that Paul, too, had somehow been involved with Alvarez. Jake had parked the Mustang so it was concealed by the saplings and tall pampas grass of the little wilderness. Then he had got out of the convertible to take up a position from where he could watch both the street and the beach. He didn't know whether the Latino kingpin had even suspected Claire's true identity. But Jake wasn't planning on taking any chances tonight— and he would do his damnedest to see that she never went back to the Flamingo Landing again to attempt to penetrate Alvarez's private rooms. Jesus. Jake's blood ran cold just thinking about it. She wasn't even a rookie cop—and two extremely experienced detectives in Narco had already wound up dead, trying to get on the inside of Alvarez's operation to obtain evidence against him.

Now, as Jake heard sounds on the deck of Claire's house and glimpsed a ghostly flutter of white, he quickly crushed out the cigarette he had been smoking and slipped deeper into the shadowy cover of the saplings and pampas grass, moving stealthily toward the beach. After a moment, he realized that despite the lateness of the hour, Claire herself was still up, had stepped outside onto the deck from what was surely her bedroom beyond. She was carrying a blanket and a towel, and as he watched, she made her way down to the moonlit shore where, after carefully smoothing out the sand, she spread the blanket on the ground, dropping the towel on top of it.

Then, utterly riveting Jake where he stood, she slowly shrugged off the gossamer, white nightgown she wore and walked naked into the sea.

The breakers frothed around Claire's ankles, her calves, and then her hips. The salty water still retained a vestige of the day's heat, so it was pleasantly tepid, washing away the sheen of sweat, born of her night mare and the humidity of the night air, which had covered her body. This was better—much better—than the shower she had also contemplated before deciding on a midnight swim instead. Exhilarated by the ocean swells that left her breathless, she waded out until she was some yards distant from the shore, so the waves covered her breasts, but not so far that her feet could no longer touch the bottom of the sea. All she wanted was to cool off—not to become the casualty of a rip-tide, as in her nightmare. Here where she half floated, the combers swept her gently back toward shore with each spumy, inrushing surge, so she knew she wouldn't be dragged under and drowned.

Once, her foot nudged something hard, and when she bent to retrieve it, she discovered that it was a beautiful conch shell, perfectly formed. Wondering how it had got there, where it had been before coming to rest in this spot, she rinsed it out, then laid it on the sand beyond the rippling waves. She and Gillian had a collection of shells they had gathered on the beach. The conch would be a striking addition. Smiling tenderly at the thought of how delighted her daughter would be when she saw it, Claire reflected idly on what other treasures she might unearth. Even if she found nothing, she was still enjoying her midnight swim, reveling in the feel of the sea slapping lightly against her bare skin, swirling around her, buoying her up.

It was, she imagined, what a baby must feel like, being rocked in a cradle. Almost, she could go to sleep out here, lulled by the waves, the murmur of the ocean. She closed her eyes, drifting languorously. How long she floated, she didn't know. But after a time, she abruptly became aware of the fact that she must actually have dozed off, and she started into wakefulness, thinking it was past time for her to get out of the water. She began to wade toward shore, then all at once halted in her tracks, glancing around warily, knowing suddenly, instinctively, that she was no longer alone on the isolated beach, that someone was watching her.

Jake stood, mesmerized, in the shadows on the strand, his groin so tight with desire that he actually ached with it. Claire was even more beautiful than he had remembered, he thought, like some elusive, ethereal mermaid frolicking in the sea, her long hair tangling like strands of golden seaweed around her, her pale skin as luminescent as a pearl in the soft glow cast by the full moon at its zenith in the black-velvet sky. All around her, the dark waves reflected the firmament above, so it seemed as though she drifted in

an ocean of stars, and the silver-white crests of the
breakers were like strands of otherworldly diamonds
draping her throat and breasts.

He wanted her so badly that he could taste it.

When she began to rise from the white-foamed sea,
it was, for him, like seeing Botticelli's *Birth of Venus*
suddenly come to life in the starry darkness.

But halfway out of the water, as though sensing his
presence, she abruptly grew very still, her mouth parting with surprise and fear, her arms crossing instinctively over her breasts, both a protective and a concealing gesture. "Who's—who's there?" she called,
and only then did Jake recognize that he stood in shadow, that she could not discern his face, only the sil-
houette of his tall, powerful figure. It was no wonder,
then, that she was afraid. Thoughts of Alvarez and the
little charade she had carried out at the Flamingo
Landing were doubtless even now chasing through her
mind. Almost, Jake was tempted to teach her a lesson
by scaring the devil out of her. It would serve her
right—except that that wasn't the kind of game currently on his mind. He wanted to play with her, all
right—just not that way.

"Didn't anyone ever tell you it's dangerous to swim
alone, Claire?" he drawled, his voice low and serrated
with desire as he stepped into the moonlight so she
could see him clearly. "That riptides and worse lurk
beneath the surface of the sea? That strangers are just
as apt as friends to take midnight strolls along the
shore?"

"I'm—I'm not so far out that my feet can't touch
the bottom," she replied, her own voice tinged with

relief and indignation and slightly breathless. "And this is a private beach, besides. What are you doing here, spying on me?"

"There's no need for you to get in a huff. It wasn't deliberate. It just...happened."

"Well, would you mind turning your back, then, so I can come out and get dressed?" Claire's heart pounded so hard in her breast that she thought Jake must surely hear it. Of all she had ever imagined, that he would show up here in this way was the last thing that had ever occurred to her. Otherwise, she would never have dreamed of going for a swim at this late hour—especially naked. She shivered with both fear and a sudden, perverse thrill of excitement as Jake's eyes, twin flames flickering in their dark depths, boldly appraised her, making no secret of the fact that he liked and wanted what he saw. "I—I don't have any clothes on."

A lazy, mocking half smile curved his mouth. "Yeah, I know—which makes for a real interesting situation, doesn't it?" Bending, he retrieved her fluffy beach towel from her blanket, casually holding it out to her. "What have you got to hide, Claire?" he taunted softly as she hesitated to reach for the towel. "Surely, you must remember that I've seen it all before."

"I—I expected better from you, Jake," she sputtered, outraged, her pulse racing at his insolent behavior.

"What a cad I am to disappoint you, then."

"Cad is right. Now, quit fooling around. I've been out here for a while, and I'm starting to get tired. Go

on up to the house, and I'll meet you there in a minute."

"It's a hot night. Maybe I'll just join you in the
water instead. God knows, despite how hard I've
fought against it, I still want you, Claire—just as much
now as I ever did before." With that, much to her
shock and mortification, Jake abruptly tossed the towel
down on the blanket and began to unbutton his short-
sleeved, white, cotton shirt.

"Surely, you're—you're not serious." Unable to
tear her gaze away, Claire stared at him, half terrified,
half peculiarly exhilarated, thinking that, certainly, he
must be teasing her, despite the fact that he had now
stripped off his shirt and thrown it down on the sand
to reveal his broad, muscular chest matted with fine,
black hair and against which gleamed the gold crucifix
she recollected that he wore always. Despite herself,
the sight of his bare chest and corded arms sent a
shudder of something she did not want to name rippling through her. Even as she watched, his boots and
socks swiftly followed his shirt. "I can't believe you
honestly mean to do this, Jake. Have you lost your
mind?"

"Probably." Deliberately, his hands fell to his belt
buckle.

Claire didn't wait to see any more. Instead, suddenly confused and unnerved by his actions, she
turned and struck out into the waves, thinking he must
be either mad or drunk, and that he was capable of
anything in such a state. Even more disturbing was her
own leaping response to him, the way the nipples of
her bare breasts peaked and tingled, sending a slow,

molten thrill rippling through her body, causing the secret heart of her to tighten and ache almost unbearably. If he got into the water, if he came after her, she knew she wouldn't stand a chance against him, that all her yearning for him—tightly harnessed but never vanquished—would erupt into an urgent, full-blown need for him, leaving her highly vulnerable to him.

But Claire had not lied when she had told him earlier that she was growing weary, and now, she made little headway against the breakers that swelled toward the shore, closing over her, engulfing her, taking her breath. In that moment, despite the fact that she knew better, it suddenly seemed to her as though her nightmare had become a reality, that she was caught by a deadly riptide that lurked in the ocean's depths, was being fatally dragged under. Sobbing and gasping for air, she strove desperately for the surface and finally broke free to find herself clasped in Jake's strong arms.

He was as naked as she, and before she realized what he intended, he burrowed his hands roughly in the sodden strands of her hair and seized her mouth hungrily with his own, his tongue forcing her lips to part and thrusting deep and provocatively between them.

In the beginning, still panicked, Claire struggled wildly against him, half beating her fists against his chest and arms as the combers carried the two of them toward shore, half clinging to him for fear she would otherwise drown. And all the while, Jake's mouth moved fiercely and insistently on hers, devouring her, his tongue ravaging the moist, inner sweetness of the lips that opened and yielded to him until she was breathless and dizzy, savaged by an ache that had nothing to do with the dreaded images that haunted her dreams or the leadenness that had, just moments ago, pervaded her limbs. She knew nothing any longer but the feel of his powerful body embracing hers, his mouth kissing her feverishly, endlessly, as at last, with a sudden, mighty rush that was like the blood roaring in her ears, the surf cast the two of them up halfway onto the beach, so Jake lay on top of her, one thigh riding between hers, the dark, frothy water swirling around them both.

One of his hands was still ensnared in Claire's soaked hair to hold her still for him, but the other roamed her body at will, teasing and taunting her in ways that wakened and incited passion long and carefully held at bay, that stirred and surged within her now like the waves that burgeoned and tumbled over the two of them where they lay, Jake pressing her down into the smooth, wet sand. His teeth grazed her lower lip, so she tasted blood, coppery and bittersweet, as he abruptly tore his mouth free of hers to mutter hoarsely in her ear. "Tell me you don't want this as much as I do, Claire. Tell me, and I'll let you up."

She opened her mouth to speak, but all she could manage was a small gasp of shock and delight as he licked her throat and breasts hotly before his lips closed over one rosy nipple, sucking greedily, sending waves of pleasure radiating through her entire body, making her arch yearningly against him. A low whimper emanated from her throat as desire and need flooded her being. It was as though the last ten years had never been, as though it were only yesterday that

Jake had held her like this, made love to her with a passion she had never before known—and had never known since. She felt as though for a very long time, she had been dead inside, and that now she was alive again, a mass of exquisite sensation, quickening everywhere he touched her.

"Tell me, Claire," Jake demanded insistently once more, his breath warm against her skin as his mouth captured her other nipple, his teeth tugging lightly, his tongue teasing it until the peak was as rigid and flushed as its twin.

In response, she wrapped her arms around his neck, her hands tunneling through his damp, glossy, black hair as she gave herself up to him, letting him do with her as he willed, knowing that some traitorous part of her had wanted this and heedless of the fact that there was no gentleness in him, that he was instead rough and urgent in his desire for her. His lips and hands were on her everywhere, tormenting and arousing her savagely, causing both fright and excitement to rush through her giddyingly as the breakers swept over them both, leaving them drenched with foam.

Jake's hard, lean body weighed her down, slick and tasting of brine when Claire pressed her mouth to his naked flesh, let her hands slide over him ardently, feeling the powerful muscles that bunched and rippled in his back and arms as he clutched her to him, setting her atremble. She was fragile and vulnerable in comparison, she knew, little more than wet sand in his strong, slender hands, his to mold and shape as he pleased, as the sea fashioned and formed the shore. His long, elegant fingers entwined with her own, pressing her arms over her thrashing head, imprisoning her as his teeth found her throat, sank sensually into her shoulder, making her feel as though a flash of Saint Elmo's fire had suddenly coursed through her. She moaned and writhed against him, seized by a hollow, burning ache at the mellifluous core of her being, wanting and needing to be filled by him.

"Jake," she pleaded. "Jake, please..."

"Please, what?" he asked thickly against her mouth.

"I want you...now..."

"Yeah, I want you, too. It seems like I've wanted you forever, Claire..."

His lips claimed her own once more, his tongue shooting deep, savoring the honeyed taste of her as he spread her thighs wide. The tip of his hard, probing maleness found her, pierced her. And then, agonizingly, he paused, inhaling sharply as he felt the moist, welcoming heat of her close around him. She felt the length of his body quiver, knew in some distant corner of her mind the tremendous amount of self-control he possessed to prolong this moment, to heighten her desire for him until she was frantic to have him fully inside her. She would have bucked against him wildly to complete his entry, but he held her down, torturing them both, his mouth capturing hers, deliberately swallowing her mewls of distress and entreaty. Then, at last, one corded arm slid beneath her, lifting her to receive him as, groaning, he drove down into her, burying himself as deeply as possible.

Crying out, Claire strained against him, her nails digging into his smooth back, as though, even now,

Jake were not close enough, had been away from her for so long that even this moment was not enough to satisfy. As he began to thrust inside her, she wrapped her legs around him to draw him even nearer, reveling in the feel of him, the strength of his supple body as he plunged into her, moving against her in such a way that the throbbing at the core of her increased unendurably, until it was like the pounding of the surf, a magnificent wave swelling and surging inside her. She rode it until it reached its crest, poising in midair for a fleeting eternity, breathless, expectant, then beginning the unstoppable, headlong tumble that finally left it exploding within her, shattering and scattering her senses. As it rippled and died away like the combers washing gently upon the shore, Jake's own release came, racking the length of his body, leaving him rasping for breath as he collapsed atop her.

After a long while, he lifted his head and kissed her lingeringly on the mouth. "I've missed you, Claire." And if his dark eyes were triumphant and satisfied, they were also tender, so she knew he had spoken the truth.

"I've missed you, too, Jake," she said softly.

Withdrawing from her, he swept her up without warning in his rugged arms and carried her to the blanket, where he laid her down gently. Then, reaching for the towel, he started to dry her off, taking his time, kissing and caressing her as he worked, so her body continued to pulsate with a slow-burning desire that he caused to flow and ebb, like the waves upon the beach. Time passed. Claire did not know how much, for it was as though it had turned back on itself, had ceased even to exist for her. She might have been twenty-one years old again, young and in love with Jake. Ten years might never have come and gone— except that they had, and she was older now, wiser, emotionally scarred by the decade, by her relationship with Jake, and with Paul. Once, long ago, she had asked nothing of Jake that he had not been willing to give. Now, she felt as though she had come full circle, were again in that place, uncertain what he wanted, if there were to be more between them than just this one night. She didn't ask—but she didn't need to. He had always read her mind.

"So...where do we go from here, Claire?" he inquired, his voice low, his mouth and hands moving familiarly, knowingly, on her body, sensuously tracing the curve of her nape, her spine, making her shiver. He kissed the small of her back, ran his hands lightly over her buttocks and between her thighs. "Where do we go?"

"I don't know. I guess that depends on you. I thought—I thought you hated me, Jake," she confessed. "We're ten years down the road, and I'm not twenty-one anymore. I'm a widow, and in case you've forgotten, I also have a daughter."

"No, I hadn't forgotten. Do you think your having a child is a problem for me?"

"It would be for a lot of men."

"I'm not one of them. As for the rest, I don't believe I ever truly hated you, Claire. I was hurt and angry all those years ago because I thought you should have trusted me, should have cared about my feelings, as I cared about yours—and you—far more than I was willing or even able at the time to admit. Deep down inside, I don't think I ever really stopped caring about you. I know I never stopped wanting you, and now, you know that, too. So I guess what I'm trying to say is that I'm more than willing to give us a second chance. Having come this far, having made love to you tonight, I'm fully aware that I didn't do it just because I could never get you out of my system and thought a one-night stand would accomplish that. I want more from you than that, Claire. But there has to be trust and commitment between us. It's just not in me to settle for anything less."

"And what about my needs?"

"Which are?"

"Understanding and compromise. You may not hate me, Jake—but you certainly loathe my work, and that's a very large part of who I am. Further, although you may not realize it, I *have* learned that in order for one to be a responsible broadcast journalist, there are lines that must be drawn, lines that must never be crossed, and over the years, I've tried hard to adhere to those, to do my job in a way I can be proud of."

"I know that, Claire—and, too, that because of what happened between us in the past, I've been hard on you when it comes to your career...probably harder than I ever had any right to be. I'm not going to lie to you and promise I'll come in time to like what you do for a living. But I can and will learn to deal with it, to respect both it and your right to do it. Is that enough?"

"For now. It's a start at least, and if we're going to

have any kind of a relationship at all, Jake, we have to begin somewhere."

"I thought we already had begun," he murmured as he gently rolled her over, his palms gliding as smooth as silk over her breasts, her stomach, the downy triangle at the juncture of her thighs, stroking and coaxing, so she trembled beneath his touch, her whole body alive and pulsing with exquisite sensations.

His indrawn breath was sharp with arousal when she reached up to draw him even closer, so her own lips and hands could explore him with equal fervor, matching him kiss for kiss, caress for caress, sliding over the planes and angles of his body until he and she were a tangle of limbs, and Claire did not know where she ended and Jake began. She closed her palm around his turgid, heated sex, teasing and stroking until his breath was an uneven rasp in her ear. Then, suddenly, he was pressing her wrists down on either side of her head, his dark body moving determinedly, exigently, to cover her own pale one, penetrating her with a single swift, hard, deep thrust that took her own breath away as she arched her hips to receive him.

In moments, a pleasure so intense that Claire felt she would die from it erupted inside her, and she clung to Jake desperately, fiercely, enfolding him, immuring him, taking him with her to somewhere that was not of this earth, but a place primordial, a place where they were both mindless, driven by sheer, blind instinct to a pinnacle that left them quivering and gasping in each other's arms.

After a while, they collected themselves and their

belongings, and they went into the house, to Claire's bedroom. By the moonlight that streamed in from the open French doors, Jake saw that it was decorated in the Victorian style he remembered from her bungalow near the university, although much more expensively and sophisticatedly. He looked at the badly rumpled bed. If he hadn't known better, he would have thought Claire had been having rough-and-tumble sex in it. A startlingly violent twinge of jealousy assailed him. He didn't want her sleeping with any other man. She was his now.

"You had the nightmare again," he asserted, suddenly understanding. "That's why you couldn't sleep, why you came outside for a midnight swim."

"Yes, but it was all right. I took your advice. This time, when the riptide started to drag me under, I reached out for the hand," she explained. "I don't know why, but it...it turned out to be yours, Jake. Maybe, subconsciously, I wanted it to be your hand all along, and was afraid it wouldn't be. But in the end, it *was* you who kept me from drowning, and then afterward, I wasn't scared anymore."

"I'm glad. I don't like to think of you having nightmares, Claire, of you being frightened." He stretched out on the bed, watching her as she placed her neatly folded blanket, towel, and nightgown to one side, then momentarily held to her ear the conch shell she had found. "What do you hear, baby?"

"Oh, most people would say the sea, I suppose. But to me, each shell is different. This one's big and beautiful in a wild, exotic way. It has a deep voice...a collective voice, really—the chorus of a thousand ancient sea creatures, howling on a wind primeval down the long, dark corridors of time. Listen." Joining him on the bed, she pressed the conch to his ear. "Do you hear them?"

"Yeah, I do, actually." Gently, he laid the shell on the night table, then drew her into the cradle of his embrace. "Did you know you have the soul of a poet, Claire, and the body of a siren—and that I want to make love to you until the dawn breaks on the horizon and we're both drained to the dregs?"

"No, but tell me more." She snuggled up against him, laying her head upon his chest, whispering even more softly, "Show me more."

They made love again and again until the sun rose in the morning sky, then fell asleep in each other's arms, only to be wakened shortly before noon, by the sound of Gillian pounding on the bedroom door Claire had wisely closed and securely locked earlier.

"Mommy, why is your door shut? Mommy, are you all right?"

"Yes...yes, punkin. I'll—I'll be there in just a minute," Claire called, fumbling for her nightgown and robe, and hastily dragging them on.

Jake, who had also scrambled from bed, was now already nearly dressed, only his boots in hand and his shirt unbuttoned, hanging open to reveal his expansive chest, his firm, flat belly corrugated with muscle, as he grabbed her and kissed her quickly—once, twice— then more slowly and deeply as her mouth yielded sweetly to his and he felt the swell of her soft, full breasts pressing against his torso.

"Mommy!" Gillian cried impatiently, rattling the

knob of the bedroom door so vigorously that Claire thought it was a wonder it didn't fall clean off.

"I'll be back later on today," Jake said as, with difficulty, he tore his lips from hers and jerked open the French doors that led to the deck beyond.

"Come for supper...six o'clock," she invited.

"It's a date. I'll be here."

"Mommy, are you locked in? Shall I go get a key?"

"Your daughter is another persistent reporter in the making, I see," he drawled, grinning ruefully as he hauled on his boots. "Anything to get the inside story. How in the hell will I ever manage you both? I don't stand a chance."

"No, I don't think you do," Claire agreed, smiling up at him tenderly.

"Well, we'll see. I'm a cop, remember? I know how to marshal my defenses."

"You do that."

"Mommy, I'll go fetch Ana Maria."

Jake groaned. "Jesus. Reinforcements. Much as it pains me to say it, I'm outta here, baby. See you at six." Then he stepped out onto the deck and strode down the beach.

Combing her hand futilely through her snarled hair and clutching her robe, Claire hurried to the bedroom door, unlocked it, and then opened it to reveal Gillian and Ana Maria standing outside in the hallway, the little girl frowning crossly, the housekeeper anxious. "My goodness, Gilly sweetheart, what's all this ruckus? You'd think I had never shut my bedroom door before."

"Well—" her daughter shrugged "—you haven't."

"Oh, punkin, of course I have," Claire insisted.

"No," Gillian declared firmly, shaking her head, "you haven't…at least, not since Daddy died. And the only times you ever closed your door before were when you and Daddy wanted to be alone together."

To her dismay, Claire found herself suddenly flushing guiltily—and didn't know whether to be relieved or mortified when Ana Maria, who had glanced into the bedroom, her gaze taking in the highly disordered bed and the open French doors, suddenly announced, "Well, everybody needs their privacy now and then, *chiquita*. Now, you let your mama have hers. Come on back to the kitchen with me and help me bake my pies. Somehow, I think maybe we have company for supper, no?"

Twenty-Five

Familiar Acts

Familiar acts are beautiful through love.

Prometheus Unbound
—Percy Bysshe Shelley

Jake had arrived for supper bearing gifts—a bottle of wine to contribute to the meal, a bouquet of flowers for Claire, and a dried starfish for Gillian's seashell collection. The little girl had been thrilled by her present.

"How did you know I collect shells, Detective Seringo?" she had asked.

"I'm a detective. It's my business to find such things out," Jake had replied, smiling, and Claire had been glad to see the rapport between the two.

After eating, the three of them had taken a walk along the beach and built a sand castle together. Then they had returned to the house, where, after Gillian had taken her bath and got into her pajamas, Jake had read her a bedtime story. Now, as Claire tucked her daughter into bed and kissed her good-night, Gillian said, "I like Detective Seringo, Mommy. He's real nice."

"I think so, too, sweetheart."

"Then are you going to marry him?"

"Oh, honey, I don't know. I hadn't even thought that far ahead yet. After all, I've only just had supper with him."

"But you've known him a long time, and you used to go out with him before. You told me so."

"I know, but relationships are...complicated, Gilly."

"Oh. Well, if you do decide to marry him, Mommy, I just want you to know I won't mind. Ana Maria said it wasn't good for you to be alone, and if you have to marry somebody, I'd just as soon it was Detective Seringo."

"Thank you, punkin. I'll keep that in mind." After tucking the summer covers more securely around her daughter and the stuffed Paddington Bear that Gillian snuggled with, Claire switched off the lamp and turned on the bedside night-light, then tiptoed from the bedroom to rejoin Jake.

"So...did you get your daughter to bed okay?" he inquired as Claire sat down beside him on the big, overstuffed couch in the living room.

"Yes, the walk along the beach wore her out. She was already drifting off to slumberland when I told her good-night."

"Well, let's hope she sleeps a little later tomorrow morning than she did today." Jake's eyes roamed over Claire in a way that brought a blush to her cheeks and made her heart beat fast. "But before I tuck *you* in, baby, we need to talk."

"About what?"

"The Flamingo Landing and that foolhardy charade you played out there last night. It was extremely dangerous, Claire. Alvarez is a cold-blooded killer. You saw for yourself that he didn't hesitate to have his bodyguards shove a gun into my ribs and escort me off the premises."

"Well, even so, you didn't seem too worried that they might actually shoot you."

"It wasn't likely—not with you standing there watching them lead me away and Alvarez not knowing whether or not you'd seen or guessed they had a pistol stuck in my side. What happened after they tossed me out of the place?"

"Alvarez bought me a drink, then took me back into the private rooms where all the gambling takes place—for all the good it did me. They search you before you go in to be sure you aren't wired or concealing a microcassette recorder or a camera or anything else like that. So even if I wanted to report the story, I wouldn't have any corroboration unless I got some of the others present to speak up, which is unlikely, considering how many of this city's so-called pillars of the community were out there boozing, taking drugs, consorting with hookers, and gambling. It's no wonder the police can't seem to shut Alvarez down. What I don't understand, though, is why they don't just raid the place, since obviously, they know damned good and well what's going on out there."

"Rumors don't constitute probable cause, Claire—

which is what you're required to have in order for a judge to issue a search warrant. It's just like you not wanting to report an unconfirmed news story. The police need some kind of evidence to back themselves up legally, and even if we got a search warrant issued, the Flamingo Landing and its grounds are riddled with high-tech security. Alvarez would know we were coming long before we ever got there. All the chips would disappear, and he'd be passing out play money, claiming the whole setup was in place for one of those Las Vegas–type charity bashes. As for the rest, Narco's tried more than once to get somebody on the inside of Alvarez's organization. So far, at least two good officers have turned up dead as a result. Vice hasn't succeeded any better. Alvarez's call girls are terrified of him—and not without good reason.''

"So he just continues to operate, and nobody does anything about it?''

"No, not quite. Piece by piece, we've built up a considerable file on him over the years, and a detailed examination of Senator Forsythe's financial records has turned up some interesting connections to Alvarez, as well. So if we can't get through the front door, we'll go through the back.''

"The senator was there last night, at the Flamingo Landing, gambling very heavily and with a woman on each arm. He certainly didn't look like a man with money problems or a grieving widower, either, by the way.''

"That's because he's not. He undoubtedly murdered his wife for her life-insurance benefits, and he's a notorious womanizer. Off the record, Claire—'' Jake's voice was dry as he eyed her intently "—we've now got enough evidence that we're very close to arresting him. We've verified a number of facts in this case. Forsythe has dug himself into a real hole financially, to the point that if he had lost access to his wife's fortune, he would have problems. And Veronica *was* going to divorce him. Worse, she wasn't prepared to wait until his re-election campaign was over to do it, but planned on filing the papers the Monday morning following his fund-raising bash. We suspect that's what their argument that night was really about and why he ultimately killed her."

"But if all that's true, how does Vanessa Hampton's death in that arsonous fire at the Seabreeze Sanatorium fit in? What about the matchbook that was discovered in the debris?"

Jake shrugged. "I don't know. It may be nothing more than that the senator accidentally dropped that matchbook from his pocket out there one evening, and Billy Oxbridge found it and used it for his own nefarious purposes."

"But you don't personally believe that?" Claire prodded, curious. "Isn't that why you were out at the Flamingo Landing yesterday evening?"

"Yeah. But I was on my own. The department hadn't sanctioned my being there, and I really didn't have any particular goal in mind when I went out there, either. I was just nosing around, baiting Alvarez, trying to see what, if anything, would shake loose. The last thing I ever expected was to see *you* there, doing an imitation of an undercover cop!"

"How *did* you know it was me, Jake? Even my best

friend, Zoey, didn't recognize me when I ran by the *Courier* to test out my disguise. What gave me away to you?''

He smiled at her lazily. ''Your perfume. It was the one thing you forgot to change—and I'd know it anywhere, Claire. It's what you call a 'signature scent,' isn't it?''

''Yes, a lot of women down here in the South use only one fragrance, either something on the market— like Joy or Chanel Number Five—which they adopt as their own, or else they have something especially blended for themselves alone. I think I told you once, years ago, that there's a small but exclusive shop in New Orleans where I have my own perfume made up. I named it Nocturne. Madame Gautier—she's owned the shop for as long as I can remember—first created it for me when I was in my teens, when Mother took Caitlin, Chelsea, and me there. It's mine alone. Once she develops a special blend for you, Madame Gautier keeps the recipe for your particular fragrance in her files, and she doesn't sell it to anyone else. She's got an extraordinary sense of smell and an incredible memory, besides, and despite that she's created hundreds of blends over the years, she has only to inhale a single whiff of any of them, and she can tell you which one it is and who she made it for.''

''Yeah, when I smelled your perfume at the Flamingo Landing, I remembered you telling me all about it once, Claire,'' Jake explained, ''and that's how I knew it was you. You're very lucky it was I and not Alvarez who penetrated your disguise. What do you think would have happened if he'd somehow unmasked your identity—especially after he'd taken you back into those private rooms of his?''

"Do you honestly believe he would have had me killed because of that, Jake? I mean, it's not as though I didn't see what numerous other people in this city who've been in those private rooms before have seen. And I didn't even have a tape recorder, much less a camera. So I've no corroboration, and not much of a story without any—at least, not any kind of a story that wouldn't smack of slander and innuendo.''

"I know, and perhaps Alvarez would view it that way, too, initially. But he's a man who doesn't like being made a fool of, Claire, which is what you basically did to him last evening. You led him to believe you were something you aren't, and you did it with ulterior motives that, if successful, would prove injurious to Alvarez. Trust me. That, he won't forgive or forget. That's why I don't want you to go back there. I just don't want you taking that kind of risk, baby. So, please, promise me you won't do it again.''

"Oh, Jake." Claire sighed. "How can I in good conscience make that kind of a promise to you? What if…what if some news story should arise that would require me to return to the Flamingo Landing? I couldn't just tell the station I wouldn't cover it—but I wouldn't want to break my word to you, either. Surely, you can see that by making such a request of me, you're placing me in an untenable position.''

"That's not my intention, Claire. I'm simply trying to protect you—the same way I tried all those years ago to keep Isabel safe by telling her to drive straight

home after work. I don't want you to wind up the way
she did, that's all.''

Claire was silent for a moment. Then she said softly,
''I'm so sorry, Jake. I didn't think about it in that
context.''

''Well, maybe you will now—if not for your own
sake, then for mine.'' Clearly, he considered that pronouncement the end of this particular conversation, for
he stood then, taking her hand in his and drawing her
gently to her feet. ''Come. I want to make love to you
now. I've thought of little else all day.''

She did not protest as he led her toward her bedroom, for the same thought had been uppermost in her
own mind since he had left her earlier that morning.
When they reached her bedroom, she closed the door
and locked it, trembling a little, her heart beating fast
as Jake took her in his arms, wrapping his hands in
her hair and claiming her mouth with his own.

Claire abruptly awoke in the wee hours of the night,
not quite sure, at first, what had roused her—except
that it was nothing frightening or threatening, as her
nightmare about the riptide had been. Instead, whatever it was had teased at the edges of her subconscious, interwoven itself like a motif through her
dreams, finally prodding her to wakefulness. She lay
very still for a moment, trying to remember, only gradually growing aware of the fact that Jake slept beside
her, his naked body half covering hers, his hand rest-
ing on her breast. By the moonlight streaming in
through the uncurtained French doors, she gazed at
him tenderly, a soft smile curving her lips. Even now,

she could scarcely believe he was real, that he lay here next to her, wanted her, cared for her. She had never thought he would forgive her for what she had done to him all those years ago, had never imagined he would someday be hers again.

She loved the feel of his hard, lean, muscular body; the taste of his smooth, bronze skin, just slightly salty and smoky; the scent of him, male and musky....

Perfume, Claire thought suddenly. That was what had disturbed her slumber. Jake had said he had known her by her perfume, that although she had altered her appearance, she had not changed her fragrance. Something about that observation had rung a bell in some dark corner of her mind, rung it so loudly that it had wakened her.

"Claire?" Jake's voice sounded drowsily in the darkness as he stirred and realized she was no longer asleep. "Is something wrong, baby? Did you have another nightmare?"

"No, nothing like that. I was just...thinking about perfume."

"What about it?"

"That's just it. I can't remember. But somehow, I believe it was important, Jake."

"Well, stop thinking about it, and maybe it'll come to you." His hand tightened on her breast, thumb rotating slowly across her nipple, which flushed and stiffened instantly, such was her body's response to him. Then he skimmed his fingers down her rib cage, her stomach, and between her thighs, where she was already wet for him. "Hmm. I like that," he murmured in her ear as she invitingly opened her legs even wider for him, the dark, secret heart of her pulsing with anticipation. She could feel his throbbing sex, big and hard with arousal, pressing against her flesh before he shifted his body to slide deep inside her, stretching her, filling her fully. "Do *you* like it, Claire?" he asked, his voice low and husky.

"Yes...you know I do," she whispered as he began to thrust lazily within her, his hand still on her mound, rubbing and exciting the tiny nub that was the key to her delight. She came in moments, gasping and arching against him as the slow, crescendoing tremors swept through her, seeming to rock her very soul. But Jake continued to move steadily within her, slipping his hand beneath her buttocks to pull her even nearer as he ground himself against her sensuously, bringing her to orgasm yet again before he reached his own climax, spilling himself inside her.

Afterward, he kissed her mouth lingeringly before drawing her into his arms, cradling her head against his chest and stroking her hair soothingly. "Go back to sleep, sweetheart."

"Yes, I will." Her eyes were already drifting shut even as she spoke. Her last coherent thought before slumber claimed her was how dear and familiar Jake felt, how quickly she had got used again to having him lying next to her in bed at night, holding her close.

His own thought was how good Claire felt, snuggled against him, how well her body fit his, as though she had been made for him, and him alone. It came to Jake just before sleep overtook him, too, that it was more than desire he felt for her, that he had loved her for a very long time.

Twenty-Six

A Choice of Justice

The quality of mercy is not strained,
It droppeth as the gentle rain from heaven
Upon the place beneath: it is twice blessed;
It blesseth him that gives and him that takes:
'Tis mightiest in the mightiest; it becomes
The thronèd monarch better than his crown;
His scepter shows the force of temporal power,
The attribute to awe and majesty,
Wherein doth sit the dread and fear of kings,
But mercy is above this sceptered sway,
It is enthronèd in the hearts of kings,
It is an attribute to God himself,
And earthly power doth then show likest God's
When mercy seasons justice.

The Merchant of Venice
—William Shakespeare

Some days later, Senator Malcolm Forsythe was arrested for the murder of his wife. At a press conference, the D.A. announced that A.D.A. Unruh would prosecute the case, which they now firmly believed would result in a conviction, based on all the evidence collected by the police. Forsythe himself blustered his way through the media's questions, proclaiming himself innocent and insisting there had been some terrible mistake. Privately, the senator worried that Lily intended to double-cross him, to hang him out to dry.

She had had nothing to do with him since the morning after Veronica's death, claiming that with him being under suspicion, it would be better for the two of them to keep their distance from each other until everything cooled down, so as not to give the police additional ammunition to use against him. At the time, Forsythe had agreed with her. But now he couldn't stop thinking about how Lily wouldn't have to share the Hampton fortune with him if he were in prison. Worse, he had nothing with which to drag her down with him in the event that he were convicted. If she had turned against him, she would deny their affair, of course, and it would be his word against hers. He had no means of putting her at the Seabreeze Sanatorium the night of the arsonous fire, since she had pretended to be Veronica during their visit; and he couldn't place her poolside the evening of his fundraiser, since she had been upstairs helping the arthritic Nadine into bed at the time of the murder and therefore had an iron-clad alibi for the time of his wife's death.

Damn Lily! He had committed murder for her, and now he felt as though he had been a fool for her.

The senator was fit to be tied, and as the police

escorted him through the clamorous barrage of media out in front of the precinct and into the station itself, he felt as though a noose had already dropped around his neck.

Some weeks after the senator's arrest, Claire finally realized the significance of Jake's observations to her about her perfume. She had, she suddenly grasped, forgotten all about the fragrance-drenched handker-chief she had unwittingly taken away with her the day of her tête-à-tête with old Mrs. Hampton and Lily D'Angelo, and subsequently tucked into her purse. Now, she recalled that there had been something about the scent that had disturbed her. It had touched some chord in her memory, she recognized, as though she had associated it with someone other than Lily D'Angelo. As a result, that morning, she took the first com-muter flight to New Orleans, to visit Madame Gau-tier's perfume shop in the French Quarter. What Claire learned there stunned her. When she returned home, she drove straight to Brett Deauville's dental office, where everything she had now begun to suspect was confirmed for her by a list of his patients' missing files.

That evening after supper, which Jake had taken to sharing with her and Gillian, Claire told him about all she had unearthed and her own deductions about it, and although he was initially incredulous, the more he contemplated what she had recounted to him, the more he realized how it supplied the answers to his own questions about the death of Veronica Hampton For-sythe.

The next day, Jake drove out to the Hampton family mansion and requested a private interview with Lily D'Angelo.

"What can I do for you, Detective Seringo?" she inquired politely as he joined her on the patio, where she reclined on a chaise longue, sunbathing.

"You can listen to an incredible story I'm going to relate to you—and then you can tell me whether or not it's all true," Jake explained as he sat down on the chaise longue next to her own. "It began more than thirty years ago, or perhaps even decades before that. Some say that during the last century, a quadroon woman—a voodoo witch—laid a curse upon her Hampton lover and all his heirs, and that this is the reason for all the tragedies with which the family has been afflicted over the years. Others not so fanciful might be inclined to place the blame upon the fact that like the rest of their blue-blooded ilk in the eighteen hundreds, the Hamptons married their own relatives—cousins and other kissing kin—to keep their bloodlines pure, and that this practice eventually, invariably resulted in genetic defects taking hold in the family. However things began is unimportant, really. It's what happened more than thirty years ago that counts."

"And what was that?" the woman now lying very still on her chaise longue asked quietly.

"Old Mrs. Hampton's eldest son, Spencer, and her only daughter, Autumn, had an incestuous affair that left Autumn pregnant. An abortion would have appeared the only decent solution, and the family certainly had money enough to have one safely, however illegally, performed. But instead, it was decided that

Autumn would give birth to the baby, who was perhaps the first full-blooded Hampton in generations. Spencer's wife, Katherine, was unable to bear a child, so it was arranged for her and Autumn to travel abroad, to Italy, where they changed identities. Eventually, Autumn delivered not one, but three babies...triplets. But the youngest, Lily, was small and sickly. It was thought she wouldn't survive. So Katherine returned home to the States with only two of the children, Veronica and Vanessa, whom Spencer and she passed off as twins and their own. Autumn stayed behind in Italy, and when, instead of dying as expected, the third triplet, Lily, lived, a husband—Eduardo D'Angelo, a notorious playboy—was bought for Autumn, and Lily was passed off as their firstborn child.

"For years, the Hamptons succeeded in keeping this terrible skeleton locked up tight in the family closet. But then, one day, somehow, Lily managed to learn the truth about her parentage. That wouldn't have mattered, except for one thing—she was quite mad, insanely jealous of Veronica and Vanessa, as well as extremely clever and cunning. She decided she was entitled to the whole of the Hampton family fortune, and she set about to eliminate anyone who stood in her way. Because she was patient and often took advantage of opportunity, she was able to carry out one bold scheme after another, without suspicion ever falling on her. Sometimes, it was only necessary for her to put events in motion, as she did one night in Tuscany, when she revealed to Vanessa and to Bruno D'Angelo their true relationship. Lily undoubtedly knew just how fragile Vanessa was mentally, that Bruno's Ferrari was conveniently parked outside, that he always left the keys in it, and that a dangerous, hairpin curve lay just below his villa. It was enough. Vanessa unwittingly did the rest herself, crashing the car, killing Bruno and winding up herself in the Seabreeze Sanatorium.

"Before then, Lily had almost certainly arranged to have Veronica's only child, Drew, kidnapped and murdered. Doubtless, Lily killed her accomplice afterward to ensure his silence. The death of the little boy drove a wedge between Veronica and her husband, Malcolm Forsythe—a wedge Lily maliciously used to her advantage by enticing the senator into having an affair with her. Together, the two of them eventually hatched a plot whereby they would get rid of Vanessa and Veronica both, leaving Lily as the sole heir to the Hampton family fortune. They decided to switch the twins, after which they planned for Veronica to die in an arsonous fire at the Seabreeze Sanatorium. They had discovered that one of the other inmates there, Billy Oxbridge, was a pyromaniac whom they could conveniently frame for setting the blaze, and the senator had already made arrangements for all the twins' dental records to disappear, just in case someone should suspect it was Veronica, not Vanessa, who had died in the fire.

"Meanwhile, Forsythe and Lily would, of course, pass Vanessa off as Veronica. Since Vanessa wasn't mentally stable, they probably intended to allow others to witness her erratic behavior, to give everyone the impression that she was gradually going crazy. Believing her to be Veronica, everybody would have assumed she was suffering a nervous breakdown, just as her twin sister had. As a result, an accidental drug overdose or some other such means of eliminating her would most likely not have aroused suspicion, but have been written off as simply another tragedy in a family known to be cursed by more than its fair share.

"But unbeknown to both the senator and Lily, something had gone wrong with their scheme. No doubt highly confused and agitated, Vanessa had somehow made her way back to the sanatorium, and Veronica—who by now had surely deduced much, if not all, of her husband and cousin's plot—had returned home in her twin sister's place. When the sanatorium was set ablaze, killing Vanessa, Veronica must have known Forsythe and Lily were responsible. Only, who would have believed her? What real proof had she to offer? The answer is, none. In fact, it was possible she would be thought crazy for voicing such accusations. So she determined to get even in her own way and her own time. Aware of her husband's financial difficulties, she let her hairdresser know she planned to divorce Forsythe, and she contacted her attorney, arranging for him to file the papers the Monday morning after the senator's fund-raiser here at the Hampton family mansion.

"Then, the night of the bash, she staged an argument with him, during which she tore one of his cuff links free. After that, she somehow lured Lily down to the pool—where she knocked her in the head with a small stone, changed clothes with her, then shoved her in to drown, tossing Forsythe's cuff link into the water to frame him for the murder. Of course, in order to avoid becoming a suspect herself, Veronica had to have an accomplice, too—and she did, her devoted grandmother, to whom she had revealed the whole truth and who provided her with an alibi for that night. As a result, everything went off without a hitch. The body in the pool was identified as Veronica Hampton Forsythe's, and the senator was arrested for murdering his wife. No one ever suspected that the corpse was actually that of Lily D'Angelo and that Forsythe had been shrewdly framed—no one, that is, except for a reporter named Claire Connelly.''

Reaching into his pocket, Jake slowly drew forth the lacy, white handkerchief that Lily had given Claire to blot up her spilled lemonade the day of their interview. ''You thought of everything, Mrs. Hampton Forsythe—everything, except your perfume. It's a signature scent, you see, created especially for you by the same woman in New Orleans, Madame Gautier, who makes Claire's own fragrance and who is apparently quite famous among the Southern debutante set. Claire took this very handkerchief to Madame Gautier's shop yesterday, and Madame was kind enough to identify the perfume as yours...Elysian Fields, I'm told it's called—while Lily D'Angelo never wore anything but her own Diamond Fire.''

Jake fell silent then, and if there were any doubts at all remaining in his mind about the seemingly fantastic scenario Claire had outlined for him, they were banished when he watched Veronica Hampton Forsythe pick up a pack of Virginia Slims 120s from the table beside her chaise longue and tear away the wrapper and box top before shaking out a cigarette and lighting up. After blowing a cloud of smoke into the summer air, she said coolly, "That is, indeed, quite an incredible story, Detective Seringo. Without any more proof than a handkerchief with a fading scent, you would have great difficulty convincing anyone of its veracity, I should think."

"Lily D'Angelo is dead—and the senator is almost certainly going to be convicted of a crime he didn't commit," Jake pointed out softly.

"So you say. But Vanessa and Bruno are dead, too—and it is for a jury to decide whether or not Malcolm is guilty or innocent of murdering his wife, is it not? In a perfect world, none of it would ever have happened. But unfortunately, we live in a terribly imperfect world, Detective, a world filled with a great deal of wickedness, and justice is seldom meted out as we would wish. Have you ever read Francis Bacon's Essays?"

"'Revenge is a kind of wild justice,'" Jake quoted, guessing her line of thought. "Shall I finish it for you? 'Which the more man's nature runs to, the more ought law to weed it out.' It is anarchy that eventually reigns supreme when people take the law into their own hands, Mrs. Hampton Forsythe."

"But when the law fails the people, what other choice do they have? Drew was only a child. I understand that you lost your wife and own baby several years ago. Tell me…did you ever get over it, Detective? Did the pain ever go away? Or is it still buried somewhere deep down inside you, a wound that has never healed? Callous as it may seem, you're still young and capable of fathering more children. But there were complications at Drew's birth, and as a result, Ronnie could never have another baby. I am the last of the Hamptons. There will be no more after me. The line—and the curse, if that is what it is—ends with me. Is that not a kind of justice, as well?''

"I don't know," Jake said, remembering his dead wife—and his son who had never been born, had never even had a chance to live. Would he not have killed for them? "Perhaps it is at that. However, it is a justice that, in all good conscience as a homicide detective, I simply cannot allow, Mrs. Hampton Forsythe."

"No, I don't suppose so. But then, it's really not your decision to make, is it, Detective? In reality, the explanation for the fragrance clinging to that handkerchief could be nothing more than that I was—that day of Ms. Connelly's interview here at the house—beset by grief, not thinking clearly, and, mistakenly believing it was one of mine, had merely picked up a handkerchief belonging to Ronnie. You cannot prove otherwise. Nor would a competent defense attorney—and I assure you that mine would be far better than just competent—have any trouble presenting other alternatives to a jury…casting that all-important shadow of doubt upon your rather fantastic theory.

"Perhaps the scenario you described did, in fact, take place, Detective. Still, it was, after all, Malcolm's cuff link the police found in the pool, Malcolm who took out the insurance policy on his wife's life, Malcolm whom Ronnie was going to divorce. And even if he were to have been framed for the murder, who is to determine whether it was Ronnie—or Lily—who did the clever deed? Neither Ronnie nor Lily was ever fingerprinted, and somehow, I have a strange suspicion that you won't be able to turn up those missing dental records, either—which would, of course, make it virtually impossible to ascertain which of them was actually dead in the pool. Perhaps one of them only knocked the other unconscious, and it *was* Malcolm who finished the job afterward. Who can tell? It is always difficult to judge what lengths a person will go to in pursuit of power and glory.

"I know only that I have an alibi for the night of the murder, Detective—and that to break it, you'd have to prove my grandmother a liar. That alone would be a formidable task, one that would ultimately fail, I should think."

"You don't intend, then, to satisfy my curiosity, Mrs. Hampton Forsythe?"

"No, Detective, I do not. You've already made up your mind, answered your own questions, have you not? Otherwise, you wouldn't be addressing me as Mrs. Hampton Forsythe. Yes, certainly, I could insist I was in fact, Lily D'Angelo, but I don't think you would ever truly believe me, even so. So what is the point? You appear to be a well-educated man, Detective. Do you know Thucydides as well as Bacon? 'But the bravest are surely those who have the clearest vision of what is before them, glory and danger alike, and yet notwithstanding go out to meet it.' Suffice to say that I had a clear vision, Detective. You must make of that whatever you will."

"I see." Slowly, Jake stood, laying the handkerchief on the small table between the two chaise longues. "As you pointed out, a scent by itself is insufficient grounds on which to base a case—although I daresay a bloodhound would take issue with that. I, on the other hand, am merely a cop, albeit a well-read one. Are *you* familiar with Polybius, Mrs. Hampton Forsythe? 'There is no witness so dreadful, no accuser so terrible as the conscience that dwells in the heart of every man.' I leave you alone now with yours. Whether or not you will ever rest easy with it is something only you and God can answer. I've done what I could, what I came here to do. Because of that, I know I'll be able to sleep nights, to look at my face in a mirror mornings."

"From birth, I had two mirrors, Detective," the woman lying on the chaise longue observed softly. "One fragile, one crazed. They're both gone now. I don't think I shall ever need another."

Twenty-Seven

Righting Old Wrongs

No themes are so human as those that reflect for us, out of the confusion of life, the close connection of bliss and bale, of the things that help with the things that hurt, so dangling before us forever that bright hard medal, of so strange an alloy, one face of which is somebody's right and ease and the other somebody's pain and wrong.

> *Prefaces: What Maisie Knew*
> —Henry James

The box Claire had removed from the shelf of her walk-in, cedar closet was ten years old. The once-sturdy cardboard had weakened, and the company name and logo stamped on the sides were faded with age. *Mariner's Clam Sauce*, it read, being a discarded box from a local grocery store. She had never opened the box since the day, a decade ago, that she had sealed it shut with packing tape. She'd had no need to. She knew what it contained…Jake and Isabel's wedding album, stacks of more casual snapshots of the two of them, and various other personal mementos of their married life together—a program from a Cinco de Mayo celebration, a cocktail napkin from a little bar over by the university, ticket stubs from a movie—the kinds of things women in love often saved to remind themselves of happy occasions in their lives.

She needed to return the box to Jake, Claire thought. She would give it to him tonight, along with the video she had made this morning. Unbeknown to him, she had followed him to the Hampton family mansion earlier, taking with her a camera with a powerful zoom lens, as well as a microphone capable of picking up conversations some yards away. She hadn't worked with Nash and McGuinness all these years without learning how to run at least some of the equipment they used. Of course, she hadn't known what would happen at the mansion, if she would even be able to obtain anything useful. But no broadcast journalist, privy to what she had known at that point, would have passed up the opportunity to try.

Fortunately, after the arrest of Senator Forsythe, media attention had shifted to him and the apartment he had rented after his release on bail, old Mrs. Hampton having withdrawn her financial and public support of him and closed the doors of her mansion to him forever. So there hadn't been any reporters cruising the streets of the Forest Gables neighborhood or parked at the curb out in front of the mansion. Still, Claire hadn't taken any chances. She had parked her jazzy, red Beamer on a side street and chosen a site well screened by tall trees and bushes to climb over the mansion's brick-and-stucco wall. The minute she had dropped to the ground, she had yanked her pepper spray from the pocket of her jeans, in case the Hamptons' dogs were running loose on the property and she needed to defend herself from them. But they hadn't appeared, and after a moment, she had recognized that they must be locked in their pens.

Surreptitiously, Claire had made her way toward the house, not knowing whether to be glad or sorry when she observed Jake being escorted by a maid out to the patio, where Veronica Hampton Forsythe had lounged in the sun. Claire had got their entire meeting, and conversation, on film. Since there wasn't any confession on it, she didn't know what, if any, use the tape would be to Jake, but she hoped that by letting him decide what should be done with it, he would finally understand that even if it *were* her job, there were some things more important to her than getting the inside story. As for the box of photographs and souvenirs, if he took it and looked through it, then she would know he had at last put the past behind him once and for all, could remember the good times he had shared with Isabel, could live with whatever pain still remained.

Groaning slightly at its weight, Claire lifted the box to carry it into her bedroom, dismayed when the cracked, yellowed packing tape that had secured the bottom suddenly gave way without warning, so the contents spilled upon the floor.

"Damn it!" she cried softly, hoping nothing had been damaged.

It was when she was repacking the box that she discovered that several of the newspapers she had used to protect the box's contents were editions of the *Courier* and contained news articles about the murders of the convenience-store clerk, Wyatt Jenkins, and Jake's wife, Isabel. Maybe it would be best if she threw those away, Claire reflected, torn by indecision. Jake had his own personal file on his wife's case, she knew, and she felt sure he had the clippings about the robbery and killings in it, so he could examine them at any time and probably had over the years. There was no point in his being compelled to see these editions— grim reminders of how Isabel had died—while he went through the box's memories of their happier days together.

Claire, however, had not read the news stories for a decade, and now, she couldn't help scanning them and dwelling on Jake's loss, the tragedy that had brought her to his apartment door that afternoon of the funerals. If not for that, she might never have met him, might never have known what it was to lie naked beside him in the darkness, the heat of him seeping into her body, her heart filled to overflowing with love for him.

She read the articles once, twice, and then a third time, her heart slamming painfully in her breast.

"Claire, what's all this?" Jake stood in her bedroom, his eyes angry, hurt, and questioning as he gazed at her kneeling there amid the pile of pictures and mementos she had only half got back into the box. She had been so engrossed in reading the stories that she hadn't even heard the doorbell ring or Ana Maria answer the front door to admit him. "What're you doing with this stuff? Damn it! I thought I told you ten years ago to throw it all away, that I never wanted to see any of it again."

"I know you did, and I'm sorry I didn't do as you instructed. But I believed you were distraught at the time and that, someday, you'd want to remember Isabel as she was in life rather than in death. So I—I kept this box for you. I was going to give it to you tonight. I thought that maybe it was time. But while I was getting it out of the closet, it broke open. I was putting everything back in when I started reading the newspaper accounts of the holdup and murders. Jake, none of these articles says anything about there being four perpetrators. *I* know there were, because I recall you telling me once about the semen recovered from Isabel's body, that it indicated four assailants. But that wasn't general knowledge, was it? It wasn't something that was ever released to the media?"

"No, why?"

"Because the other night at the Flamingo Landing, Manolo Alvarez said you'd been a loose cannon on the police force ever since your wife had had her throat cut after being raped by four men presumed to be gang members. How could he know there were four, Jake—unless he were there, unless he were one of them?"

"He couldn't, Claire," Jake said grimly after a moment. "He couldn't."

In the beginning, it had been all Claire could do to restrain Jake from driving straight out to the Flamingo

Landing and physically attacking Manolo Alvarez. But as she clutched him fiercely, so he couldn't shake her loose without hurting her, she at last managed to persuade him that taking the law into his own hands was not how to deal with the Latino kingpin, that Alvarez belonged behind bars for life, or else in an electric chair.

"We can get him! We can get him another way, Jake! But not like this. Think about your career, for God's sake. You've got ten years on the force, and you're one of the finest homicide detectives the police have. Think about the life you've built for yourself. Isabel wouldn't have wanted you to throw that all away for her. *I* don't want you to throw it all away! I love you. I love you, Jake, and I won't let you do it!" By then, Claire was so upset and sobbing so hard that she was scarcely even aware that he had stopped trying to make his way down the hall while dragging the dead weight of her clinging figure with him.

Instead, he had abruptly halted in his tracks, grabbing hold of her arms so tightly that she knew she would have bruises on them tomorrow. He stared down at her intently, a strange, leaping light in his dark, dangerously smoldering eyes. "What did you say?" he demanded, his low voice harsh, serrated with emotion.

"I love you," she whispered, her tear-filled eyes falling in sudden confusion before his and color staining her cheeks. She swallowed hard. "You—you must have known that, Jake."

Yes, deep down on some instinctive level, he had, he realized now. "Yeah, I suppose I did. But you've never told me so before, Claire. Nor, in all the time we've known each other, that you've slept in my bed, have you ever asked anything of me before, not even once.'' Jake paused for a moment, reflecting soberly on that. He glanced down the hall toward her bedroom, at the box she had saved for him for so long, at the precious, scattered contents that another woman in her position would have been more than happy to toss into a garbage can years ago, not wanting to compete with a ghost, not caring that there would, in fact, come a time when he would want to remember Isabel the way she had once been—young and full of life. "Didn't you ever think you were entitled to something more from me than just sex, Claire?" he queried quietly.

"Oh, Jake, yes, of course I did. But after Isabel's death, I knew you needed time and space, and then when you found out about my miniseries, you walked out of my life with hardly a word, and I thought I'd never see you again. So what I had wanted didn't matter anymore—at least, not to you."

"It matters now, Claire." Cupping her chin in his hand, Jake tilted her face gently up to his own. "I think that deep down inside, I've known that for a very long time. I loved Isabel, and because of that, she'll always have a place in my heart. You understand and respect that, I know, or you wouldn't have saved all those pictures and mementos I told you to throw away. And no matter what I said, I'm grateful that you *did* keep them. But I love you, too, Claire. You're in my heart, as well—you and Gillian, both—and I don't want to lose you."

"Then, please, don't go off half-cocked like this after Alvarez," she entreated earnestly, tears welling in her eyes once more, even as her heart spilled over with joy and love for him. "I don't want to lose you, either. I—I just don't think I could bear that a second time, Jake. You said I'd never asked you for anything before. But I'm asking now. Call Remy and Captain Nichols. Please. We can get Alvarez legally. I know there must be some way."

There was, in fact, a way—but Jake hadn't liked it one single bit, and now, as he gazed down into Claire's pale face, he liked it even less. "This is crazy," he insisted stoutly, a muscle working in his taut jaw, so she knew how worried he was. "Getting Alvarez isn't worth risking your life over, Claire. We don't know what kinds of security measures he may have in place inside. You could be killed before we're able to reach you. I've changed my mind. I'm not going through with this. I'm just not going to let you do it, Claire!"

"Yes, you are. It'll be all right, Jake. I'll be fine, you'll see. My goodness, Captain Nichols has a whole S.W.A.T. team out here, for heaven's sake. Nothing's going to go wrong. I may not even be able to finagle Alvarez into repeating what he told me that night about Isabel having been raped and killed by four men—in which case, I'll simply leave, and we'll have to try and think of some other plan."

Still, despite her words of reassurance to Jake, Claire was more nervous than she had ever before been in her entire life as, after taking a deep breath, she got into her convertible, which was parked on the verge down the road a piece from the Flamingo Landing, and started toward the hotel. She wasn't a police officer. She wasn't even carrying a gun. The only thing standing between her and Alvarez was the wire she wore beneath the sexy outfit she had donned earlier that evening, along with her curly, dark-brown wig and tortoiseshell, tinted glasses. As her alter ego, Cocoa Saint John, she was about to give the performance of her life—and there weren't even going to be any cameras in sight to capture the event for *Inside Story*.

She was bait—and Manolo Alvarez was the big fish she hoped to hook, for Jake's sake.

"I sure hope you guys can hear me," she said softly as she turned into the parking lot of the Flamingo Landing, praying that the wire was working properly and that the police officers in the van down the road were picking up her transmission. "I'm at the hotel now and about to go inside. Keep your fingers crossed."

All hell had broken loose at the Flamingo Landing. From the tunnel beneath the old plantation, Claire could hear the sounds of police sirens wailing, of automatic weapons firing, and of people screaming and running. When she had embarked upon this escapade, she had never imagined anything like this, had thought the S.W.A.T. team was only a precaution, to cover the hotel grounds in case Alvarez should attempt to escape before he could be arrested. She'd had no idea that the Latino kingpin would abduct her as a hostage, that a full-scale raid of the premises would ensue as a result.

Everything had appeared to be going so smoothly. Alvarez had professed delight at seeing her once more, been all smiles and charm as he had led her into the bar, where they had sat at one of the dark booths in the back, only the candle flickering at their table illuminating his thin, ratlike visage. He had ordered drinks for them, and they had talked, Claire gradually and, she hoped, naturally working the conversation around to Jake, and to his wife's murder.

"I can understand your sympathizing with Detective Seringo, Manny," Claire had stated, "but really, at the very least, I should think you would notify his superiors about his behavior in your hotel. At best, the man's most likely an alcoholic. At worst, he might be a corrupt cop on the take. I was never so insulted in my life as when he propositioned me and put his hands all over me. I declare...I don't know what I would have done if you hadn't happened along to rescue me. But afterward, I figured you were just being nice... You know, because you own the hotel and all, and since I didn't want to run into that detective again, that's why I didn't come back out here right away. If the truth were but known, he probably killed his poor wife himself in a drunken rage! Oh, but that can't be right, can it? Didn't you say she was raped and murdered by four gang members during a robbery at a convenience store?"

"*Sí,* that was the police's theory at the time," Alvarez had agreed, shrugging carelessly.

"I wonder what made them think that, why they never investigated Detective Seringo as a possible suspect, what with him being such a loose cannon and all?"

"He was on duty that night, so his partner could vouch for him. I believe it was, in fact, the two of them who discovered his wife's body."

"Well, maybe his partner was in on it with him— for the insurance money or because the wife knew they were bad cops or something, and she was going to turn them in," Claire had suggested darkly. "Things like that are always happening on TV shows, cops accepting bribes, stealing dope and loot from crime scenes and property rooms. I mean, if there weren't any witnesses, how could the police possibly know there were four men and not just two?"

"Traces of semen in the wife's body, I should imagine. She had been raped, after all, the gangbangers taking turns on her. She was a very pretty, young girl, perhaps only twenty-three or -four at the time, and her white nurse's uniform and pregnancy made her look like a Madonna. She was even wearing a crucifix at the time—not that it or her prayers did her any good. Still, it is easy to understand why the gangbangers wanted her before they cut her throat from ear to ear. But who cares about all this now? It was a long time ago, and the police are unlikely to make any arrests in the case at this late date—although you are quite right that steps should be taken with regard to Detective Seringo. However, as you say, one has pity for what he has suffered, the way in which he lost his wife and unborn child."

"Yes, one does." Claire had wondered anxiously if Alvarez had confessed enough to be indicted and bound over for trial. That Isabel had been dressed in her nurse's uniform and wearing a crucifix around her neck at the time of her death weren't details that had been released to the media, either. Why hadn't the police shown up to arrest the Latino kingpin? Claire had asked herself. Maybe they were waiting for her to leave. Picking up her handbag, she had got to her feet. "Well, thanks for the drink, Manny. But I need to be going now."

Alvarez, too, had stood. "You do not wish to stay and play blackjack again this evening, *señorita?*" he had asked, a tiny, puzzled frown knitting his brow, so she could almost see the wheels churning in his brain as he thought back over their conversation. Then, suddenly, his black eyes had narrowed to hard, glinting slits, and without warning, he had grabbed hold of her wrist cruelly, growling softly, "You are a far cleverer woman than I thought." Clapping his hand over her mouth to stifle any sound she might have made, he had swiftly dragged her through a rear door of the dim, smoky bar, into a narrow hallway beyond, where, after slamming her up against the wall, he had thrust his hand down the bodice of her low-cut dress to rip away the wire taped beneath her breasts. Then, despite her struggles, he had hauled her down the corridor and, eventually, into the dark, dank tunnel in which the two of them now slogged through the slimy, rat-infested water that was ankle deep within.

"You won't get away with this, Alvarez," Claire warned him half nervously, half defiantly now as she strove mightily to yank free of his ironlike grasp, stumbling as he jerked her along savagely behind him.

"The police know all about the gambling, prostitution, and drugs that go on out here in your private rooms, and obviously, since you tore off my wire, they're aware that something's gone wrong. They're swarming all over your hotel even as we speak. This time, they'll have enough evidence to send you away for life."

"My dear Ms. Connelly—*sí*, I know who you are, despite that wig and those glasses. The next time you choose to disguise yourself in order to get a news story, you should provide a background for yourself that stands up to investigation and rent a car, so your license tag can't be traced back to you. It was all too easy to uncover your true identity, and then, of course, I assumed you wanted to learn what your late husband had been up to out here, or else to attempt to expose the hotel's illegal activities. My mistake. I had no idea until just a few minutes ago that it was really the murder of Detective Seringo's wife that interested you."

"It wasn't, at first. But you slipped up, Alvarez. Your sort always do, sooner or later. Only the police and I knew there were four men connected with the robbery and killings at the convenience store—and once I realized you were one of them, the rest of your operation, even Paul's possible involvement with you, was unimportant. That I could get you for murdering Jake's wife and unborn child was all that counted."

"Too bad you won't succeed. I've a launch moored at the end of this tunnel, you see. By the time the police realize I'm no longer in the hotel, you and I will be long gone, and you, Ms. Connelly, will be bait for the sharks—just like my arrogant, unsuspecting father, Leon Gutierrez.''

Claire's heart hammered horribly at these revelations as Alvarez continued to drag her through the tunnel, the dim lamps that glowed in its ceiling giving his lean, hard, pocked visage a diabolical cast. He was sweating profusely in the muggy atmosphere, as was Claire herself, and once, his breath coming in labored rasps, he halted briefly to strip off his suit jacket and roll up his shirtsleeves, slapping her across the face, sending her glasses flying and knocking her to her knees when she tried to run away from him. Then, snarling his fingers in her riotous mass of dark-brown curls, swearing foully when her wig came off in his hand, he snatched her up by the blond hair of her head, nearly breaking her neck before he half hauled, half shoved her to the end of the tunnel, where an iron ladder bolted into the wall led to the top.

"Start climbing," he ordered angrily, pulling from his boot a knife that gleamed menacingly in the half light. "Or I'll kill you right here and now—and give you something to remember me by on your way to hell before I do it!"

Utterly terrified, her heart in her throat, cutting off her breath so she gasped for air, Claire did as he had demanded, her shaking hands and heeled sandals slipping precariously on the scummy, iron rungs as she ascended the ladder. She didn't dare look down, or even think about trying to kick Alvarez in the head as he followed her up. The reason she was a white-knuckles flier was because she was afraid of heights, and there wasn't a doubt in her mind that if she attempted to smash her foot into Alvarez's face, he would grab her leg and jerk her off the ladder to fall to the bottom of the tunnel below.

When, finally, Claire gained the top, she pushed open the trapdoor above and scrambled out, thinking to flee from Alvarez before he could climb out himself. But clearly anticipating this, he caught her ankle, tripping her up so she stumbled and sprawled headlong onto the wharf she had exited onto, and before she could stagger to her feet, he was on her, hauling her upright so violently that he almost wrenched her shoulder from its socket. Brutally, he pinned her arm behind her back, his wickedly flashing knife at her throat as he pushed her down the dock, toward the motorboat moored at its end.

"Hold it right there, Alvarez!" To think that had it not been for Toussaint's unearthing the original blueprints for the plantation, Jake would never have known about the two tunnels—Alvarez's escape routes. The Latino kingpin would have got away with Claire; he might still, too. It was only the luck of the draw that had put Toussaint at the stables and Jake here at the landing, to witness Claire's plight, to attempt to save her.

Hearing the shouted demand, the Latino kingpin pivoted abruptly, shielding his body with Claire's own as he turned to confront the pursuer who had without warning materialized behind him on the wooden pier. Jake's dark, handsome face was grim with fear and determination in the moonlight as his gaze took in Claire's ashen countenance, her wide eyes filled with fear, the lethal, single-edged blade pressed to her slender, white throat.

"It's over, Alvarez. Let her go."

"Not a chance. Put it down, Seringo." Alvarez motioned tersely at the automatic pistol Jake gripped expertly in his strong hands. "And step back, or I'll cut your lovely, blond *gringa's* throat from ear to ear, just like I did your wife's."

The black skull tattooed on Alvarez's forearm seemed to grin at Jake mockingly, so he remembered of a sudden the young, Latino woman he had found stabbed to death in a dark alley of the barrio so many years ago, recalled her face and Alvarez's arm wrapped around her, his hand at her breast. The two of them had been laughing, staggering drunk down a cracked sidewalk of the barrio together. Of course, the girl had been Alvarez's whore, Jake realized now— too late.

To hammer home his deadly intentions, the Latino kingpin had jabbed the point of the knife into Claire's tender flesh, drawing a bead of blood and causing her to whimper with pain and fright, her head lolling helplessly against his shoulder.

Her small mewl of terror tore hideously at Jake's insides. His pulse raced, adrenaline pumping wildly through his tense body. He had lost Isabel. There was no way in hell he was going to lose Claire, too. But if he laid down his gun, let Manny Alvarez drag her on board the launch, Jake knew she was dead, that he would never see her alive again. Claire understood that, too. He could see the dreadful knowledge of it in her tearful eyes.

"I love you, Jake," she cried out softly, then. "I trust you with all my heart. Don't do what he says. Take your best shot."

Oh, God, how could he? Jake asked himself, stricken with horror. His hands were trembling a little, he recognized in some obscure corner of his mind. What if he accidentally hit Claire instead? He had insisted on her trust and commitment, and she had given him both without reservation by laying her very life in his hands. It was far more than he had ever wished for; if he had it all to do over again, he would never speak those damning words. He had only seconds to decide what to do.

You must learn to have faith and put right the wrong. When the betrayer offers trust, believe in it, and you will not falter... The words of the mysterious quadroon woman who had perhaps been only a ghost echoed suddenly in his mind, and in that moment, trusting blindly to faith, Jake fired.

Epilogue

Suffer a Sea-Change

Full fathom five thy father lies;
Of his bones are coral made:
Those are pearls that were his eyes:
Nothing of him that doth fade,
But doth suffer a sea-change
Into something rich and strange.

The Tempest
—William Shakespeare

Twenty-Eight

The Sands of Time

Grow old along with me!
The best is yet to be...

Rabbi Ben Ezra
—Robert Browning

A Small City, The Gulf Coast, The Present

So long as she lived, Claire knew she would never forget that moment when Jake had pulled the trigger of his gun, shooting Manolo Alvarez straight through the head. The impact of the bullet had been such that Alvarez had staggered back violently, dragging Claire with him, blood from his wound spattering them both, warm and red and sticky in the heat of the summer night. They had lost their footing, tumbling backward off the end of the landing into the muddy river beyond, and in that moment, as she had felt the dark, swift-flowing water close over her, engulfing her, Claire had not known whether she was dead or alive.

Somehow, it had been her nightmare come to life.

And then Jake's hand had reached out to her, just as it had in her dream, and captured her own, pulling her from the river before she had been swept away and drowned.

Alvarez's decomposing body had washed up onto the riverbank a few days later. His entire operation had been shut down with a vengeance, and his cohorts were all currently under criminal indictments. His second set of books—the ones in which he had recorded all his illegal dope dealing and money laundering, had surfaced during a search of the Flamingo Landing.

Senator Malcolm Forsythe's name had figured prominently in the accounts. That he would be convicted of murdering his wife now appeared a virtual certainty.

A little earlier this evening, Claire had finally given to Jake the video she had filmed of his conversation with Veronica Hampton Forsythe at the family mansion—or had it really been Lily D'Angelo all along whom he had talked with? In the end, it was impossible to say with real certainty, beyond a shadow of a doubt. Since the confession Claire had hoped for had not been forthcoming, the tape was thus probably, despite all her good intentions, of little or no value or assistance to Jake. What he had done with it, she didn't know. But now, as she stood on the beach beyond her house, gazing silently out over the vast, grey-green sea reflecting the glitter of the countless stars in the night sky, she sensed she was no longer alone, that he had joined her on the shore.

"Even without knowing whether it's Veronica or

Lily you captured on film, even lacking a confession, it's still the news story of the century, Claire,'' he announced quietly as he came to stand beside her, the video in hand. ''You could have run with it, made a fortune, written your own ticket to any broadcasting studio in the whole damned country. So why didn't you?''

''Because you were right all those years ago. Sometimes, we *do* have to ask ourselves, 'What price glory?' Under the circumstances, it was just too high a price for me to pay. The truth is that I don't want to be responsible for destroying somebody's life just because of a fragrance on a handkerchief and what might be nothing more than sheer, unsubstantiated speculation on my part. That's not journalism—at least, not the sort I've always believed in. Rather, it's lurid, tabloid sensationalism, and I don't want to be a part of that. And maybe revenge *is* a kind of wild justice, just as she told you. I don't think so, but…if I hadn't been standing on that wharf, with Manolo Alvarez's knife at my throat, if it had just been the two of you, alone, would you still have fired that shot, Jake?''

''I've already asked myself that same question a hundred times, Claire—and the answer is that I don't know for sure. I'd like to think I'm better than that…that ultimately, my conscience would have compelled me to uphold the kind of justice I believe in, and that I think you believe in, too. Otherwise, you wouldn't have given me this video. You'd have used it for your own gain instead. I'm glad you didn't, Claire. I admire your decision, the fact that you've drawn a line in the sand, so to speak, and stuck to it. Deep down inside, I know it was always there, from the very beginning of your career. I just never could see it before.'' Slowly, deliberately, Jake began to pull the tape loose from the cassette until there was nothing left on the reels. Then raising his hand high, he let the film go to stream away like the tail of a kite in the wind before casting the empty cassette into the sea. ''I've come to respect your work—just as you always have mine—to be able not only to live with it, but also to appreciate it for the good it can accomplish. What I can't live with, what I can't bear even to think about, is not having you beside me—no matter what—for the rest of our lives. I know that now.'' He paused for a moment. Then, his voice low and earnest, hoarse with emotion, he said, ''Marry me, Claire.''

''Yes,'' she answered softly, breathlessly, her heart filled to overflowing as he took her in his arms then, his mouth descending upon hers fervently to seal their love and pledge, while the breakers white with foam rushed in upon the sandy shore, and the melodious cries of two seabirds winging their way in perfect flight across the midnight-blue horizon echoed sweetly in the stillness of the summer night.